THE BLACK QUEEN

JUMATA EMILL

DELACORTE PRESS

Text copyright © 2023 by Jumata Emill
Jacket art copyright © 2023 by Adekunle Adeleke

All rights reserved. Published in the United States by Delacorte Press, an imprint of Random House Children's Books, a division of Penguin Random House LLC, New York.

Delacorte Press is a registered trademark and the colophon is a trademark of Penguin Random House LLC.

Visit us on the Web! GetUnderlined.com

Educators and librarians, for a variety of teaching tools, visit us at RHTeachersLibrarians.com

Library of Congress Cataloging-in-Publication Data
Names: Emill, Jumata, author.
Title: The black queen / Jumata Emill.
Description: First edition. | New York : Delacorte Press, [2023] | Audience: Ages 14+. | Audience: Grades 10–12. | Summary: When Nova, Lovett High School's first black homecoming queen, is murdered the night of her coronation, her best friend, Duchess, finds an unlikely ally in her search for the killer—her prime suspect, Tinsley, the white rival nominee for queen.
Identifiers: LCCN 2022006228 (print) | LCCN 2022006229 (ebook) | ISBN 978-0-593-56854-5 (hardcover) | ISBN 978-0-593-56855-2 (library binding) | ISBN 978-0-593-56856-9 (ebook)
Subjects: CYAC: Mystery and detective stories. | African Americans—Fiction. | Race relations—Fiction. | High schools—Fiction. | Schools—Fiction. | Contests—Fiction. | Murder—Fiction. | LCGFT: Detective and mystery fiction. | Novels.
Classification: LCC PZ7.1.E4745 Bl 2023 (print) | LCC PZ7.1.E4745 (ebook) | DDC [Fic]—dc23

The text of this book is set in 11-point Calisto MT.
Interior design by Ken Crossland

Printed in the United States of America
10 9 8 7 6 5 4 3 2 1
First Edition

Mama,

You are my first true love.

My Forever Black Queen.

CHAPTER ONE

DUCHESS

OCTOBER 5

9:46 A.M.

NOVA AND I are walking in unison, leading the crowd that followed us out of B-Building to witness for themselves what's about to go down. I don't know how word got out. I can only assume Nova told other people about the text Tinsley McArthur sent her last night. Tinsley asked Nova to meet her between first and second periods today by the courtyard—the middle point between our opposite worlds on this campus.

I can see Tinsley strutting toward us in the distance—the crisp breeze ruffling the hem of her plaid skirt and her shoulder-length chestnut hair. A crowd of people are following her as well. It's like that part in *She's All That*—the original one from the '90s that I pretend to hate every time my girlfriend wants to watch it—when Taylor Vaughn, that story's resident mean girl, meets face to face in the hallway with Laney Boggs, the frumpy-turned-semipopular pet project of Taylor's ex-boyfriend, as their heated contest for prom queen in the movie nears its climax. But it's not the prom queen crown fueling this little rivalry between Nova and Tinsley. It's homecoming queen, which Tinsley feels entitled to because three generations of her family have worn the crown before her. And she has no chance in hell of winning it this year unless Nova drops out of the race. Which is why she requested this meetup. To somehow convince my homegirl to step aside, because God forbid Tinsley doesn't get something she wants.

Spoiler alert: That ain't happening.

I inhale a deep breath that has me feeling taller and we all stop a few feet from meeting in the center of the covered breezeway. The racial undertone of what's happening could not be more evident. Pretty much all the kids behind us are Black, and Tinsley's crowd is predominately white. The chatter on both sides simmers to hushed whispers as Tinsley looks Nova up and down. I don't need to check to know Nova is glaring back at her.

"Tinsley," Nova says, fiddling with the silver, flower-shaped diamond pendant she's worn every day since getting it for her birthday last semester. It's fake, but it looks hella real. "What's this about?" she adds, sliding her hands into the pockets of her high-waisted jeans.

You could hear a pin drop.

"I won't belabor this," Tinsley says, tugging at the strap of the messenger bag hanging on her shoulder. "I'm pretty sure you have assumptions about why I summoned you."

"Summoned?" I hiss.

Nova laughs, shaking her head at this entitled trick.

Tinsley is literally a carbon copy of Taylor Vaughn, but

with a Southern twang. She walks around here with her slender nose pointed in the air like she owns everything and everyone. And yeah, her family is one of the richest and most influential in this town, *and* her dad's construction company built our school, but that's beside the point. Tinsley is self-entitled and hella obnoxious. She can be cruel, and she knows she can get away with it. The white kids don't wanna cross her because they're either country club brats like her or they don't want to be excluded from her social circle. And lots of the Black kids' fathers, uncles, and older brothers work for her father in some capacity, so they're scared that pissing her off could mean unemployment checks for their families. It's mad annoying.

But I know at least one person besides me who isn't about to back down to the spoiled princess today: my girl Nova.

She might be the Laney Boggs in this scenario, but she ain't *nothing* like ol' girl in that movie. My girl isn't some awkward pretty girl who needs a makeover to realize her worth. Nova showed up here junior year already looking like a freaking goddess. Dudes were losing their minds, and girls were losing theirs in jealousy. A dark-skinned, statuesque Black girl with iridescent blue eyes. Everyone was gawking at her like she was a freaking unicorn.

Apparently, blue eyes are so rare in Black folks that our biology teacher taught a whole lesson on genetic coding to highlight the few instances when dark-skinned people like Nova are born with eyes like that. According to Mr. Holston, there were three possible ways Nova got her stunning eyes: (1) one of her immediate relatives is white; (2) she has some rare disease that makes her albino only in the eyes; or (3) there's some kind of mutation in her bloodline. We've always joked it has to be the latter. Having some sort of genetic mutation sounded too cool not to embrace.

"I would have preferred to do this one-on-one; you know, woman-to-woman," Tinsley says, looking more at me than Nova or the crowd behind us. "Did you really need an audience?"

"Did *you*?" I retort, nodding at the sea of white faces I hardly know.

If Tinsley is the Taylor Vaughn in this scenario and Nova is Laney, that makes me Gabrielle Union's character. The chick who started out as Taylor's friend first but flipped to becoming Laney's BFF. There was a time when I considered Tinsley a friend. A long, *long* time ago. I would never trust her snake ass again.

"We're here to protect Tins," Giselle says to me. She's one of Tinsley's best friends. Lana, her other best friend, flanks Tinsley on her left, like some CW bodyguard.

Giselle's Black, one of the few Black kids in Tinsley's orbit, or in the sea of faces behind her. Giselle's family has the money to belong to the country club. All her friends are white. Every dude she's been linked with has been white too. We call her Candace Owens.

"Protect her from what?" I snap.

I definitely know what the Black White Girl is implying.

"Who knows. You can never be too careful with these *transplants*," Lana says.

"Girl, if you don't—"

Nova holds a hand up, stopping me. She's right. Me cutting up would feed into the little stereotype they're trying to push on us. I bite my lip to stop myself from saying something else.

"Why are you trippin' about the crowd?" Nova says. "Don't like doing your dirt in public?"

Tinsley flinches. "Excuse me?"

"I'ma cut right to it," Nova says. "'Cause what we're not about to do is pretend this is something other than yo' weak-ass attempt to intimidate me into dropping out of the election."

Tinsley's brow creases.

"Sorry, boo-boo, but I ain't Kim Hammerstein," Nova continues, eliciting gasps from a few people and confused looks from everyone else.

Kimberly Hammerstein was Tinsley's rival for captain of the cheerleading squad junior year. We ran into her last week at Jitterbug's, the hamburger spot Nova and my girlfriend work at. Kim spilled some hot tea to us after she overheard us talking about Nova running for homecoming queen.

Kim said she'd been the favorite for captain, being the more skilled cheerleader and all, though she admitted it helped that her mother was the coach's best friend. Kim said Tinsley pulled her aside after practice the day before Ms. Latham, the cheerleading coach, was going to pick the captain and warned her that if she didn't tell Ms. Latham not to consider her, she'd be forced to tell our principal about how Kim sneaks her nineteen-year-old boyfriend onto campus to smoke weed under the bleachers of the football stadium during school hours. When Kim called her bluff, Kim said Tinsley pulled out her phone, and showed her the pictures she had of them in the act. Like I said, the chick is a snake.

Tinsley tilts her head. Little Miss Blackmail is probably wondering how we found out about Kim.

"Whatever you think you know—you don't," she says.

"I know you're naive enough—no, make that delusional enough—to think I'd let you intimidate me," Nova replies.

Tinsley sighs. "You're new here, so you don't understand what this means to me. I've been dreaming about being homecoming queen since I was a little girl. My—"

"Your grandmother, mother, and sister were queens too," I finish for her, rolling my eyes. "She knows. I told her. Next."

"Y'all wouldn't be this cocky if we were having a *real* election this year," Lana says. "Everyone knows she'd never beat Tinsley in a fair vote."

"That's only because *y'all* outnumber us," someone behind us says.

Nova and I both turn back just as our homeboy Trenton steps out of the crowd, and it suddenly hits me how word got out about this showdown. Nova probably mentioned Tinsley's text to him. He's linked to both the Black kids and the white kids since he takes AP courses. He knows the white kids from class, but still hangs with us. He also despises Tinsley, more than I do. He ran his mouth for sure.

"It's a historical fact—y'all don't support us unless we cooning for y'all," I say, looking directly at Giselle.

She actually tries to step up to me like she's 'bout that life. Tinsley's right arm shoots out like she's some soccer mom shielding her kid after throwing on the brakes. She clearly doesn't want this to escalate into something physical. She cares too much about her image.

"Can we *not* bring race into this?" Tinsley says. "That has nothing to do with me wanting to be queen."

"Funny you say that now," Nova answers, "'cause wasn't

you the same student council president who argued that our new election policy is basically *reverse racism* to try and persuade the rest of the council into lobbying the administration to rethink doing it this year?"

Nova's comment excites chatter on both sides. Accusations and insults are flying back and forth. Too many for me to tell who's saying what. I'm just listening to make sure I don't hear the N-word come out of anybody's mouth on Tinsley's side.

"Hold up! It wasn't anything like y'all are making it seem," Tinsley yells, shifting her weight from one foot to the other. "Don't paint me as some bigoted, tiki-torch-carrying, let's-whitewash-history, right-wing conservative because I voiced *concerns* about the racial quotas this school has implemented. Look, I was only saying the policy is another form of discrimination. I definitely think we're all equal. And should be treated fairly. Everyone here agrees, Black lives matter. I blacked out my social media along with everyone else during the police reform protests."

Is this chick serious?

"Yeah, performative activism at its finest," I retort.

"Nooooo," she croaks with an exasperated expression. "However, being excluded from something solely because of my skin tone, which *you* guys say you've had to endure all these years, is kind of unfair to us as well, right?"

A few kids behind her nod and mumble in agreement.

"That's not how this works," I say. "That's not how *any* of this works."

"My only goal in bringing it up to the council was to start a conversation," she says after the chatter subsides. "You're captain of the dance team, Nova. Didn't you hate having to pick a certain number of white girls for the team this year, regardless of how talented the other Black girls were who tried out?"

"Are you admitting that we dance better than y'all?" Nova says, inciting laughter from our side.

"Why don't y'all throw hands and whoever loses drops out!"

That dumbass suggestion came from Jaxson Pafford, who's perched on one of the courtyard's round concrete tables with some of the other football players. His dirty-blond hair looks ten shades lighter underneath the morning sun's warm glow.

"We don't need commentary from the Fuckboy Gallery," Tinsley responds, maintaining eye contact with Nova.

"You wasn't saying that sophomore year," he says, his entourage high-fiving him.

Never would have thought Tinsley would slum it with him. Jax and his family are *way* below her tax bracket.

"Name your price," Tinsley says to Nova.

"My price?"

"Yeah. There has to be something you want more than that crown. Something I can give you instead." Tinsley tucks some of her hair behind her ear, seriousness entering her pale face. "I heard you've been spending your weekends organizing cleanups at the old slave cemetery in your neighborhood. I think that's so noble. So selfless. That place is in such disrepair—"

"How would you know?" someone behind us yells. I have to strain to keep myself from bursting out laughing.

"What if I made a large donation toward its revitalization?" Tinsley continues, unfazed. "I could have my father write the check tonight. Pulling up weeds and picking up trash can only go so far. You're right, history that important deserves respect. Respect I can help you give it. Think of how good it'll look when you can afford new headstones and better landscaping, repair the crumbling graves, maybe even install landmarks and signage."

Some of the pride I've been feeling slowly seeps from my chest like a deflating balloon. Nova's pensive expression has me worried she's really considering it. This I didn't factor, Tinsley trying to bribe Nova into dropping out. Nova's been spending a lot of time cleaning up that cemetery. She even roped me into helping a few weekends, which is when I usually play ball with my Pops. I rarely cancel on him. It's become a passion project of hers. But she has run into a lot of walls when it comes to raising money to really give it the attention it needs.

No. No. No. This is *not* how this was supposed to go.

"You're the only Black girl on the ballot," Tinsley says, her tone even and compassionate. "If you drop out, it'll be impossible for this new policy to be implemented. Which is okay. They can pick a Black girl next year; no harm done."

I know Nova can feel my eyes burning a hole in the side of her face. That's why she's refusing to look at me.

"I heard you weren't even all that excited about being nominated at first," Tinsley continues. "That has to mean something. So how about it? I get you a check for whatever amount you come up with, and you use it to honor your ancestors. You know I can make it happen. Is the crown worth that much to you?"

The three-minute-warning bell goes off, but none of us move. I have to remind myself to breathe.

"Come on, Nova. We're going to be late for class." Trenton places a hand on Nova's shoulder, pulling her out of whatever thoughts Tinsley's proposition has unlocked. "You McArthurs are something else," he says to her. "Is this the only way y'all can get on top? By stepping on someone you think is weaker? Using money to get what you want?"

"What's it gonna be, Nova?" Tinsley says, ignoring Trenton.

Nova blinks, and the hardness she had in her face when we marched up to Tinsley returns. "No, Tinsley. I'm not dropping out."

My chest loosens and I let out my breath.

"And that's that on that," I say with a smile.

"I'm seeing a lot of students who'll be getting detention if this breezeway isn't cleared—and fast!"

Everyone knows that voice. The crowd disperses like ants scattering from a disturbed mound. Mrs. Barnett is standing off to the side with her hands propped on her hips.

"Ladies, do you not have class?" our principal says to us. Giselle and Lana remain at Tinsley's side, just like me and Trenton remain next to Nova. "Mr. Hughes, what's this about?"

"Nothing but our student council president trying to tamper with the homecoming elections," Trenton responds.

"Tinsley? Nova?" Mrs. Barnett's gaze ping-pongs between them.

"No worries, Mrs. Barnett," Nova says. "I think Tinsley understands."

Mrs. Barnett steps up to us. "Understands what?"

"That she'll be homecoming queen over my dead body," Nova says.

Then she spins around and takes off toward B-Building.

Trenton and I follow, leaving Tinsley and her minions standing behind us with Mrs. Barnett.

"I bet Tinsley's seething," I say when we're out of earshot.

"Let her," Trenton says. "We're about to crown this school's first Black queen."

Nova is beaming as we enter B-Building together.

I am too.

My Pops always says that when one of us wins, we all win. I've never felt that more than right now. Taylor might have won in the end of *She's All That,* but in our version, Laney's getting the crown.

CHAPTER TWO

DUCHESS

OCTOBER 7

1:15 P.M.

LOVETT HIGH IS really two different schools masquerading as one. Most of the people who deny that are white.

This school has never had a Black homecoming queen, student council president, or prom queen. Any schoolwide elected positions have always gone to *them*—the white kids. They outnumber us. They've known one another and attended school together since kindergarten. That makes it hard to win any of this school's popularity contests. A fact us Black kids had to accept since we were forced to go here after Hurricane Katrina.

The student population was 95 percent white before Katrina. Everyone focuses more on the damage the storm did to the city of New Orleans, but Katrina wrecked shop along the Mississippi Gulf Coast too. It leveled our town and all the others that dot the coastline. All kinds of tornadoes tore through here, flattening entire neighborhoods, businesses, and our two high schools—this one and Booker High, the school us Black kids used to attend. The school district wasted no time allocating the money to rebuild Lovett back then. But Booker . . . that was a different story.

They *claimed* that it wasn't feasible to reconstruct Booker because of its poor academic performance and extensive building damage. Translation: the all-white school board wasn't about to pour a whole bunch of money into rebuilding a school for the Black kids who consistently whipped their majority-white sports teams here. They had a better idea: close Booker and split up the student body, busing half the students to a high school in the next town and sending the rest to Lovett, where they spent millions on top of millions to expand so they could accommodate all the new Black faces who would coincidentally become the star athletes that transformed the school's weak-ass sports program into the multidivision champions they are today.

For the past decade, the leaders of the local NAACP have publicly called out all the disparities the situation created. Their efforts finally got some traction after the nationwide police reform protests, or as I like to say, when white people finally wanted to acknowledge that systemic racism exists. The school's administration folded to the calls for change, implementing racial quotas for all clubs and after-school activities, starting this year.

The homecoming court got expanded so that it would include two slots for all the grade-level maids—one girl from the standard curriculum and another enrolled in the school's AP curriculum. For queen, the student body would have to elect a senior girl from the standard curriculum one year and the next choose a girl from the AP side, alternating each year going forward, starting with the election of a senior girl from the standard curriculum this year.

It's basically the school ensuring the court will be composed of one Black girl—or person of color, though around here, that color is mainly Black—and one white girl at each grade level, with the crown for queen being passed between a white and Black girl every other year since most of the Black kids make up the "standard" students and all the white ones are the AP kids.

My girl Nova has already got the crown locked up. But white folks are funny to me. As long as everything is swinging in their favor, all you hear from them is "Work hard and you can achieve anything." The minute we get even a crumb tossed at us, suddenly they lose their mind and wanna play victim, the way Tinsley McBitchy is.

Let her be butt-hurt. It's entertaining. This is *our* year, and no one can take it away from us.

"Would you ever mess around with a white dude?" Nova's voice pulls me out of my head and into the present.

I'm doodling in my art sketchbook. I sit up straighter on my stool, scrunching my nose at her. "Girl, really?"

"Forgot who I was talking to," she says with a chuckle. "How about a white girl? Could you see yourself ever dating one?"

Hell to the no! And she should know why.

"Bih, you know me better than that," I respond, looking back down at the entangled set of lines, shapes, and shading I've spent all period working on. The abstract drawing Mr.

Haywood assigned that I've decided is my interpretation of the mental struggles I have of being a queer Black woman in this country. He's probably not going to get it.

"Stop capping. You know I know you've kissed one before."

She catches my eyes shift over to the art table where Tinsley and Jessica Thambley are seated, two rows behind us.

Introduction to Drawing and Painting is the only class where I see any white faces who aren't faculty or staff. It's like that for most of us Black kids. Electives are really the only classes we share with the AP kids. The NAACP recently called attention to that as well, accusing the school's administration of discouraging us from testing into advanced placement courses. We all know they only created the AP curriculum to appease the white parents who pretended they were concerned the teachers would have to spend too much time catching up the Booker High transfers when the school first reopened. In reality, they just don't want their kids mingling with us. Separate but equal is still as Southern as iced tea.

"Don't even try and bring that up, trick," I say to Nova, whose smirk lights up her pretty eyes. "I was eight. It was innocent. And it taught me why I'll never trust any of them again."

I still feel Nova watching me after I go back to scribbling in my sketchbook.

I pause. "What?" I say to her.

She leans closer and whispers, "I heard she asked Mrs. Barnett to take her name off the ballot."

"Who?"

"Tinsley," she replies, nodding her head in her direction.

I smack my lips and go back to my drawing. "Girl, I'll be

so glad when homecoming is over and you can stop obsessing over her. We won. Let's enjoy it and not worry about her. You act like she slept with yo' man and you need to get revenge."

"I'm teaching her a lesson, that's all."

"Uh-huh."

"I'm hearing a lot of talking over there," Mr. Haywood says, looking over at us as he's meandering around the room to see what everyone else is working on. "I assume you'll both have finished your drawings by the time I get over there."

Nova and I bend back over our sketchbooks, biting our lips to keep from laughing.

"Mr. Haywood, I'm done," Jessica Thambley announces, waving her skinny arm in the air. "Wanna come take a look at mine?"

"Oh God, here she go again," Nova whispers.

"Wannabe teacher's pet," I reply, rolling my eyes.

"Nah, wannabe teacher's little ho."

"*Ew,* he's old . . . and engaged."

"I don't think Vanilla Barbie cares."

We both giggle, which draws a stern look from Mr. Haywood.

It's kinda funny how all these chicks be fawning over him. I mean, it's understandable, I guess. Dude's not bad-looking, and he's not *that* old. He only just graduated college. He sort of looks like Adam Driver, oozing that awkward, unconventional handsomeness girls somehow find hot. He lightly touches the small of Jessica's back as he reaches her. I almost burst out laughing again because I catch Jessica deeply inhale when he leans over to look at whatever she drew.

"Why'd you ask me that?" I whisper to Nova now that Mr. Haywood is distracted.

"Ask you what?"

"About messing around with a white person."

She stops shading with her pencil a brief second, her eyes quickly flicking my way, then returning to her notebook. "Briana was giving Nikki a hard time the other day about dating Chance. Saying she can't really be pro-Black dating a white dude." Nova rotates her sketchbook and tilts her head to the right, studying her drawing with a furrowed brow. "Just wondered what you thought, that's all," she adds with a shrug.

Briana and Nikki are my girlfriend's friends who we've been hanging around a lot lately. Even though that sounds like something Briana would say, something about the way Nova's tone changed when she said it feels inauthentic. Pops says I have a sixth sense about these types of things. Says my ability to sense when someone is trying to hide things is why I would make a good police investigator. Spent most of childhood thinking I would prove him right.

The chime of the school's intercom system stops me from hounding Nova for the truth.

She shoots up straighter on her stool the second Mrs. Barnett's raspy voice echoes from the loudspeaker above the whiteboard in front of class. I forgot the homecoming election results were being announced today. A smirk pulls on my lips. It's going down in the one class we have with Tinsley. Nice.

"I bet she's back there about to lose it," Nova says, reading my mind.

I fight the urge to look over my shoulder to see if that's true.

After some dry speech about everyone being winners re-gardless of the results, Mrs. Barnett starts reading off the names of the court, starting with the freshmen. A few people in class clap when Jessica is announced as one of the junior maids, shocking no one. She's one of the pretty/popular girls. Tinsley Jr., if you will. Cheerleader. Country club brat. I think she's been on the court since freshman year too, like Tinsley. She'll probably be the queen next year.

"And finally, our esteemed queen this year is Nova Al-bright, who I know will serve the title well as this school's first Black queen," Mrs. Barnett says.

"Yeeeaaaahhh," Nova and I sing in unison before poking our tongues out at each other in our best Cardi B impressions.

"And because the only other girl nominated from the senior class dropped out at the last minute, there will be no senior maid this year," Mrs. Barnett continues. "Congratulations to all the winners."

Half the class looks back at Tinsley, who is shrugging her messenger bag onto her shoulder as the bell rings to end class.

"Congratulations, Nova," Mr. Haywood says as he walks past our table on his way to the front of class. "It'll be great when we can move past having semi-rigged elections to foster inclusion."

No he didn't.

Tinsley walks by, her nose pointed at the ceiling. Nova steps out of the crowd, blocking her path to the door.

"Tinsley, aren't you gonna congratulate me?" Nova teases.

Tinsley steps up to her with that resting bitch face that has a lot of these white girls around here scared of her. I push through the crowd to stand next to Nova.

"Good luck getting a ball gown for your coronation," she says matter-of-factly. "I doubt you'll find anything grand enough that your mother can afford, you know, since Klarna isn't an option."

Everyone within earshot howls.

Nova doesn't get the chance to respond. Tinsley pushes past her and stalks out of class.

When Nova turns around to me, I can tell she's trying to blink back tears. She's never said it, but I know she's embarrassed her mother barely earns above minimum wage working as a cashier at one of the neighborhood grocery stores.

"Fuck that bitch," I say, grabbing Nova by the wrists and looking in her eyes. "*You* are the queen. That's all that matters."

CHAPTER THREE

TINSLEY

OCTOBER 7
4:12 P.M.

"**SO YOU'RE GIVING** me the cold shoulder because you're upset with her?"

"Nathan, don't," I warn.

After a few seconds of stilted silence he says, "Excuse me for trying to be supportive."

"A *supportive* boyfriend wouldn't be pressuring his girlfriend to talk after she distinctly told him she didn't want to when she got into said boyfriend's truck."

I knew I should have taken Lana up on her offer to give me a ride home after cheerleading practice. I didn't drive to school today. My mother had to take my car to the dealership for brake repairs. Lana would have at least commiserated with me over the Nova situation. Nathan, on the other hand, thinks I need to "accept it and move on."

"Babe, it's not the end of the world." He takes one hand off the steering wheel of the new silver Ford F-150 his parents gifted him for his senior year. He attempts to place it on my knee, but I snap my leg over before he can make contact. "Come on, chill, Tins. You knew she was going to win."

I have to look out the passenger window and count to myself to keep from going off on him. Conversations like this don't make me regret cheating on him while I was on vacation in France with my family this summer.

"Babe, seriously—"

"Nathan, please stop talking." I yank off the elastic that's been holding my ponytail since practice, using my other hand to shake my hair loose. "You made your point loud and clear. This is all a joke to you."

"That's not true. I'm just bored by how much of a big deal everyone in this freaking town makes it. You'd think it was the Miss America pageant or something."

Lovett High's homecoming queen practically becomes this town's version of Miss America. Her reign goes far beyond just being paraded out on the football field with her father during halftime at one game. Not only does she become the pseudo–student spokesperson for the school alongside the student council president, she also serves as a social ambassador for the town's tourism office. For twelve months she acts as hostess at various festivals and city-sponsored events. She gets invited to fancy parties with state leaders. Lovett High's homecoming queen has become an institution.

And Nathan knows that. His aunt held the title two years after my mother. Every time I see the woman, she brags about all the political connections she made while being queen, and how they led to her becoming our current lieutenant governor. I intended to use the title as a springboard to become a social media influencer. Something the infusion of followers and public appearances being queen could have easily helped me achieve.

Fuck you, Nova!

"Babe, all I'm saying is—"

"Can you please *not* say . . . anything?"

He doesn't until we turn on Main Street, which puts the blinking skyline of the hotels and casinos that dot the eastern end of Beachfront Boulevard in his rearview mirrors. He offers me a weak apology before asking me to go somewhere with him this weekend. I barely hear him because my attention is focused on the array of cafés and boutiques we're whizzing past. My wandering gaze freezes on two people seated at one of the wrought-iron tables in front of Frozen Delights. A sight that causes my breath to catch in my throat.

"What d'you say, babe?"

I poke my head out the window, craning my neck to the right as Nathan zooms by. My heart starts to race. I definitely saw what I saw.

"Does that sound like a plan?"

"Yeah, whatever," I mumble, settling back in the passenger seat.

I press my hand to my chest to steady my breathing.

"Babe, what's wrong?" Nathan asks. "Tins?"

I can't speak to answer him because I can't comprehend why *my father* is sitting at a table downtown eating frozen yogurt with Nova Albright.

The crown is heavy, darlings, so just leave it where it belongs.

Ever since Lisa Vanderpump, my favorite Real Housewife, started to use it as her tagline, it's been mine as well. I say it to myself every time I try on one of the three crowns we keep in a glass display case in our formal living room. I whisper it now as I place my mother's crown on my head.

My grandmother's crown and scepter are perched on the top shelf of the display case. I'm still shocked my mother hasn't moved it to one of the lower shelves, given how much she despised my father's mother—a feeling that was completely mutual.

My mother's crown and scepter take up the second shelf, and my sister's sit just below it on the third. I daydreamed my own would get placed beside hers—or that my mother would buy a new display shelf to house the four sets. The reality of that never happening makes lifting my arms to remove my mother's crown a little harder.

The crown and engraved scepters every Lovett High home-coming queen receives aren't the run-of-the-mill plastic tiaras you see at nearly every other high school. A family-owned local jeweler has crafted and donated the pieces to our high school's queens since the daughter of the family's patriarch won the title two years before my grandmother. The designs of the crown and scepter have varied over the years, but the quality remains the same. The sparkling accessories are made of sterling silver and adorned with hundreds of cubic zirconia crystals.

After replacing my mother's crown on its tiny red velvet pillow, I pick up her scepter, appreciating the weight of the fifteen-inch wand in my hand. Rachel got grounded once for hitting me with hers after she caught me playing with it. She chipped one of my teeth and cracked her scepter's glass orb by batting me in the mouth with it. The crack catches the overhead lighting in the display case, almost winking at me as I replace my mother's scepter. I make sure it's positioned in the holster so that my mother's name, engraved on the metal piece connecting the glass and cubic zirconia orb to the wand, as it is for every winner, can be read through the glass door—just like my sister's and grandmother's.

"Tinsley!"

I spin around, thinking I'll find my mother standing beneath one of the two archways to the room.

"Dinner's ready!" she yells. "We're in the dining room, sweetie."

My brows knit.

We? That must mean my father's home.

I take a deep breath before charging out of the room and across the foyer.

What in the hell was he doing today with Nova?

My frown immediately dissolves and my mouth slackens once I enter our dining room. The "we" my mother was referring to is actually Rachel and my three-year-old niece, Lindsey, who are seated with their backs to me. They must have arrived while I was upstairs showering and changing out of my practice uniform.

"Where's Nathan?" my mother asks from her seat at the head of the table.

I return the enthusiastic wave my niece gives me before replying, "Home. Sorry to deprive you of the opportunity to fawn over my boyfriend, but I wasn't in the mood for his company." As I round the table I add, "Rachel, you're here . . . again . . . eating with us instead of at the house you live in with your husband. It's only been three years. Don't tell me Aiden is that sick of you already?"

Rachel is seven years older than me. She made our mother one of the happiest women in the world the day she married Aiden Prescott on her twenty-first birthday, two months after he graduated from Ole Miss. The Prescott family made most of their fortune in real estate. My sister's relationship with Aiden, which was basically arranged by their mothers, has been financially beneficial to my father's construction company, where Aiden became the chief administrative officer shortly after they were married.

Our mother appointed herself architect of our social lives at birth, her driving force being her daughters wouldn't have to fight so hard to maintain the lifestyle she had to marry into. Ironically, that involved us marrying into other well-to-do families who frequent the country club with us. For Rachel she picked Aiden Prescott; for me, Nathan Fairchild, who also comes from one of this town's oldest and wealthiest families.

"How did the election go today? Oh wait, I already know," Rachel says as I drop down into the chair opposite her.

I feel like picking up my knife and slicing the smirk off her face.

"Girls," my mother warns.

"Is Aiden working late again tonight? That's usually code that your husband is hooking up with someone younger and hotter than you, which in your case would mean he could be sleeping with someone who goes to school with me," I say.

That takes care of the smirk. Her shoulders tense as well. I've struck a nerve. Good. How dare she bring up the homecoming election like that?

"Tinsley, I know you've been on edge all week over that mess at school, but let's not take it out on your sister, okay?"

"I don't see how she should be feeling any sort of way, really." Rachel pulls a lock of her hair, which she dyed jetblack last month, behind her ear. "She's had the whole summer to accept the inevitability of it all."

My jaw clenches. "You're so right, Rachel. Maybe I should have sought counseling at Abundant Life, like you did at my age, to sort through my emotions."

My mother's gasp echoes through the room. My sister's nostrils flare.

Abundant Life is a clinic in Harrison County approximately seventy-five miles outside Lovett. It offers various health care services to women, most of whom are low-income or impoverished, but it specializes in providing discreet abortions, like the one my sister had when she was sixteen.

"Tinsley, I swear to God," my mother snaps, her French-manicured fingertip pointed at me. "You breathe another word about *that* and you'll regret it."

"Then tell your daughter not to provoke me," I retort.

"*Both* of you, enough!" my mother shouts. "I didn't go through all the trouble of having this nice meal prepared and setting the table for y'all to bicker. I thought having a family dinner could soften the disappointment of what Tinsley had to deal with today."

It's typical of my mother to think a pretentious meal would somehow make me feel better.

Jalapeno-stuffed catfish and crawfish Alfredo are steaming on two silver serving dishes in the center of the table. I lift my gaze from the food and lock eyes with Rachel. She quickly picks up her phone and pretends it's more interesting than we are. Bringing up her abortion was a low blow. But I was clearly joking about Aiden having an affair. Rachel usually isn't that easy to rattle.

"Tinsley, you wouldn't be in this predicament had we pushed back harder when this new policy was being discussed." My mother picks up the glass of wine sitting in front of her. "But no, you didn't want everyone to think we were racists."

"I wasn't the only one. I don't remember any of the other white parents speaking out against it either—at least not publicly."

"Well, it's offensive, if you ask me," she says after taking a sip of wine. "I swear, all we seem to talk about in this country anymore is race. Focusing on it so much is what has us divided."

Definitely agree with her on that.

Having me serve as homecoming queen meant bragging rights for her as much as it did for me. The day I told her Nova was threatening our legacy, she actually shattered the wineglass she was holding. Nothing bonds us like our shared contempt for someone.

"What's done is done." My mother puts down her glass and claps her hands. "Let's eat before all this food gets cold."

"Granny, I thought you said we had to wait for Grandpa."

My mother gives Lindsey a warm smile. "I did, sweetie, but it looks like Grandpa is working late too, so we might as well dig in."

The image of Nova and my father together flashes through my mind.

"Rachel, we're at the dinner table," my mother says after reaching over to spoon some of the crawfish Alfredo onto her plate. "Please put the phone down."

"Hold on a sec. I'm reading an article. Looks like they finally caught that guy, Curtis Delmont, who the police think killed that family in Jackson."

I use my fork to lift one of the stuffed catfish off the platter. "That guy they spent three days looking for?"

Rachel nods, her eyes still on her phone.

"Thank God! What he did to that poor couple and their little girl is just awful," my mother says.

While I've been obsessing over Nova and the homecoming elections, everyone else was wrapped up in the murders of Noah and Monica Holt, which have dominated the local news all week. And not just because the couple was fatally shot in their home along with their eight-year-old daughter, but because the Jackson, Mississippi, police think the person who entered their house midmorning and killed the family execution-style is their gardener—a man who worked for the family for years and had some kind of dispute with the husband the day before the murders. The racial undertones of the crime have intensified news coverage. The Holts were white, and the gardener is a Black man.

"There's no solid proof yet he killed them, Mama," Rachel drawls.

"Then what do you call several neighbors who saw that man running out of the house shortly after hearing the gunshots?"

"One neighbor also told police she saw Curtis Delmont

enter the house around ten-fifteen, which conflicts with every-one who said they saw him run out of the house not too long after that. He couldn't have shot three people that fast."

"Oh please, Rachel," my mother replies, rolling her eyes.

"His family and friends say he doesn't even own a gun—and has never shot one," Rachel counters. "The police are charging him with murder without any real evidence. It's crazy."

"Only an animal could do that," my mother says. "There's no telling how that man was raised. I read somewhere he didn't grow up in the best surroundings, if you know what I mean." My mother widens her eyes when she says that last part.

I stuff a bite of catfish into my mouth. I want no part of this conversation once I see the look on my sister's face as she puts down her phone.

"By that standard, you're capable of doing horrible things too, Mama. You know, since you grew up in that trailer park."

I nearly choke on my catfish. A vein is protruding along my mother's neck. Her past has always been a touchy subject, one she has chosen to ignore since marrying my father. In her mind, the moment she became Charlotte McArthur, she was no longer "white trash," as she had been called growing up. Unfortunately, it took the people in my father's world a lot lon-ger to accept her, including his mother.

"My past has *nothing* to do with this." My mother twirls the noodles from her crawfish with her fork. "I wasn't raised around violence. *That* man was. There's no telling how that affected him."

"You don't know that—"

"Rachel, drop this, okay? I knew it was a mistake letting you attend LSU. You came back with all these liberal *ideas*."

The front door slams as Rachel opens her mouth to respond.

"Sorry I'm late, ladies." My father seems to cut through the tension as soon as he enters the dining room. He pauses to squeeze Rachel's shoulder before leaning over Lindsey's chair to kiss the top of her head. "We had a bit of good news I had to stay behind and take care of."

I have my lips pinched when he comes over to kiss me on the cheek. Knowing that he just lied knots my stomach.

He gives my mother a tight smile and a curt nod before taking the seat at the opposite end of the table.

"What good news?" she asks.

"Found out we got that affordable housing project over in the Avenues," he replies, unfolding the cloth napkin tented in the middle of his plate and spreading it across his lap.

"Excuse me?" my mother says.

I'm surprised to see frown lines across her forehead. I know she had a Botox appointment two weeks ago. She's holding her fork in midair. "I thought the Hughes brothers were at the front of the line for that project."

My father forks one of the stuffed catfish onto his plate, his eyes nervously shifting toward my mother a few times. "Yeah, I think they might have been."

"I thought you were done stepping on Clayton's toes."

"This wasn't about that, Charlotte."

My mother puts down her fork. "Then what is it about?"

I glance over at Rachel, who looks as confused and uncomfortable as me. All I know is Clayton Hughes is Trenton's father. He used to work for my father until they had a falling-out.

"I think it's a great thing, Daddy," Rachel says. "Mama was just complaining about unhealthy environments sparking violent behavior in *some* people. Glad to see somebody in the family can acknowledge certain needs and work to address them."

I stuff a crawfish in my mouth to hide my grin.

"I appreciate that, honey. But it's gonna mean a lot of late nights for Aiden. This project will have a lot of moving parts to it."

Rachel's face goes slack when she hears that.

"Charlotte, this fish is excellent," my father says, stabbing the second-to-last catfish fillet off the platter. "Please give my compliments to whoever you had cater it. I might need to take a run after dinner."

I gulp down some water to help me swallow the bite of crawfish that now tastes like cardboard. This is the window I've been looking for.

"I can't believe you have such an appetite, Daddy, since you already had dessert this afternoon."

My father slowly lowers his fork, side-eyeing me. "Huh?"

"Was that not you I saw with Nova Albright this afternoon?" Some of the color drains from his face. "You were eating yogurt outside Frozen Delights, am I right?"

My mother's fork clanks against her plate and we all whip our heads in her direction. If she had the power to set things on fire with her eyes, my father would be singed right now.

"Virgil, what in the hell is Tinsley talking about?" she says.

"*Oooooh,* Mommy, Granny said a no-no word," Lindsey says.

"It's not what you think, Charlotte," my father says.

"What could she possibly think?" I interject. "How could you do this to me? Why are you entertaining the girl who stole the crown from me?"

"She didn't *steal* anything, she won it fair and square," my father responds.

"I'd hardly call it fair," I protest.

"Why are you defending *her*?" my mother demands. "And more importantly, how did it happen? Did she reach out to you?"

My mother's voice trembles slightly.

My father drops his fork and then lifts his cloth napkin to wipe his mouth. "She reached out. She asked if my company would serve as her sponsor."

My mouth drops open.

Getting local businesses to help pay for the gowns and accessories it takes to maintain the pomp and circumstance of being Lovett High's homecoming queen isn't uncommon, especially for girls who win but can't afford it. But to my knowledge, my father has never sponsored a queen, unless you count my sister.

This must be Nova's way of getting back at me for what I said to her in class today. I've been underestimating her.

"There's no way in hell I'm going to allow you to sponsor that girl," my mother says.

"*Allow* me?" my father says before I can chime in.

"What did you tell her, Virgil?" my mom asks.

My father casts a nervous glance in my direction. "Said I'd think about it."

"Are you freaking kidding me!" I wail.

"You will not give that girl a cent," my mother follows.

"She only asked, all right?" my father yells. After several seconds of silence he adds, "I won't do it, okay?" which he says more to me than to anyone else.

They eat the rest of their dinner in silence. I just push my food around on my plate. The only thing I've got a taste for is revenge.

CHAPTER FOUR

TINSLEY

OCTOBER 12
4:05 P.M.

CHEERLEADING PRACTICE ENDED up lasting an extra thirty minutes today. Ms. Latham felt our stunts were sloppy. Her annoyed gaze landed on me when she said it. She made us run through them all afternoon and I felt like I was going to throw up the whole time.

When we were finally done, some of the girls serving as hostesses at the coronation Friday night lingered to discuss final details. When me, Lana, and Giselle told Ms. Latham earlier that we were opting out this year, she nodded with a tight smile, understanding why we wouldn't want to do it.

"I'm sorry, what?" I say to Giselle as we plod off the football field toward the gym. I use the end of the towel around my neck to blot the sweat off my forehead.

"I *said* Jennifer Stansbury told me she saw Nova in Exquisite Designs last night, getting her coronation dress fitted."

Giselle uses her hand to fan herself. "She *claims* the dress is gorgeous—Jen's words, not mine."

It's been five days since Nova was officially announced homecoming queen, and she is all I've been thinking about since then.

Since my useless friends couldn't find anything I could use to blackmail Nova into dropping out of the elections, I'm dedicating the rest of the semester to bringing her down. That involves turning her into the most embarrassing queen this school ever has. Exposing any secrets she has and circulating whatever rumors I can to smear her name is one way I can do that. Petty but effective. Like this town, our school thrives on gossip.

"I wonder who her sponsor is," Giselle says, reading my mind. "Exquisite Designs is expensive. You definitely don't think it's your father, right?"

"He knows better," I say.

My parents argued for at least an hour after our dinner Friday night. I couldn't hear everything they were shouting at one another, but I did hear my mother threaten to expose how my father scored some of the development contracts with the town if he gave Nova one cent. I can only assume his childhood friendship with the mayor has something to do with it.

"Maybe it's that older dude I saw her arguing with in front of school," Lana says.

"What older dude?" Giselle and I both ask.

"I don't know," she replies with a shrug. "The guy looked old enough to be her father."

"How do you know it wasn't?" I press.

From what we've heard about Nova, she's never met her

father. I heard she's told people he abandoned her mother before she was born. Apparently, that's why her mom moved away. She only moved back here to live in the house her grandmother left her mother when she died a year ago, according to Lana and Giselle.

"No way that man was her father," Lana says. "Not the way he was leering at her, even after she stormed off."

"Girl, when did you see this?" Giselle asks.

"I saw it all go down as I was walking on to campus this morning. They were on the sidewalk, a few feet from the main gates." Lana takes a swig from her canteen. "She looked embarrassed to see him."

"And you're *just now* telling me this?" I snap. "I can never depend on you to deliver when I need you to."

Nova in an inappropriate relationship? This is the type of dirt I could have used *before* the elections. I need better friends.

"Can you at least work on perfecting your toe touches since they're still trash?" I say to Lana as I yank open the door to the gym.

I come to a stop in the doorway.

There are people everywhere. Jaxson Pafford and some of the other football players are moving tables and arranging folding chairs. Girls are hanging paper streamers along the wall and bleachers, which are retracted. Mrs. Barnett is barking orders off to the side, a clear clipboard clutched in both hands. This is where the coronation dinner will take place, after Nova is crowned at the ceremony in the auditorium.

The girls who returned to the gym with me push past me and file through the door. I go in last. We gather near the black baseline of the basketball court.

My eyes narrow on Nova, who's at the center of the court in the hunter-green running shorts and T-shirts the girls on the dance squad wear for practice. A few of the other Black girls on the squad are gathered around her, all of them gawking, as if watching the gym's transformation is this miraculous thing. The same girls who assured me after the new election policy was announced that none of the Black girls in standard curriculum were interested in being homecoming queen this year. Lulling me into a false sense of security about being able to hold the title despite the new policy.

Seeing them cackling together unlocks a new streak of rage in me.

I take off in their direction, focusing on Nova.

"Tins, what are you doing?" Giselle whines behind me.

I can hear the rest of the girls at my back as well.

Nova notices me approaching a few yards before I reach her. She steps in front of the girls standing with her.

"Everything looks beautiful, huh?" she says with a smirk that lights up her turquoise eyes.

My girls fan out to my left and right, mirroring the way the girls from the dance squad are lined up on either side of Nova.

"*Beautiful* isn't the word that springs to mind. More like *common*," I say, looking her up and down. "Decided who's escorting you on the field yet? We know it won't be your father. Perhaps that guy you were arguing with this morning? Lana was just telling me how . . . *friendly* y'all looked."

Nova's shoulders fall and her cocky grin deflates.

So the queen does have a secret after all.

A sneer pulls at the corners of my mouth. "Lovers' quarrel? God, I hope not," I say with a mocking frown toward the girls on my side. "From what Lana said, that guy looked old as fuck. You got some serious daddy issues, girl."

"You don't want to go there, Tinsley, trust me," Nova says through clenched teeth.

"Oh, sweetie, I know all about your desperate attempt to get my father to sponsor you. Nice try. Guess your sugar daddy is paying for whatever gaudy gown you're getting from Exquisite Designs, 'cause my *actual* daddy sure ain't."

"That was my uncle, bitch!" Nova steps forward. "But it's good to know I'm living rent free in your mind."

"Calm down, girl." I press a hand to my chest in faux concern. "I was only worried our homecoming queen might be in an inappropriate relationship. Everyone on the squad thinks it's a little suspect, that's all. I'd hate for a nasty rumor to get out of control and taint your victory."

Nova cuts her eyes to my left. I follow her gaze, which is pointed at Jessica Thambley. She's one of the girls who stayed behind to talk to Ms. Latham about working at the coronation dinner. Jessica and the rest of them are now lined up to my far left. I didn't notice them join us.

"Is that true?" Nova has an eyebrow raised.

Jessica's eyes drop to the floor. "Can you guys leave me out of this?" she mumbles.

"Of course we can," I say. "Nova's the one who's deflecting. It's clear you're hiding something about this *uncle* of yours. Maybe I should let the school's administration decide whether it's appropriate or not."

Nova thumbs her diamond pendant. There's an unsettling coldness behind her glassy eyes. "When I started school here, I thought we could be friends. You know, the kind that seem more like sisters. But I realize now I could never be close to a chick like you. You're too insecure."

My heart is pounding in my ears.

"Girls, what's going on over there?" Mrs. Barnett shouts from across the gym. Neither Nova nor I break eye contact.

"Look, bitch, please don't let being homecoming queen go to your head. I still rule here."

Nova rolls her eyes. "I advise you to step the fuck back before—"

"Before what?" I snap. "Watch your mouth, unless you want everyone at this school to hear about your scandalous affair with your *uncle*."

The next thing I know, red-hot pain lashes across my face.

If my ear weren't ringing, I'd be able to hear the gasps I see on everyone's faces.

My hand clenches into a fist. "That was a mistake," I say, right before slamming it into Nova's face.

Before I know it, she and I are rolling on the floor clenching handfuls of each other's hair. Everyone's shouting suffocates us. Hands are pulling at me from all sides. And I scream, "You're dead, bitch!" before Mrs. Barnett and Jaxson can tear us apart.

Neither of us has said a word since Mrs. Barnett ordered us to take a seat outside her office while she called our parents. I'm seated on the stiff wooden chair closest to her door. Nova is slouched in an identical chair on the opposite side of the entrance to the school's administrative offices. Aside from Mrs. Barnett, whose door is closed, we're the only people here. The persistent ticking of the wall clock on the other side of the room fills the silence.

My cheek still burns. My ponytail is lopsided; errant strands of my hair shoot in every direction. The collar of my crewneck is ripped. Every slight movement seems to expose a new scratch or bruise I begin to feel more and more as the adrenaline leaves my blood.

"Fighting? You know I can't afford to be taking off work for this!"

I turn and there's a woman in the doorway who bears a striking resemblance to Nova. She's wearing a bright orange vest with the words *Quick Mart* stitched in blue across the right-side chest, over a loose-fitting T-shirt and skinny jeans.

"I raised you better than this," Nova's mother says as she steps in front of her daughter.

Ms. Albright's dark face hardens as soon as she notices me, and she turns back to Nova.

"Didn't I tell you to stay away from her?" she says, eye level with her daughter. Her index finger is pointed in Nova's face. "I knew it was a mistake moving back here. You're acting out again."

Again?

"*She* got up in *my* face," Nova says, sitting up straighter. "I wasn't stuntin' her ass!"

"Watch yo' tone," Ms. Albright snaps.

"Do me a favor and use this same energy to keep yo' brother away from me," Nova says, and glances over at me. "Then I won't have to deal with her and her friends trying to start shit about him."

Ms. Albright cringes as she slowly straightens her posture. The air is feeling heavier suddenly.

"Where did you see him?" Ms. Albright asks, her voice trembling a little.

"He was waiting for me outside school this morning," Nova replies.

"What did he want?"

"What do you *think*?" Nova retorts.

To the best of my ability, I keep facing forward while casting sideways glances at Nova and her mother. Ms. Albright is pulling at the strap of the tattered black purse hanging on her right shoulder as she stares down at her daughter. Just as she's about to say something, she closes her mouth.

I shift in my chair and realize that my mother is now standing in the doorway. She's wearing a white polo and matching tennis skirt. That means Mrs. Barnett's phone call interrupted one of her pseudo tennis games with her friends at the club. They're really more an excuse to drink wine during the day.

She looks at Nova first and then Ms. Albright, her nose scrunched as if they're rancid garbage stinking up the room. I can't help but smile at her dramatics.

"Let me guess, you're the mother?" she says to Ms. Albright, who appears somewhat confused by the question. "You put her up to attacking my daughter because my husband refused to give her the money she practically got down on her ashy little knees and begged for?"

"That's *not* what I did," Nova snaps.

"*Hush!*" her mother hisses.

"Let me clear up the confusion."

Mrs. Barnett has stepped out of her office. She's still looking as pissed as she was when she pulled me and Nova apart in the gym.

"The girls are here because Nova slapped Tinsley and Tinsley retaliated by hitting her back," Mrs. Barnett explains.

"Like I said, it was an attack," my mother taunts Ms. Albright.

"Tinsley isn't innocent in this," Mrs. Barnett interjects. "Nova slapped her after Tinsley made antagonizing remarks."

"*That* girl has been antagonizing my daughter ever since you let her become homecoming queen!" my mother shrieks, pointing at Nova.

"That's a lie!" Nova shouts, standing up from her chair.

"Nova, be *quiet*!" her mother orders. She looks at Mrs. Barnett and says, "That girl tried to bully my daughter into dropping out of the homecoming race. Why didn't y'all do anything about that? Don't y'all have some kind of antibullying policy?"

"Both girls are at fault here," Mrs. Barnett responds.

"I hope that doesn't mean my daughter is getting suspended for defending herself," Ms. Albright says.

Nova's face folds into a pained look. It's registering for her what being suspended would mean. She wouldn't be able to participate in any extracurricular activities, meaning the coronation Friday. It would all be so perfect if I weren't in danger of getting suspended too.

"I called you mothers both here to discuss alternative punishments for the girls," Mrs. Barnett says. "I don't think it would be right or fair to suspend Nova in this instance, given she's our queen and—"

"You're protecting *her*?" My mother is seething. "The

McArthur family built this school, and this is how you treat our daughter?"

Mrs. Barnett folds her arms across her chest. "You act like you did it for free. Your husband was paid—very well, I might add—just like any contractor would be had they been awarded the project."

"Mama, chill," I beg her.

Given the tantrum I threw to be removed from the homecoming ballots, I'm definitely not one of Mrs. Barnett's favorite people right now.

"I don't intend to suspend Tinsley either, although I probably should," Mrs. Barnett says more to me than my mother.

I don't realize how tense I've been until a wave of lightness ripples through my body at her words. My blemish-free disciplinary record will remain intact.

"I can understand why emotions have been high this week between the girls, but I also can't let them go unpunished." Mrs. Barnett weaves her fingers together and drops her hands in front of her stomach. "They'll each have a month's worth of Saturday detentions. That's nonnegotiable."

Okay, I guess not completely blemish-free anymore.

My mother grabs me by the wrist, yanking me out of my chair. "Whatever. We're leaving, Tinsley. I have half a mind to drop out of the coronation ceremony."

The school invites former queens to participate in the coronation every year. The previous queens usually serenade the newly crowned queen with our school's alma mater. Both Rachel and my mother have agreed to participate, according to my mother, "out of obligation."

"That would totally be up to you, Charlotte." Mrs. Barnett

cocks her head. "We have a number of former queens who I'm certain would love to contribute in a greater capacity if you're not in the way—I mean, so eager to be involved."

My mother mumbles something I can't hear as she yanks on my arm. She pauses in the doorway, casting a venomous look over her shoulder at the Albrights, before pulling me with her out the door.

CHAPTER FIVE

DUCHESS

OCTOBER 14

8:03 P.M.

"IT NEVER FAILS. White people will find a way to center themselves in our progress."

Evelyn lifts her head and follows my sight line across the gym, where my girl Nova is surrounded by the mayor, his wife, and Mrs. Barnett.

"Chill, bae." Ev looks back down at her phone. She's bored. "Isn't this what the newly crowned queen supposed to do at this reception? Take pictures with all these pretentious-ass folks?"

"It doesn't annoy you how they've been taking ownership all night of something we waited so long to get?" I say. "The inflection in their voices when they kept calling her *their* first Black homecoming queen. She's not theirs. She's *ours*. They acting like it was their idea to finally do the right thing by us."

"You gonna give yourself an aneurysm," my girl says. "Remember, when one of us wins, we all win."

"Yeah, *us,* not them."

Nova has been paraded around this reception like she's a show pony, the white folks hogging all her time with requests for selfies I'm sure they've posted on their social media to prove how "progressive" they are by supporting Lovett High's first Black homecoming queen. #ItsNotAboutRace.

The fact that articles with headlines that read THE FIRST BLACK PERSON TO . . . are still being published should be embarrassing to them. Tonight, during her opening remarks at the coronation ceremony, Mrs. Barnett told the audience that implementing the school's new "fairness policies" was a "much-needed step in the right direction." I wanted to stand up and shout, *Thank y'all for finally making us feel like we matter after othering us since y'all forced us to come here!*

I take a deep breath. Ev's right. Can't let anything spoil the Black girl magic of this night.

My girl has been handling it with grace. Maintaining a perfect smile through all the "Come here and say this to that person" and "Stand here and do this" she's been getting since being officially crowned. Anyone can attend the coronation ceremony, as long as they secure one of the limited number of tickets the school makes available. But only invited guests and friends and family of the newly crowned queen are allowed to attend the reception afterward. Apparently, the school is using the guest list from previous years. There are hardly any Black community leaders or business owners here. I purposely said "us, not them" loud enough for Mrs. Barnett to hear as we were sitting down at Nova's table. How could they not invite the very people who've been celebrating her victory all week? Thankfully, Nova did manage to Meghan Markle the coronation ceremony by weaving some of our culture into the program. She walked out to a New Orleans–style brass band, was serenaded to "She's Your Queen to Be" from *Coming to America,* and had the school's gospel choir sing "Amazing Grace" after she was crowned.

Nova is looking like a Disney princess tonight. I gasped when she first came onstage. The tulle of her white ball gown shimmers in the spotlight. She still hasn't told me what business she got to sponsor her. I'm betting it was Jitterbug's.

I lean over to Ev. "I really need these folks to fall back," I say. "We've barely gotten to talk to her all night."

"And I'ma need you to calm down, all right?" Ev strokes the back of my head with a smirk. "Your girl is queen. Let her do her queen tingz. You're gonna have to get used to sharing her."

I catch the older white couple at the next table staring at us as I'm about to reply. The woman has this stank expression on her face. I realize it's because Ev is still stroking the back of my head as she looks down at her phone. They don't turn away until I purse my lips at them and tilt my head. I couldn't care less how uncomfortable they are seeing two girls be affectionate with each other in public. One thing my mother drilled into me before she died: never let anyone make you feel ashamed about who you are. She told me that so I'd take pride in my brown skin and kinky hair. Making her proud, even though she's gone, trumps everything.

Ev and I are the only people at Nova's table in the center of the gym, which—thanks to all the balloons, special lighting, and decorations—hardly looks like the place where I'm forced to sweat for an hour three afternoons a week. The longest Nova has been at the table is when she got here to put her purse down and have Ev touch up her makeup. Nova's mom, Ms. Donna, was seated with us too, but she made a quick exit shortly after dinner. Mrs. Barnett, and Trenton were also invited to sit with us. Trenton ducked out a few minutes ago to help the IT guys with some glitch in the lighting.

There's no telling why Ms. Donna dipped so quickly. Nova and her mother are a hard pair to comprehend. One minute they're lovey-dovey, and the next they'll act like they're only tolerating each other because they have to. Things have seemed more strained than usual since Nova's uncle moved back here a month ago, after he was released from prison. I haven't asked her about it yet. He's a *very* touchy subject in their household.

"Bae, Nikki's calling," Evelyn announces, squeezing my forearm.

"What time is it?" I ask. "She probably wanna know if we still coming."

We're supposed to meet up with Ev's friends at some kick-back later tonight, and I'm ready to go. This reception is lame. But with us being some of the only melanin-endowed people at this reception, I'm trying to be here for my girl as long as I can.

"Let me see what she's talking about," Evelyn says as she accepts the call.

"Bet. I'm 'bout to rescue my girl from these white folks," I reply, standing up.

Nova has just gotten her photo taken with the mayor and his wife as I approach her. The second our eyes meet, her mouth flies open and she steps away from whatever the mayor's wife leaned in to say to her.

"Girl, perfect timing," she says, having to practically shout over the string quartet nearby. "The mayor's wife asked if she could feel my hair. 'I can't believe they managed to get the crown to fit all of it,' she said."

"No that bitch didn't," I blurt.

Nova grabs me by the arm, pulling us away from the band and out of earshot of the mayor and his wife.

"I'm going to scream if I have to take another picture with some pasty white person," Nova says. We both fold over with laughter.

We pause near the table holding the punch bowl and the large ice sculpture carved in the shape of the school's initials. Nova recenters the crown Tinsley's mother pinned into her curly Afro earlier.

"We've barely gotten to chop it up all night," I say. "You know I've been dying to be petty."

Nova looks over at our table and frowns. "Where's my mama?"

"Left a little while ago," I say, surprised she doesn't know. "She ain't say nothing to you?"

"Nope. And I ain't stuntin' it." Nova shifts her expression, losing the frown.

"Everything good between y'all?" I ask.

"It's whatever." She takes a step back and looks me up and down. "Girl, I'm really liking how this tux ensemble came together," she says, waving her scepter in a circular motion at me.

Good deflection, girl. I'll let it slide since this is your night.

"These country-ass folks wasn't ready for your girl tonight, hun-tee," I say, strutting in a semicircle around Nova. "Real talk, thanks for putting this together for me. You really something sick with that sewing machine."

The dress code for the coronation and reception is semi-formal. But I don't do dresses, so I got Nova to alter this old tuxedo I picked up at a local thrift store. She tailored it to fit my body and added some embellishments to modernize it. I decided to rock it with some black heels and a tuxedo shirt unfastened to show off a little cleavage. There's nothing I love more than giving the kids a li'l butch-fem realness.

"Bump what I got on, though." I bend over to lift the train of her ball gown. "Girl, this look is ever-re-*thang*! You gon' tell me who your sponsor is or what?"

"They wanna remain anonymous for now," she replies with a coy grin.

My gaze shifts across the room to where the McArthurs are seated. Tinsley definitely inherited her mother's resting bitch face. Her sister, who emceed the ceremony tonight alongside Mr. Haywood, has been a little less bitchy. Mr. McArthur has been kind of aloof, clearly here only out of obligation to his wife.

"I kinda wish you could have talked Tinsley's father into doing it," I say. "You would have gone down in the Petty Hall of Fame for that one."

Nova shrugs. "Oh well. Still got what I needed and managed to piss her off. Win-win."

She starts telling me about some of the awkward conversations she's had to endure, but her phone chimes and she pauses, pulling it out to see who texted.

Jessica Thambley walks in my line of vision as I look around the room. She and most of the cheerleading squad are serving as hostesses for the reception, which involves refilling water glasses, showing guests to their assigned tables, and a lot of standing around looking pretty. Didn't surprise me at all that Tinsley and her minions opted out. Jessica is glaring at the table where Mr. Haywood is seated, next to a woman I assume is his fiancée. I think she's in grad school at Mississippi State.

I'm about to make fun of Jessica's obvious crush on our art teacher but stop when I see the worry shadowing Nova's face. "What's going on?" I ask her.

She jumps, looking up from her phone as if she forgot I was standing here. "Oh. Nothing, girl," she replies, sliding her phone back into the pocket I didn't know was folded into her ball gown.

"It don't look like nothing. You seem a li'l—"

"Fine, I'm fine," she cuts me off.

I want to press further, but Ev's suddenly at my side.

"You wouldn't happen to be ready to bounce, huh?" she says to me. "Nikki is summoning us to this party. Apparently, Chance and Briana aren't entertaining enough."

"Y'all can go," Nova interjects with a smile that conflicts with the tension clouding her iridescent eyes. "As your queen, I beseech you to go and turn up."

Ev playfully bows. "As you wish, my queen."

I can't help but notice how Nova's deflecting again.

"We can stay a little longer," I say. "I'm getting major *Get Out* vibes here. Don't wanna leave you defenseless around all these white folks."

I'm not really joking, but Nova laughs. "Girl, bye. It's cool. I'll text y'all once this is over."

I search her face for some hidden appeal for me to stay, but there's nothing.

"How you getting home?" I ask.

"I'll catch a ride with Trent." She looks around the gym. "He's still here, huh?"

"Yeah," I tell her, "he's in the auditorium helping them do some nerdy thing with the lighting." I rub Nova's arm. "Girl, seriously. We can stay. You look kinda—"

"Girl, I told you I'm fine." Her tone is still pleasant, but I can hear the annoyance at the edges. "I'ma holla at you later, okay?"

I frown at her. I feel Ev staring at me, waiting for me to move.

"I'm serious," Nova says with a nervous laugh. "Look, I'll download you on some stuff tomorrow. Nothing I'm trying to get into tonight."

"What kind of stuff?" I ask.

She looks down at her scepter, avoiding my inquisitive frown. "Stuff you'd have to promise you wouldn't tell anyone else."

Nova quickly glares at Ev, who doesn't catch it because she's sending a text.

"You know I got you. Always," I reply.

"I promise, I'll tell you tomorrow," she says. "I just wanna enjoy tonight. Live in the moment."

We say our goodbyes with a round of hugs and air kisses, and my stomach gets heavier as we walk away. As we're leaving the gym, we run into Trenton reentering, looking a little disheveled.

"Y'all bouncing?" he says.

I nod, then add, "Hey, you not leaving anytime soon, huh?"

"Nah, why?" he says.

"Something's up with Nova," I tell him. "She got a text and started acting a little weird after she checked her phone."

Trenton sighs. "She'd tell you before she tells me anything."

True. But knowing she still has someone here who has her back would make me feel a little better about leaving her. "Do me a favor and make sure she good, all right?" I say.

He grins before nodding.

After weaving my fingers with Ev's, I glance over my shoulder. Nova's in the same spot we left her, looking down at her phone.

Did I just make a promise I won't be able to keep?

CHAPTER SIX

TINSLEY

OCTOBER 14
8:26 P.M.

I CAN'T TELL if the picture my mother just texted me is blurry because whoever took it (probably my father) did a bad job, or because of all the vodka I drank. Whatever the case may be, I wrinkle my nose at the image of her and Rachel goofily smiling in their shimmery evening gowns. This has to be the twentieth photo she's sent tonight from the coronation. It almost feels like she's enjoying reminding me that I'm not there. That she and my sister are a part of something I couldn't be.

I toss my phone down beside me. "God, my mother is being annoying as fuck tonight. If she sends me one more picture . . ."

"Just mute her, for crying out loud." Giselle props herself up on her elbows on the beach towel beside me. "That's what I do whenever my mom is doing the most."

Lana is sprawled on her stomach on the towel in front of us, scrolling through her phone. She raises an eyebrow in our direction. The shadows cast by the fire crackling in the hole Nathan and his best friend, Lucas, dug in the sand give her face a sinister vibe.

Nathan and his best friend are clowning around near the water's edge a few feet away. I guess the Gulf's rolling tide is somehow more entertaining than we are, which is crazy, since this little beach party was *his* idea.

Nathan's let's-distract-Tinsley-from-the-coronation party is set up in one of the secluded nooks along the beach that serves as the southern border of the towns along the Mississippi Gulf Coast. We're shielded from most of Lovett by the hotel casino to our left. To our right, the quiet beach stretches into the darkness for miles, to Gulfport, Mississippi, in the distance. The sound of traffic whizzing behind us on Beachfront Boulevard competes with the slapping of the Gulf's waters against the beach as the tide rolls in. Our town's population swells by as much as two thousand people during the summer, when tourists flock here to frolic in the Gulf's warm, steely waters and frequent any of our many casinos, historic museums, and restaurants, plus various festivals we host each year. The side of Beachfront Boulevard we're on almost mirrors a California-like snapshot, with a white-sand beach and palm trees. The opposite side has all the backdrops people love in Southern Gothic fiction: antebellum architecture and trees draped in Spanish moss.

The wind curling the Gulf's waters brings with it periodic whiffs of sulfur from the industrial site jutting from the northwest extension of the beachfront. The steel cranes and metal cargo crates stacked in the distance are reminders that the oil and gas industry rules this state's economy.

I lie back on my beach towel, woozily gazing at the starless black night canopying our pitiful party. Lil Boosie's "Wipe Me Down" is blasting from Lucas's portable speaker. This was *supposed* to get my mind off the coronation. But thanks to my mother and the pathetic company I have right now, the coronation is all I can think about.

I pop back up and crawl over to the ice chest five feet away. As I untwist the cap on the bottle of Tito's Nathan snuck from his parents' liquor cabinet, Lana whines, "Tins, you drove us here."

"Yeah, I know," I snap while pouring more vodka into my pink Solo cup. "Stop trying to kill my vibe, bitch."

I toss a fleeting glance at Nathan, who has Lucas in a headlock. It looks like he's trying to toss Lucas into the Gulf's black waters, a battle Lucas is close to losing.

My phone chimes again. I sip my drink and wiggle my toes into the cool sand. That's likely another picture from my mother. I'm not about to let her further disrupt my peace.

I hear Nathan and Lucas coming before I sit up and actually see them bopping our way.

"I pull up at the club VIP, gas tank on E but all drinks on me . . ."

"Wipe me down!" Lucas inserts, hanging off Nathan's shoulder.

"Fresh kicks, fresh white tall tee, fresh NFL hat, fresh baus with the crease—" Nathan continues, his curly bush of sandy-brown hair flapping in the wind as he crouches, thrusting his arms to the song's beat as they advance toward us.

"Pussy niggas wanna hit me with they heat . . ."

Every muscle in my body tenses. "Nathan!"

"What?" He pauses near the ice chest, giving me the same dumbfounded look as Lucas.

"The N-word?" My gaze flicks to Giselle, who's still lying on her back with her eyes closed. "You know better."

Nathan drops down in front of my towel, stretching his lanky frame across the sand. "Chill, babe. Just singing along."

Lucas snickers as he takes a seat on the lid of the ice chest.

"And?" I snort. "First, just because it's in a song doesn't give you the right to say it. And second, it's offensive to Giselle."

"It's fine, Tins," Giselle says. "I know Nathan didn't mean it like *that.*"

I narrow my eyes at her. Do I use her apathy as an example of why a lot of the Black kids at school call her Candace Owens?

"See! Giselle ain't trippin'." Nathan throws up his arms to catch the beer Lucas tosses to him. "You watched one lecture by that Ta-Nehisi Coates dude and wanna act like you're so woke. Which is hypocritical as fuck since you literally tried to hijack this year's *inclusive* homecoming elections."

It's not the cocky smile he flashes at me that causes something inside me to snap. It's seeing the amusement on everyone else's faces that sends me over the edge.

"I thought we agreed Nova's name wouldn't be brought up tonight."

"*Technically,* he only said—"

"Oh, shut up, thirst bucket!" I snap at Lana. I almost tumble backward from standing up so quickly. I awkwardly tug on the flapping ends of Nathan's powder-blue button-down, which I put on over my bikini to keep me warm. Trying to button it as the gusts of wind keep ripping it open further irritates me.

"Nova Albright's irrelevant!" I slur as my world starts to tilt a little more to the left. "You know why her being homecoming queen doesn't matter? Because that's it for her. She's a girl who'll peak in high school. Whereas I'm a fucking McArthur. I don't need a crown to be queen. Never did!"

I hold out my right arm, hoping it'll stop me from feeling like I'm walking a tightrope suspended thousands of feet in the air. Unfortunately, it doesn't. "She'll be the girl at our ten-year reunion no one remembers because she looks like she's been rode hard and put up wet."

I take another sip. A few of the seagulls that have been hovering nearby all night start squawking.

"Nah, I think everyone will always remember the chick that slapped the piss outta Tinsley McArthur, no matter how bad she looks," Lucas teases.

"*Dude,*" Nathan protests while attempting to hide a grin.

"Fuck Nova Albright!" I spill some of my drink on Nathan when I jerk my cup in Lucas's direction. "I should have killed her and dumped her in that slave cemetery she loves so much."

Giselle gasps.

"Oh, *that* offends you, but not hearing Nathan casually say the N-word?" I tug on an end of Nathan's shirt again. "It would have served the bitch right if I'd killed her for stealing my fucking legacy!"

"Babe, chill, like, for real." Nathan stands up just in time to stop me from tripping forward. "This is dark, even for you."

"Yeah, that was some fucked-up shit," Lucas says.

Lana still has her phone in both hands, but now she's sitting on her beach towel with her knees pulled into her chest.

"What?" I bark at her. "You don't like what I said either?"

She looks down at her phone instead of replying.

I push myself out of Nathan's arms. "You know what? Y'all are fucking boring."

"Where are you going?" Nathan asks after I toss my cup aside and bend over to yank up my beach towel.

"Anywhere but here," I say.

I stuff my towel into my beach bag, which takes longer than normal because my vision is so fuzzy. Nathan keeps telling me to calm down.

"Tins, what are you doing? You're our ride," Giselle says.

"Call a Lyft," I tell her.

Nathan's hand closes around my wrist and I jerk away, almost falling backward. Storming off would be so much easier if I didn't have to work so hard against the sand pulling at my feet.

"Tins, hold up!"

"Leave me alone!" I scream.

"You're drunk. I'm not about to let you drive like this."

I keep staggering toward the parking lot, which feels more than the actual thirty feet away.

"Tins, stop! I'm serious."

Nathan pulls at my wrist again. I jerk free of his grip and spin around to face him. "Must you always be a pathetic little puppy chasing after me?"

His mouth twists. "What?"

"Can you just leave me alone? Can you do that? Or do I

have to be the bad guy and say you definitely won't be the husband I show up with at our ten-year reunion?"

"Tins—"

"What?"

"I'm sorry, all right? I'm sorry I brought her up."

"You're always sorry, Nathan. You're a sorry individual I only date because my mother wants me to. But you'll never be my husband. I'm starting to question if I even want to stay in this relationship until graduation."

Nathan's eyes widen and he furrows his brow at me.

"Yeah, I said it."

He doesn't try to stop me when I turn and walk away. Toward the car that he's right I have no business driving.

CHAPTER SEVEN

DUCHESS

OCTOBER 15

7:18 A.M.

SATURDAYS ARE THE only day I *kinda* get to sleep in late. I say "kinda" because my Pops still wakes me up early, but usually not until after nine a.m. Our weekly Saturday routine involves me cleaning up around the house while he's out working in the yard. It's been that way since my mother died. I got to share some of the burden with my two older brothers when they still lived here, but now it's just me.

Today my phone wakes me up. At first, I figure it's a spam call, 'cause anybody who knows me *knows* not to call this early on a Saturday. I finally poke my head from under the covers after about the twelfth time the phone vibrates on the nightstand. The scant sunlight that has managed to bully its way through my dark curtains stings my eyes.

Everything feels ten pounds heavier than usual. I barely made it home last night before curfew. The kickback was super lit by the time Ev and I arrived. I wouldn't have got here in time if she hadn't pulled me away from a spirited game of Spades against some of her classmates. Pops was sound asleep on the sofa when I got home. Had I been one minute late, he would have sprung up out of his sleep the second he heard me trying to quietly shut the front door. It's like he has some internal alarm that's set to go off if my foot crosses the threshold after ten-thirty.

As soon as my hand finds my phone, the vibrating stops. Since I'm already up, I snatch it off the nightstand and sit up in bed to see who I need to curse out. I rub the sleep from my eyes with my free hand and freeze when I see all the notifications listed down my phone screen. Seventeen missed calls? And beaucoup texts!

What the hell could I have slept on this early in the day?

I expand the grouping of missed call notifications. Most of them are from Pops. He's been calling since a quarter to seven. Why didn't he just bang on my bedroom door?

"Pops!" I shout, continuing to scroll through the call log. "Pops! You doing wake-up calls now?"

Silence.

I got two missed calls, back to back, from Ev. And one from Trenton ten minutes later. A text from Pops folds down from the top of the screen. What it says pulls my brows together.

CALL ME! PLEASE!

My heart swells, pushing against my rib cage like it wants to break free from my chest.

I rip the covers off. Pops has never used all caps in a text before. He teases me when I do it. "Who you think you shouting at, li'l girl," he'll joke. The unusual silence still taunting me starts scratching around in my stomach. As I'm about to press my finger on Pops's contact tab, my screen morphs into a picture of me and Briana.

"B, let me hit you back in a minute," I answer as I'm stepping out of bed. "I need to holla at my Pops."

"Bet. What's he saying about what happened to her?" she says, sounding out of breath. "Girl, I can't believe this is real."

"What is real?"

"Nova."

"What about her?" I ask.

The silence stretches out so long that I hold my phone up to see if the call dropped.

"Hello? B?" I say. "Whatcha talking about?"

"Wait. You haven't—you don't know . . ." The tremble in her voice rattles me.

"Know what?" I yelp, getting super annoyed.

There's another brief silence before Briana stammers, "It—it—it's all over the news."

I'm already reaching for the remote on my nightstand. I have to push aside my copy of *The New Jim Crow* to get to it. I bought the book a week ago, hoping it will help me decide if criminal justice is really what I want to major in at college. Still haven't gotten around to reading it. I'll start it tonight, I tell myself, as I point the remote at the flat screen mounted on the wall facing my bed.

"Like, how could this have happened?" Briana says. "Go talk to yo' dad, and call me back once you know something more."

But for some reason Briana doesn't hang up, and neither

do I. I keep the phone pressed to my ear as I click to Fox 6, one of our local news channels, and read the words on the bottom of the screen. *Body found in cemetery identified* scrolls below Judy Sanchez, the station's lead crime reporter.

I aim the remote and turn up the volume. Drowning out the room's menacing silence. Briana's breathing on the other end of the line is getting louder in my ear.

". . . the body of seventeen-year-old Lovett High senior Nova Albright was discovered around six a.m. today in the Sacred Hearts Slave Cemetery right behind me."

Judy's words yank my stomach to my feet.

My knees buckle. My collapse sends my basketball rolling across my bedroom floor.

"B, what happened?" I yell.

"They don't know," Briana replies, tears straining her voice. "Duch, this is so messed—"

"Shhhhhh," I hiss, increasing the volume on the TV.

There's no way I heard Judy right. She can't be talking about *my* Nova. This has to be some other Nova. One who lives here too and goes to school with us. My Nova is alive. My Nova is just fine.

The camera pans left, revealing a knot of uniformed police officers gathered around a headstone that's marked off with yellow crime-scene tape. It suddenly dawns on me why my Pops has been blowing up my phone. And why he's clearly not here right now.

"Police haven't released any details regarding cause of death, but we do know the girl was last seen alive around nine-thirty last night at Lovett High, where the school hosted its annual coronation ceremony and homecoming reception. An hour earlier, the victim had been crowned this year's queen, becoming the first Black student in the school's history to hold the title."

The more Judy talks, the wider this icy emptiness grows in my gut.

"Duch, Duch," Briana pleads in my ear. "Duch, you okay?"

I don't want to answer her. Acknowledging her concern would make this real.

The television cuts from Judy to shaky video footage. I lean forward on my knees, studying the wobbling person who now fills the screen. I stand up, one leg at a time, as I begin to recognize the bikini-clad girl struggling to maintain her balance in front of what looks like one of the lifeguard stands along the beach in town. Whoever filmed Tinsley did so without her knowing it.

"This video has gone viral on social media overnight. It features Tinsley McArthur, daughter of prominent businessman Virgil McArthur, ranting about wanting to murder the victim," Judy Sanchez explains in a voice-over. "We must warn you, this video contains graphic language."

"[Bleep] Nova Albright!" Tinsley yells to Giselle, and—by the looks of the other silhouette sitting on the beach at the edge of the video frame—her boyfriend, Nathan Fairchild. *"I should have killed her and dumped her in that slave cemetery she loves so much."*

The screen switches back to Judy Sanchez. "That video was posted on TikTok by one of Tinsley's friends approximately an hour before the victim was last seen alive. Tinsley McArthur was the victim's rival for homecoming queen. It was a rivalry that got physical just days before the murder—"

My mind flashes back to the look on Nova's face after she checked her phone last night. Whoever posted that video of Tinsley must have sent it to her too.

"Duch, this is all too surreal—"

"B, let me call you back," I say, and hit end before she can protest.

I mute the TV and call Pops. He answers on the first ring.

"Duchess—"

"Pops, please tell me this isn't true," I say, pacing in front of the silent TV. My room feels even smaller than it already is. "All I wanna hear is this isn't real. That she's not dead. Please tell me she's not . . ."

The rest of my words get stuck in the back of my constricting throat.

I can hear the murmur of conversation on the other end of the call, but nothing from my father.

"Pops!" I scream.

"Baby girl." He sounds drained. "I can't tell you that. She's, she's . . ."

The dread that's been crawling over my skin needles my neck.

"No, Pops! Not Nova," I say, pain gathering behind my eyes. "It can't be Nova."

"Duchess, I'm gonna be home as soon as I can. Just try and hold it together—"

"*NO!*" I scream, falling to my knees again.

On the nightstand sits a framed picture of my mother. The

last good photo she took before the cancer started eating away at her. Her smiling face watches me sprawled on the floor, crying in agony as my heart rips from my chest. The same way it did the morning Pops told me my mother was never coming home from the hospital.

CHAPTER EIGHT

TINSLEY

OCTOBER 15

8:17 A.M.

I TAKE OFF running as soon as I see my father's Range Rover turn into our driveway.

I've spent the last thirty minutes pacing the balcony off my parents' bedroom. It overlooks the front of our property and the rest of our subdivision, making it the best way to see when they get back from wherever they've been all morning.

I barged into their bedroom seconds after watching Judy Sanchez's breaking-news report on Nova's murder. I was barely conscious when I crawled out of bed to answer Rachel's call—which was her fifteenth this morning.

"Turn on the news! *NOW!*" she screamed after my weak hello.

Everything that followed is a whiplash of emotions. Stomach-clenching disbelief dissolved into heart-pounding rage before my anxieties opened up and swallowed me whole.

Nova is dead. Murdered, they're saying. And everyone thinks I did it.

My parents' room was empty, their bed unmade and the clothes they wore to the coronation ceremony last night flung over various pieces of furniture, when I rushed into their room. I thought about calling them but didn't want to turn my phone back on. Although not being alerted every time someone leaves a comment on the video hasn't made it any easier *not* to stress.

She's an entitled, evil brat! someone said about me on TikTok.

This is disgusting!!! someone else wrote.

Bitch is canceled!

Nothing to see here, people, just another white person doing what they always do when something doesn't go their way: whine about it and then threaten violence.

I've always hated this privileged bitch. Glad the world is seeing the truth.

Why hasn't she been arrested yet? She's pretty much admitting she did it!

Someone oughta strangle this ho and dump her body! Fucking Karen!

Yes, what she said was horrible, but can we wait until all the facts have come out before condemning her? Innocent until proven guilty! I was grateful at least someone had my back. That was until I read all the replies to that comment basically attacking the person who wrote it, while at the same time asserting that I'm a racist for what I said about dumping her body in a slave cemetery.

That sneaky witch Lana! I can't believe she recorded me, and worse, posted what I said all over social media. I need my parents—mostly my mother. She'll know what to do. She always does.

She's stepping out of the Range as I barrel out the door. She doesn't see me racing toward her, but her face is already twisted by a scowl.

Rachel probably called and told them what's going on, I realize.

Knowing how much they despise any news about our family they didn't have some hand in curating, I should have called my sister and told her to keep her mouth shut until I had a chance to explain everything to them.

"It wasn't me! I swear!" I yell.

My outburst startles my mother, who comes to an abrupt stop at the rear bumper of my dad's SUV. She rolls her neck after she looks at me. I'm still wearing my bikini from last night, and Nathan's pastel button-down. The warm concrete pinches my bare feet.

"Tinsley, you look like hell," she says.

My father appears at the back end of the driver's side, a frown distorting his bearded face.

"I don't give a damn what I look like," I snap.

"What's going on?" my father asks.

"What do you mean, *'What's going on?',*" I say. "Didn't Rachel tell you?"

"Tell us what?" my mother replies.

"It's all over the news! She's dead, and they think I did it!"

My parents exchange these looks that seesaw between bewilderment and angst.

"Tinsley, my God, you're shaking." My mother grabs me by the shoulders. "Who's dead? What on earth are you talking about?"

"Where were y'all? I've been freaking out," I say, my voice shaky.

My father steps up beside me. "We were having breakfast at the club. What's got you so rattled?"

"Nova Albright was murdered last night," I say, shrugging off the arm my father tries to snake around my shoulders too. "Everyone thinks I did it!"

"Why on earth . . . would they think that?" my mother says, casting a confused look at my father.

I open my mouth to tell them about the video. I shut it as a tan and white police cruiser turns into our driveway.

My stomach drops to my feet. My mother clutches my father's forearm. The three of us watch the Lovett Police Department cruiser come to a slow stop behind my father's car. I don't pull away this time when he drapes his arm over my shoulders.

I know the dark, chiseled face of the uniformed officer who steps out the cruiser. He shares his deep ebony skin with his daughter. As he approaches us, I realize Duchess also has her father's deep-set eyes and full lips.

"Virgil, Charlotte," he says, acknowledging my parents with a nod.

I can barely hear him. My heart is pounding in my ears.

"Why are you here?" my father asks, stepping in front of me and my mother. "This early? On a Saturday?"

Mr. Simmons briefly looks at me, then steps up to my father with both hands on his duty belt. "There was a murder last night. Nova Albright was killed. She was my daughter's best friend."

"Sorry for your loss, but what does that have to do with us?" my father replies, his voice trembling a little.

"We need Tinsley to come down to the station and answer a few questions," Mr. Simmons says.

My mother steps forward. "What for?"

Mr. Simmons lets out a breath and says, "Because she's the only person we know who wanted her dead."

The Lovett Police Department is housed in what used to be our county hospital. After Katrina, county leaders used millions in federal grant money to build a bigger medical facility across town, and the old hospital was given to the police. I have never seen the inside of this place before today. My parents haven't left my side since we got here.

"She's not being arrested," Mr. Simmons explained. "But we need to understand why she said what she said in that video. No need to get attorneys involved yet."

The way he emphasized *yet* lifted the hair on the back of my neck.

The three of us have been sitting in an interrogation room for the past forty-five minutes. The wall behind me is covered in a collection of electrical outlets that were used to power hospital equipment. The faded outline of where a flat-screen TV used to hang discolors the steel-gray paint of the wall in front of me. Dark fabric roller shades block the sun from pouring in through the large rectangular window to my right. The shades cast a drab overlay on everything, making the large metal table and chairs in here look dull. The room is so cold.

I tug on the sleeves of the sweatshirt I threw on with a pair of jeans before leaving the house. Cocooning my chilly fingers within the ends of the plush cotton doesn't stop the shivers rippling through my body.

"What is taking so long?" My mother shuffles over to the door, on my left, to peer through the narrow glass window in its center. "I really think we should have called a lawyer, Virgil," she says as she spins back around to us. "I have zero faith they won't try to pin this on our daughter."

Thanks to the news, my parents have seen the video of my rant on the beach. Lana and her mother are now on my mother's shit list too.

"Charlotte, can you sit down?" my father pleads. "You're making me nervous. I already have enough on my mind, for God's sake."

"But what if they—"

The door opens, interrupting my mother. A brick of tension rolls around in my stomach as I watch Duchess's father enter the room. He's clutching a brown folder with both hands. Another man walks in behind him. When our eyes meet, I realize it's the police chief. I've only ever seen him on the news. Chief Barrow's hardened gaze flicks toward my parents. He presses his thick lips into a tight line when he does. The head of the police department leans against the wall in front of me, folding his arms across his chest, while Duchess's father lowers himself into the chair across from me. I hear my mother drop into one of the seats behind me as Mr. Simmons—well, *Captain* Simmons, according to the gold name tag pinned to his shirt—clears his throat.

After thanking us for being patient, Captain Simmons tells me to walk him through everything I did last night.

"Don't leave anything out," he adds, like I'm a toddler who has trouble comprehending.

My mouth is so dry my tongue feels heavy. I take my time explaining my night. Who I was with, why we were there. I even tell them we were drinking. I blame the alcohol for what I said about Nova. "Everyone there knew it was a joke," I say. Chief Barrow and Captain Simmons remain emotionless. I hear my father shifting in his chair behind me when I admit to driving home drunk after blowing up at Nathan.

"If you can't fully remember how you got home last night, why should we believe that you didn't drive over to the school after you left your friends?"

My heart sinks as my mother's gasp fills the room. Chief Barrow's brow knits. He seems annoyed by her outburst.

"I—I—I didn't kill her," I stammer, desperate to make him believe me. "I wouldn't do something like that. Plus, I was too *beyond* wasted. I could barely stand up straight—even this morning."

"Yet you were capable of driving yourself home?" Captain Simmons quizzes me.

I pull on the ends of my sleeves. Drunk driving hardly requires the motor skills you'd need to kill someone and dump a body. But I'm too afraid to argue, with the way Duchess's father is glaring at me across the table.

He must hate me as much as his daughter does. His wife lost her job at the country club after I told my mother Duchess kissed me one day while we were playing on the tennis court. We were eight. I didn't know my mom would go to the manager and express her "concerns." I didn't find out about it until the following weekend, when neither Duchess nor her mother were there. The incident led to the club's current policy prohibiting employees from bringing their children to work with them.

"I thought my daughter was here to answer questions, not to be accused of murder," my mother says.

"Chief, I can handle this," Captain Simmons says over his shoulder to his boss. "Tinsley, let me walk you through what we know so far." Captain Simmons weaves his fingers together and places his hands on top of the folder in front of him. "Eyewitnesses at the coronation ceremony say they saw Nova check her phone before leaving the gymnasium around nine p.m."

"She did leave," my mother interjects. "We were there. She couldn't be found when it was time to see off some of the distinguished guests."

"Charlotte!" my father snaps. "Please. Let the man talk."

Captain Simmons waits a few seconds before he resumes. "The groundskeeper of the cemetery discovered Nova's body around five-thirty this morning."

Captain Simmons opens the folder. He takes out an 8" x 10" photo and gently places it in front of me. I don't make it past the bloodstained white ball gown before I look away. Vodka-tasting chunks bubble up in the back of my throat. Nova is really dead. Like, someone actually killed her.

This can't be happening.

"She had multiple head wounds," Captain Simmons continues. "Looks like someone struck her head from behind and she fell."

"Hit her? With what?" I ask.

"We think her scepter," Captain Simmons replies. "The coroner found glass fragments in her skull. Nova's scepter is missing, along with her cell phone." He picks up the photo of her body and returns it to the folder, which he closes. "We have to piece together what happened in the hours between nine p.m. and when her body was found. I know you said you don't remember, but is it possible you could have encountered her somewhere?"

"No! No way! I was wasted. Just ask my friends—Nathan Fairchild, Giselle Joubert, Lana Malone, and Lucas Hutchins. They were all with me. They know me. They know I'd never do something like this."

"You and Nova had a talk a few days ago, didn't you? Before the homecoming elections?" Captain Simmons says.

"When I asked her to drop out?"

"You say *ask*, but I've heard it wasn't that polite." Captain Simmons's face is blank.

I shift in my seat. "It wasn't hostile either."

"Did you try to bribe her?" he asks. "You offered her money to fix up the Sacred Hearts Slave Cemetery, but she turned you down?"

"Yeah." *How is that relevant?* I have to wonder.

"That upset you?"

"I mean, I wasn't glad she didn't take it. Everyone knows how much being queen . . ." The back of my throat tightens. It dawns on me why the chief's and Captain Simmons's eyebrows both rose after what I just said. "Hold up. Are you trying to insinuate I dumped her body out there because I was angry she didn't take the money? That would be *soooo* messed up— and also not true."

"No one said anything like that," the chief says with this smug look.

"And you don't recall what time you made it home from the beach?" Captain Simmons follows.

I shrug at him. I realize that maybe I should lie. But my mind is so scrambled right now I can't figure out what time would make me look the most innocent quickly enough.

"What time did y'all get home last night?" Captain Simmons asks again, only he's looking past me now.

I turn in my chair. My father's shoulders draw up as he sits straighter. And I can't tell if it's the lack of sunlight that has the color draining from my mother's face or if it's because the determination of my innocence has landed on her shoulders.

"Um, well, I had a few drinks at the coronation," my father says, scratching at his beard. He turns to my mother. "What time was it when we rolled in, sweetie?"

My mother crosses her legs, steeling her expression. "We got home between ten and ten-thirty. And our daughter's car was parked in the driveway."

"So you saw her at the house when you got home?"

"No. Her bedroom door was closed. Like she told you, she was sleeping the rest of the night."

"All night?" Chief Barrow says.

I turn back around. He's standing up straighter now, looking at my mother like she said something offensive.

"What are you implying?" my mother asks.

"Tinsley, let me be honest," Captain Simmons says, sitting back in his chair. "This is very personal for me. Nova . . . well, she was like a daughter to me. She spent *a lot* of time at my house, so . . . let's just say I'm aware of how *tense* things got between you two over the homecoming elections."

I roll my shoulders, sensing what he's about to say next.

"For instance, I know that you two got into what was described to me as a pretty heated fight earlier this week—"

"Is that what Duchess told you?" I fire back.

"I heard there were a few tense conversations between the two of you before she was killed," Chief Barrow adds. "I've also heard that you've gone to extremes in the past to get what you want. Like the captain spot on the cheerleading squad?"

Who in the hell told him about that? The only person that makes sense is Duchess, I realize, thinking back on how she and Nova threw Kim Hammerstein in my face.

"Using someone's secrets against them hardly means I'd kill someone," I respond.

"But you're a very popular girl, Tinsley," Captain Simmons says. "A lot of people want to be your friend. Get in your good graces. Please you, even. Someone could have seen that video, which your friend posted approximately an hour before Nova left the coronation ceremony, and carried out your wishes."

"Are you kidding me?" I say. "I don't have that kind of power."

"That's not entirely true," Captain Simmons replies with a tight expression.

He doesn't have to say it; I know he's referring to what I did when I was younger and how it affected his family.

"You'd be surprised the power teenage girls can have," Chief Barrow chimes in. But he's looking at my mother, not me, when he says it.

The scraping of metal across tile pierces the silence that follows.

"Can't y'all trace her phone or something?" my mother

says, suddenly standing next to me. "That'll prove that girl was nowhere near my daughter."

"We're already on top of that, Charlotte," Chief Barrow says. "Don't need you telling us how to do our jobs."

"Well, I can't tell," my mother replies, verbalizing what I'm too afraid to even let them see me think right now, out of fear it might incriminate me.

My father stands up before he says, "I swear to God, Charlotte, if you don't keep your damn mouth shut . . ."

Captain Simmons and Chief Barrow appear surprised by this rare public display of my parents' dysfunction. I know my parents are on edge, but now is not the time for their marriage to implode.

"If it's not you who did this, Tinsley, you have any idea who might want to hurt Nova?" Captain Simmons asks.

I look down at my fingers, which I've been weaving together and pulling apart in my lap for the past few minutes. "No," I tell him. "You clearly know we weren't friends."

"Are we about done here?" my father says, appearing at my side.

If anyone can shut this down, I know he can.

"We just have a few more questions, Virgil," Captain Simmons says.

"No, I think we're done here." My father pulls me out of my chair by one arm. "I don't like the accusatory tone in your boss's voice. I won't let his prejudice against me and my wife affect my daughter."

My brow furrows. I'm confused by the turn this is taking. Prejudice against my parents?

"And you better believe the mayor will be hearing from us about this," my mother adds as my father pulls me across the room, then pushes me toward the door.

Chief Barrow steps into my path, stopping me short. "Go right ahead, Charlotte," he says. "I don't work for the mayor. I work for the residents of this town. *All* of them. Not just y'all. And one of them was murdered last night and dumped in a cemetery like she was a piece of trash. I'm not going to stop until I find the person who did it—no matter who it is."

The chief's gaze turns from my mother to me. The way he's looking at me makes me want to vomit.

He steps back and opens the door, allowing us to file into the lobby. There's a woman standing at the circular reception desk. A uniformed officer is beside her, his hand pressed against the middle of her back as she's bent over signing the visitors' log sheet.

I stop, causing my parents to stop too. I know who she is before she turns around and her puffy eyes lock on me from across the lobby.

Ms. Albright's face hardens the second she notices me. My knees get weak. But it's Ms. Albright who drops to the floor. And with a trembling finger pointed at me, she shouts, "What did you do to her?"

A news van follows us from the police station. We ride home in silence. My father doesn't even turn on the radio. There are two more news vans parked on the street outside our house when we pull up. One has the Fox 6 logo splashed across its side. From the backseat of the Range, I see Judy Sanchez shut the mirrored compact she's using to check her makeup as my father turns into our circular driveway. The other van is from one of the stations in Jackson.

The van following us screeches to a stop in front of the Fox 6 van. A reporter and a cameraman jump out to catch up with Judy, who's leading the pack of interlopers up our driveway.

My father is first out of the car. With a finger pointed in their direction, he yells, "All of you, get the hell off my property! *Now!*"

The knot of people stops in the middle of the driveway. That's the last thing I see before my mother uses her leather jacket to shield my face from their cameras as she rushes me past them into the house. Before she slams the front door, Judy Sanchez shouts, "Tinsley, did you kill her?"

"God, that woman is relentless," my mother says, adding, *"Bitch!"* for punctuation. Then she turns to me with a forced smile. "Everything is gonna be okay, sweetie. I promise. No one really thinks you . . . you know . . ."

I could show her the hundreds of messages people have sent me on social media saying the contrary, but I don't. And that was only the first time I looked. I'm not ready to turn my phone back on and face all that.

I'd rather ask the question that's been on the tip of my tongue our entire ride home.

"What was all that back at the police station?"

"All what?" my mother replies, innocently blinking at me as we stand in the middle of the foyer.

"Between you and the chief. What was with all the tension and major 'tude he was giving you?"

The empty foyer's acoustics amplify my mother's nervous

laugh. "Oh, just some lingering high school drama, nothing you need to worry about."

I frown at her. "What did you do to him?"

The silence that hangs between us answers my question. She did something. Something bad enough that he's still angry. And he's ready to pass his disdain for her on to me.

"Are you going to answer me?" I snap, causing her to jump.

The front door opens behind her and my father steps inside. He looks as frustrated as I am.

"I'll call Joel, see if he can do anything to keep them off the street." He doesn't look at either of us as he stalks away.

"He can't do anything about that, Virgil; he's the mayor, not the police," my mother says, finally breaking eye contact with me.

My father mumbles a response as he disappears down the hall. I spin around and take off in the same direction.

"Where are you going?" my mother calls after me.

"To think," I say over my shoulder.

My father is shutting the door to his office as I turn the corner and I dash into our library across from it. The book I'm looking for is exactly where it always is, on the third shelf of the floor-to-ceiling bookcase that stretches across one wall. A few seconds later, I'm bouncing up the staircase that curves toward the second floor, hugging the thick hardcover I plucked from the shelf.

"What are you doing?" my mother asks, appearing at the bottom of the staircase just as I'm reaching the top. "Don't you want to talk? I have some ideas on how we should—"

"Nah, I'm good," I say, cutting her off.

I go straight to my bedroom, slam the door, and drop the

1994 Lovett High yearbook on my bed. I flip it open to the senior class and search for Fred Barrow, not caring to pause on the grainy images of my parents. I've seen them before. Seen how much I resemble my mother.

But I can't find the chief. I flip to the index at the back of the book. It doesn't take long to spot his name in the B section. Only there's another Barrow. Regina.

Regina Barrow.

The name somehow feels familiar. It even sounds routine as I repeat it to myself. There are at least a dozen pages listed beside her name. I turn to the first one and discover that Regina Barrow was a cheerleader, and very pretty. She's at the bottom center of the pyramid the squad built for its yearbook photo. Her narrow nose, thin lips, and sandy-blond hair remind me of Chief Barrow. The teenage version of the police chief appears in the third photo of Regina. No wonder I didn't find his name among the senior class; the caption reveals that he was a sophomore back then, and a cadet on the school's JROTC drill team. Seeing them standing side by side, their arms draped over each other's shoulders, amplifies the shared characteristics in their features.

Regina Barrow is one of several students in the fourth picture I flip to. It looks like it was taken in the cafeteria, during lunch, and she's surrounded by people I can only assume are her friends. The boy kissing her on the cheek with his arm around her neck elicits a gasp from me.

It's my father.

Faint echoes of long-ago conversations click into place, just as I spot my mother within Regina's group of friends. Regina Barrow must have been the girl my father dated before he started going out with my mother. The girl my mother claimed my grandmother wanted my father to end up with. The girl my mother described as a drop-dead-gorgeous cheerleader from a good family.

The hairs on the back of my neck rise. The last index entry I flip to is a full-page black-and-white headshot of Regina Barrow marked *In Memoriam*.

"She died?" I say to myself, pressing a hand to my mouth.

There's no information explaining when the photo was taken, but it's in the yearbook, so it must have been before they graduated.

I jump off the bed to grab my laptop from my desk. I type *Regina Barrow* into an Internet search engine. Most of the hits I get aren't her, but the fourth page of results lists an article about Fred Barrow that was published in our local newspaper eight years ago. It's a profile written shortly after he won his first term as police chief. An alt + f search for his sister's name takes me to the spot where he mentioned her. The reporter asking how her suicide in high school affected him.

Suicide?

Fred Barrow told the reporter his older sister's decision to take her own life served as the catalyst for him joining the military at a time when his life felt like it was spiraling out of control from grief.

The sadness that clouds Barrow's eyes as he talks about Regina shifts the mood in the room, the article reads. *After a short silence, Barrow says advocating for more sexual education in high schools is the campaign promise he's most passionate about keeping.*

"If I can save one girl from having to go through what my sister did—that will truly honor her," he said.

When asked to elaborate further, Barrow only said, "She trusted someone she shouldn't have."

The thick mass that has been lodged in my chest all morning expands. Did my parents fall in love behind Regina's back and that sent her over the edge? It would explain why the chief doesn't like them. And why he's so determined to pin Nova's murder on me.

CHAPTER NINE

DUCHESS

OCTOBER 15

5:52 P.M.

"**BAE, STILL SURE** you don't want me to come over?"

I've lost count of how many times Ev has asked me that today. I deeply inhale to keep from snapping on her. I know she's not trying to irk me. She's struggling to comfort me. But nothing she says or does, here or on the phone, will ease this numbing pain.

"Nah. I'm good. Waiting on my Pops to get home," I reply matter-of-factly, eyeing the foyer that leads to our front door.

We sit on the phone in silence. Something we've done more than once over the course of this hour-long conversation. Although, saying our calls today have been conversations is a stretch. This makes our fourth. The longest we've held our phones in silence was over an hour this afternoon. I think Ev just wants to hear me breathe. Make sure I'm not the babbling ball of emotions I was this morning when I finally answered her call.

I haven't cried again since then. Which is odd, since the pain of it still aches in my bones. It's like my tear ducts have dried up. Maybe they're as weak as me. They lack the strength to properly function. I wish it could have been like this when my mother died. The tears were endless then. Every day. Seemed like every hour. For three months. Having to watch cancer slowly suck the life out her was a roller coaster of lows and godawful despair. By the time her suffering ended, she'd become a shriveled version of her former self. Maybe that's why I haven't cried much today. I exhausted my eyes then.

I tug on one of the loose threads poking from a tattered section of upholstery on our sofa. My parents bought it before I was born, like most of the furniture in this house. The cushions are sunken, and the pillows are stiff and discolored from years of us sleeping on them. Some of our friends have teased that the inside of our house looks like the set of a sitcom from the late '90s. Pops can afford to get new stuff, but he, my brothers, and me have never entertained the thought. Not after my mother died. She decorated this house. Getting rid of the things she picked out would feel like we were erasing her legacy. And none of us wants to do that.

Maybe I haven't cried much because my grief is entangled with rage and confusion. I've been on autopilot. Moving around the house in sweats. Taking naps in the misguided hope I'll wake up and realize this is all a nightmare. Watching the news for updates on Tinsley's arrest. Texting and calling my father when there are none. Seeing her on Fox 6 leaving the police station with her parents, trying to look all distressed, really set me off. I've never wanted to jump through a TV more. I immediately called Trenton.

"You see this bullshit?" I shrieked as soon as he answered.

He shared my outrage. That was a little comforting. Then he reminded me about how Tinsley tried to use the slave cemetery to bribe Nova into dropping out of the homecoming elections and I got angry all over again. She's playing in our faces. This is all a game to her.

"She'll get hers. Trust that," Trenton said before we hung up.

Pops said he'd explain everything. He's barely had time to chat today. Said he's been tied up interviewing people who were at the coronation and talking to Nova's mother. I asked how Ms. Donna was holding up. "She's . . . existing," he replied. Pops said we're visiting her tomorrow. He suggested we bring her food. "One less thing for her to worry about," he explained over the phone. Seriously doubt she's thinking about eating. I know I haven't at all today.

"This is so messed up," Ev hisses on the other end of the line.

For a quick second I think she's talking about Nova's murder. Then I see the mug shot of a distraught-looking middle-aged Black man pop up on the TV. I stop pulling on the sofa threads.

We're watching the national news together. The chyron says *Gardener charged in the murders of Jackson, MS, family.* Nova's murder hasn't made national headlines yet, but the slaying of that white family has.

Why am I not surprised?

Learning that Curtis Delmont, the family's gardener, was charged today on three counts of first-degree murder, even though they still don't have any concrete evidence, is really sending me. They're actually going to put this man in prison, for who knows how long, over some shoddy eyewitness accounts from neighbors who say they saw him there? But here, this hateful, spoiled princess gets recorded saying she wants to kill my girl, and then it happens, but she gets to walk out of the police station like nothing happened. I'm dying to hear Pops justify that!

"The police ain't even following up on that claim from the wife's coworker who overheard gossip around the office the woman was having an affair with another one of their coworkers," Ev says, as if I'm not watching the same thing she is. "And you know why not? Because she was a Christian white woman who *supposedly* loved her family? Here they go again pushing this poor white woman narrative."

She's right, but I can't muster up the strength to agree. Not when I suspect Tinsley likely weaponized her white tears at the police station to get out of being arrested. What could she possibly have said to get Pops to release her? My right leg starts shaking as I sit on the edge of the sofa. A picture of Nova and me clowning around at the state fair last year stares back at me on the coffee table.

"Watch this man get life," Ev rants. "When is the justice system going to work for us? When are the boys in blue gonna stop incarcerating and killing us and do better jobs trying to protect us?"

My heart twists into a knot.

My father is one of the "boys" she's talking about. Even though she didn't name him specifically, what she said cuts. Not because I'm offended; I agree, but have been conditioned to never say it to anyone. Not when Pops is one of the only Black police officers on the force. He's in a supervisory position he's afraid of losing for any slight infraction—which includes anything I might publicly say or do.

My leg bounces harder as heat rushes to my face. I want to believe Pops is out there doing whatever he can to get justice for Nova. But here we are, almost twelve hours since her body was discovered, and still no arrest of the girl everyone knows did it. Ev's right. When is the justice system going to work for us? For Nova?

I hear the front door close. The sofa springs squeak when I stand up.

"Ev," I stage-whisper into the phone, "my Pops just walked in. Let me holla at you lata." I end the call while she's mid-sentence.

The top button of his uniform shirt is already undone when he appears on the threshold between our tiny foyer and the living room. Fatigue shadows his face. Grief clouds his eyes. The sight of him dissolves the tension from my shoulders, along with my pent-up frustrations. I lumber across the room, shoulders slumped. Dragging my feet along the threadbare carpet. He holds out his arms when I'm halfway there, wrapping them around me the second I step into them.

"Baby girl, I'm so sorry," he keeps repeating, squeezing me tighter every time he says it.

I close my eyes, letting his warmth wash over me. His strength steadies the world that got kicked off its axis this morning. I still don't cry.

"Come here, talk to me," he says, dropping his arms and nodding toward the kitchen.

I follow him, my bare feet feeling like they're being weighed down by heavy shoes. I sit at the dining table as he's opening the fridge and watch in silence as he spends at least a minute staring inside. He grabs a beer and the container of leftover Chinese food he ordered last night. How can he eat at a time like this?

The chair he jerks out from the table scratches against the tile. He pops the cap off his beer as he collapses on it. After taking a long gulp, he sighs, then finally meets my anxious gaze. His deep-set eyes are glassy and red. He hasn't looked this drained since Mama.

"Baby girl, I know today has been a lot for you, but I need you to be strong and walk me through what you remember about last night," he says, ripping off the lid to his leftovers.

"It's fine. I'm ready to talk." I sit up straighter. "I've been running everything over and over in my head all day."

I feel like the worst friend ever for leaving last night. I can't help but think if I'd stayed, Nova might still be alive.

Pops uses his hands to eat the cold sesame chicken as I tell him everything I remember. I know the drill. Know that any minute detail could be important to him piecing together how Tinsley did it. I always pay attention when he talks about conducting investigations. Watch and listen to enough true crime documentaries and podcasts. I used to want to be like him. Be a cop. That was until so many of them started fatally shooting so many of us and getting away with it, claiming they felt threatened.

I push that frustration aside to focus on Nova and the night of the coronation. I can't leave anything out. I tell him how she looked, what everyone said, who all she interacted with, how certain things made me feel. He nods in agreement when I mention how vexed Nova looked after checking her phone before we left.

"Did you happen to see what caused her reaction?"

I shake my head. "I can only guess that someone must have sent her that video of Tinsley on the beach."

"Were she and Lana Malone friends?"

His question catches me off guard.

"Lana? Tinsley's friend?"

He nods.

"No. What does she have to do with this?"

"That's who recorded that video and posted it. She would have had to send it directly to Nova at the time you said you left last night. It didn't get posted until fifteen or twenty minutes later."

I'm shocked. I'm not friends with Tinsley's besties on social media. But nearly everyone I *am* friends with from school reposted the video today, so I couldn't help but see it. Lana and Giselle are Tinsley's ride-or-dies. At least, I thought they were. I would never have suspected one of them of outing her like that. Not when they've each played integral roles in her takedowns of other people.

"I told Trenton to keep an eye on her when Ev and I bounced," I tell Pops. "You talk to him yet?"

He pushes the container of leftovers aside. "Yeah. He said some of the same. That Nova was preoccupied with her phone before she dipped out of the reception without him noticing."

I flash back to last week, when Tinsley asked Nova to meet her in the courtyard. She had texted her the night before. Saying they needed to have a "one-on-one" about "some things." "Some things" being the homecoming elections. I knew what was up the second Nova mentioned it.

That means Tinsley coulda been hitting her up that night on some foul BS. I know she had Nova's number. She was clearly drunk in that video. I'm betting alcohol turns her into an even meaner bitch than she already is. One who would bash someone over the head when she didn't get what she wanted.

"Nova's phone is gonna be key," I say, more to myself than to my Pops.

"That or finding the scepter," Pops says. "I'm betting the killer took it because it would have incriminated them."

"Come again?" I say. Does Pops really think anyone *but* Tinsley could have done this?

The sound of the TV I forgot was still on in the living room fills the silence that's eroding the connection of our shared grief.

"Why you talking like we don't know who did this?" I say. "We got her on video, admitting what she did."

Pops sighs. "No, someone recorded her saying what she would have liked to see happen in a moment of anger, but we don't have proof that she actually did anything."

My hands curl into fists on the table. "Is that why you didn't arrest her today? 'Cause you don't have enough *proof*? How much proof do you need?"

My dad shakes his head. "It's not that simple, baby girl," he says.

"No, it's not that complicated," I fire back.

"Look, none of the people who were at the reception last

night said they remember seeing Tinsley there," he says. "And yes, since it appears Nova might have left, that means she could have met up with her somewhere else last night."

"What did Tinsley say to you today?" I press.

He picks up his beer and takes a swig. "That she drove home drunk after leaving her friends at the beach. And passed out once she got home."

She passed out! How convenient. Pops is supposed to be smarter than this.

"And y'all believe her? That girl lies and manipulates people as easily as we breathe."

"We're checking her story, don't worry."

"And she gets to sit at home, *free,* while you do that?" I stand up, take a few steps away from the table, and spin back around. "Why is video evidence never enough to convict white people of killing us, but suspicion alone is enough to gun us down and lock us up?"

Pops's face tightens. "Duchess, don't go there with me."

"What is it going to take?" I say. "The same tireless advocating, millions of texts and phone calls to state leaders, and petitioning it took to get those three white men who murdered Ahmaud Arbery arrested—*two months* after they killed him?"

"This is not the same, and you know it," he replies.

"I want her arrested. She should be arrested! Why didn't you arrest her?" I shout.

"Watch your tone with me, girl," he barks. "I know you're emotional right now, but I'm still your father."

"Let me guess, your boss is too scared to go up against the almighty McArthurs?" I say, ignoring his threat.

He scratches his nose. "Actually, the opposite. Chief would

have locked her up if he could. But that family has friends in higher places than us. No judge will sign an arrest warrant until we have solid evidence she's involved. That video is circumstantial."

"Circumstantial evidence hasn't stopped the Jackson police from charging Curtis Delmont with murdering that white family," I argue.

Pops scrubs his face with his hand, but it doesn't remove the frustration building in his eyes.

"Money and white privilege always win," I fume, throwing my hands in the air. "This girl is really gonna get away with what she did."

"I'm not going to let that happen," my Pops says, his voice growing louder. "Whoever killed Nova, I'm gonna find out. I promise you that."

"Yeah? Like you promised me Mama would be okay?"

The way his eyes cloud and his brow furrows, I know my comment did the damage I meant it to. I don't care. My friend is dead. And the girl who did it is sleeping peacefully in her bed.

I run down the hall into my bedroom before Pops can curse me out. Tears prick my eyes as I'm slamming the door. Apparently, it took blinding anger to get my ducts working again.

CHAPTER TEN

TINSLEY

OCTOBER 16
5:45 P.M.

THE SUCCESSION OF light taps on my forehead pulls me from the peaceful darkness. My eyes flutter open, only for me to squeeze them shut again at the blinding sting of the overhead light. I have to blink a few times before my niece's chubby face becomes recognizable.

"Lindsey?" I yawn, stretching my arms over my head. "What are you still doing here?"

"Waking you up, silly." She gives me this goofy smile that would irritate me had it come from anyone else. "You been asleep a long time, Auntie Tinsley."

"Apparently," I say, casting a quick glance at the burnt-orange glow of the skyline filling my bedroom window.

I don't remember dozing off. But it was sometime after we got home from church, which my mother forced us to attend as a family today.

"We have to be there. It won't look good if we're not," she said as she pulled me out of bed this morning. "Innocent people don't hide. They walk around with their heads held high."

Easy for her to say. It wasn't her face plastered across the front page today under the headline *Viral Video of Teen Threatening Violence Linked to Murder Investigation.*

"Mommy said you aren't feeling well," my niece says as I sit up in bed. "Is it because you didn't like going to church today? You looked like you weren't having a good time."

No, I didn't have fun feeling everyone watching me throughout service. And I *definitely* didn't like seeing my boyfriend ignore me with his arm draped across the shoulder of one of my backstabbing best friends. Lana and Nathan left before I could talk to them. It's understandable why Lana's avoiding me. She's worried about the payback she rightfully deserves for posting that video. She definitely has that coming. But her and Giselle's support would mean a lot right now. Something familiar to quiet all the hate people are posting about me online.

Nathan is clearly punishing me for what I said to him on the beach Friday night. Which, okay, fine, he has a right to be mad. But doesn't me being wrongly accused of murder overshadow a bruised ego? If he can't pull it together enough to be at my side comforting me through this hell, he should at the very least be storming the police station with my friends to proclaim my innocence.

I pick my phone up off the nightstand. He still hasn't responded to the *Can we talk?* text I sent before I fell asleep. Neither of the girls has reached out either. Like, WTF, Giselle? I haven't done anything to *her.* What's up with the radio silence?

I drop my phone beside me on the bed. "Y'all been here all day?" I ask Lindsey.

She nods.

She and Rachel met us at church with my brother-in-law, Aiden, in tow. My sister and niece were here all yesterday evening too.

I climb out of bed and Lindsey follows me into the bathroom connected to my bedroom.

"You don't look sick," she says.

"I'm not that kind of sick," I tell her, turning on the faucet.

She asks question after question in her attempt to diagnose my fake illness as I wash my face.

I'm grabbing my toothbrush when she says, "You look tired."

"I am. Of you being so nosy," I tease, bending over to squeeze her button nose.

As I'm brushing my teeth, she grabs the tube of lip gloss I left on the sink counter. Watching her smear some of it on her lips amuses me. I rinse out my mouth, and then I pick her up, placing her on top of the toilet lid.

"Here, let me help you," I say, squatting in front of her dangling legs.

I pluck the tube of gloss from her tiny hands. I have to use a piece of tissue to wipe up what she smudged all over her mouth and chin.

"Why did your friends use a tray of bees at you?" she says as I smooth the gloss evenly across her pink lips with my finger.

I stop, trying to make sense of what she just said. "Huh?"

"I heard Grandma and Mommy talking—I acted like I wasn't listening"—her shrug and raised brow pull another laugh out of me—"and they said your friends gave you a tray of bees."

The words come together, and I understand what she's trying to ask. "Oh. They said my friends *betrayed* me," I explain.

"What does that mean?" Lindsey asks, rubbing her lips together like she must have seen her mom do after applying lipstick.

I stand up. "That they did something bad to me," I say.

"Are you going to get in trouble?" she asks.

"I might," I reply, the muscles in my neck tightening.

I turn to the mirror and apply a coat of gloss to my own lips. As I admire it, Lindsey says, "My friend Allison did something bad to me one time."

"Oh really?" I say, turning back to her. "What was that?"

"She pulled my hair while I was playing on the swings. It made me cry."

I return the tube of gloss to the counter. I long for the days when hair pulls on the playground were the extent of the drama I had to deal with.

"Why didn't you tell me?" I say, bending over so I'm eye level with my niece. "I would have beat her up for you."

Lindsey giggles. "I got in trouble 'cause the teacher told Mommy Allison did it because I skipped in line to get on the swings before her."

"Well, did you?"

"Yes! But I was just really excited. I didn't mean to hurt her feelings."

"Are you still friends with Allison?"

She nods. "But I had to apologize. And Mommy said I had to really, really, really mean it to make Allison feel better."

I pick Lindsey up off the toilet lid and put her down, then turn off the light and gesture for her to follow me out of the bathroom. "Did it work?" I ask.

"Yep."

It'll probably take more than a heartfelt apology to make things right with Nathan and my friends. *But* it's worth a try, I guess. I need them on my side. Now more than ever.

I grab my phone off my bed and am hustling my niece down the stairs when she says, "Can I have a Popsicle, Auntie Tinsley?"

It's then that I realize I haven't eaten all day.

"You can have anything you want," I reply, giving her a quick smile before looking down at my phone.

Still no reply from Nathan, but dozens of notifications about social media comments fill my lock screen.

"Auntie Tinsley, did you hurt your friends' feelings?" Lindsey asks as we're entering the kitchen. "Is that why they did something bad to you?"

The answers knot my stomach, quashing what little appetite I have. I open the freezer to avoid my niece's inquisitive gaze. I can't face her, just like I don't want to face the reality that I might have brought this on myself. Luckily, she stops questioning me as soon as I hand her the Popsicle she asked for.

I go through my phone's settings to turn off all the notification alerts for my social media accounts. The thousands of unanswered messages, status updates, and comments are still chiming in, and they are definitely not good for my mental health right now.

I head into the den to find Rachel sprawled across one end of the sectional. Her intense faux-black hair is fanned across the pillow she has propped beneath her neck as she watches the flat-screen TV mounted above the fireplace.

"Look, Mommy!" My niece waves the Popsicle in the air

as we step down into the room together. "Auntie Tinsley let me have a Popsicle!"

"I thought I told you not to wake her up—and that you couldn't have any more sweets tonight." Rachel mutes the TV with the remote as she sits up.

I plop down in the middle of the sectional. "Where are the parentals?" I ask.

"Mama's been locked up in her room for the past two hours. I assume doing more damage control."

Meaning she's probably telling everyone this was all some big misunderstanding, and that Lana posted that video because she's jealous of me (which isn't actually a lie, I think).

"Dad hasn't been out of his office since we got back," Rachel continues. "You should see all the news vans parked outside now. The Uber Eats guy could barely drive up earlier."

"Great," I sigh, dropping my phone in my lap. "Hey, you remember Regina Barrow?"

Rachel's forehead wrinkles. "No. Should I?"

"She's Daddy's ex-girlfriend from high school."

"You talking about that girl he dated before Mama, the one she was friends with?"

I nod.

"What about her?"

"She's the police chief's sister, and she killed herself. I found that out after we got home from the station yesterday. I did some research because Mama wouldn't tell me why the chief was being such a dick to them."

"What does this have to do with your stuff?" Rachel asks.

"I think the chief is going to take out whatever vendetta he has against them on me," I say. "Depending on when they got together, he might think Daddy falling in love with Mama sent his sister over the edge. Wouldn't be the first time a girl did something crazy because of a boy."

Rachel presses her mouth into a thin line as her gaze lowers to her lap.

"What?" I ask.

She waits a few seconds before she says, "It's crazy to think he hates them so much he's willing to pin a murder on their daughter out of spite."

"Why is that crazy?" I say, narrowing my eyes at her.

"I understand why the police questioned you, but at the end of the day, that video doesn't prove anything," Rachel says.

"Tell that to the court of public opinion," I reply. "No one cares what the truth is anymore. You get caught doing or saying something horrible, they cancel you and then discredit any explanation that comes out after."

I know better than anyone. It's how I won student council president last year. I eliminated the strongest contender, Ethan Callaway, by digging up old tweets of him crassly joking about banning attractive girls from joining the school's chapter of the National Honor Society around the time the #MeToo movement was gaining momentum. It didn't matter that he later posted other tweets sympathizing with the victims, which he brought up after I made sure the bad tweets got "leaked" to our student newspaper. The damage was done. I won by a landslide.

What's happening to me now must be karma for me spending two days scrolling through his tweet history until I found something I could use against him.

"Tins, you can't let—"

"Rach, can we *not* get into this right now?" I interrupt, picking up my phone to signal the end of the conversation. "You know I'm right. And you pretending that I'm not to try and make me feel better will only do the opposite."

I can feel Rachel watching me, so I glue my eyes to my phone screen. My finger hovers over Nathan's text thread. Needing to hear his voice feels foreign.

Rachel's gasp stops me cold. I lower my phone, following her shocked gaze toward the TV, where Judy Sanchez's stoic face is staring back at us. The words *new details surrounding the death of Lovett High homecoming queen* are scrolling across the bottom of the screen. A shot of our dimly lit house is framed in the background.

"Turn it up!" I shout at Rachel.

". . . a source within the police department has confirmed investigators are still questioning witnesses and trying to piece together the last few hours of Nova Albright's life," Judy Sanchez says, her face looking like the flawless end to a YouTube makeup tutorial. "The same source tells me police have spoken to at least two of Tinsley McArthur's friends and her boyfriend since yesterday, but the details regarding why and what they might have told police are still unknown. . . ."

"They told them there's no way I could have killed her!" I interject while scooting up to the edge of the sectional.

"The video of Tinsley proclaiming she wanted to kill the victim has been shared over a million times on social media, drawing outrage from local Black leaders, who are upset that Tinsley still hasn't been charged in connection to the victim's death."

After a quick shot of me leaving the police station with

my parents, the screen cuts to an older Black woman I don't recognize. The identification tag that flashes at the bottom of the screen tells me it's Reverend Joyce Mable, president of the county's chapter of the NAACP.

"An innocent Black man was charged with three counts of murder yesterday with little to no evidence," Reverend Mable practically screams into the Fox 6 microphone being held in front of her mouth. "But this rich white girl, who was filmed talking about killing one of us, gets to continue enjoying her freedom while the police twiddle their thumbs? You'd think after everything we been through—all the talk of racial harmony and police reform these last few years—that we'd be past this. We want charges and we want 'em now, or else we'll take to the streets until we get justice!"

"Oh my God." I press both hands to my forehead and pull my hair back from my face. "Why are they spinning this into some kind of Black Lives Matter issue?"

"The victim's mother wouldn't talk on camera, but stopped short of agreeing with Reverend Mable," Judy Sanchez says in a voice-over as various shots from the cemetery where Nova was found flash across the screen. "Cheryl Barnett, principal at Lovett High, was quick to downplay that accusation."

The screen cuts to Mrs. Barnett, who's seated behind the desk in her office.

"It's reckless to make such inflammatory accusations when, one, we don't have all the facts, and two, this is a delicate situation," she says. "These are two seventeen-year-old girls from vastly different backgrounds but with the same potential to have bright futures. This is a tragedy. A horrible cloud that now hangs over this school and this year's homecoming festivities, which were supposed to be a moment of racial harmony, not more division."

"Friends of the victim aren't blaming race for Nova's death, but they are blaming Tinsley McArthur," Judy Sanchez announces right before Trenton's face pops up on the screen.

His eyes are red and puffy. The harsh light from the camera completely washes out his honey-colored skin.

"Tinsley tried to intimidate Nova into dropping out of the homecoming election because she felt the title belonged to her. And when Nova didn't, she resorted to bullying her, and spreading lies about my friend," he says. Trenton is barely making eye contact with the camera. "She doesn't care about anyone but herself," he adds.

"Tinsley?" Judy Sanchez asks off camera.

After a few seconds, he nods. "Nova was one of the only people at school who wouldn't bow down to her, and look what happened when she didn't."

"Do you think Tinsley McArthur could have really done this?"

The screen goes black.

"What the hell?" I yell, turning to Rachel.

She drops the remote in her lap. "Fake news. All of it."

"Why was that boy saying that stuff about Auntie Tinsley?" a small voice says.

I forgot my niece was in the room.

"My life has turned into a literal hell within forty-eight hours." I stand up. "Every little thing I've ever said or done is getting twisted. I'm already on trial!"

"Tins, those were biased interviews," Rachel says. "No one with any credibility in this town will believe anything they said. Trust me."

I roll my eyes at Rachel before I walk out.

Right before I make it to the grand staircase, my phone chimes. It's a text from Nathan. A slow smile stretches across my face.

'Sup? it reads.

Can I come over? I immediately send back.

I stand at the foot of the stairs, biting my lip as I watch the three dots pulsate for what feels like forever. My heart shrivels when they vanish without a response.

I stomp up the stairs, trying not to think about the way Nathan had his arm draped around Lana in church. I can't jump to conclusions. Lana, at least, knows better. She doesn't want my wrath. My phone chimes as I'm entering my room.

Yeah, he writes, leaving me to wonder whether he typed out something else and then deleted it before sending his one-word answer.

I take less than ten minutes to change into a pair of skinny jeans and a V-neck T-shirt Nathan likes because it accentuates my breasts. After slipping into a pair of wedged heels, I punch my arms into my beige cropped leather jacket. I quickly brush my hair as I'm racing down the stairs, my car keys clutched in my hand.

"Where are you off to in such a hurry?" my mother asks from the second floor as I'm stepping off the bottom step.

"Nathan's," I say without slowing. "I'll be right back."

As I'm rushing out the front door she shouts, "Tinsley, wait! You shouldn't be out in public by yourself!"

My mother's warning makes sense the second I shut the door behind me. Camera flashes go off like crazy as I dash to my car. I speed out of our circular driveway before anyone has a chance to jump into their news van and follow me.

Nathan lives in the Garden District, one of the town's oldest and most affluent neighborhoods. It's where my father grew up, before he moved out of his family's generational home at nineteen when he defied his father's wishes by not going into the family business. After traveling the world with my mother, and marrying her, he returned to Lovett and used a portion of his trust fund to start his construction company. My grandfather never got to see my father become the thriving businessman my grandfather claimed he would never be: my grandfather died a year before Rachel was born.

I use the drive to rehearse the apology I'm hoping will lure Nathan back into my orbit. Hoping it can work for me like it worked for my niece. I can barely keep a firm grip on the steering wheel.

As I pull up to Nathan's house, the outer ring of the setting sun is peeking over his roof, and the orange glow cocoons it in an intimidating shadow. I step out of the car as soon as the front door opens. Nathan is already halfway down the narrow path from their wraparound porch to their mailbox. He's barefoot and wearing a pair of khaki shorts that stop at his knees. He has the collar popped on his olive-green polo.

We meet in the middle of the pathway.

"Hey."

"'Sup?" His tone is flat.

"Can we go inside and talk?"

Nathan rakes a hand through his messy curls. "Um, yeah.

About that. Look, I'm not trying to hurt your feelings but . . . well . . . look, my dad thinks we need a little space right now. You know, until everything calms down."

All I can do is blink as he talks, giving me some bullshit explanation about his father not wanting to tarnish the image of their family business by having him associated with all the "drama" going on with me. I'm trying to control my breathing, talk myself out of pushing past Nathan and marching into that house to ask his father if he's man enough to say that to my father's face. To the man who has been his friend for years and who has made substantial investments in his business ventures.

"Tins, you all right?" Nathan asks, pulling me from my thoughts.

"You're kidding, right?"

I can tell by the way Nathan keeps looking down at his feet that he's not.

"Of course you'd do this to me," I say, shaking my head.

The apprehension dissolves from his face, which rearranges as his nostrils flare and his eyes harden. "What were you expecting? Me being a pathetic little puppy?"

"Is that what this is really about? You're still in your feelings about what I said? I was drunk, Nathan. I'm sorry. I'm really sorry."

It's not the apology I rehearsed on the way over, but I mean it. I'm a little surprised by how much. Having his familiar arms around me right now would feel so good. So . . . normal.

"Are you, though?" he says. "Or are you here because you finally need me, but you realize you fucked up, and that's why you're wearing that shirt? Like me seeing your cleavage will turn me into a chump and I'll fall in line."

I timidly pull one side of my jacket over my chest. Nathan's voice is trembling with a resentment I've never heard before.

"I'm not here to fight, all right?" I say, shifting my weight from one foot to the other. "I mean it, Nathan. I'm sorry about what I said that night. I know I can be . . . *a lot.* But I'm not the kind of person who would do what the police think I did. You know that. You've known me my whole life."

He looks away. "Tins, why are you here?"

"To say—"

"Stop with the apology tour," he cuts in before I can finish. "You wanna know what we told the police, don't you?"

Now I'm the one who can't stop looking down at my feet.

"You wanna know what we said?" he asks. Then he leans into me with his teeth clenched. "We told them the truth. That you're a manipulative, self-centered bully, and a liar."

My breath catches in my throat. "A liar?" Why would he say that?

"What would *you* call a person who can lie straight to her boyfriend's face about how much she missed him over the summer, when she was being a slut and hooking up with some dude on her family vacation?" he replies. "Would *THOT* be a better word?"

A wave of rage washes over me. *Fucking Lana!* She's the only person I talked to about my summer fling.

"Is that what Lana said to get you to wrap your arm around her in church today?" I narrow my eyes at him. "Was that your way of punishing me? Please don't tell me y'all are hooking up now."

He gives me a blank stare.

"This is my life y'all are messing with! This is serious! It's not some petty high school game, Nathan. They're trying to accuse me of murder."

"Yeah, it sucks. But there's nothing I can really do to help." Nathan jerks his head to the side, whipping his hair out of his face. "We told 'em what we know: that you were pissy drunk and angry at the world Friday night and left us at the beach to go who knows where."

"I went home," I say.

He shrugs. "We don't know that. And I'm not going to lie for a girl who could give two shits about me."

My heart pounds. "How would you feel if I turned the tables? I could easily plant the seed that y'all killed Nova and are trying to frame me as retaliation for all the bullying y'all *supposedly* suffered from me. Let's see how your father handles that PR nightmare."

Nathan smirks at me. "Go right ahead," he says. "The cops already know we were at Jitterbug's most of the night after we left the beach. The employees already confirmed we were there until closing. And our parents have told them what time we got home and that all of us were in bed all night."

A knot the size of my fist pushes against my stomach. "Please, don't abandon me. Not now," I say, and my voice sounds small, like it's coming from far away. "Not like this."

Nathan shoves his hands into his pockets. "You said you wanted me to leave you alone. Well, I'm just giving you what you want."

"Fuck you!" I shout, spit flying from my mouth. "You're going to regret this when I clear my name!"

I speed-walk to my car. I can feel the tears building behind my eyes, and I refuse to let him see me cry.

CHAPTER ELEVEN

DUCHESS

OCTOBER 17

9:18 A.M.

AFTER MY MOTHER died, I wanted someone to blame. Thirteen-year-old me needed to make someone pay for taking her away from me. That's what sucked so much about cancer. I couldn't have that. Cancer wrecked my life and then just up and moved on to upend some other family the way it did mine. And there was nothing I could do about it.

That's not going to happen with Nova. Her killer is a walking, talking, breathing bitch I'm not about to let get away with murder.

If it's solid proof Pops needs to arrest Tinsley, then I'ma make sure he gets it—whether he knows it or not. And in this case, he doesn't.

That's my sole purpose for even showing up at school today. Ain't no other way I would have dragged myself out of bed with how I'm feeling. The hollowness that took root in my chest Saturday morning keeps growing. Being on campus without Nova only makes it worse. But here is as good a place as any to help Pops prove Tinsley's guilt.

Things are still tense between us. We hardly said anything to each other yesterday. Didn't play our weekly one-on-one game of basketball. Went to church together in silence. Visited Ms. Donna afterward. Checking in on Nova's mother was the most we said all day, but it was a lot of talking to her and not each other.

Several folks stopped by Ms. Donna's house while we were there. Despite it being filled with people, it still felt cold and empty without Nova there. Neighbors, church members, and parents from school were there. Ev and some of Nova's co-workers came too. Everyone brought food. Ms. Donna was polite, even though I could tell she really didn't want any of us there.

I've been waiting outside the front entrance to A-Building for the past ten minutes, anxiously glancing up and down the crowded breezeway every few seconds. I'm praying I don't see Tinsley. Ain't no telling how I'm going to react when I run into her again. I still have five more minutes before I'll need to book it back to B-Building if I want to avoid being late to my next class. If Trenton came to school today (like I'm hoping he did), I should catch him any second. His first block on Mondays is a study break. He usually spends it in the robotics lab doing the nerdy stuff he likes. He's one of about a dozen Black kids who primarily take AP classes with all the white kids. The school couldn't have discouraged him from testing into the curriculum if they tried. My boy had a near-perfect score on the practice SATs he took in ninth grade. Trenton has gotten a few early admission offers from colleges already. Boy is too smart for his own good.

And that's precisely why I need him.

I spot his slender brown figure among the cluster of white faces shuffling in my direction. He's walking with his head down and doesn't make eye contact with me until he's a few feet away. He maneuvers his way through the crowd.

"Surprised you're here today," he says as he approaches.

"Same," I reply.

Our eyes connect for barely a second before he looks off in another direction. Doesn't look like he's been getting much sleep either. His eyes are puffy.

"You holding up okay?" I ask.

His shoulders lift in a weak shrug. "I've gotten a lot of 'atta boys' this morning from folks who saw the news last night."

"From *them* or *us?*"

He flips his hand over, rubbing the inside of his palm with his index finger, indicating he's talking about the white kids.

"Never would have thought so many of them shared my contempt for that family." The right side of his mouth curls just a little before straightening into a line again.

Seeing Trenton struggling with Nova's death is a reminder that I'm not alone in this grief. I feel like hugging him, I probably should, but I remind myself why I'm here. For something that could help us numb this pain eating away inside us.

"Look, I need to holla at you right quick," I say in a serious tone.

"'Sup?"

"Need you to do me a favor," I tell him.

"What kind?" he asks, stepping aside so the other kids can

more easily walk past us as they funnel into and out of A-Building.

"Can you hack into the school's security system again? I'm trying to get my hands on some surveillance footage."

He finally makes eye contact with me, incomprehension creasing his forehead. "What for?"

"Thinking maybe one of the cameras posted around school might have caught Nova leaving Friday night," I explain, lowering my voice. "Maybe even a shot of her with you-know-who."

"Your dad hasn't done that yet?" he asks, scratching the side of his neck. "I mean, that's something the police would do, right?"

"I'm trying to help him, on the low, break through all the red tape he's gotta go through to arrest that trick." I quickly glance over my shoulder to ensure no one is listening. "Didn't you hack into the system before?"

"Yeah, in tenth grade—for fun. Some of my best work, actually." A fleeting glimmer of superiority ripples across his face, giving me a ghost of his usual disposition. "But I can't help you, Duch. Sorry."

"Why not?"

"School put up a new firewall after some kid ran their freaking mouth about what I did," he explains. "I can't afford the software it'll take to get in without them knowing."

"Dammit," I hiss.

"Just press your dad to do it. This is a criminal investigation. He should be able to subpoena the footage—if there is any."

That bitch's father probably has people in his pocket at the courthouse. Meaning they might not grant my dad a warrant if he requests it.

"Things are kinda rough with Pops and me right now," I tell Trenton instead.

"What happened?" he asks.

Don't wanna talk about it. Trenton would definitely take Pops's side. They have their own bromance.

"You sure you didn't see Tinsley up here Friday night?" I ask to change the subject.

He looks down at his feet. "Nah."

"Why'd you leave without making sure Nova had a ride home?" I ask, trying to keep the edge out of my voice. I know Trenton must think I'm about to go off on him; otherwise he'd look me in the eye.

"I texted to see if she was good when I noticed she wasn't at the reception anymore, but I never got a response." He kicks at a rock on the ground. "Thought maybe she left with someone else and would hit me up later."

"But you didn't see her—leave with someone else?" I press.

Trenton takes a deep, pained breath. "I fucked up, didn't I?"

"Whatcha mean?"

"Go on and say it, Duch, I know you want to. That if I was a good friend, I would have made sure she was okay. Especially after you asked me to."

I grab his wrists. "If that's the case, I fucked up too by leaving even though I knew something was off with her."

As I say it out loud, it hits me that I'm trying to convince myself of that more than him. I cannot allow myself to think like that. It won't help me prove Tinsley is guilty.

"What's done is done. We can't change the past," I tell Trenton. "I don't blame you for what happened to her. No cap."

"Still . . . ," he mumbles.

The two-minute warning bell goes off, and Trenton's bottom lip trembles. I pull him into my arms. We hug until the final bell for next period goes off. The hollowness inside me expands a little more.

Trenton's right. Pops does know what he's doing. He's just not doing it fast enough. He'll know to pull that footage. I can help by connecting the dots elsewhere in case the school's cameras didn't catch anything incriminating. Although a lot of the Black kids didn't attend the coronation reception, some might have seen Nova somewhere later that night. Or more importantly, some might have seen Tinsley doing something that doesn't align with what she told the police. That's an area where I can help my dad cover ground.

I spend all morning asking kids if they saw Nova or Tinsley Friday night. Prodding them for any detail they can think of, even if they don't think it means anything.

I start questioning a new batch of students as soon as I walk into US History.

"Ariah, let me holla at you for a min," I say as I slide into my desk.

Ariah looks up. She was on the dance team with Nova. "Hey," she says softly. She's giving me the same *Are you gonna be okay?* look I've seen from everyone today.

"You didn't happen to run into Nova anywhere Friday night, did you?" I ask. "You know, after the coronation and before . . ."

I let my sentence trail off, and Ariah presses her lips to-gether and shakes her head.

"What about Tinsley?" I ask.

"Girl, please. I live in the Avenues," Ariah responds. "You know she ain't rolling through there after dark."

I resist the urge to point out the inaccuracy in her statement by reminding her Tinsley had to roll through her hood that night to dump Nova's body in the cemetery. I lean forward in-stead and tap Lorenzo on the shoulder. He's sitting in the desk in front of Ariah.

"Yo, Renzo," I say when he turns around. "You see Nova or Tinsley anywhere Friday night?"

"Why you asking?" he says, his eyes narrowing. "Yo' daddy 'bout to let us down again?"

A few of the kids sitting close by turn around.

"What you trying to say?" I ask, a lump forming in the back of my throat.

I grip the sides of my desk with both hands. Hoping this fool isn't about to say what I think he's going to say.

"That yo' old man still tap-dancing for them racist-ass cops he works for and not stepping up for *us* like he should."

The kids around us are nodding or mumbling. I don't know why, but I look over at Ariah for a lifeline. Her eyes drop to her textbook and she squirms around in her chair. Clearly, she agrees with this fool.

"My Pops ain't no coon—don't even try to play him to the left like that," I huff, my grip around the edges of the desk tightening.

"Girl, please, tell that to one of these other niggas who don't know," Lorenzo snarls. "Them white boys ain't stop rolling through our hoods, harassing us every chance they get. They still waiting around with handcuffs after football games, pulling *us* over so that they can 'check our insurance' if we're driving nice cars."

He makes air quotes when he says that last part.

I bite down on my lip, my leg shaking. I should be saying something. Shutting him down. But him using Nova's murder to voice the frustrations I've suspected some of my classmates are harboring about Pops being a cop has my mind spinning.

"What yo' *Pops* doing to stop that? Not a gotdamn thang," Lorenzo continues.

The chorus of grunts from everyone who agrees makes it harder to latch on to a whiplashing thought I can use to shut this down.

"They just got your daddy there to check their diversity box," he says. "That nigga hasn't done anything for the community. He probably the one selling us out to them."

"That's a lie!" I bark.

"Then why isn't anything any different with him there?" Lorenzo replies. "What good is it to have a cop that looks like us if it ain't making our lives any more valuable to the rest of them? He letting us get killed and letting them go free. Letting his daughter do his job for him, ain't that right?"

The memory of what I said to my Pops the other night heats my face. Maybe that's why I'm struggling over how to defend him right now. Because I'm afraid to admit there's a part of me that agrees with Lorenzo.

"I don't see how no self-respecting Black man could ever put on the uniform of the system that was literally created to enforce segregation and uphold white supremacy," Lorenzo's homeboy, Khalid, chimes in.

"How can you even respect him when he letting the chick who might have killed your homegirl go free?" Lorenzo says.

"Murder investigations take time," I assert, gripping the edges of my desk so hard my knuckles are turning white. "This ain't *Law and Order.* Shit don't get wrapped up in an hour. My Pops is doing what needs to be done."

I say that with conviction. More for myself than for them.

"If that was true, you wouldn't be up in here trying to interrogate us," Lorenzo says. Then he rolls his eyes and turns around in his desk.

The shrill ring of the bell stops me from responding, and Mr. Pattinson immediately starts class while I sit there fuming.

As Mr. Pattinson leads a discussion on the War of 1812, I stew over all the things I should have said to Lorenzo. Things I know to be fact. Like how my Pops became a police officer thinking he could change the system from the inside, then got somewhat demoralized when he realized what he was up against: a problematic culture built on bigotry, a union that doubled down on those beliefs, and constant resistance to reform. And yeah, the timing of his promotion is suspect, given it happened after George Floyd's murder, when police forces everywhere were getting scrutinized. But Pops worked hard behind the scenes, using his new position to do the very thing Lorenzo is accusing him of not doing.

I should have said something about the Know Your Rights seminars he held in the community so Black people could learn how to not be manipulated into incriminating themselves during their interactions with cops. Or all the work he's been doing with the district attorney's office to grant early releases to folks convicted of nonviolent offenses, most of whom are poor and Black and couldn't afford good lawyers like many white offenders. I could have told him my Pops has handed down strict disciplinary consequences to officers he's been able to prove used unnecessary force or who have been caught posting, saying, or doing anything remotely racially insensitive. That wasn't happening at all before he became a captain.

But I doubt it would have made a difference. I know the change Lorenzo is talking about. He, and a lot of other Black people, won't be happy until having more Black officers like my Pops means our unarmed Black men are no longer getting gunned down in the streets by trigger-happy white police officers. Until Black people aren't getting prison sentences for the same thing white people get probation for.

As for me, I need Tinsley arrested to resolve the conflicted emotions I'm feeling toward Pops because of Nova's murder.

As soon as the bell goes off at the end of class, I jump out of my seat and bolt out the door. I need to get as far away as I can from that conversation.

I get caught up in the throng that has formed in the middle of the hall. Everyone seems to be clustering together to watch something up ahead.

"What's going on?" I ask the kids around me, standing on my toes to try to see over the crowd.

"The police are going through Nova's locker," a girl answers. Recognition registers on her face as she realizes who asked the question. "I think your father's up there."

I push my way to the front of the crowd, and sure enough,

Pops is at Nova's locker with two white officers. He's got his back to me, watching one of them place a crumpled sheet of paper in a plastic bag with a gloved hand. After sealing it, he hands it to my father.

"I wonder what they found," someone behind me says.

My own curiosity pulls me forward.

The other two officers start putting all the stuff they pulled out of Nova's locker back in. The memorabilia that students have been placing out front all day as a mini shrine is now piled off to the side.

Pops turns around as I'm walking up.

"What did y'all find?" I ask.

His mouth is fixed in a hard line. He stalks past like he doesn't even see me, disappearing into the crowd gathered on the other side of the hall.

The hollowness in my chest swells again. He's hurt. *I* hurt him. And that feels like a death too.

CHAPTER TWELVE

TINSLEY

OCTOBER 17

10:47 A.M.

MY MOTHER LETTING me stay home from school today was a god-send. It's the last place I want to be, given my fight with Nathan last night, coupled with the fact I still haven't heard from Lana or Giselle, who I suspect are icing me out, if their description of my character to the police aligns with Nathan's. Not having my boyfriend or my best friends at my side will only make me look more guilty.

My father has barely spoken to me since Saturday. He's hardly talking to my mother either. The bottles of Pinot Grigio and whiskey are rapidly disappearing. When my parents get like this, it usually means they're disagreeing about something involving me or my sister. And instead of talking it out like adults, they drink heavily and avoid each other.

I didn't crawl out of bed until after nine, and all I've done is take a shower and wander downstairs to force myself to eat a few pieces of fruit and half a bagel that tasted like cardboard. I've been sprawled on the sectional in the den ever since. Luckily, neither of my parents is here to make me feel worse than I already do.

Nova's murder wasn't the top news story this morning. The series of demonstrations and street marches in Jackson have somewhat eclipsed our scandal. Black leaders there have taken to the streets, demanding that the charges against Curtis Delmont be dropped and he be freed until police can produce more evidence that he could have killed the Holts. Things are peaceful now, but one of the local pastors expects them to escalate if Mr. Delmont isn't released from police custody soon.

Apparently, there was a new Judy Sanchez interview that aired this morning, featuring Chief Barrow answering questions about their continued investigation into Nova's murder. In the clip my sister texted me, Judy got Chief Barrow to say they're "looking very closely" into the actions of a "person of interest" to see if that person somehow "influenced" what happened to Nova.

My stomach tightened when Judy asked, "How close are you to making an arrest?"

Chief Barrow looked directly into the camera and replied, "I will not comment on that at this time."

His faint smirk sent a chill down my spine.

Chief Barrow is determined to make people believe I played some part in Nova's death, whether it's true or not. The sobering thought causes me to sit up straighter on the sofa. I didn't kill Nova, but someone did. Someone who obviously hated her. And I refuse to believe they did it because my drunken rant inspired them to. Which means Nova must have had a secret.

That's always what gets girls killed in TV shows and movies. If I can find out what it was, maybe I can save myself from being targeted by the police like Curtis Delmont.

I grab my phone. My pulse speeds up as I log back into my Instagram account for the first time since turning off notifications Saturday. There are over three hundred alerts waiting for me. Hundreds of people who likely took time out of their day to tell me how much they despise me. I purposely ignore the tiny red flags over my DM box and notifications tab and tap the search bar with my index finger. I only have to type the letters *N* and *O* before Nova's profile pops up in the list of people I follow. The first photo on her page is from that night. She's posed outside the gym, wearing her white ball gown. Hundreds of RIP messages are posted underneath the image. I click on the icon that will pull up photos she's been tagged in.

Dozens more from the night of the coronation fill my screen. In the first, she's standing on the auditorium stage, looking beyond gorgeous in her beaded sweetheart-neckline ball gown. It almost looks like she's getting married instead of being crowned homecoming queen. Her puffy Afro is haloed by her sparkling crown. She's cradling her scepter in both hands like it's a newborn baby. Her crown and scepter are pretty much identical to the three in my family's display cabinet.

Photo after photo serves as a glimpse into that night. Since Friday, people who were there have been posting and tagging Nova as some morbid way to involve themselves in her tragedy. Captain Simmons said Nova was last seen alive around nine p.m. He said she checked her phone before she walked out of the gym.

I mute the television as I swipe through the rest of the images. Nova's killer could have been there or showed up later. And maybe, just maybe, someone took a picture of the person without them knowing.

I pause on a close-up of Nova with Mrs. Barnett, another picture that was taken in the auditorium, shortly before the ceremony moved into the gymnasium for the sit-down reception. The lights are catching in her turquoise eyes and reflecting off the flower-shaped silver-and-diamond pendant dangling from her neck. I continue swiping, stopping briefly on a photo featuring my mother and Rachel with Nova and the six other past queens who attended, all in identical poses, crowns perched on their heads, holding their respective scepters. My mother is on Nova's right, a strained smile stretched across her heavily made-up face. A bunch of candid shots follow, some of which Nova is tagged to but not featured in. Those I pause on for several seconds, studying the background, taking inventory of who all was there.

I spot Jessica Thambley and the cheerleaders who served as hostesses. Lots of faculty and staff, including Mr. Haywood, who posed with Rachel for a picture. I forgot that they emceed the coronation ball together. Lots of images of Nova in pictures with kids I know, and with honored guests like the mayor, various city councilmen, and her friends. In one, Nova is making silly faces with Duchess and another girl with a blond buzz-cut fade who I've never seen before. I can't be certain, because the photo severs them at the waist, but it looks like Duchess was wearing a men's tuxedo jacket with a feminine-looking white button-up shirt.

Trenton Hughes pops up with Nova a few pictures later. I almost don't recognize him in his tailored tuxedo, with his mini Afro buzzed to perfection. He and Nova look like the couple he probably wished they could have been.

She doesn't care about anyone but herself. His words about me on the news echo in my mind.

I keep swiping, and the next dozen photos are of folks standing around drinking and talking, eating, and adoring Nova. I spot my dad lurking in the background of one. He looks bored, almost tortured. I pause on the next picture, one of Nova and her mother. The ebony-skinned woman and her carbon-copy daughter look like they couldn't love each other more. Far different from the way they acted in the main office the day we got into our fight.

I lower my phone. Who am I kidding? I'm not a detective. But I am Charlotte McArthur's daughter. My mother has this saying: *Perception is reality.*

"If you want people to believe something about you, you have to make them," she always says.

That gives me another idea. One that involves Nova's mother.

I find Nova's house by using the master call list the band director and Ms. Latham put together in Google Docs. The list has the names, contact numbers, and home addresses for every member of the school's band, dance team, and cheerleading squad. It's mostly used by the faculty when there are changes or last-minute updates they need to tell us about. We have access to the shared folder as well, in case we need to call one another for rides or whatever else we deem important.

Nova lived in the Avenues, which is about ten miles southwest of downtown. It's a primarily low-income, predominately Black neighborhood. I can count on one hand the number of times I've been there. The neighborhood definitely needs that affordable housing project my father's company is doing.

Two blocks from her house, the Sacred Hearts Slave Cemetery comes into view, and my breath catches in my throat. The yellow crime-scene tape still blocks off the section of graves where her body was discovered, one end flapping in the wind. Instead of turning right, like my phone GPS is telling me to, I turn left and coast along the fence line on the east side of the cemetery's entrance. I've been here once before, for a class field trip. I think I was in the seventh grade.

The cemetery takes up an entire block and is surrounded by a wrought-iron fence featuring an entrance gateway on Avenue F that is flanked by life-size statues of a Black man and woman reaching toward the sky and breaking free of the chains that once bound them. It's hard to believe Nova spent weekends organizing cleanups out here. The grounds are so unkempt. There's litter everywhere. Many of the aboveground concrete tombs are crumbling, exposing the rotting coffins inside them. The rusted wrought-iron fence is drooping and misshapen in spots. The crime-scene tape adds to the cemetery's decaying atmosphere. In other words, it could really use the money I offered her.

I pull over and park near the spot where she was found. I get out of the car and walk up to the fence, squeezing its skinny wrought-iron rods as I peer into the cemetery from the sidewalk. Gnarled branches from a trio of oak trees canopy the section of the cemetery that is now a crime scene.

Standing less than twenty feet away from the unmarked

graves where she might have taken her last breaths sends a chill down my spine. The image of a lifeless Nova returns to my head. I squeeze my eyes shut, desperate to bury it. But Nova's bloodstained white ball gown only becomes clearer. When my eyes pop open, it's like I can literally see her lying there, across three graves, the one in the center marked by a cross-shaped wooden grave marker that's partially covered in moss and lichen. I look away, trying harder to push the image from my mind.

My unsettled gaze lands on the entrance, which, as I realized when I drove up, isn't locked. That means anyone could have gotten access at any time of the night. And given the proximity of the cemetery to the surrounding homes, I'm thinking she had to have been dead, or close to death, when she was brought here. Nova was a fighter; I know that firsthand. I have to assume she would have fought back if she could.

"What you over there looking for?"

I spin around. There's an older Black woman peering at me from the porch of her shotgun-style home across the street.

"Um, nothing, ma'am," I answer, my heart racing as I scurry back to my car.

The woman's inquisitive eyes remain on me as I start my car and pull away. Through my rearview mirror I can see her on the porch, watching as I continue on to Nova's house.

The house matching Nova's address could fit in our backyard. The sand-colored-brick home has a messy front yard and a discolored roof with shingles fading from black to ash. Butterflies are jackhammering against my stomach as I squeeze my Mustang in next to the older-model gray Honda Civic parked in the two-car driveway.

I turn off the car and sit there, staring at the screen door. What if Ms. Albright falls to her knees as soon as she sees me? What if she screams at me like she did at the police station? What can I possibly say to get inside and do what I came here to do? Getting Nova's mom to believe in my innocence would force the police to admit they jumped to conclusions about zeroing in on me as a suspect. If Ms. Albright doesn't think I killed her daughter, it'll be difficult for the rest of this town to believe I'm guilty. It's a long shot, but the only option I have.

You got this, girl, I tell myself as I unbuckle my seat belt and climb out of the car. *You're Tinsley fucking McArthur. You. Make. Shit. Happen.*

I press the lighted doorbell and drop my hands to my sides. My stomach falls as the door swings open on the other side of the screen. The expression on Ms. Albright's dark face shifts from shock to confusion to anger within two seconds. She leans forward, casting nervous glances to the right and left of me before she pushes open the screen door.

"You on the wrong side of town, huh?" She eyes me up and down so hard my ribs start squeezing my lungs. "You definitely at the wrong house. 'Cause ain't no way you'd show up on my doorstep."

I try to swallow the lump in my throat. When I open my mouth to speak, the words I practiced on the way over get lodged in the back of my throat, so Ms. Albright speaks before I can.

"Y'all McArthurs are coming out the woodwork today, ain'tcha?"

"Excuse me?" I mumble.

Ms. Albright puts her hand on her hip, pursing her lips at me. Her brittle hair is pulled tightly into a ponytail held by a green rubber band. She's wearing house slippers and a pink terry-cloth robe paired with jeans and a lazy-fitting V-neck T-shirt. Her outfit mirrors the distressed confusion in her eyes when she says, "Why you here, li'l girl? To tell me you didn't kill my daughter?"

"I—I—I didn't." I pluck off my shades so she can see the sincerity in my eyes. "Ms. Albright, I promise. I swear on the Bible. On my grandmother's life. I didn't kill Nova."

Her hardened gaze has my heart knocking harder against my chest.

"I know this is asking a lot, but can I please come inside and talk to you?" I blurt out before the anger I can see simmering behind her dark eyes sends me back to my car. "I know you don't owe me anything after everything that went down between Nova and me, after everything I said about her, but you and I want the same thing—I promise."

"And what's that?"

"To find out who killed your daughter."

Her brow furrows, I hope because she's letting what I said roll over in her mind. I maintain eye contact with her, even though I want to look away. I can't stand to see the sadness there.

"Go home," she hisses, swinging the door closed.

I quickly jam my foot in the doorway to stop it from shutting, wincing from the dull ache that shoots up my leg when the door hits me.

"Girl, what is yo' problem?" Ms. Albright says, pulling the door open and glaring down at my foot.

"Please, Ms. Albright."

"Please what?" she barks.

She's definitely slamming the door harder in my face if I don't give her a compelling reason not to.

"Would I be here if I *really* killed her?"

"White people like to think they can do anything and get away with it."

"That may be true, but that's not me."

The look she gives me says *Girl, please!* without her having to verbalize it.

"Please hear me out!" I yell as she starts to shut the door again. "I did say some hurtful things about Nova. Things that were born out of my jealousy. But I really, really, *really* didn't kill her, ma'am. And I'm going to prove it. But I need to talk to you. Please. Just five minutes."

She waits a few seconds before dismissively waving me inside.

I'm hit by a familiar scent as I enter. The woodsy aroma tickling my nostrils doesn't match the muted feminine charm that greets me when I step into an open-plan living and dining area. Although the furniture in the living room is somewhat outdated, it's in good condition. I'm pretty sure I've seen the polyester sofa, love seat, and brass-and-glass three-piece table set in one of those rent-to-own furniture ads that are always in the Sunday newspaper. A round, five-piece wood dining table sits to my immediate right. Beyond that, a narrow kitchen. An archway a few feet away appears to lead to the rest of the house. Ms. Albright walks past me and turns toward the dining area.

It's when she's turning around to face me that I notice the

two mugs on the table. One is still steaming and filled to the rim. The other looks half-empty.

"I'm sorry. I didn't realize you had company," I say, pointing to the mugs.

"I don't." Ms. Albright picks up the steaming mug, the one closer to me, then goes to the kitchen and sets it in the sink. As she returns to the table, she says, "The person just left. Surprised y'all didn't run into each other." With a raised eyebrow she adds, "That would have been something."

My eyes shift toward the slender bookcase flush against the wall next to me. Its shelves are cluttered with framed pictures and knickknacks all covered in a thin film of dust.

"Is this Nova's grandmother?" I ask, pointing to the largest framed photo centering the shelf at my eye level. I take a step forward, squinting at the sickly-looking woman seated in a folding chair in front of the house. "She died from the coronavirus, right?"

Ms. Albright rolls her eyes before replying with a curt nod. "Suffered with so many complications from diabetes and kidney disease for seventeen years. That damn virus comes along and kills her within a week."

I can empathize. It killed my dad's mother too.

"You and Nova moved in after she died, right?" I ask.

"You talked your way in here to ask me a bunch of questions you already know the answers to, li'l girl?" she says, her face tightening.

I frown at her. "I'm sorry, what?"

"Nova told me how you and yo' li'l friends tried to get all up in our business." Ms. Albright pinches her robe closed and drops into the chair in front of the coffee mug she left on the table. "That li'l Black girl she said hangs with you sweet-talked one of the stock boys y'all go to school with to tell her all about me and my mama and why we moved back here from Virginia. Were you hoping we were running away from something?"

The sneer on her face is reminiscent of the one on her daughter's the day I tried to talk her into dropping out of the homecoming elections.

"Don't come up in here trying to act all innocent," she continues. "You met your match with Nova, didn't you? That girl wasn't afraid to go up against the devil himself for something she wanted."

My stomach feels like lead. I wonder if that stock boy told Ms. Albright all the other stuff he let Giselle know about them. Like how Nova's grandmother used to complain to the cashiers for years that her children never visited her. And how her daughter, Nova's mother, thought paying for her expensive medical treatments and medications sufficed.

"I can only imagine what you must think of me—"

"I don't know what to think yet," she interjects, leaning forward, propping her elbows on the table. "But I know the police are breathing down yo' neck because of that video. And the fact that yo' daddy was sponsoring Nova definitely establishes a motive for you wanting her dead, from what Captain Simmons told me."

I freeze. I must have just misheard Ms. Albright. "My father didn't sponsor Nova. My mother told him not to."

"And I wish he had listened to her. There were dozens of Black-owned businesses in town willing to do it, but Nova wanted him 'cause she knew it would get under yo' skin."

I retract my arms from atop the table. If Ms. Albright is

telling the truth, that means my father paid for that beautiful ball gown Nova was murdered in. How could he do that? *Why* would he do that?

"You didn't know," Ms. Albright says, pulling me from my thoughts. "Guess that daddy of yours is good at keeping secrets from his family."

I lean forward. "Did Nova have any?"

"Excuse me?"

"Secrets," I say. "Could there have been a *reason* someone would want to hurt her?"

Ms. Albright raises an eyebrow in my direction.

"Besides what you just said," I add, "because *I* didn't kill her."

"I'll tell you like I told the police: Nova and I . . . we weren't close like that. It wasn't always like that, but it stayed like that after . . ." She drifts into silence.

"After what?" I prod when the silence drags on too long.

Ms. Albright shifts in her chair. "I made a mistake when she was a little girl. A serious one. Didn't try to understand why she used to act out in school. Refused to believe her after I found out why. And things just never got better after that."

"I'm not following, Ms. Albright."

"All you need to know is that my daughter has had a difficult life," she responds, her shoulders stiffening. "I did the best I could as a single mother, but it was never good enough. Then we moved back here, into this house, and she became obsessed with a life she could never have."

Ms. Albright's eyes are fixed on mine, intensely.

"What did you do that was so horrible?" I ask.

After a beat Ms. Albright looks away and responds, "I brought her into this world."

Her statement creates a wall I know I won't be able to break through. Her faraway gaze falls into her lap. The thought of what happened to her only child is likely what drew it there. My ambitious, or more like misguided, attempt to convince her of my innocence is headed toward failure. I side-eye the archway that leads to the rest of the house. My stomach hollows. Guess I will have to try to Nancy Drew my way out of this.

"Um, can I please use your restroom, Ms. Albright?" My lips stretch into a nervous smile when she looks up. "I had one of those forty-four-ounce Slushes from Sonic on the way over."

The tears glistening in her eyes make me roil in my chair.

"Bathroom is the first door on the left." She points at the archway. "Right across the hall from Nova's bedroom," she adds helpfully.

She watches me stand up and I can feel her gaze burning into my back as I leave the room and head into the dark, narrow hallway. There are four doors, two on each side. I pause at the bathroom to look over my shoulder and make sure Nova's mother isn't following me. I stand there, my heart racing, until the faint sound of running water drifts toward me from the kitchen; then I lean into the bathroom to find the light switch and flip it on, shut the door, and dash across the hall to Nova's room.

My frantic gaze bounces from the queen-size bed to the messy mirrored dresser to the photo-adorned accent wall. I don't know how much time I have to search, but I have to assume it's not a lot.

I'm sure the police department has already been here. But I'm thinking Chief Barrow sent them to find something that would make *me* look guilty, not to shine a light on whoever it is that *really* killed Nova. That, and I highly doubt the Lovett police force would know where to look for the secrets a teen-aged girl could have been hiding.

I'm hit with a flash of numbing guilt that I'm in a dead girl's bedroom, getting ready to rummage through her personal life. As if I haven't already violated her enough.

There's a small desk against the wall next to her closet. That will be first. There are a few textbooks piled up, and a small tower of loose papers is neatly stacked in the left corner. A velvet board above the desk is cluttered with various articles, glossy pages torn from magazines, and what at a quick glance look like sticky-note reminders of dates and deadlines she didn't want to forget.

My gaze lands on drawings tacked to the wall beside the mirror. Was Nova into fashion design? I step around the corner of her bed to get a closer look, and they're actually pretty good. It makes me wonder whether she designed some of the unique clothes she wore. I let the sewing machine tucked in the corner to my right serve as my answer.

I glance at the doorway before peeling back the lavender comforter on the bed, then lift her mattress. The maids who clean our house periodically flip the mattresses when they change the sheets on our beds. I didn't realize they did it until I was twelve. That's when I stopped hiding my diary, and anything else, *under* my mattresses and started hiding stuff *inside* it instead. I haven't kept a diary since I was fifteen. The space I sliced open now serves as my hiding place for weed.

I walk around Nova's bed, running my hand along the side of her top mattress, gently applying pressure, on the off chance she and I thought alike. I make it to the other side of the bed without feeling anything, dropping the top mattress as quietly as I can and then fishing out my phone.

I drop down to my hands and knees and tap on the flashlight feature to take a quick glance underneath the bed. Of course, she probably wouldn't hide anything there—it's too obvious. And if she did, the police have no doubt looked and already found whatever she was foolish enough to think she'd hidden. But what if she *taped* something to the bottom of the box spring? That's what I did in the seventh grade when I didn't want my parents to find one of my progress report cards. I got two Fs weeks before my thirteenth birthday party, and there was no way I was going to let my disinterest in social studies and math stop me from having *the* party of the year.

There's nothing under Nova's bed except dust mites and shoe boxes.

Still on my knees, I look up at the lavender accent wall to my right. A string of white lights borders the wall where it meets the popcorn ceiling. Each vertical string hanging from the main line running along the top of the wall is ornamented with tiny photos that were taken with one of those novelty Polaroid cameras. There must be more than fifty pictures clipped to the strings cascading down the wall. A waterfall of memories Nova's collected that I don't have the time to scan through now.

I realize then that I no longer hear the faraway hiss of the kitchen faucet. My armpits are damp as I push myself up off the floor, beelining for Nova's closet. I contemplate dashing across the hall to the bathroom to flush the toilet or turn on the faucet, anything to make Ms. Albright think I'm still inside in case she's wondering what's taking me so long. A mental picture of her standing at the archway, peering down the hall toward the closed bathroom door, pops into my mind, but I still haven't found anything.

I yank open the closet door and jab my free hand into the pockets of the jeans and jackets hanging in Nova's closet, but there's nothing. Not even loose change or forgotten bills, like I used to find on my father's side of the closet when I was little.

A shrill bell echoes throughout the house, nearly causing my heart to rip from my chest.

I freeze, watching the doorway. The doorbell's chime echoes through the house again. A few seconds later, I hear Ms. Albright ask, "Who is it?" Her voice nowhere near the hallway or, more importantly, Nova's bedroom.

I strain my ears as another few seconds tick by; then I hear the front door crack open and I can exhale.

I dash across the room and poke my head out the doorway. Whoever it is will buy me another minute or two at least.

I feel sweat beading across my forehead and along the back of my neck. When I spin back around, my eyes stop on the exposed vent near the dresser. I have to cool myself off. Ms. Albright will know I was up to something if I emerge looking like I just completed a Zumba class.

I drop to my knees, crawling toward the vent and the coolness I'm craving. But there's nothing, not even when I press my face to the metal screen hiding the small rectangular hole cut into the wall. I can hear air wheezing from the vent, but with nothing close to the force it should be.

I glance over my shoulder to make sure I'm still alone before lightly slapping the vent. The thin metal screen pops off, startling me, but I catch it before it hits the floor. There are no screws. I grin, realizing what that means. With no screws holding the screen in place, someone can take it on and off easier. That someone being Nova, who found a better hiding place for her secrets than I have.

I look inside the ventilation shaft, and sitting in the center, there's a medium-size box.

Ms. Albright's voice rises an octave, but I can't make out what she or the person at the door is saying. I pull out the box and set it on the floor in front of me. It's covered in a hideous pink, green, and yellow floral fabric. The lid folds back but remains attached by metal hinges, similar to how my grandmother's crystal keepsake box opened.

It's filled with stacks of small papers folded into tiny squares. I pick one up, frowning at the yellowing slip of looseleaf paper fraying at the edges. I unfold it, revealing the short, jagged letters of a handwritten message.

You look beautiful today, it says.

I drop the slip of paper on the floor and pluck another from the box. It's the same handwriting.

I think I might love you.

I look down at the rest of the folded slips of paper stuffed in the box. So Nova *was* seeing someone! Who apparently was in love with her! But without a date or a name, it's hard to know how old these are. They could be from a boyfriend in her school back in Virginia. Whoever it was, she didn't want her mother to know about him—or maybe her? I mean, we *did* think she and Duchess were dating when they first started hanging out.

The next note I pick up says *I wish I could kiss you right now.*

The fourth: *Your smile makes me weak.*

I wish last night didn't have to end.

No matter what, please know I'll always love you.

I would give you the world if I could. I roll my eyes at that one.

The next: *I want you.*

If only this was easier . . .

That one makes me pause. Why wouldn't loving Nova be easy?

As I'm reaching down to pick up another note, something hidden at the bottom of the box catches my eye.

The back of my throat tightens. It's a brochure. The same one Rachel got when my mom took her to Abundant Life for her abortion. I dig it out of the box, my hand trembling. The glossy foldout tries to dispel any concerns and answer any questions a woman considering an abortion might have.

Does that mean Nova *had* an abortion, or was she just thinking about getting one?

"You can't come in because this is my house now!" Ms. Albright shouts, pulling me back to the present.

I turn around to the bedroom door. The voice that responds is gruff. It's definitely a man's.

Frantically, I stuff all the notes and the brochure back inside the box and close the lid. I return it to the air shaft, snap the vent cover back in place, get up, and leave Nova's bedroom, pausing at the archway to the living room so I can listen to the conversation Ms. Albright is having at the front door.

"I grew up in this house—just like you!" the man says.

"But Mama left it to me," Nova's mom responds.

"I ain't here to cause trouble, Donna. I just wanna be here for my big sister," the man says, his tone softer. "I know you must be going through it right now."

"I am. But I ain't up for company," Ms. Albright replies.

"Oh really? Then whose car is that in the driveway?" the man retorts, the pitch of his voice rising again.

My heart skips a beat.

"None of your damn business, Leland!" Ms. Albright yells.

"It better not be him!" the man fires back.

I take a step back from the archway, thinking he might be trying to look past Nova's mom to see inside the rest of the house.

"He has every right to be here if it was," Ms. Albright says.

"Please! I was practically that girl's father!" the man scoffs.

"Fathers don't do what you did," Ms. Albright replies, her voice trembling.

I slowly peer around the archway, straining to see who Ms. Albright is talking to. Her back is to me, but I can see that the man is dark-skinned, like her, and built like Dwayne "The Rock" Johnson. I snap my head back just as his eyes drift past Ms. Albright's shoulders. It has to be the guy Lana saw Nova arguing with outside school. The man Nova said was her uncle.

"Leland, leave before I call your probation officer," Ms. Albright says.

"That's messed up, sis. You real messed up for that," I hear him say. "Can a brother make up for his past mistakes by being here for you?"

"I don't need you," Ms. Albright asserts.

"But you did when her daddy didn't want nothing to do with her, or *you*." Leland Albright's tone is laced with contempt. "And what did I do when you came knocking on my door in Virginia, broke and pregnant? I was there for you! When Mama turned her back on you. And this is how you treat me?"

"Worry 'bout staying out of jail, keeping yo' job at Fatbacks," Ms. Albright says. "I don't need you worrying about me."

The entire house shakes when she slams the door.

I emerge from the archway as Ms. Albright is turning around. "I should probably go," I say. "I've intruded on you long enough."

"Make this the last time you do," she replies.

CHAPTER THIRTEEN

TINSLEY

OCTOBER 17

7:07 P.M.

I BARGE INTO my father's office. He's seated behind his desk, his back to me. My stomach has been in knots since I left Nova's house. When I haven't been thinking about Nova's possible secret pregnancy and abortion, my mind's been preoccupied with whether Ms. Albright was telling the truth about my father sponsoring her daughter. I would have confronted him as soon as he got home from work had I been here instead of at Rachel's babysitting Lindsey while she was out running errands.

"Daddy, we need to talk," I announce.

He doesn't move or respond. I round the right side of the desk and discover he's not staring out the large window overlooking our moonlit backyard.

He's sleeping.

His head is tilted slightly to the side, his mouth open. One of the crystal tumblers that belongs to the set adorning the minibar tucked in the corner of the room dangles from his limp hand, the empty glass in danger of shattering on the hardwood floor if his hand relaxes any more.

His whiskey breath burns my nostrils as I lean over to gently pull the tumbler from his hand. As I'm doing that, I realize he's clutching something in his other hand as well. It's a few crumpled sheets of paper that are stapled together. He must have been in the process of balling them up before he passed out. It looks like some kind of contract.

I cast a curious glance at his face, making sure he's still sleeping, before I slowly lean over to get a better look at them. His breath tickles the side of my neck once I'm close enough to read the bold words at the top of the first sheet.

NONDISCLOSURE AGREEMENT

I have to lean in closer to make out the name scribbled in the first blank space.

"What are you doing in here?"

His voice sends my heart into my throat and I jump back.

My father's blue-green eyes are narrowed at me.

"You scared the living daylights outta me," I say with a nervous laugh.

"Didn't I tell you a closed door means I don't want to be bothered?" he croaks, clenching his jaw.

He yanks open the bottom right drawer to his desk and shoves the nondisclosure agreement inside, then eyes me squarely. "Why are you in here?" he says. "Is something wrong? Has another one of your friends filmed you doing or saying some stupid thing?"

There's the anger I've been expecting. But I'm not about to let him flip the script.

I step around to the front of the desk to look him in the face. "We need to have a conversation," I say, my stomach quivering as I watch him reach for the crystal decanter sitting amid the stacks of papers and construction drawings splayed across the desk.

"About what?" he growls.

I briefly shut my eyes and exhale. "It's about Nova."

My father, glass tipped to his mouth, stops and slowly lowers his drink. "What about her? Did the police find some new evidence?" he says with a wrinkled brow.

I hope they have. Anything that clears me of suspicion. "They were at school today, searching her locker, according to Judy Sanchez," I say.

His expression clears. "Maybe that means Fred has dropped the ridiculous notion you had something to do with what happened to . . . her," he says. Then he downs the entire glass of whiskey in one gulp.

It's now or never. He's given me the perfect opening. But the words get caught in the back of my throat.

"What?" He pours himself another shot of whiskey. "Just spit it out. What do you want? 'Cause I can tell you want something. It's the only time you act like you give a damn about what me and—"

"Is it true you were sponsoring her?" I blurt out.

His thick brows lower as he lifts the tumbler again. But he doesn't drink. Instead, he holds it inches from his mouth, silently watching me over the rim. After a few seconds he finally takes a sip and then asks, "Where'd you hear that?"

"That doesn't matter. Is it true or not?"

He sighs before rocking back in the chair and raking a hand through the dark brown curls framing his rugged face. "Yeah. It's true."

It takes a few seconds for me to catch my breath. "Daddy, why did you do that? Especially after Mama told you not to."

"She's *your* mother, not mine," he barks.

I can feel my face heating up. "Never mind how doing it is a total slap in the face to me," I say, "but given what happened to her, don't you understand how this makes me look? If the police know too, they're gonna try to say I killed her out of jealousy."

I pause to try and steady my breathing. The adrenaline shooting through my body feels like fire. How is it possible that a dead girl is wreaking more havoc on my life than she did when she was alive.

"Don't you know I already thought of that?" my father replies.

"Then why do it?"

My father slams his hand on the desk. "How was I supposed to know you'd be foolish enough to let your friends record you talking stupidly—and then . . . what happened happens!"

"You had to know that would hurt me—even if someone hadn't killed her." I bite my lip, blinking to hold back the tears pricking my eyes. "She only came to you to get back at me."

"Tinsley, don't!" He rolls his eyes, as if the sight of me is too much for him. "Not everything is about you."

"Then why'd you do it?"

"Why not?" he barks. "Because I was supposed to blindly

support your silly little vendetta against her? She was the school's first Black homecoming queen. It was a good look for the company—hell, *any* white-owned business nowadays needs to publicly show its support for racial equality initiatives."

"But it wasn't public," I remind him. "You did it in secret."

His shoulders slump. "I made her agree to wait and announce it later, during her reign. After you would have gotten over your hurt feelings and moved on to the next vapid thing you'd get obsessed over."

"So screw how it would make me feel?" I respond with a shrug, swiping at a tear running down my cheek. "As long as McArthur Construction gets its gold star for supporting diversity, that's all that matters to you."

My father turns his head, eyeing the decanter of whiskey instead of me. The daughter he's always treated like an afterthought. He would have *never* done something like this to Rachel. His favorite daughter. The child who shares his acumen for business. The one who was practically his shadow until she went off to college and got married. He's the reason Rachel and I have never been close. He punishes me for clinging to my mother. Taking out on me whatever resentments he has for her. I don't care what he says; she told him not to do it, and he did it anyway. And as usual, I'm the collateral damage in their strife.

"I thought it could help me get ahead of some business mistakes—not that I owe you an explanation," he says somberly, pouring himself another shot of whiskey.

"And scoring that new affordable housing project wasn't enough? Or was that part of your diversity outreach too?" I say, pursing my lips.

My father glares at me. "Kinda felt I needed to do a little damage control after your theatrics last week about the elections."

He pops his head back, downing another shot in one gulp.

"You can't walk around town saying whatever ignorant thing you want anymore, Tinsley," he continues. "That damn video. You trying to sabotage the elections. My God! You have any idea how that might hurt the company I've spent half my life building from the ground up? Everyone in this town probably thinks I'm a bigot now. And in this PC climate, the slightest perception of racism can ruin someone. You trying to ruin me?"

And just like that, this is all my fault.

"No, Daddy," I start, "I wasn't thinking—"

"That's right! You weren't thinking!" he bellows, cutting me off. "So don't come in here questioning me about . . . *that.*"

I look down at the floor as he rakes his hand through his hair. This is *not* how this was supposed to go. He should be feeling like shit for what he's done, not me.

"How did you find out?" my father says, interrupting the silence that's thickened the air in the room.

Do I tell him I went to Nova's house today? That I talked to her mother? And when he asks why, what lie do I tell because I don't want to tell him the truth?

The doorbell rings.

"I'll get that," I quickly say, darting out of the room.

I'm tired of this. Tired of him.

My mother is already at the door when I get to the foyer. "Oh God! What is it now?" she fumes when she opens the door.

I come to an abrupt stop in the middle of the foyer the second Chief Barrow looks up. His accusatory gaze locks on me beyond my mother's shoulder.

"Just here to do my job," he responds while keeping his eyes on me. "We're here to search your daughter's room."

I stop breathing.

My mother opens the door wider, revealing the two uniformed officers standing behind the chief, both with solemn looks.

"I think not!" my mother fires back.

"I ain't asking." Chief Barrow breaks eye contact with me to pull a folded piece of white paper from his back pocket. He shoves it in my mother's face. "We got a warrant."

"For what?" I cry out as Chief Barrow pushes the door open wider and walks into the house.

"That, I don't have to tell you."

"Virgil!" my mother shouts as she reads the warrant she jerked out of the chief's hand. "Y'all can't just come into my home like this. Not without our lawyer here."

"Actually, we can." Chief Barrow turns to the two officers and says, "You know what we're looking for. Gather as much stuff as you can that we can analyze against what we found at the school today."

My mother scrambles in front of the two officers, blocking their path to the staircase. I join her.

"No. Hell no!" she shrieks. "Y'all can't do this—*Virgil!*"

I whip my head around toward the hallway, desperately waiting for my father to emerge from his office. The second he does, I turn back to the chief.

"When are you going to get a clue and realize I didn't kill that girl?" I say to him as he stands near the doorway with both hands on his duty belt.

"Funny, 'cause those friends you desperately wanted us to have a chat with claim you were so upset Nova wouldn't drop out of the elections that you made countless remarks about harming her."

Shocker, I think with an exasperated look.

I take a step toward him at the same time my father is entering the foyer. "You're not going to find anything in my room proving I killed her."

"If that's true, then you have nothing to worry about."

His cocky smirk knots my stomach. What could they have found at school, in Nova's locker, that would lead them to my house? Her locker was in B-Building, where I hardly ever go. Even still, I'm mentally combing my bedroom as my mother snips at the two officers. Wondering if there is anything in there this bastard could use against me.

"Fred, what is the meaning of all this?" my father says.

"He got a warrant to search Tinsley's bedroom," my mother explains, dashing across the foyer waving the paper at my father. "This is borderline harassment," she hisses at the chief.

Chief Barrow watches with amusement as my father's glassy eyes scan the paperwork. When I look over my shoulder, the two police officers are halfway up the stairs.

"Enjoy your little visit?" Chief Barrow says to me after I turn back around.

"Excuse me?" I say, confused.

"Your visit over in the Avenues." Chief Barrow joins me in the center of the foyer. The smugness flashing in his eyes sends a chill through my body. *He knows I went to Nova's,* I realize before he asks, "What could you possibly have had to say to Donna Albright earlier today?"

Both my parents' brows are knitted by the time I turn and look at them. My mother's scowl seems fueled by her disbelief, while my father's conveys a different emotion entirely. Now he knows how I found out he sponsored Nova.

"What is he talking about, Tinsley?" My mother joins the chief and me in the center of the foyer. "Why on earth would you go talk to that woman?"

Another question I'm not about to answer tonight. Not when I have the opportunity to call Chief Barrow out.

"I know why you're doing this to me," I say, ignoring my mother. "Why you won't even entertain the notion that I'm innocent. It's to get back at her, right?" I point my thumb at my mother.

My mother gasps.

"Tinsley, stop talking *now!*" my father shouts, appearing to my left.

"No, Daddy! He's trying to put me in jail because his sister, your ex-girlfriend, killed herself after you fell in love with my mother."

"Tinsley, don't," my mother protests.

"Is that what she told you?" the chief says calmly. He looks at my mother and then me. "Because your mother did more than go behind my sister's back and start dating your father."

My mother steps in between me and the chief. "How many times must I tell you it wasn't my fault? How could I have known what would happen? And I won't tolerate you trying to blame me for that. Not in my house."

"Then stay out of my way and let me do my job," the chief says, pushing past me to stomp up our staircase and join the officers I can faintly hear rummaging around in my room.

My mother is still standing with her back to me. I notice that her hands are trembling.

"Mama," I murmur, softly laying a hand on her shoulder.

She recoils from my touch as if it burned, then retreats into the kitchen. My father has a pained look on his face. I'm so confused.

"I'm gonna go watch over them, make sure they aren't trying to plant any evidence," he says, and climbs the steps two at a time.

The need to understand my parents' tension with the chief pulls me into the kitchen, where I find my mother seated at the island. A half-full glass of Pinot Grigio sits in front of her, the rest of the bottle beside it.

"Mama," I say quietly. But she doesn't acknowledge my presence. She just sips the wine robotically. I amble to the island, sliding onto the empty stool next to her. "Mama, what does the chief think you did to his sister?"

Her initial silence snakes around me, hardening my stomach. She takes a slow, delicate sip of wine, then turns her head, finally looking at me. Her eyes clouded by what I can only assume is guilt. I've never seen it before from her.

"Mama," I say gently, "what did you do?"

"Marrying your father, I thought it would make things easier," she says. "After going without for so long, having it all is *supposed* to be better. And it is, I guess. Compared to where I came from. The thing I sometimes struggle with is how tiring it is to keep up appearances. Be the socialite. A distinguished lady who lunches. It won't be as hard for you and your sister. Y'all were born into this. But me . . . every day can be a struggle."

"What does that have to do with Regina Barrow?" I say, even more confused.

My mother lets out a breath. "Shame is a big part of why I don't talk to you girls about my life before marrying your father," she says. "But it's not the shame y'all must think I have knowing what people still say about me behind my back—while smiling in my face because they want our money. I've always wanted my daughters to see me in a *certain way*. I convinced myself that would never happen if you knew about Regina."

I sit in silence, anxious for her to continue. I have so many questions, but I've never seen my mother so vulnerable and I don't want to disrupt this moment. She starts twisting the stem of the wineglass between two fingers. Her distracted gaze pointed at its translucent contents, as if the wine is reflecting whatever memory she's been afraid to share.

"The Barrows weren't an affluent family. Despite that, they still moved in the same social circles as your father's family, since Fred's dad was chief of police back then," she begins in a soft tone. "Regina was *the* girl. She was you: pretty, popular, and envied. She was . . . perfect. At least, that's what she wanted everyone to believe, and they did. Even me for a while. We became friends junior year. We sat next to each other in home economics. Our friendship blossomed quickly. There weren't many places she went without me, even the country club sometimes. It shocked me that Regina wasn't as stuck-up and pretentious as she seemed to most people. She had done a very good job of being who everyone wanted her to be, 'everyone' being her family, your father, and his country club posse."

My mother looks over at me and says, "What a lot of people didn't know was that she had a wild side too. Looking back on it, I think she expected me to have one as well. That's why she so readily fell into an unlikely friendship with me, the girl from the run-down trailer park across town."

I lean forward, resting my elbow on the island countertop and cupping my chin with my hand. Eager to learn this new information about my mother's former life.

"Regina was dating your father, which your grandmother loved, but she got a kick out of flirting with my friends. You know, the 'bad boys' from the wrong part of town," she says, making air quotes when she said "bad boys." "A friend of mine was throwing a party one night and Regina talked me into letting her tag along, despite me telling her that it wasn't her crowd and she wouldn't know anyone there besides me. Your father was away that weekend, visiting family out of town, I think. Anyway, Regina was wild that night. Drinking. Grinding up on different guys. Doing drugs, you name it. I was dabbling too—no sense pretending I was this innocent church girl."

The side-eye she gives makes me smile.

When she shifts her weight on the stool, her face darkens. "We got into an argument that night after I said I was ready to go and she wasn't. When I brought up your father and how he might react if he knew how she'd been acting that night, she turned vicious. Calling me white trash, a leech. Everything I'd always been afraid she and her friends thought about me. I was so angry I left. Told her to find her own way home."

My mother deeply exhales. "What happened after I left was all everyone talked about at school on Monday. It involved Regina and several of the guys from the party . . . yeah. When your father found out, he was furious. Called her a slut, broke up with her, even though she claimed she had been slipped something and taken advantage of that night."

My brow furrows. Regina was raped?

"She tried to lean on me for support. But I was still angry about what she said, so I didn't give her the support she obviously needed. Oh God, this is horrible." My mother's eyes start to glisten. "I had convinced myself that if what everyone was saying was true, then somehow she deserved it. No good person would ever treat their friend the way she treated me, I told myself. As if that made it better. I had no idea how much she was suffering, or maybe I just didn't want to know. And I never got the chance to realize how wrong I was. The gossip. The fall from grace. All of it drove her to do what she did."

"And Fred, oh God, he was angry," my mother continues, wiping away the tears dangling on the tips of her eyelashes. "He blamed me for leaving her at the party. To him, it didn't matter what she'd said to me. His sister was my responsibility. He blamed your father too, for turning on her. Us starting to date months later just exacerbated Fred's disdain, which I realize now has never gone away, given what he's so clearly trying to do to you."

My mother places a hand on my thigh. "Sweetie, I'm so sorry. He's only doing this because I wasn't the friend I should have been when Regina needed me. But I was young. And stupid. And petty. I don't want you to suffer for my mistakes."

I blanket my hand over hers. Wishing there was more I

could do to heal the guilt she's been carrying around for so long. "I'm not going to let him win, Mama. You taught me better than that."

"What does that even mean?" my mother says after sniffing back tears.

That if Chief Barrow won't find out who really killed Nova, I will.

CHAPTER FOURTEEN

DUCHESS

OCTOBER 18

7:30 A.M.

MY HEART IS knocking around hard in my chest as I tiptoe out of Pops's room. The key in my clenched fist pinches my palm as I softly close the door. I've only got ten minutes to do this and return it—fifteen tops if he decides to shave in the shower too.

I dash down the hall to Pops's office, watched only by the family photos covering the beige walls. It takes a few seconds to get the key in the lock, my hands are trembling so much.

There was a time when I didn't have to do this, sneak around to look at Pops's case files. A time when I used to think police officers were *always* the good guys. That's why I wanted to be one. He started locking this room when I was in the seventh grade and began to understand and question the complexities of the world. Specifically, it was after I embarrassed this boy who kept calling me a dyke by telling everyone he was living with his grandmother because his mom was a drug-addicted sex worker. Something I learned after seeing his last name among my Pops's work files.

Since that day, he's locked his office. As soon as I heard him start the shower, I crept into his bedroom to swipe the key. I haven't been interested in gaining access until last night, after seeing him come home with a brown accordion folder tucked underneath his arm. *Albright* was scribbled across the front in black Sharpie.

That folder is lying on its side in the center of his desk. I dart over to it. The array of photos and framed certificates chronicling Pops's career in law enforcement watch over me from the wall behind the desk.

I have to know what they found in Nova's locker yesterday. Pops and I are still barely talking to each other, though I doubt he'd tell me even if we were. This tension between us is compounding the chill that has attached itself to me, and to this house. If my Moms were still alive, she'd make me apologize to him.

" 'Honor thy mother and father so that you may live long,' " she used to say whenever my brothers or I didn't do something we were told.

I never heard of her disrespecting my grandparents, but she wasn't granted a long life. Maybe if she had called them out when they needed it, she'd still be here. Then everything would be different. Pops would probably be different. I would be too. Our blowup would never have happened. Nova would still be alive too, and hopefully still my best friend.

I swear my heart is about to explode as I'm pulling out the stack of papers stuffed inside Nova's file. I flip past the coroner's report and typed witness statements. I close my eyes and shuffle past the black-and-white pictures of her lifeless body sprawled out in that cemetery. I leaf through diagrams, a copy of a warrant to search Tinsley's bedroom, school disciplinary papers for both Nova and Tinsley, documenting their fight. Guess the chief hasn't been lying to the press about seriously looking into Tinsley. Good.

What I don't find is the evidence bag that officer gave Pops in the hallway. Not even when I turn the folder over and shake it to make sure there's nothing else inside.

The five-minute timer on my Apple watch starts beeping and I jump.

Shit!

Frantically, I start shoving everything back into the folder. I can't risk him catching me. Not after what I said the other night. He'd bring down the wrath of God if he thinks I'm trying to interfere in their investigation. Him angry still scares me. That's really why I'm not trying to face him yet.

I've gotten nearly everything back inside when something on the coroner's report catches my eye and I pause, thinking there's no way I saw what I think I saw. I even hold the paper up to my eyes 'cause I'm convinced my eyes are bugging.

They aren't. Clear as day. In black-and-white. My blood goes cold in my chest and I drop into the chair behind me.

Nova was pregnant?

The shrine at Nova's locker has grown. It's plastered with photos, sympathy cards, and handwritten notes. Now people have to walk around the collection of candles and mementos arranged in front of it on the hallway floor. Eventually someone will need to clean this up, clean out her locker, and give everything to Ms. Donna. Somehow, I know it will probably be me.

I'm standing in front of it all, forcing people to step around me while I stare at the photo in the center of the collage on her locker. It's an 8" × 10" of the yearbook photo she took last year. Her eyes match the turquoise background we all had to pose in front of. How could this girl I called my sister, my ride-or-die, have been pregnant and not even told me? I thought we told each other everything. I always told her. So what was up with her keeping that from me? Or had she tried to tell me and I didn't pick up on it?

I think back on what she said to me at the coronation reception. *Stuff you'd have to promise you wouldn't tell anyone else,* she said when I left that night. *I promise, I'll tell you tomorrow.*

And then, that day in Mr. Haywood's class, when she'd asked me about dating a white dude. Was that her way of letting me know she was boo'd up? Nah, there's no way she could have kept a whole relationship from me. It had to be just a hookup. A hookup that led to her being pregnant.

This is too much.

A sudden shift in the volume of the chatter buzzing around me pulls my attention from Nova's smiling face and toward the crowd forming on my left in my peripheral vision.

"Hey, I really need to talk to you," Tinsley says, suddenly all up in my personal space.

I turn, and I'm a little thrown by her appearance. She's not as put-together as she usually is. Though I guess trying to beat a murder charge will do that to a person. And yet, even though her chestnut-colored hair is a little disheveled and her face naked of makeup, she's still got her preppy, ice queen vibe going, in jeans, loafers, and a blazer over a sweater I'm certain cost a few hundred bucks.

"Unless you here to confess, you ain't got *shit* to say to me," I fume.

Everyone starts gathering around us.

"I didn't kill her," she says with this pained look.

"Oh really?" I say. "Then why talk about doing it?" I look her up and down, suck in a breath through my teeth. "You have the audacity to walk yo' privileged ass up in here and approach me after what you did."

This is why I didn't want to run into her. My anger is vibrating in every limb of my body.

"Duchess, come on. We used to be—"

"That's right," I stop her, "*used to be*. Until you shitted on that too."

"Can you just listen to what I have to say?" she asks, her voice shaking. "What I need to ask you. It's serious."

"You think I'm 'bout to sit up here and entertain some foolishness from you?"

All I see is red. I need this girl out of my face. I need her in handcuffs.

I take several deep breaths, clenching my fists. I'm having a hard time resisting the urge to smash her in the face. It's not justice, but it would make me feel better. At least temporarily.

"You need to fall back, for real," I warn.

"Get in her ass, Duchess!" someone shouts from the throng of people around us. The energy from the crowd is fueling my anger. They want justice for Nova just as much as I do. And I want to give it to them, any way I can.

"Duchess, please." This girl leans in closer instead of

backing up off me. Seriousness enters her expression. "This is about Nova. You have every right to be pissed at me. But I want to make it right by finding out who really did kill her."

"Girl, fuck you!" I yell.

I spin on my heel. Walking away is the only thing that will stop me from getting suspended. Pops would ground me until graduation for fighting at school. I've already pissed him off enough this week.

"Wait! Please," she shouts.

I turn back around, my nostrils flared. On second thought, maybe the suspension is worth it. Nova's dead. This chick has ruined everything we had planned for our senior year.

"You gon' molly-whop her ass or not?" one of our spectators shouts.

"Who was Nova dating?" Tinsley blurts out before I can threaten her again. "I wasn't aware she had a boyfriend—at least, not one who goes to school with us."

A chill trickles down my spine. She shouldn't be asking me this. *Why* is she asking me this? Could she somehow— Nah, ain't no way. If *I* didn't know, ain't no way she did.

"Nova wasn't boo'd up," I reply, straining the muscles in my face so my uncertainty doesn't show.

Tinsley's brow knits. "Are you sure?"

I purse my lips at her.

"Then who wrote her all those love notes?"

"What love notes?"

"The ones I— Look, I know her secret."

A knot hardens the back of my throat.

Tinsley glances around before taking a hesitant step toward me. I already know what she's about to say. She knows. But how? Did Pops mention it while he was questioning her? If that's the case, though, why hasn't he asked me about it?

"Clearly she had to be seeing someone if she had an abortion," Tinsley whispers.

My mouth falls open.

Abortion? That's not right. The coroner's report said Nova was still pregnant when she died. Where this trick getting abortion from? Is she trying to spin some narrative to somehow make herself look less guilty?

"Girl, if you don't want me to drag yo' white ass up and down this hall I bet not *ever* hear you repeat that!" My voice is trembling, I am so angry.

Even though Nova's gone, I still want to protect her. At least, her image.

"I'm not lying, I swear," she says, her eyes desperate and her chin quivering. "Duchess, I found—"

"Haven't you taken enough from us?" I hear someone say.

Trenton steps between us, looking more pissed than me. I'm confused about why he's in B-Building until I look down and see the photo of him and Nova he's clutching in his hand. His contribution to her locker shrine, I presume.

"We're not gonna let you get away with what you did," he says, his voice filled with conviction.

"I didn't kill her!" Tinsley shouts, looking more at the crowd than at us. "You know I could sue you for defamation after what you said about me on TV."

"Of course you will, because that's what your family does: take, take, and take some more," Trenton hisses through his clenched teeth. "Do y'all ever get tired of having to lie, cheat, and steal to keep the rest of us down?"

"All of this"—Tinsley waves her arm at Nova's shrine—"has nothing to do with the bad blood between our fathers."

Trenton snorts. "Whatever."

"Look," she says, "I know you probably had some unrequited thing for Nova, but cool your jets, Poindexter."

Oh no this girl didn't!

"Nah, princess, you need to check yo'self," I interject. "We ain't got nothing here for you, so strut yo' ass back over to A-Building with your kind. Enjoy the last little freedom you have."

She straightens her shoulders and bites down on her lip, then storms off in the direction she came. Leaving me to wonder how Nova's secret might somehow be linked to her.

CHAPTER FIFTEEN

TINSLEY

THIS MIGHT HAVE been a mistake. Coming to school.

Being here seemed like the most logical (and safest) place to approach Duchess about Nova's pregnancy. And doing that— *huge* mistake too. However, that convo fades into the back of my mind as I enter A-Building. It's like time slows as everyone watches me walk down the hallway. Their stares a form of intrusion foreign to me.

Before, I reveled in this kind of attention. Considered these halls my personal runway. The looks of contempt and the side-eyes I'm getting now have my throat feeling like sandpaper. The buzzing conversations among different knots of friends aren't bolstering my posture the way they usually do. Everything feels different. Disjointed. Like suddenly I don't belong somehow.

I think I overhear someone say, "How can she even show

her face here?" It feels like I'm walking in a live-action version of the comments section of a social media post. How can any of these idiots think I really killed Nova? They've known me my whole life. I mean, they know I can be mean, maybe vengeful sometimes. But murder?

I knew this would happen. I told Rachel it would be like this. They don't want to see the truth when the scandal of it all is more entertaining.

I make eye contact with some of the AP officers on the student council. They're gathered at the locker of Kyle Bakeman, the vice president. I acknowledge them with a strained smile and a timid wave. They're just the refuge I need. Something familiar to anchor me to the life I had before that video and Nova's unfortunately timed murder. I start to squeeze through the clusters of people to make my way over to them. Having the public support of my council, the other student leaders on campus, is a good look. It'll prove I haven't lost the respect of my peers. That they see me as innocent.

Kyle leans over and whispers to the others before sneering at me and shutting his locker. I come to an abrupt stop. The group scatters in different directions down the hall. There's an outburst of laughter behind me. Having the power to turn invisible (or telepathically burn this place to the ground) would be clutch now.

Don't react, I tell myself. *Just keep walking.*

It would be so much easier if I had my friends walking beside me. I glance down the hall, desperate for their faces. Any friendly face, really. A lifeline that can pull me out of this sinking feeling of powerlessness.

I need to walk. Faster. Get to my locker.

"Look who graced us with her presence: the future ex-con!" someone shouts.

The back of my neck heats up.

"From head cheerleader to homecoming queen killer," someone else taunts. "She's a Lifetime movie waiting to happen."

People start laughing, and the back of my neck feels like it's on fire.

I whip my head in the direction of the insults, my defensive instincts on autopilot. A group of football players are pointing at me. It's the one person among them who *isn't* that catches my attention.

Jaxson Pafford actually looks annoyed by his teammates' jokes. We lock eyes. I'm taken aback by how bloodshot his are. And it looks like he slept in the clothes he's wearing.

"Can y'all chill the fuck out?" he says.

Jaxson slams his locker shut and storms off, leaving his teammates behind with their dumbfounded looks.

Wow. He's the last person I ever thought would come to my defense. I pick up my pace, darting between people, trying to look unbothered. The crowd thins as I turn onto the hall where my locker is located.

Chief Barrow and his goons left our house last night with several of my notebooks after spending at least an hour ransacking my bedroom. From what I can tell, those notebooks were the only things they took. And of course, Chief Barrow wouldn't tell us why.

"You'll hear from us if they shed light on the investigation," he said with a mocking grin as he was leaving.

I stop abruptly again.

Lana, Giselle, Nathan, and Lucas are all walking together up ahead. I should feel a sense of relief. But I don't. Seeing how they're laughing together, as if they've already moved on from me, scratches at the back of my throat.

I dip into the girls' bathroom on my left, desperate to avoid any more public humiliation. A lightness washes over me the second the door clicks shut at my back. Then a breath catches and twists into a knot in my chest. Jessica Thambley and two other girls are standing in front of the long mirror that stretches over the four sinks lining the wall in front of me.

The three of them silently stare at me in the mirror's reflection for a few seconds. I don't know where to look, how to act, or what to say. Jessica decides for me.

"You showed up . . . *here* . . . at school." She lowers the tube of rose-colored lip gloss she was in the middle of applying when I stormed in. "Guess I owe you that one hundred dollars, Brooke."

Brooke Haughton, a junior and fellow cheerleader, cackles along with Jessica and Chelsea Grant, another junior.

I purposely don't break eye contact with them. I can't show them any weakness.

"This is what innocent people do." I clear my throat, hoping it'll strengthen my voice. "Continue living their lives with nothing to hide."

"Riiiiiiight," Chelsea drawls with a smirk.

Jessica spins around to face me. "It's just, no one thought you'd be brave enough to show up here, given the fallout. It's not a secret how much you love to assert your authority in your various roles on campus."

"What fallout? What are you talking about?"

She gasps with melodramatic flare. Not understanding why she's taunting me right now churns my guts.

"Well, that explains it. She doesn't know," Jessica says, looking at Brooke and Chelsea.

"Know what?" My gaze flits between their condescending looks.

Jessica has never been like this with me. She's usually passive; I'd even say obedient. Always laughing at my jokes. Eager to participate in our conversations. Complimenting everything I wear. Now, though, there's this maliciousness flickering in her porcelain features as she stands with her friends. The three of them looking like generic versions of me.

"I doubt this is how they wanted you to find out, but it is what it is," she says. "Yesterday the student council adopted a motion to censure you for what you said in that video."

Tinsley, don't react, I tell myself. *Don't. React.*

"And I heard from Kyle they have enough votes to adopt a motion of no confidence, which I'm sure you're aware would force you to resign from your position as president," Brooke says. "But that's probably good, with everything going on in your life right now. It'll give you time to focus on that. Sort it out."

"Murder suspect is kinda not a good look for the student body leader, you know?" Chelsea adds.

I dart into the first empty stall to my left. Slam and lock the door. I won't let them enjoy the punch in the gut they just delivered. Censure? No confidence? That would force me to step down from cheerleading captain and all the other leadership roles I have. I'd basically be a nobody.

I press my forearm to my mouth to muffle the scream I have to release.

Everyone is turning on me. Like it's nothing. Like this is the moment they've been waiting for. My downfall.

Jessica and her friends are still whispering, but I can't make out what they're saying. I drop down on the toilet lid. Tears building behind my eyes. I so want to open the stall door and cut Jessica and the Nobodies down to size. Remind them I'm still *that girl*. But doing that might play right into the narrative everyone is building based on that video. Of course, acting meek might come off as guilty behavior as well, like I have something to hide. I'm damned if I do and damned if I don't. Whatever I say, whatever I do, these assholes are going to make me the villain. And why not? It's not like I got popular being America's sweetheart, like my sister. I've always known my social status was forged by money and fear. It was never threatened, because I knew how to leverage other people's secrets and insecurities. Something my mother taught me how to do.

For the first time, other people at this school have the power to take away everything I've built my identity on.

I wait until Jessica and the other girls leave before I emerge. I hardly recognize the timid person staring back at me in the bathroom mirror.

How did I get here?

Hiding in bathroom stalls. Getting heckled in the halls. Avoiding my friends. This is all some kind of twisted karma.

The hall is nearly empty by the time I exit the girls' restroom. Good.

I need to focus on finding out who got Nova pregnant if I want to salvage any part of my life. Duchess clearly won't be any help in that regard, but it occurs to me there's someone else who could be.

—

I snuck off campus to wait for Nova's uncle to show up for work, and there's nothing I hate more than waiting.

I have no intention of going back to school until I've given the police someone else to focus on—the father of Nova's unborn child being the most logical choice.

A secret babydaddy would be hard for them to ignore. True-crime documentaries have taught me it's almost always the boyfriend, the husband, or the scorned lover who commits homicides against women. My ex-friend, and Nova's best friend, may not know who she was seeing, but I think I know who does.

It better not be him! The words ring through my head.

I'm assuming Nova's uncle was talking about whoever Nova was secretly dating. The only other things I can remember from the exchange, besides her uncle's obvious disdain for whoever he was referring to, are Ms. Albright's calling her brother Leland and her mentioning his job at Fatbacks.

Fatbacks is a soul food diner on the west side of town, on the outskirts of the Avenues. It's Black-owned and a popular tourist draw. I've never been here before, but I think my father has. A hazy memory of him talking up a fried-chicken-and-red-beans platter haunted my thoughts on the ride over.

I've been crouched in a booth for the last two hours, my hair tucked underneath the Ole Miss baseball cap Nathan left in the backseat of my car. The quaint diner was pretty packed when I first got here. My entrance garnered a few curious glances from within the cluster of brown and Black faces packed in the dining area. After mumbling to the woman who greeted me at the door that I only needed a table for one, I pulled the bill of my cap down a little lower to hide my face. I have to assume a lot of these people wouldn't be kind if they realized who I am. And being one of the only white faces here makes me stick out even more.

I learned from my server, Tiffany, who doesn't look that much older than me, that Leland Albright is late for work today. I asked for him while she was taking my drink order.

"He better get here soon before Mrs. Anita fires his trifling behind," she said as she handed me a menu.

Tiffany let me sip on a glass of water for about an hour before she asked, slightly irritated, if water was the only thing I came here for, so I ordered the fried-chicken-and-red-beans platter even though I'm too nervous to eat. I've done nothing but pick at the heaping plate of food as I wait for Nova's uncle to show up, and I've been here so long that the diner is now almost empty.

I'm biting into the drumstick, which surprisingly is still warm, when a dark, brawny man strolls into Fatbacks and the fuzzy memory I retained from my quick glance of Leland Albright in the doorway to Nova's house sharpens into a solid picture. I watch him move through the dining area seemingly without a care in the world. His solid, muscular frame is squeezed into a white V-neck T-shirt, dark jeans, and tan unlaced combat boots. He has a stained white apron slung over one shoulder. There are remnants of Nova in his features. Only an idiot like Lana wouldn't have picked up on them and realized that Nova was related to the man.

When he disappears through the aluminum swinging doors

that lead into the kitchen area, I realize Tiffany is watching me from the register on the other side of the diner.

My eyes immediately fall to my plate. I break off another piece from the drumstick, stuff it into my mouth, and chew frantically. Tiffany's curious gaze continues to periodically shift to me as I force myself to eat more of the red beans and chicken. Do I ask Tiffany to get Leland for me? And what story should I tell about why I'm here? Maybe that I want to offer my condolences about what happened to his niece. Tiffany hasn't given me any indication that she knows who I am, which means she must not watch the news. The lie could work.

"Would you like some dessert or something?" Tiffany asks, appearing at my table after I've eaten nearly half of the food on my plate.

I'm the only person in the restaurant now.

"No, I—"

The rest of my reply gets caught in my throat as I see Leland push through the double doors. He uses the back of his hand to wipe away the sweat glistening on his forehead.

"Going to grab a quick smoke, Mrs. Anita," he shouts over his shoulder.

"Better not be longer than five minutes! Yo' behind was already late today!" I hear shouted back at him from the kitchen.

A mental picture of a short, no-nonsense older Black woman whose voice is probably bigger than her body pops in my head for Mrs. Anita.

Leland casts a fleeting look at me right before he walks out the front entrance.

Tiffany has one eyebrow raised when I look up at her.

"He takes his smoke breaks near the dumpster around the side of the building," she says with a coy grin.

"I promise, I'm not leaving." I scoot out of the booth. "I just need to ask him something. Then I'll pay my bill and be out of your hair."

"Uh-huh," Tiffany murmurs, and purses her lips.

I find Leland exactly where Tiffany said I would, sucking on the end of a cigarette, after I round the wooden fence encasing the diner's dumpster on the side of the building. I try rolling my tongue around to relieve the stickiness that starts spreading in my mouth as I approach him—this source of tension between Nova and her mother that I'm still struggling to understand. I remove Nathan baseball's cap and comb my fingers through my hair. Leland doesn't notice me until I accidentally kick a pebble across the parking lot from dragging my feet.

My sudden presence makes him jump.

"Girl, don't be sneaking up on a brotha like that. That's how fools get got." Leland exhales a cloud of smoke through his crooked smile.

I mumble a weak apology, but struggle over what to say next. Do I offer my condolences to get the conversation started? Maybe telling him I'm innocent is the better icebreaker. I should have rehearsed while I was waiting.

Leland's eyes narrow before he cocks his head, taking me in. "You Virgil's daughter, ain't you? The one everybody thinks killed my niece."

It's a little off-putting to hear how comfortable he is calling my father by his first name. And since he already knows who I am, I should probably tell him now that I didn't do it.

"How long you been sitting in there waiting for me?" He

flicks the ash off his cigarette. "I seen you bent over in that booth when I got here."

"A while," I say. There's no anger flashing behind his eyes, which eases some of the tension knotted in my chest. Still, I add, "I'm not here to cause trouble, sir. I just want to talk; ask you something, really. About Nova."

Leland sucks his teeth. "You came to the wrong person for that. Nova and I wasn't all that close."

"But I heard you tell her mother you were like her father."

"When you heard me . . ." His mouth drops open. "So that was *your* car parked outside my mama's house yesterday." After taking a drag from his cigarette, he adds, "What were you doing over there? Throwing money at your mistake—y'all McArthurs good at that shit."

Why he thinks that—despite its being accurate—is a mystery for another day. This is about his niece, not my family.

"I was there to prove my innocence," I say.

Leland chuckles. "I bet you were."

"Mr. Albright, I think the boy your niece was dating might have killed her."

"What boy?" he replies with a blank look.

"The one you thought I was yesterday."

A pensive look shadows his already dark face. It's only there a second. Then his mouth relaxes into an obnoxious grin. After taking another drag from his cigarette, he says, "I don't know what the hell you talkin' 'bout, girl."

"I don't believe you."

"You can believe whatever the hell you want. I could give a fuck. I don't owe you shit."

"Mr. Albright, I know she was seeing someone; I just don't

know who. But whoever it is, I have a feeling they wanted her dead because of something she did or didn't want to do."

Leland flicks more ash from his cigarette. "Does yo' daddy know you're here?"

What's up with this dude? He's all over the place. Yesterday he claimed to be a father figure to Nova. Now he's saying they weren't that close. He's annoyed by me asking questions about something he said but didn't display even a flicker of anger toward the girl everyone thinks killed his niece. This must be why Nova told her mother to keep him away from her that day in Mrs. Barnett's office. He's super shady. Which now has me wondering, why was he pestering Nova and her mother so much?

"Don't you want to know who did that to Nova?" I ask.

"Look, I already told you, my niece and I weren't close, so I don't know nothing about no boyfriend."

"Then why did you come to our school to see her two days before she was murdered?" I say.

"You da cops or some shit?"

"No, but do they know you were there?" I fold my arms across my chest. "From what I heard, y'all were arguing about something."

"I was more of a father to that girl than her real one. He wasn't man enough to do it," Leland says, jabbing his thick index finger at me. "But now my sister treats me like I ain't shit, after all I did for them when she showed up and interrupted *my* life in Virginia."

"What happened between y'all?"

"Nova." Leland drops his cigarette on the concrete, steps on it, and then twists his foot like he's killing a bug. "Never could keep her mouth shut. Her mouth is probably what got her killed."

Leland leaves me standing near the dumpster, stunned by his words.

The sun has almost set by the time I get home. I have three missed calls and two unanswered texts from my mother.

After leaving Fatbacks I drove around town for an hour, my strange interaction with Nova's uncle replaying itself on a loop in my mind. I ended up parking at the beach and sitting in my car, watching the Gulf in the distance. Got woken up a few hours later by a meter maid tapping my window to let me know I was in a no-parking zone.

My body aches a little as I step out of my car. I'm grateful there are no media vans parked outside our house tonight. I plod toward the front door. It's like everything I've been through these past few days is starting to take its toll on my body.

My phone vibrates in my hand. I look down at it. The notification illuminating the screen makes me gasp.

It should have been you, not Nova.

Sent to my school email account. There's no signature, and I don't recognize the address of the sender: sickofkarens@ evermail.com.

"How did you know?" someone shouts behind me.

I spin around, my heart leaping into my throat. Duchess is halfway up our circular driveway.

"Where did you come from?" I ask, my hand pressed to my chest.

"I've been waiting for a while." She steps into the halo of light above our front door. "I wanna know how you found out."

"What are you talking about?" I ask, my thoughts still attached to the cryptic email I just received.

"Nova," she says. "Why do you think she had an abortion?"

I sigh, contemplating whether I should tell her the truth or lie. The flicker of desperation that flashes in her eyes pushes me to be honest. I tell her about the brochure I found in Nova's bedroom yesterday.

"You were snooping around in her room?" Duchess barks. "For what?"

I roll my eyes. "Why are you here? You refused to listen when I tried to tell you this earlier."

Her face softens a little. "I didn't know she was pregnant. Found out this morning when I . . . That's not important. But you were wrong. She didn't have an abortion. She was still pregnant when you—when she got murdered."

"Oh my God." For some reason this revelation hits me harder than I would have guessed. Makes me sadder.

"But I don't understand how that happened," Duchess continues, her voice cracking a little. "Nova wasn't caught up with no dudes—at least, not any I knew about."

"Will you come inside with me?" I respond.

CHAPTER SIXTEEN

DUCHESS

OCTOBER 18

5:27 P.M.

GUESS SHE WASN'T expecting me to accept her invitation. Tinsley has this dazed look on her face.

"Are we going inside?" I ask after we've been silently staring at one another for a little too long.

"Oh yeah," she says, blinking out of whatever thoughts she was having. "Come on."

I take a deep breath. *There's no turning back now,* I tell myself. *Justice for Nova. That's what all this is about.*

Had to keep repeating that to myself the entire drive over here. This entitled, insensitive brat is the last person I want to be around. But I'm thinking she might be the only person who can help me get to the truth. Our blowup at school today has had my head reeling. Tinsley might actually be innocent.

Her mother is standing on the other side of the front door when Tinsley opens it.

"Where have you been? The school called and said—"

Her sentence dies when she sees me standing behind her daughter. Tinsley waves me inside after I pause in the doorway in an intense staredown with Mrs. McArthur. I have to remind myself again why I came here to resist the urge to back out of this house before Tinsley has a chance to shut the door. This woman still makes me feel insignificant and unwanted. The same way she did when it was her daughter I called my best friend instead of the girl everyone thinks she murdered. I think it's her resting bitch face. The woman must have been born with it.

I wonder, does she even remember who I am? Probably not. She seems like the kind of woman who got a lot of folks fired from that country club.

"You can't be yourself around some of *them,* Duchess. They'll use it against you," my mother said to me the night she got the call she was being let go due to several guests' complaints. But it was only one guest. The one standing in front of me. Looking like an older, colder version of her daughter. The same woman who twisted an innocent kiss between two little girls, one of whom was still trying to figure themselves out, into something she claimed her daughter felt threatened by.

"What's this about?" Tinsley's mother says with a dismissive wave toward me.

"School was too much, so I left," Tinsley replies.

"That doesn't answer my question," Mrs. McArthur responds, side-eyeing me.

Tinsley starts walking toward the biggest staircase I've ever seen in a house that wasn't on TV. "Come on, Duchess. We can talk in my room," she calls back to me.

My feet don't move, even though I'm mentally screaming at them to follow Tinsley. The way Mrs. McArthur is still scrutinizing me has me frozen in place.

"Duh-chess," her mother repeats in an icy tone. "I thought you looked familiar. You're the little girl Tinsley used to play with at the club. Your mother, she used to wait tables there, right?"

No, bartend, bitch! I want to say, but I know that correcting her won't do any good. Bartender, server, it's all just hired help to her.

"Tinsley, is there something going on here I should know about?" This woman actually scrunches her nose at my baggy overalls and neon-colored Vans. When Tinsley doesn't answer her question, she turns to me and says, "How is your mother? Doing well, I assume."

Some of the color drains from Tinsley's already pale face. I'm not breathing. My throat is clenched tighter than my fist.

"Mama, excuse us. We need to talk about a group project for class." Tinsley snatches my wrist, pulling me with her to the staircase.

Her mother is still watching us when I look back over my shoulder. I finally let the air out of my lungs once we're inside Tinsley's bedroom with the door closed.

"God, why are mothers the absolute worst?" She stops, realizing what she said and to who. "Sorry, didn't mean to— Breast cancer, right?"

Not gonna lie, I'm shocked. Didn't think my mother's death would land on her radar. Especially since we weren't friends and didn't even go to the same school when Mama died. Has this chick been keeping tabs on me? I'm not pressed enough about it to ask. I'm not here for her fake sympathy.

"What's on yo' mind that you couldn't tell me outside?" I say to change the subject.

She drops her messenger bag on the floor near the desk centered under the arched window to my right, then plops down in the recliner by her closet, which looks like a dressing room at a department store.

I try to look unimpressed as I stand in the middle of her room. It's big enough to fit all three of my house's bedrooms in. And I've never been somewhere so feminine and bougie. Everywhere I look there's lace, frilly pink embellishments, and sparkly things. Her bedroom feels like a fully realized Baroque aesthetic off Pinterest.

"Can I ask you something first?" she says, her brow furrowed.

I respond with a reluctant nod. I have a good idea what she's about to say.

"Why are you here?" Her head tilts to the right. "At school today, you were ready to drag me down the hall, convinced I killed her." She narrows her eyes at me. "But you wouldn't be here, standing in my room, if you really believed that. What gives?"

I shove my hands into the front pockets of my overalls. The sobering truth to her question slowly dragging my stomach into my feet. Clinging to the notion that Tinsley killed Nova just because I can't stand this girl won't give Nova the justice she deserves. I need that more than anything. I won't let whoever did this to her get away with it. I can't sit back and grieve helplessly again, like I was forced to do with my mother. So I swallow my resentment toward this chick and decide to be real with her. Admit I was letting my raw emotions over losing Nova prevent me from seeing things objectively.

"My Pops told me once that guilty people do whatever they can to avoid getting caught in the crosshairs of investigations connected to their crimes," I say, looking past Tinsley's shoulders into her closet but not really seeing it. The memory of ten-year-old me seated at our dining table with my mother, two brothers, and Pops is all I'm envisioning. One of many dinners where Pops's job was the topic of conversation. "He said they tend to do that out of fear they might say or do something that could incriminate themselves, especially the ones who aren't career criminals who get off on lying to police."

My eyes lock with Tinsley, whose brow is still knitted.

"You just told me you went to visit Nova's mother yesterday. And today, you approach me at school," I continue. "Two people who are grieving the hardest over her death, you're running up on with all these questions. The way you were talking, the look on your face in the hallway today. I never seen you look so desperate. Desperate to understand what was going on with a girl you hated. Once I calmed down, I kept replaying everything you said to me over and over in my head. And I can't make sense outta why you would be doing all of this if you really killed her. If what my Pops said is true, you'd be off in the cut somewhere, lying low. Scared you might do something to throw even more suspicion your way."

Tinsley's mouth, a tight line before, slowly stretches into a smile. This has to be the first time someone, outside of her family, has expressed any belief in her innocence.

"I know this is about nothing but self-preservation for you,"

I say. "You didn't give a damn about Nova. And that's fine. I do. And I want the same thing you do. And the more I've thought about it today, the more I think finding her killer might still be connected to you."

Tinsley's frown pulls tighter, and her posture stiffens. "Excuse me?"

"You've spent the past three years being a straight-up bitch to everyone." I pull my hands out of my pockets, counting my next points off with my fingers. "You have blackmailed, manipulated, bullied, and messed over a grip of people. Any one of whom could have been among the first hundred or so people who saw that video yo' girl posted of you on the beach."

"I'm still not following where you're going with this," she says, drawing her head back slightly.

"Somebody trying to get back at you could have killed Nova," I snap. "It's too much of a coincidence she was killed a few hours *after* you said it. The only two logical explanations are that you did it *or* someone who wanted revenge on you killed her as the ultimate takedown."

Tinsley shakes her head. "I don't believe someone would go to that extreme."

"You got another plausible theory?"

She stands up. "Maybe you're half-right. My video gave someone a smoke screen to hide what they did. But I think whoever killed Nova did it because they wanted her dead."

"How so?"

Tinsley drops back down in the recliner. "Unless Nova got pregnant through immaculate conception, she had to be hooking up with somebody," she says. "And that someone murdered her. You didn't pick up on *any* clues who that might be?"

I shake my head.

"It's usually the boyfriend, you know," Tinsley says.

Nova's comment in Mr. Haywood's class about dating a white person pops into my head.

"She wasn't boo'd up with anybody—that I know of," I say.

"How did she manage to keep a secret like that from everybody in this town?" Tinsley says as she peels off her blazer and tosses it across the back of the recliner. "Oh. Sorry. You can have a seat." She waves at the chair at her desk.

Guess since she now knows I think she's innocent, she's being more hospitable.

"I tried talking to her uncle today, thinking he might know who it was," she says as I'm dropping into the antique chair.

"Leland? *He* wouldn't know." I yank off my beanie, raking my hand through my pixie cut. She wouldn't talk to her uncle if her life depended on it. "Nova avoided his nasty ass like the plague."

"Why?"

"That degenerate use to molest her when she was younger," I say before I can catch myself.

Tinsley's mouth drops open.

Nova swore me to secrecy. She only ever talked about the sexual assault once with me, during a sleepover. With a tearstained face she gave me all the graphic details about what she endured while she and her mother lived with Leland back in Virginia. The ordeal is why her and Ms. Donna's relationship was so messed up. Nova said her mother didn't initially believe the things she told her Leland would do to her every time he babysat. Nova started acting out at school because of it, getting the attention of a counselor, who coaxed her into revealing the abuse. Child protective services almost took her away from her mother and Leland was sentenced to prison.

"How young was she?" Tinsley asks quietly.

Nova, please forgive me.

"Happened in elementary," I answer.

"Gross," Tinsley murmurs, curling her upper lip.

"Leland was supposed to do ten years but got out this summer through some early release prison reform movement the governor in Virginia championed," I explain. "He moved back here, even though there was a protective order prohibiting him from going anywhere near Nova. The perv still tried to make amends, though. Nova's mother even asked her to give him a chance to apologize. But Nova wasn't having that."

"That explains why he had zero compassion about her murder when I talked to him," Tinsley says. "Plus, he's so . . . *intimidating.* I had a feeling he was hiding something."

I grind my teeth as I remember how emotional Nova got whenever she talked about him. Leland deserved to be in a coffin six feet under, not prison.

"I was waiting for that fool to slip up," I say. "The second I see him within one hundred feet of a kid or a school, I'm reporting his pedophile ass."

Tinsley leans back into the recliner. "You already missed that opportunity. Lana saw him talking to Nova outside school a couple days before coronation. According to her, the convo looked heated. Although she misinterpreted it and thought he was Nova's sugar daddy."

"What would make her think that?" I say with a frown.

"She claimed Leland was leering at Nova in some suggestive—wait a minute!" Tinsley stands up and starts pacing in front of me. "What if she *tried* to keep her uncle away, but he . . . um . . . ignored her."

"Nah, that ain't happen," I assert.

"You know that for sure?"

"She would have told me."

At least, I think she would have. Nah, I'm *sure* she would have. She knew I hated Leland as much as she did. Or . . . was Leland, or something related to him, the *stuff* Nova promised to tell me but never got the chance to?

Tinsley pauses, raising an eyebrow. "Oh, like she told you about being pregnant? Or her uncle showing up at school? And don't lie and say you knew about that," she adds as I'm opening my mouth to respond. "You were surprised just now when I told you."

Ugh, this chick!

"Why you even going there with this?"

I thought we were trying to figure out who Nova was having sneaky links with. Not talking about Leland's disgusting self.

"Think about it." Tinsley resumes her pacing. "Neither of us knows of anybody she was dating or hooking up with. But she did have a pervy uncle who may have wanted to pick up where he left off. And now that he couldn't easily manipulate her, he forced himself on her."

I steel myself for what she's about to say.

"He could have gotten her pregnant."

My mouth drops open, but I can't wrap my head around what she just said fast enough to craft a response.

"A baby would be irrefutable proof he violated the terms of that order," Tinsley continues. "And if he didn't want to go back to prison, which I'm sure he didn't, and if she wouldn't get an abortion, killing her was the only way to make sure that didn't happen."

The twisted scenario she's spinning opens a simmering rage in my chest that my quickening heart starts pumping through my body. Just the thought that Leland could have hurt her again—

"All I need to show is that it's possible he could have killed her to make it harder for the chief to pin it on me," Tinsley says, seemingly more to herself than to me. "If I tell them what I found out today and what you just told me—"

I shoot up out the chair. "Hol' up, hol' up, hol' up!" I say, my hands raised. "I'm not about to let you do that."

"Do what?"

"Put all that stuff out there about what went down between Nova and Leland." I stab myself in the chest with my index finger and add, "She was *my* best friend! She revealed that to me in confidence. *I* know how it went down. You don't get to control how that comes out. Not on my watch!"

Tinsley's shoulders droop, the excitement draining from her face.

I take a deep breath, calming myself. "You said the chief wants you to go down for this," I say, my voice softer. "That man is like a dog with a bone. My Pops is your only hope of getting someone on that force to truly listen to you. He was crazy about Nova. And he doesn't let his personal feelings get in the way of what is right. He'll believe us more if I'm there, trust me."

"Us?" Tinsley replies, her chin pointed down and brows lifted. "You wanna do this together? Go to the police?"

I wait a few seconds before I nod.

Her face lights up. "Okay. We do it tomorrow morning. Deal?"

My phone chimes as I'm nodding again. Tinsley's quiet as I pull it from my back pocket. It's a text from Ev.

Please rethink working with that girl, it reads.

Before I can type my response (which was going to be *too late*), another text from her pops up. This one says, *I don't trust her!*

"Everything okay?" Tinsley says, pulling my mind back into her bedroom.

I give her a weak smile. "Yeah, it's all good."

I really need this to be one of those times I prove my paranoid girlfriend wrong.

CHAPTER SEVENTEEN

TINSLEY

OCTOBER 19

7:05 A.M.

I PICTURED THIS going a lot differently.

And in that scenario, Duchess's father would first give us a horrified look when he learned why Nova's uncle served time in prison. Then he would listen with intensity as I talked through my theory on how Nova got pregnant and why Leland was motivated to kill her. Our conversation would end with Captain Simmons profusely apologizing for all the unnecessary stress and embarrassment the department caused me and my family. I'd leave the police station with my head held high. Then I'd give Judy Sanchez the exclusive interview on how I went from suspect to unlikely hero in the murder investigation that rocked our small town.

It's looking like that's not going to happen.

Duchess's father has had this pinched look since we mentioned Leland's arrest. He even rolled his eyes at my theory about why Nova's uncle could have murdered her. Chief Barrow is here too, standing behind Captain Simmons's desk with a wad of tobacco knotted in the front corner of his chapped mouth. He followed us into Captain Simmons's office after spotting Duchess's father escorting us through the police station.

"Is this what you talked about with Donna Albright?" Chief Barrow interjects as I'm explaining how Nova's pregnancy could have sent Leland back to prison. "Is that how you found out Nova was pregnant? And that her uncle molested her?"

I fold my arms and sit back in my chair. "No, it's not," I reply, sneering at him.

"Then how'd you find out?"

Duchess shifts her weight in the seat next to me. Why isn't she saying anything? She had a lot to say in my bedroom last night. Things I *never* thought I'd hear her say. Like that she believes in my innocence. Finally, someone besides my family with common sense in this town.

"That's not important. The fact that it's true is," I say to the chief.

Captain Simmons gestures at me. "Is that where you snuck off to last night—to her house?" he says to Duchess. He's seated behind his desk, which is cluttered with stacks of folders and papers and framed pictures of his family.

Duchess gives me a pensive look. There's this crazy tension happening between her and him right now. He seems very irritated by her presence. She said her being here would help. I'm starting to think it's doing the opposite.

"Pops, doesn't it make sense that Leland could have done

it, given what he did to Nova when she was a kid?" she says. "I heard you on the phone this morning saying you think her killer had to be someone she knew or had an intimate relationship with, since the person stole her necklace."

Wait. That's new. I look at Duchess. "That flower-shaped pendant she always wore?" I say, then turn back to Captain Simmons. "You didn't tell me the killer stole that. Is that what y'all were searching for in my bedroom the other night?"

"This is an ongoing investigation," Chief Barrow says, "so we can't answer that."

"Why were you listening in on my conversation?" Captain Simmons snaps at his daughter. "Didn't we already have this discussion a long time ago about you *not* involving yourself in my work? You're not a little girl anymore. It ain't cute. The stakes are higher. You should know that, given how *passionate* you were the other night about me doing my job."

"And how's that going?" Duchess says. "Looks like *we're* working harder than—"

"Do *not* disrespect me again!" Captain Simmons barks, slamming his hand on the desk.

The room is silent for a few moments until Duchess speaks. "She was my best friend," she says, her tone softer.

"I know that," her father replies with a tight face.

"You might want to limit your time around people right now," Chief Barrow interjects, looking directly at me but, I'm pretty sure, speaking to Duchess. "Can't have our investigation getting compromised like I suspect it already has. Now, I want to know how you found out Nova was pregnant, and considering an abortion, you say?" He spits a glob of tobacco juice into the garbage can.

There's no way in hell I can tell him that.

Chief Barrow raises his shaggy eyebrows at me and I shift in my seat so that I'm facing Captain Simmons, with the chief in my peripheral vision.

"Captain Simmons, what about Nova's uncle?" I say. "You can't ignore our theory."

"Y'all are way off base," he responds.

"How can you say that?" I ask.

Captain Simmons rocks back in his chair, rubbing the back of his neck. "I've already been down this road, all right?" he says, suddenly looking tired. "The other day I dropped in on Leland at Fatbacks as well, after I learned about his background. He was working the night of the coronation, the late shift. His boss confirmed it."

"Fatbacks closes at ten, though," Duchess beats me at pointing out. "You said Nova was murdered between nine-thirty and about midnight, based on what was said on the news."

"I also got confirmed statements from several eyewitnesses who say Leland was at a local bar on the west side of town, selling them hot goods," her father adds.

"And you're going to trust people who bought stolen goods?" I argue.

"I have no reason to think they lied to me." Captain Simmons scratches his head. "And I have something to hold over Leland if I need more information. Selling stolen goods is clearly a violation of his probation."

"I didn't give you authorization to chase that lead. I asked you to track *her* whereabouts," Chief Barrow snaps at Captain Simmons, while pointing at me. "Have you made any headway on finding Nova's cell phone?"

"Sir, I—"

"I need to know what *she* was doing in that window of time!" the chief barks at Duchess's father, stabbing his finger in my direction again.

Heat rushes to my face as the chief's voice grows louder.

"Chief," Duchess's dad begins, "I know you have the local NAACP pressuring you for a quick resolution that fits the narrative they're pushing—"

"That has nothing to do with you being insubordinate, Simmons," Chief Barrow interrupts, ready to explode, "and not doing the job I asked you to."

Captain Simmons seems to grow smaller in his chair. "Yes, sir," he mumbles.

I'm gripping the arms of my chair so hard I'm surprised the tips of my nails haven't broken off. Finally, I can't keep my mouth shut anymore.

"This is so insane!" I erupt. "Nova was freaking pregnant. Something that you, Chief Barrow, somehow made sure didn't leak to the press, unlike a lot of other stuff. Why haven't y'all gotten a paternity test done on her fetus? Can't you do that? They do it all the time on *Law and Order*. Don't you think finding out who the father of the baby is would be a better use of your time than, I don't know, trying to pin her murder on me?"

"We're waiting for the results from the county lab, Veronica Mars," Chief Barrow says with a sneer.

"Yes," Captain Simmons adds. "We're hearing that could take a few days, since they've got a backlog of cases. Now"—he turns to his daughter again—"let's circle back to you thinking you can play detective."

Duchess sits back and folds her arms as he launches into a

lecture about how we need to let the police do their job. It's not until he finally says "The truth always comes out, but you can't try to rush it" that I lean back in my chair too, giving him an exasperated look.

I stop myself from making a snide comment and tune him out. I walked into this station feeling proud about everything I uncovered yesterday, only to have it all immediately dismissed by a man who's now telling me I have no business trying to save my own ass.

To my left, a door I haven't noticed suddenly swings open, interrupting Captain Simmons, and a uniformed officer pokes his head into the room.

"Chief, need to borrow you for a sec," the officer says.

The officer does a double take once he realizes Duchess and I are in the room too. He quickly looks away, and it dawns on me he was one of the officers who showed up at my house the other night with the chief.

"What is it, Johnson?" Chief Barrow says to him.

"Um, some—something related to . . . you know"—the officer cuts his eyes at me—"our active investigation."

Chief Barrow's arms drop to his sides. "Gotcha."

As I'm watching the officer step back into whatever room is connected to Captain Simmons's office, a chill punches me in the gut. Beyond the young officer's shoulders, I see my face. The photo is grainy because it has been blown up five times the size it is on my school ID. The door shuts, but not before I can also see that my photo is taped to what appears to be a dry-erase board with lots of scribbling and more pictures I can't make out.

"Listen to your father, Duchess," Chief Barrows says, then

turns to me. "And you, don't leave town." Then he opens the door to the mysterious whiteboard room.

I respond to the chief's warning with a fake smile.

As he turns to leave, I scoot forward in my chair, hoping to catch another glimpse of the board with my picture on it. But Chief Barrow opens it just wide enough to squeeze through before slamming it shut, like he knows what I'm trying to do.

"Come on, girls, I'll walk you out so you're not late for school." Captain Simmons stands up and walks around to the front of his desk.

Hundreds of butterflies are fluttering in my chest. I think I know a way I could get a better look at what's on that board, which I'm thinking is a snapshot of whatever case the chief is trying to build against me. I look down at my messenger bag as Duchess bends over to pick up her backpack off the floor. I stand up along with her, giving Captain Simmons a benign smile while I covertly kick my messenger bag farther underneath my chair. I exhale when neither of them notices I didn't pick it up as I follow them out of the office.

I make it a point to lag a few steps behind the father/daughter duo, who begin what sounds like a stilted conversation about how she's coping with Nova's death. I'm sure seeing her walk into the police station with me this morning has set off all kinds of alarms for him. But that's not my concern. I need to figure out my next move. As my mother would say, I need to play chess, not checkers. I need to see that board.

Halfway down the hall I stop and say, "Oh crap!"

Duchess and her father both stop and turn to see what my problem is and I continue, "I left my bag in your office, Captain Simmons."

"I'll go get it," he says.

"No! I can run and grab it," I say, holding out my hands to stop him. "You keep talking. It'll take me a second."

I turn around and go back to the office, straight to the door to the adjoining room. I quickly check to make sure nobody followed me, then pull my phone from my back pocket. My hands are trembling as I key in the code to unlock it and open my camera app, quickly checking to make sure the phone is on silent so the camera shutter doesn't sound. My palms are so slick I wipe my hand on my jeans before grabbing the doorknob. My heart is pounding like a freight train in my ears.

I'm literally not breathing as I gently push the door forward, praying the hinges don't creak. Through a slim crack I see Chief Barrow. He's bent over reading something alongside the officer who poked his head in earlier, but his back's to me. I squeeze the doorknob harder, silently pushing the door open a little wider.

I slip my phone around the door until the board comes into view on the screen. The second it does, I snap a picture, then quickly pull my arm back and ease the door shut.

Immediately, I pull up the picture, frantically studying the image I managed to capture.

"Whatcha doing?"

I almost drop my phone from jumping.

Duchess is framed in the other doorway, her brow furrowed.

"Getting my book bag, *hello,*" I reply, stuffing my phone in my back pocket. Duchess has this intense look as she watches me walk over to the chair and grab my messenger bag off the floor. I catch her perplexed gaze dart toward the door to the adjoining room. "You really shouldn't frown that hard. It'll give you wrinkles," I say as I breeze past her, as nonchalant as possible.

Neither of us speaks until we're walking out of the station and Duchess says, "You going to school?"

"Maybe," I reply weakly. All I can think about is my phone in my back pocket and getting to a place where I can see the photo I took.

I say a quick *bye* and take off in the opposite direction. I'm practically speed-walking. My skin is tingling. I somehow feel more alive than ever, but anxious at the same time.

By the time I make it to my car, and inside, my stomach is in knots. I pull up the image and the first thing that stands out is a wrinkled sheet of notebook paper that's taped to the dry-erase board next to my picture. Written beside it is *Found in victim's locker.* It looks like a note. I have to expand the image to read the sentence scribbled in the middle of the crumpled sheet.

I suck in a breath when I realize what it says.

Don't do it! Or I'll make you regret it!

CHAPTER EIGHTEEN

DUCHESS

OCTOBER 19

3:39 P.M.

I HAVE NO idea why Mrs. Barnett wants to see me—she only said it was "something important"—but she's over thirty minutes late. I'd be pissed, but waiting here is better than being at home. Alone. The quiet makes it harder to ignore the void that has attached itself to my insides. Plus, I'm being entertained at the moment by this sophomore who's waiting for her alongside me. She's here for some disciplinary reason. I know that because she's been talking so loudly on her phone.

"Yes, I caught that nigga at her house," the girl announces to me, Mrs. Barnett's secretary, and the person she's on the phone with. "Yeah, guh. I downloaded Find My Phone onto his phone but linked the account to my computer. Then tracked his ass over there Saturday night without him knowing."

I can hear whoever's on the other end howling with laughter. Mrs. Barnett's secretary is glaring in this direction from behind her desk. Normally I'd be annoyed too, but this girl's lack of decorum is taking my mind off my grief.

"Jaz, I was about to snatch that ho by her lace front in biology today," the girl continues. "She lucky Mr. Glasper's crooked-eyed self held me back."

Mrs. Barnett rushes through the double doors. "Duchess!" she says. "So sorry I'm late. Had to tie up a few loose ends, took longer than I expected."

I stand up. "It's cool."

"Let's step into my office," she adds, gesturing to her door. She follows me inside, pausing in the doorway to look back at the sophomore, who's still on the phone. "Tori, I'll deal with you in a minute," she tells her. "And *get off the phone*." Then Mrs. Barnett shuts her office door.

"Again, my apologies," she says as she's rounding her desk. "How have you been holding up?"

Concern is coated thicker on her face than her makeup. God, I wish everyone would stop asking me this. It's like a fresh reminder Nova's gone.

"I'm good—well, not *good*," I say, rubbing the back of my neck. "I'm . . . *here*. That counts as good, right?"

"Yes, of course," she replies with a soft smile. Then she folds her hands on the desk in front of her. "I'll get right to the point. We're putting together a tribute to honor Nova at Friday's game. The community is in such mourning over this tragedy, I thought it fitting we set aside halftime for a memorial service in addition to parading out the court. Nova's crowning was such a monumental step toward inclusion and diversity here, and I hate that it was tarnished like this."

It feels like she's about to ask me for something. I brace

myself for whatever it is and choose to let the insensitivity in her last remark slide. Nova was a person, not just this school's diversity poster child.

"Lining things up for this is why I was late. I've met with the band, the dance squad, and the cheerleaders, who all agreed to participate and put together a special performance."

I sit up straighter. That would mean Tinsley's involvement as well.

"The cheerleaders? Including—"

"I've asked Ms. McArthur to sit out, for obvious reasons. She made no objection when we spoke a few moments ago at practice."

The tension dissolves from my shoulders. *Good,* I think. Even though I don't believe that she killed Nova anymore, she still said all that effed-up stuff about doing it. Wouldn't feel right having her included in something like this.

"I was hoping you'd say a few words," Mrs. Barnett says. "You were Nova's closest friend. I thought it fitting you be involved. Help people understand how special she was, as only you could."

I had no intention of attending the game or the dance this weekend. Without Nova, it didn't feel right. We had planned to go hard. Our senior year, her the first Black queen. We had outfits, knew where we were going to afterparty. It was going to be epic. Beyond memorable. But there's no way I would let them do a memorial and not be there to talk about her. I knew her best, despite the secrets she was apparently keeping from me. Someone needs to be there who can make sure she's honored as a whole person and not just this school's token queen. *I* can make sure that happens.

"Sure, I can do it," I tell her.

Mrs. Barnett nods. "I appreciate that," she says.

Loudmouth Tori is still talking away on her cell as I'm leaving the administrative offices. I look at her phone in her hand as I pass her and think about her dumbass boyfriend when something comes untethered in my mind.

Nova's phone.

I take off running down the empty hall toward B-Building. I need the laptop I left in my locker. And Mrs. Barnett mentioned Tinsley being at cheerleading practice right now. After I grab my laptop, I book it to the gym. I know how we can track Nova's phone.

"Wait. Are you serious?"

I barged into the gym and waved Tinsley over from cheerleading practice to tell her what I figured out. Her face lacks the angst it would probably have if she were guilty. Her wide-eyed disbelief reassures me that I'm not making a mistake by doing this with her.

I step up onto the set of bleachers behind us, plopping down in the third row. "Yes, I'm serious." I rip open my book bag and pull out my school-issued laptop. "But if you got better things to do, don't let me interrupt you. Forgive me for wasting your time on something that could help clear your name."

"You caught me off guard, that's all," she says. "Your timing is perfect, though. I need to stop showing up to this place. Ms. Latham pulled me aside a little while ago and suggested I step down as captain for a few weeks, 'until the dust settles.' I only came to school today hoping I could suss out who wrote the . . ."

Her eyes quickly drop to where I'm balancing my laptop across my legs.

"Sorry," she says, her cheeks flushed. "Didn't mean to dump on you like that."

I pause for a second, studying her. She's standing in front of me with this nervous grin on her face. She obviously almost slipped up and said something she doesn't want me to know. And she was acting just like this at the police station this morning when she went back into Pops's office. I shake my head. I'll circle back on the doubt knotting my stomach later. Finding Nova's phone is clutch now.

"If you stop whining and get up here and help me, we can stop all that from happening when we find her real killer," I say, waving her up to join me.

She steps up onto the bleachers and plops down next to me as I'm turning on my laptop. "This isn't just about Nova, is it?" she says.

I frown. "Who else would it be about?"

She waits a few seconds before she says, "Your dad."

I slowly turn to her, worried she's about to rehash some of the things Lorenzo and my classmates said about Pops this week. *Lord, please don't let this girl go there with me,* I silently pray. I'm liable to *really* drag her ass for making any ignorant assumptions regarding my Pops.

"The chief comes off as the micromanager from hell, based on what I witnessed at the police station this morning," she says. "I'm still fuming over how he bit your dad's head off just for doing actual detective work instead of carrying out his witch hunt against me. You're doing this to help him too, aren't you? Because he might lose his job if he doesn't do it the way the chief wants him to."

I focus on my laptop, watching the screen blink to life as I let what she just said sink in. Her words shake loose some of the resolve I've built up within myself to seek justice for Nova, and to do it with a girl I despise. That same girl who has some understanding of my father's struggles, something only a few people know. She's wrong, but not really. This isn't about doing the job the chief won't let my father do, and at the same time, it kind of is. I just didn't realize that until she said it.

A tightness in my chest melts. I feel her gaze pinned to the side of my face as I continue staring blankly at my laptop screen. The girl may not be as shallow as I thought. Hope that means she can handle what I have this strong inclination to tell her.

I look up at her. "Did you know this town didn't have its first Black police officer until fifteen years ago?"

I wait until she acknowledges my question by shaking her head before I continue.

"My dad was, like, the third Black officer to enter the force out of the academy, and he's the first and only one that's been promoted to a supervisor position," I say. "As you saw this morning, he still has to tiptoe around Chief Barrow, who stays on ready to undermine his decisions. He's under ten times more pressure than any of the other supervisors because he's the first. And let's not even get into the scrutiny he takes from the Black community for even putting on that uniform."

I look back down at my computer. "Whatever beef the chief has against you, it is blinding him from letting my Pops properly do his job."

"And that's where you're gonna step in?" she asks.

"Don't be condescending," I snap.

"I'm not. But he seemed pretty adamant about not wanting you involved."

"He'd probably also prefer it if I was into dudes," I lie. Pops literally shrugged it off when I came out to him at fourteen. "Chief concentrating solely on you could hinder the truth coming out about what really happened to her."

"One thousand percent," she agrees.

I sigh. "But real talk: Me doing this wasn't about all that. I started out of anger toward my Pops, which is none of your business," I add when I see the curiosity flashing in her eyes. "Just know now we're here, and after seeing for myself how much of a buster the chief is being, yeah, you might be half-right."

We share quick grins, and for a second, it feels like we're still those same little girls chasing one another around the country club, naïve to everything that made us different. It's only a moment, and then my home screen pops up, pulling our attention to the computer, and it passes.

I click in the Search box and quickly type in the words that will pull up the application I need.

"So how are you gonna do something even the police can't?" she says as I'm logging in to my account on the Find My Phone app. "Don't they have some way they can track cell phones?"

"The usage, yes, but not exactly where a cell phone *is*. The police can only subpoena phone records and track usage by seeing where a phone pings off various cell towers," I explain. "That doesn't tell them exactly where the phone *itself* is, just the area it was used in. It's how they prove if someone was in a certain part of town committing a crime—people are too dumb to realize they should actually turn their phones completely off so the signal isn't pinging off nearby towers, because they're receiving notifications even when it's not in use."

"Okay," she drawls, raising an eyebrow in interest.

"But we can pinpoint exactly where Nova's phone is through the Find My Phone app."

"Doesn't that only work if you have the feature activated?"

I nod. "Which Nova did. It also helps that I know her password, since she had to use the feature on my laptop. That girl couldn't keep up with shit."

Remembering all the times she misplaced her keys, her phone, even her pens and pencils pulls at the edges of my mouth. I'd give anything to waste hours of my day helping her find something again.

"Wow, guess this detective stuff runs in the family," Tinsley says. "You following in your father's footsteps?"

"I was, and then too many of the ones who look like you started unjustly killing too many of *us*—and getting away with it," I say.

Now I'm headed to college with no idea what I wanna do with the rest of my life, I finish in my head.

"Um, Nova was murdered Friday night," Tinsley says to fill the awkward silence that's settled between us.

The cheerleaders she left behind when I called her over disperse from their huddle on the other side of the gym and start heading toward the girls' locker room.

"Surely her phone battery is dead by now," she adds.

"Doesn't matter. The Find My Phone app uses Bluetooth location to track a missing device."

"What does that mean?"

"That even if a phone's battery is dead, the app will track the device's last known location before the battery died."

Her eyes light up. "That means we'll either know where Nova might have been killed, or where her killer might be—if the person didn't toss her phone in a trash can, or the Gulf—God forbid."

"Exactly."

"Why didn't you think of this before?" she says.

"I've had other stuff on my mind," I reply with a little more edge in my voice than I intended. "She didn't mean anything to you, but Nova was like a sister to me."

"Yeah, I know," she says, wincing.

"Plus, I just remembered I could do this," I say honestly.

She scoots closer as I start typing. I press enter and wait as a map materializes on my computer screen. I click the Find Phone button and the map expands as the app zeroes in on the signal Nova's phone last emitted before it went dead. The memory of her distressed face the night of the coronation flashes in my thoughts.

I turn the screen so Tinsley can better see it, and the tiny phone icon lands. I frown when I see where it appeared.

"Great! That didn't tell us anything we didn't already know," she complains.

It's blinking on top of the rectangle representing our school on the map.

"We know she was here for the coronation that night. This was useless," she says.

"Calm yo' tits." I press control and the plus sign at the same time and the map expands, which consequentially causes the phone icon to shrink until it lands on a specific building on campus.

We both lean forward at the same time, squinting at the screen.

"Where is that?" she says, pointing at the small square building.

I twist the laptop counterclockwise so that we can better ascertain our location in reference to the phone icon. Together our heads slowly turn toward the gym's rear entrance. The map is telling us that the last place Nova's phone was is in the building connected to the gym and auditorium.

I yank hard as I can on the handles to the double doors that I'm almost certain lead to the storage room behind the auditorium stage. They don't budge.

"Fuck!" I shout.

My outburst echoes within the hollow womb of the covered breezeway connecting the rear entrance of the gym to the auditorium.

"What's in there?" Tinsley asks behind me.

I frown at the screenshot of the Find My Phone map I sent to my phone. "If it's what I think it is, I know another way we can get inside. Come on."

"Where are we going?" she says, following me as I reenter the gym right as some of the cheerleaders are emerging from the girls' locker room.

"It's a storage room," I explain. Tinsley's close on my heels as I jog through the covered breezeway leading to the courtyard. "We can get to it through the auditorium."

We round the cafeteria building to get to the mini courtyard in front of where Nova was crowned Friday night. I'm surprised Tinsley doesn't know about the storage room. I assumed a lot of people that go here did.

I'm panting by the time we reach the auditorium's glass doors.

"How do you know what it is?"

Something moves in my peripheral vision, and I pause as I'm about to pull the door open. I glance over my shoulder, but the dark blur I thought I saw near the edge of the cafeteria building is still. I almost thought we were being followed.

"This senior who was in the drama club used to bring me back here *all* the time when I was a sophomore," I explain, leading Tinsley inside and through the backstage area. I used to come back here at least once a week to meet up with Dani. No one knew about us. She liked to play straight to protect her Southern Baptist image. "A lot of kids duck off in the storage room to smash during school—or after."

"Not me," she says.

Guess rich kids don't have to worry about their parents catching them having sex since their rooms aren't practically on top of their parents', like ours.

I maneuver through the confusing maze of doors and narrow walkways by memory. My heart is racing. Finding Nova's phone would mean getting an answer about what had her so distracted at the reception. *What was she gonna tell me if she hadn't died?*

My stomach heaves from the coppery odor that hits me as we enter the dank room. It's never smelled all that great in here, but this is the worst stench I've been hit with in all the time I've been sneaking back here.

"Ewwww," Tinsley groans. "What is that smell?"

A knocking sound from the endless darkness behind us causes me to freeze.

"What was that?" Tinsley says, slamming into my back.

"*Shhhhh,* hold on," I tell her.

It takes a few seconds for me to feel around in the dark for the light switch I know is next to the entrance. I flip the switch and Tinsley's still standing where I left her. She eyes the large set pieces the drama club used last year for their production of *Into the Woods.* Her perplexed gaze scours the room. Whatever we just heard falls from my thoughts as we take in the cluttered mess.

"If Nova's phone is still here, how are we gonna find it in all *this*?" she says, waving her arms at the cluttered confusion surrounding us.

There's no rhyme or reason to the way things are arranged. Old football helmets share shelf space with wigs and other extravagant headdresses. For every piece of athletic equipment I step over, there's some elaborate set piece I have to squeeze around. The eight-foot-tall metal shelves arranged side by side create rows that divide the center of the room into three walkways.

"Is this for the drama club or the athletics department?" she asks, picking up a deflated basketball from the shelf she's near.

I walk down the center aisle.

"Both," I say, "and the robotics club, apparently." I inspect the plastic and metal robotic-looking dog at eye level on the shelf to my left. It reminds me of some of the stuff I've seen in Trenton's room. "Her phone might not actually be in here.

Remember, the app only pings the last location it was in before it died—or was turned off."

The farther I walk into the room, the stronger the coppery odor gets. Tinsley has her practice-uniform T-shirt pulled over her nose. "So that means either she was here or her killer was."

"Or both," I say. "But I don't see why Nova would have come in here that night." We meet back up on the other side of the room at the end of our respective aisles. "You see anything?"

Her shoulders slump and she shakes her head. "You can't set off an alarm or something on her phone through that app? I mean, we'd have to tear this room completely apart to find it in all this junk. And I don't know how much longer I can stand this smell."

"You ain't lyin'." I can taste it in the back of my throat.

"Smells like someone left ground beef out too long."

There's another thud. Closer this time. We both still. My stomach drops. Tinsley and I exchange paranoid looks. We slowly turn in the direction of the noise—just beyond the entrance to the storage room. There's giggling, and then what sounds like the shuffling of feet.

Someone's here. We *were* being followed!

Two shadows detach from the darkness gathered at the entrance. It's Lana and Giselle. Or as I like to call them, Tinsley's minions. However, it's looking like that label may no longer be applicable. The smirks on her friends' faces are laced with malice, and a vein is already protruding along Tinsley's neck at the sight of them.

"It's insane how so much about a person's life can change

within a matter of days," Lana says, tossing an inquisitive look in my direction. Giselle, or rather Ms. I Think I'm White, follows her friend's gaze as they come closer. "Last week you're with Nathan and the self-proclaimed Queen Bee, and this week you're a murder suspect who's slumming it with Duchess Simmons?"

I'd be insulted if I really gave a damn what they thought of me.

Tinsley takes a deep breath. Like she's mentally preparing herself.

"Lana, Giselle, I've been wanting to clear the air with y'all," she says, her voice cracking like it did the day she approached me in the hall asking about Nova's pregnancy. "I got some advice this week that apologizing to you two could help us move past this rough patch we're in."

Tinsley is barely making eye contact with her friends. She's fidgeting a lot too. I can see the desperation gradually building behind her eyes. She wants her minions back. Which has me feeling some type of way.

"Apologize? For what, exactly?" Giselle says.

"Everything. Like, for real. How I've treated you guys." She takes a few timid steps forward. "I know in the past I've made both of you feel like I take you guys for granted—and I think I did. Okay, I know I did. That's why I have no choice but to forgive you, Lana, for posting that video. Maybe I deserved it. And you had no way of knowing what would happen. I just really miss y'all. I miss *us*. I could use my friends right now. Like, *bad*."

'Cause having only one person on her side—me—would

never be enough for this trick. I start pursing my lips as I watch them.

"I've been so lost without y'all these past few—"

"So this is what happens to a person who's about to lose everything they never deserved," Lana interrupts. "I kind of like seeing you this . . . pathetic."

There's a flash of anger in Tinsley's eyes. She closes them and takes a deep breath. "Lana, I know—"

"You know nothing," Lana fires back. "Save the apologies. We don't want them. You wanna know the truth? I posted that video so everyone could see who you really are. The you you are with us. Nova actually turning up dead, that was a lucky coincidence that made this takedown more epic."

Oh hell no. "What I'm *not* about to let you do is talk out the side of yo' neck about my girl!" I interject.

Tinsley's left arm shoots out, blocking me from running up on Lana and catching me off guard. "Duchess, don't," she says.

"The climate has changed," Giselle says. "Now *you're* the outcast. You taught us well."

"Once the student council strips you of your title, you're done here," Lana adds. "I'm gonna make sure you're out as captain of the squad next."

"That's what you've never understood about me." Tinsley steps all the way up in Lana's face. They're so close it almost looks like they're about to kiss. "Nothing will hold me down for long. And once my name is cleared, mark my words, the both of you are over. Your betrayal will not go unpunished. Just know it didn't have to be that way. This is me *trying* to make it right."

This chick's superiority complex is outta control. But I have to admit, after what Lana just said, I'm kinda glad to see some of the old Tinsley resurface.

"Deep down," Tinsley continues, "you must be worried that once this is all over, everyone will be groveling to get back in *my* good graces. You wouldn't be trying so hard to be me if it weren't true. It must worry you, Lana. Knowing you'll never be more than a vulture nibbling on my leftovers—like Nathan."

I barely dodge Tinsley as Lana shoves her backward and she flies into one of the shelves, causing it to tilt, sending its contents crashing to the concrete floor along with her.

"You fucking bitch!" Tinsley screams.

Lana and Giselle take off running out of the storage room, the door clanging behind them.

I have to press my lips together to stifle the laugh that wants to escape from my gut. "Princess, let me give you some more advice," I say. "Given how quickly things have gone left between y'all, those chicks were *never* your friends."

"Will you just help me up?" she barks.

I look down at her with an *Excuse me?* look.

"Please?" she adds.

I grab her outstretched hands and pull her to her feet. When I let her go, she spins around, checking herself for injuries.

"Uh, you got something on yo' shirt." I grab her forearm and point to the brownish stain trailing down her back.

"What is it?" She stretches her neck to try to see over her shoulder.

"Looks like dried paint, or . . ."

The chill in the room enters my body.

"Or *what?*" She reaches around her back, running her hand down her shirt, and holds it up. Muddy brown flakes cover her fingertips. "What the hell is this?"

I glance down at the dark puddle staining the concrete. It'd been hidden by the metal shelf Tinsley knocked over. I kneel to inspect it closer.

"This looks like . . ." I slowly reach out to touch it but stop seconds before my fingers meet the floor. I snap back up. "I think that's blood."

"Blood? From where . . ."

Our eyes meet. Then our mouths drop open as we arrive at the same thought.

Nova.

I use my feet to push the toppled shelf back more to expose the rest of the stain.

"Look, there are smear marks here," I point out. "Someone tried to clean up. Whoever it was couldn't reach under here, or wasn't strong enough to move the shelf."

"Duchess."

"What?"

"Look."

Tinsley is pointing at something on the floor behind me. The thing that brought us in here.

Nova's phone.

CHAPTER NINETEEN

DUCHESS

OCTOBER 19
5:00 P.M.

TINSLEY IS IN the shower. She said she was still feeling "icky" even after changing out of her bloodstained T-shirt. I glance over at Nova's phone, which is sitting on Tinsley's nightstand, connected to her charger. I promised not to turn the phone on until Tinsley got out of the shower so we could go through it together. But everything inside me wants to lean off the edge of her bed and grab it. All the answers are right there. Just two feet away. Justice for Nova.

Fuck it! Tinsley will have to get over it. I need answers now.

Her bedroom door flies open right as I'm lifting the phone off the nightstand. I jump back onto the edge of the bed. My heart punching up into my throat.

Mrs. McArthur is standing in the doorway. One hand gripping the doorknob, the other propped on her hip. She does a double take at me sitting on the corner of Tinsley's bed, trying to look innocent, and narrows her eyes.

"What are you doing here . . . *again*?" she asks. She takes a step forward, peering around the door. "Where's Tinsley?"

"Sh-she's in the shower, ma'am," I stutter nervously, scooting back farther on the bed. "We have more work to do on that . . . group project we have."

No one was home when Tinsley and I got here. I'd thought I'd avoided another run-in with this woman.

Her mouth presses into a hard line. "How about you come downstairs and wait for Tinsley. It'll give us a chance to catch up."

The thought of being alone with her makes me want to throw up.

"Um, I think she's almost done," I say, praying I'm right. "Wouldn't want her to think I left—"

"I insist," she retorts.

It's clear that this woman does not like me. Her grin is laced with gut-wrenching hostility. The way she's staring at me screams *I don't want you here!* There's no need to say it out loud. That's cool. I don't like her snobby ass either.

She eyes Nova's phone; then her icy glare returns to me.

"Come on, dear," Mrs. McArthur presses, waving me toward her like I'm some stubborn dog who refuses to obey.

I get up and slowly make my way across the room. If I move slow enough, maybe Tinsley will appear and save me from this woman. I walk past Mrs. McArthur, out the door, and she closes it behind me, her mouth fixed in a plastic smile. She leads me downstairs, where there are several Hispanic women gathered in the foyer, all wearing matching powder-blue lab coats and each holding a different cleaning tool.

"Go on, ladies, you can get started," Mrs. McArthur says to them. "I'll be in the dining room entertaining our unexpected guest if you need me."

One of the ladies nods before turning to say something in Spanish that makes the other women scatter out of the foyer to begin cleaning and polishing.

"How about we sit in here." Mrs. McArthur stretches an arm toward the formal dining room. I squeeze past her and the faint smell of alcohol wafts from her breath as she says, "You can have a seat over there. Would you like something to drink?"

"Water is fine," I reply, rounding the rectangular dining table. I sit in the first chair facing the foyer.

My leg starts to bounce under the table as I wait for Mrs. McArthur to return from the kitchen. From where I'm sitting, I can see one of the women from the cleaning crew wander into the room on the other side of the foyer. I assume by the plush sofa and love seat that it's the formal living room.

Of all the drunk housewives my mother overserved at that country club, she hated Tinsley's mother the most. Even before she had my mom fired, Mama said Mrs. McArthur treated her and the rest of the staff as if they were there only to serve her.

"That woman invented the term *nice-nasty*," she said to me one day on our drive home after one of her shifts. "You be careful around her daughter. I've seen how that woman watches y'all play together. She doesn't like it—she thinks she's better than people who look like us. She'll look for any reason to turn her daughter against you. Mark my words."

Mama's words echo in my head until Mrs. McArthur's footsteps bring me back.

"So sorry to learn about what happened to your mother," she says as she reenters the dining room. The glass of water she places in front of me hits the table with a hollow thud. "Cancer is such a horrible disease."

She pauses, studying my face. The reference to my mother's death has me tightening my grip around the water glass. Tinsley must have told her that my mom died after I left the first time I was here. Mrs. McArthur waits for my reaction, probably hoping I'll share one of the most painful moments in my life with her. But it ain't gonna happen. I'd rather tell her to keep my mother's name out of her mouth.

The hum of a vacuum dragging across the floor in one of the rooms downstairs fills the silence thickening the air between us.

"Tell me about this group project y'all keep referring to." Mrs. McArthur gently places her manicured hands along the curvy edge of the back of the chair at the head of the table. "You're not an AP student. There are so few, you know, Black kids in that curriculum. Not too difficult to keep up with who's who, you know?"

I gulp down three huge sips of water to stop myself from saying what just popped in my mind. It included the words *bitch* and *fuck you,* but not necessarily in that order.

"What classes could you possibly be taking with Tinsley?" she presses.

"Art," I croak, which isn't a lie.

"Interesting," she purrs. "You must be a very dedicated student."

"Very. Dedicated enough to be in AP, if I wanted."

The corners of her mouth lift into a disarming smile. "That's not what I mean." Her head tilts to the side. "Weren't you close friends with Nova Albright?"

My stomach drops and my leg stops shaking under the table. Why is this woman asking me this?

"Given the absurd accusations against my daughter surrounding that poor girl's death, and your father telling us how close you two were, I'd think working in a group with Tinsley would be rather difficult for you at this time. From what I've gathered, some of the people in this community are dead set on seeing my daughter punished for Nova's murder. Am I not wrong to assume you think the same—given your close relationship with Nova?"

Well, there it is. This is what this little one-on-one is about. She thinks I'm up to something underhanded against her daughter. Let me go ahead and squash this right quick.

"I'm a leader, not a follower," I say, looking her directly in the eye. "Tinsley and I are definitely not as close as we used to be—"

"Of course not," she interjects.

"*But* I was raised to believe in innocent until proven guilty. And since I know what you're getting at: I don't think she had anything to do with my friend's murder. Me being here should prove that."

"Good to know," Mrs. McArthur says. "Tinsley is in such a fragile state right now. Her judgment skewed by the betrayals of her friends. I, however, still see things *very* clearly. Especially when it comes to my family. Hopefully you can understand why I'm somewhat wary of your reappearance in her life. The police department has an agenda, and your father works for said department. So forgive me for being paranoid that you're here with some ulterior motive."

I am curious why Tinsley hasn't told her mother that I believe she's innocent. I can only assume she's worried that her mother might try and stop her from getting involved in the investigation the same way Pops did. And if that's the case, maybe it's best I don't blow up Tinsley's spot.

"I'm just here to complete an assignment, Mrs. McArthur," I say.

I can't tell if she believes the lie. Her jaw is set as she studies my face.

"I hope that's true," she says a few seconds later. "I'll choose to believe it is. Your father, I'm sure, raised you right. I'd hate for something you did to affect him . . . somehow."

A chill ripples through my body. I'm pretty sure that was a threat on Pops's career if I do anything to hurt her daughter.

"Hey, what are you doing down here?"

We both turn at the voice to find Tinsley standing in the archway to the foyer. She's wearing baggy sweats and an oversize T-shirt, and her hair hangs limply on her shoulders in damp strings. She tosses a distressed glance in my direction, then squints at her mother, confused.

I slump in my chair. Never thought I'd be this relieved to see her.

"Uh, your mom asked me to wait down here while you were in the shower," I say with a tight smile.

"Sweetie, you know it's rude to leave guests unsupervised in this house," Mrs. McArthur says.

"She was in my room," Tinsley says. "You've never had an issue when I've left anyone else in there alone."

Mrs. McArthur side-eyes me. "Yes, but I *knew* them."

I roll my eyes. Mama was definitely right about this lady.

"Come on," Tinsley turns and says to me. "We need to finish that . . . assignment."

I stand up and turn to go, but Mrs. McArthur stops me.

"Duchess, this was informative, getting reacquainted," Mrs. McArthur says. Then, as I pass her to get to Tinsley, she adds, "You're more than welcome to join us for dinner tonight. I'm sure your father doesn't have time to cook a good meal if he's out doing his job, making sure my daughter's name is cleared."

Tinsley gives me an apologetic look as I squeeze by her.

"She's busy, Mama," she says. "I'm sure she doesn't have the time to suffer through one of our family dinners."

I'm almost at the staircase when I realize I don't hear Tinsley behind me. I turn around and she's still in the archway. Her mother is gripping her by the arm and whispering in her ear, and Tinsley looks annoyed by whatever she's saying.

I manage to read Tinsley's lips before she snatches her arm away from her mother. "I know what I'm doing."

"Everything good?" I ask as Tinsley joins me at the bottom of the staircase.

"No, Margaretta!" her mother calls out, preventing Tinsley from answering. "I told you *not* to touch the display case!"

I turn to see an older Latina woman standing in front of this huge glass case, looking as bewildered as I feel. Mrs. McArthur's heels click against the hardwood floor as she stomps into the middle of the foyer.

"You people *do* understand English, right? Did you not hear me before?"

You people?

"Yes, ma'am," the woman replies with a nod, scurrying into the foyer with the white dust rag clenched tightly in both her wrinkled hands.

The lady mopping the foyer says something in Spanish to Margaretta, who immediately retreats down the narrow hallway to my right and disappears into another room.

I purse my lips at Tinsley, who grimaces so hard that deep creases distort her face.

"I think it's time to find a new cleaning service," Mrs. McArthur says to us, willfully oblivious to the tension she created. "A few things around the house have come up missing lately. I'm limiting the help's access around here."

Tinsley grabs my wrist. "Come on. We need to get on that . . . thing."

I really don't wanna be up in this house. The place is a palace of bigotry. No wonder Tinsley is the way she is. Look who her mother is. Finding out what's on Nova's phone is the only reason I'm letting this chick lead me back up to her room.

"Sorry about that," Tinsley says as we walk in. "I swear she isn't always like that with them."

"Your Moms is . . . *intense*" is all I can say. I take a deep breath, swallowing the rage simmering in my chest. "She's like you, but on steroids."

Tinsley has this pinched look as she shuts her bedroom door. She's probably not liking the comparison, given how her mother just acted.

"What did she say to you?" she asks.

"She was curious about our assignment," I say, then add, "Don't worry, I covered after I realized you didn't tell her the real reason we've been sort of hanging out."

"Sorry, *again.*" Tinsley makes a beeline to the nightstand, where Nova's phone is still connected to the charger. It doesn't look like she tampered with it while I was downstairs.

I sit back down in the same spot her mother found me in earlier.

"Everything I'm going through is affecting my parents differently," she says. "My father is turning into an alcoholic, and my mother is becoming even more of a helicopter mom. None of it is helping."

This flash of vulnerability is a bit off-putting.

She yanks Nova's phone off the charger and hands it to me before tucking one of her legs underneath her butt as she sits next to me on the bed. I stare at the phone for a few seconds, biting my bottom lip.

"What are you waiting for? Turn it on," she prods.

She scoots a little closer as the phone blinks to life. She smells like apples and jasmine.

I enter Nova's four-digit passcode, awakening the home screen. The selfie Nova took during lunch on the first day of the semester is still her backdrop.

Almost immediately the phone starts vibrating as notifications pour in. Alerts for text messages, emails, missed phone calls chime through in rapid succession. I pull up the text-message app. The newer messages that were sent while it was dead push down all the older messages.

"We need to scroll to the day of the coronation, see who all she was talking to right up until she was crowned," Tinsley says.

"I'm trying, but all these damn new messages keep popping

up," I reply. "Jesus Christ, how is a dead girl's phone blowing up more than mine?"

I keep swiping my index finger across the screen to scroll down to Friday night. Most of the texts echo the heartfelt sentiments people have been posting on Nova's social media accounts. Honestly, it's kind of morbid. Why were folks sending texts to a dead girl who'll never get to read them?

Finally, I get to one from me and I stop. "Okay, this is from Friday night; I texted her how pretty she looked during the coronation."

"You felt the need to text her that while you were there, watching her get crowned?" Tinsley says with a raised brow.

"Look, I'm not in love with her or anything—"

She holds up her hands, trying to hold back a smirk. "Did I say that? I did not say that."

"But your little evil-ass mind was thinking it." I press my lips together to stop myself from grinning too. "I wanted to lift her spirits. She seemed a little uncomfortable that night."

I sit up straighter once messages from Friday night start rolling up the screen.

"Here's a text she got at nine-oh-two p.m. From somebody she has saved as 'Bae,'" I say.

This confirmation that Tinsley was right—that Nova was secretly boo'd up with someone—sinks like a brick in my stomach.

Tinsley leans in. *"Meet me in the storage room,"* she reads aloud.

We look up at one another with furrowed brows. This is the text that summoned Nova to her death.

"What does it say before that?" she asks.

I scroll up the message thread. "Seems like they were arguing about something."

"Whatever it was, *Bae* wanted Nova to do something she didn't want to do."

"Look at this message from three days before she died: *How much is it gonna be?*" I lower the phone. "He has to be talking about the abortion."

Tinsley presses her index finger to the button that pulls up additional contact information for "Bae." We both frown at the phone number. It has a local area code, but I don't recognize it.

"I can't believe this," I mumble, scrolling farther.

"You recognize the number?"

"No. I can't get over her having a whole-ass relationship behind my back. These messages go as far back as the summer."

"And she never even mentioned liking anyone to you?"

I shake my head.

"Wait! What are you doing?" she yells when she sees my finger hovering over the call button on Bae's contact profile.

"Let's call and see who the hell this is," I say with a shrug.

Tinsley stands to grab her phone off the nightstand. "Right idea, wrong execution. I highly doubt that whoever it is will answer a call from a dead girl."

She dials the number and hits speaker so we can both hear. It rings four times before someone answers.

"'Sup?"

The voice sounds familiar, but I can't immediately place it.

"Hello. Who is this?" Tinsley asks.

"Jax. Who dis?"

My heart leaps into my throat.

"Jax? You mean Jaxson Pafford?" Tinsley says, looking up at me, eyes big.

"Yeah. 'Sup?"

"Sorry, wrong number," she says, and quickly ends the call.

The room becomes so quiet I can hear a vacuum downstairs. I'm breathing heavily, clenching my fist. Jaxson Fuckboy Pafford killed Nova?

"Nova was pregnant by Jax?" Tinsley says.

Would you ever mess around with a white dude?

"*That's* who she was talking about?" I yelp.

CHAPTER TWENTY

TINSLEY

OCTOBER 20
7:05 A.M.

WE AGREED TO confront Jaxson together before first period. The goal: get him to confess, then go to Duchess's father with everything we uncovered yesterday. We figure we have more than enough—between the text messages and Nova's pregnancy—to coax Jax into admitting he killed her.

It's understandable why Jax kept their relationship under wraps. Everyone knows his parents are tiki-torch-carrying, gun-toting right-wing conservatives. He's spent a lot of time trying to distance himself from them and their bigoted views after pictures surfaced of them at a white supremacy rally; he's constantly professing support for the Black Lives Matter movement and reminding everyone how many Black friends he has. I honestly think people only tolerate him because of his talent on the football field.

Their relationship being a secret is likely why he was pressuring Nova to abort their baby. Duchess thinks Nova didn't want the abortion and they got into an argument about it. An argument that led to her death.

Don't do it! Or I'll make you regret it!

The thing I don't get is why he wrote that note the police found. I still haven't mentioned it to Duchess, because I know she'll think *I* wrote it, to scare Nova into dropping out of the homecoming elections. It probably wouldn't even matter that the handwriting is nothing like mine. I don't want to risk her doubting my innocence. She's the only person, outside of my family, who I have in my corner right now.

The police must know I didn't write it. They have my notebooks, and the writing doesn't match how I write. That's why they haven't arrested me. Why did Jax make the threat, though? That's the only piece that doesn't fit yet.

I look down at my phone to confirm what I already know: Duchess is late. She was supposed to meet me in the student parking lot at 6:55. I got here ten minutes early and have been standing near the gate that funnels the commuter students onto campus, looking like the pathetic outcast I've become. Clearing my name is the only reason I keep showing up here. I spent the entire day yesterday sneaking glances at as many classmates' handwriting as I could. No matches. That could be because the person I'm looking for doesn't take AP classes. If we're wrong and it's not Jax, I might be forced to show Duchess the photo of the note.

But I'm not gonna think like that. It's him. It has to be. I'm ready for this nightmare to end.

The bell for first period will go off in ten minutes. I charge through the fence toward A-Building. I really don't need her anyway.

I find Jaxson exactly where I expected, rummaging through his locker. He's wearing his football jersey with the matching sneakers he and the other starting players all wear. The football team and cheerleaders always wear their uniforms to school on Spirit Day homecoming week. I would have mine on if I were participating in the pep rally this afternoon. I'm not, for obvious reasons.

"Jaxson Pafford, just the person I've been looking for."

I tilt my head back as I approach him. I'm feeling something I haven't felt since waking up five days ago to the news that Nova was murdered. I'm feeling a little like myself again. The version of me who walked these halls like they were mine.

Jaxson pokes his head out from behind his locker door. His sandy-blond brows knit together. There are dark circles under his eyes. I know why he hasn't been sleeping well.

"Tinsley, really not up for talking right now," he says, reaching into his locker to grab a textbook.

"Oh, but I'm here to offer my condolences," I say with a grin. "You know, given how much Nova meant to you—or thought she meant to you, anyway."

He clears his throat. "Excuse me?"

This boy needs to work on his poker face. He can barely look me in the eye right now. I take a satisfied breath. *I got him!*

"I know you're a fuckboy, but please don't tell me you've already forgotten about her. She's not even in the ground yet. She was your babymama, for God's sake."

His hazel eyes widen and his shoulders stiffen.

Jaxson shuts his locker, casting a nervous look behind him while he shrugs his book bag onto his shoulder.

"You've been sniffing too much of that expensive perfume you wear," he says with a nervous laugh. "You always coming up with some crazy shit."

"How long were y'all secretly dating?" I press.

"Dating? You making shit up 'cause everyone hates you now?" he says, shoving his hands into the front pockets of his jeans. "Was I trying to smash? Yeah. But that ain't dating. If it was, I was dating you too."

His usual cockiness is back, but I can tell it's a facade. He has to be shitting in his pants right now. Of course he's trying to deflect. He doesn't know I have the evidence to back up what I said. But he's about to find out.

"That's how you're gonna play it? Straight-up lie to my face?" I say.

"I ain't got time for this. I'm gonna be late for class."

"I have proof you wanted Nova to get an abortion," I blurt out as he turns to leave.

A few girls within earshot turn in our direction. Jaxson gives them a tight smile.

He takes two steps forward to narrow the distance between us. "What the fuck game you trying to play?"

I jab my index finger into his rock-hard chest. "You should know I *never* just make things up," I say. "I know you and Nova were dating since this summer. Just like I also know you got her pregnant and wanted her to get an abortion, which she didn't do, so you killed her."

"What?" Jaxson says.

"You asked Nova to meet up with you in the storage room the night of the coronation."

Jaxson's jaw clenches. Now he definitely knows I'm not lying. I bet he's wondering how I know all this. He's gripping the strap on his book bag so hard his knuckles have turned white. I fold my arms across my chest with a slow grin. What's he gonna say to get out of *this*?

The ear-piercing chime of the first-period bell echoes through the hall. It's immediately followed by the bong of the intercom system. Jaxson and I continue staring at one another in silence as Mrs. Barnett's voice blares through the halls.

"Good morning, students. Due to an unforeseen emergency, all classes and extracurricular activities are canceled today."

Jaxson and I break eye contact as the few students remaining in the hall start cheering, momentarily drowning out Mrs. Barnett's voice.

". . . and those who ride the bus must wait in first period until we reroute all the busses back to the school," she says after some of the faculty has shushed at everyone to simmer down. "We'll be sending a text to parents to let them know they can pick up those students who get dropped off. We will make a decision about the rest of the week by noon today."

I turn back to Jaxson, who's looking as confused as I feel.

"And can Tinsley McArthur please report to my office . . . *now.*"

Everyone turns to look at me. Everyone except Jaxson, who is halfway down the hall when I turn back around.

———

Mrs. Barnett is waiting for me in the doorway to her office. She's pressing her mouth closed so tightly her lips have disappeared. She steps aside so I can enter, and Duchess is sitting in one of the chairs in front of her desk.

"Where were you?" I say. "I tried waiting . . ."

The rest of my sentence gets caught in my throat when I see that Chief Barrow and Duchess's father are also here. Both men are standing to the side, their faces twisted in the same severe frown as our principal's.

"What's going on?" I ask Duchess.

She doesn't look at me. She sits there and keeps staring straight ahead out the window overlooking the school's courtyard.

"Tinsley, sit down." Mrs. Barnett closes the door. I do. After she is seated behind her desk she says, "The police are here to talk to you."

Chief Barrow appears on my left. "Where's the phone?"

He holds out his hand, palm up. I blink at it at first, then start shaking my head once it dawns on me why Duchess is being so cold.

"You. Little. Snake," I hiss at her. "My mother warned me not to trust you."

She still won't look at me.

"What happened to our agreement?" I say.

Duchess whips around in her chair, narrowing her eyes at me. "How can I trust you when I know you lied to me?"

Lied to her?

"About what?"

"Why you went back to my Pops's office yesterday, for starters."

I shift in my seat, darting my gaze around the room to avoid all the eyes I feel on me.

"Why did you really go back? 'Cause I know it wasn't just to get your bag," Duchess says.

Captain Simmons steps closer to Duchess's chair.

"I told my mother she was wrong," I say, "that you weren't playing me, but that's exactly what's been going on, isn't it? You haven't been trying to help me find out who killed Nova. You were helping them set me up."

Captain Simmons places a hand on Duchess's shoulder, and she shuts her mouth. She slowly exhales and goes back to staring out the window.

"Well, the truth is out now, and I'm glad it is," her father says. "We can't risk that crime scene getting even more contaminated than it already is."

"What truth?" I say, confused. Then I turn to Duchess again. "You told them *everything*?" I yell.

"Yes," Mrs. Barnett says. "That's why we're shutting down campus today—and possibly tomorrow. The police need to process the scene."

"Why did you go back to Captain Simmons's office?" Chief Barrow says.

"Not important." I bend over, reaching into my bag to pull out Nova's phone. "So I guess y'all are going to arrest Jaxson."

"And seeing that text message was the first time you knew about Nova going to that storage room?" Chief Barrow asks, taking the phone from me.

I flinch back in the chair, brows furrowed. "What type of question is that?"

"Jaxson Pafford is quite popular here. Just like you." Chief

Barrow perches on the corner of Mrs. Barnett's desk. "I suspect you two ran in the same social circles."

"We didn't. Not really. And what does that have to do with him killing Nova?"

Mrs. Barnett gasps. "Jaxson? No! He couldn't . . . he wouldn't—"

"He did," I interject.

"How can you be so certain of that?" Chief Barrow says.

I turn to Duchess. "I thought you told them everything?"

"He's implying you and Jaxson could be in cahoots," she responds dryly.

"You gotta be kidding me!"

Chief Barrow's gaze shifts to Duchess's father, who is holding a glossy white sheet of paper in one hand. He extends his arm to hand it to the chief. Chief Barrow turns it over to briefly study it before holding it out so I can see that it's a grainy picture of a girl driving what appears to be a brightly colored car.

It's only when I scoot forward and squint at the image that I understand why he's showing it to me. My blood chills. I'm the girl in the picture. And I don't need them to say when it was taken. I'm wearing Nathan's button-down shirt in the photo. The one he let me wear while we were on the beach that night.

"This was captured on the surveillance camera of a business near campus," Chief Barrow says. "Within the window of time Nova was last seen at the reception."

"Why were you on this side of town?" Captain Simmons says. "You told us you drove straight home, drunk, from the beach that night. Your house is nowhere near here."

"It's not completely out of the way to take Route 715 to get to my house," I reply. "Given how messed up I was, I probably drove near here out of reflex, since I do it every day."

"So you weren't coming here to meet up with Jaxson Pafford that night?" Chief Barrow asks.

My heart is pounding in my throat. He's turning everything around on me. Damn you, technology and vodka.

"You are relentless," I say at the chief. "Jax killed Nova. He got her pregnant and she didn't want to have an abortion! That has nothing to do with me."

"If you knew that, though, one could argue that you used the secret to get Jaxson to kill the girl who took something you wanted," Chief Barrow retorts.

Mrs. Barnett's pensive expression causes something inside me to snap.

I spin in my seat to face Duchess. "I don't understand why you would do this to me! Do you still hate me that much?"

"Get over yourself," she says in a measured tone. "I ain't thinking about you like that."

"Tinsley, we're trying to understand what happened that night," Captain Simmons says.

After taking a deep breath, I calmly scoot back in the chair and cross my legs.

"I'm a minor. You can't talk to me without my parents or a lawyer present." I tilt my head toward Chief Barrow. "Got that?"

"You okay?"

Rachel asks the question from the other end of the sectional in the den right after we hear the front door shut.

I lean over to the coffee table and pick up the TV remote. "I had to spend the last hour and a half discussing my legal strategy in case I get arrested for a murder I didn't commit. How do you think I feel, Rach?"

"But Mr. Hubbard says the judge won't sign an arrest warrant until the police produce solid proof you were involved in Nova's murder. That's . . . something."

Mr. Hubbard is the attorney I didn't know my father has had on retainer since Saturday. I learned about him when my mother burst into Mrs. Barnett's office this morning and told everyone I would no longer be answering any of their questions without my attorney present. I've been locked in my bedroom since I got home. My parents forced me to come downstairs when Mr. Hubbard arrived. Rachel showed up with him. She's been here almost every night this week, sometimes until late into the night. I'm too worried about my own shit to question her about it.

"I hope he wasn't charging Daddy for that hour, because that entire conversation was pointless." I aim the remote at the TV to turn it on. "The police department doesn't *think* I'm the killer, they *want* me to be. The chief is doing everything he can to create that narrative."

"Oh, turn it up!" Rachel shrieks, pointing at the TV. "The riots have made the national news."

On the screen a news anchor is standing in a street that looks like a war zone. Last night, in Jackson, the protests demanding Curtis Delmont's release accelerated, and people started vandalizing businesses and tossing firebombs at the police, who made more than a dozen arrests. The footage shows police officers dressed in riot gear tussling with screaming protesters. Apparently, Curtis Delmont's lawyer has obtained signed affidavits from several people with knowledge that Monica Holt was having an affair with a man named Thomas Edgemont. These people claim Thomas had a violent streak. Everything exploded yesterday when the information went public— Jackson police still haven't questioned this Thomas dude.

"You know what's sad?" I say. "I highly doubt anyone will be rioting in the streets like that for me if I get arrested."

Rachel finally pulls her gaze away from the TV. She tilts her head at me with pursed lips. "Tins, stop. You know Mama and Daddy won't let that happen."

"Our parents are part of the reason it *will* happen," I say.

"It seems Fred was serious about keeping an eye on you," my mother says, reappearing in the den with my father two steps behind her. "There's an officer camped outside. Maybe that'll deter you from playing detective with that man's daughter. I told you not to trust her—"

"Mama, don't."

It's all she's been saying since we left school. She was right: Duchess was *not* to be trusted. But if she's waiting for me to admit that out loud, she'll be waiting a long time. I refuse to give her the satisfaction.

"Your mother is right—for once," my father says. Rachel scoots over so he can sit next to her. "You heard what Mr. Hubbard said. You don't need to give them any reason to believe you're somehow trying to sabotage the police investigation."

Now *he's* siding with *her*. Could this day get any worse?

"That's not what—"

"You heard your father," my mother interjects. "It stops today. I don't want you anywhere near all of this, and certainly nowhere near Captain Simmons's daughter."

A picture of Lovett High flashes onto TV and I sit up

straighter. At some point while my parents were presenting their annoying—and uncharacteristic—united front, the national news transitioned to the local news. I turn up the volume.

". . . police wouldn't give us an official word on why students were told to go home today," Judy Sanchez says as various images of the school cycle across the screen. "But trusted sources tell me bloodstains were discovered somewhere on campus and police shut it down to process the scene. They think the blood could be that of Nova Albright, whose murder Friday is still under investigation."

The screen cuts back to Judy, who's standing in front of our vacant campus for her live shot.

"Police have confirmed they are questioning a new person of interest in the girl's murder: the school's star quarterback, Jaxson Pafford, who they fear could have conspired with Tinsley McArthur to murder the victim. Tinsley is the student in the viral video linked to this murder investigation."

"This is ridiculous!" my mom exclaims, and I hiss at her to be quiet.

"The bloodstains could be the first indication that Nova was murdered somewhere on the campus of Lovett High, shortly after she was crowned homecoming queen. Speaking of homecoming, school officials have given no indication that tomorrow night's game will be canceled in light of recent events. But the dance that was set to take place in the gym following the game could be postponed, something many parents shared frustrations with us about."

The segment switches to a taped interview with some of the heartless parents the reporter mentioned, and I turn off the TV.

"She didn't even mention Nova's pregnancy, or that Nova and Jax were dating," I say.

"Nova was pregnant?" my father says.

I nod. "By Jax."

"How do you know?" My mother casts an anxious look across the room to my father.

"Because I was being a foolish detective," I reply.

"Tins is practically getting crucified in the media," Rachel fumes. "The police are twisting facts and spoon-feeding anything to the press that calls her innocence into question. Kinda like they do anytime a white police officer shoots an unarmed Black man."

That's all I can take. I stand up and leave the room.

I've been one of those people who, after seeing news reports involving white police officers shooting unarmed Black men, have thought, and sometimes verbalized to others, that the police must have had been justified in responding with force. My sentiments toward the victims were in part fueled by the criminal histories, unflattering photos, and socioeconomic backgrounds the media would present. I never once considered that law enforcement could be shaping a narrative to justify the cops' actions. But these last few days have shown me firsthand how manipulative and biased the police can be if they want something to be true.

I'm sitting at my desk when I hear light taps on my bedroom door. I know it's my mother: I heard her heels on the stairs a few seconds ago. I'm not trying to hear whatever she came up here to say, so I continue scrolling through the article on internal bias I googled after I walked out of the den. I've been toggling between it and the Fox 6 News webpage, where I keep getting disappointed there isn't a breaking news alert announcing that Jaxson has been charged for Nova's murder.

My phone chimes. As I'm picking it up, my bedroom door creaks open behind me. I tap the message from "Unknown" and it sends my heart into my stomach. It's a picture of me driving home after our early dismissal from school today. And it says *Watch your back!*

I immediately put the phone facedown on my desk.

"Tinsley?" my mother says.

"What?" I bark, trying to steady my breathing.

"You stormed out of the den in such a huff earlier. Are you okay?"

"Why does everybody keep asking me that?"

How can I be okay? People are threatening to do who knows what to me because of what happened to Nova.

"Sweetheart, you know your father and I will *never* let them arrest you. *Ever.*"

I wait a few seconds before turning around in my chair. She's poking her head through the small crack in the door.

"Can we not do this right now?" I say.

"Fine. Then I have something that might take your mind off things a bit." She opens the door wider and steps inside, revealing that she's holding a brown 11" × 17" envelope in her other hand. "Ms. Latham stopped by a few minutes after the news was over to drop this off."

I think back. I don't remember hearing the doorbell.

"She said these are all the fundraising suggestions the squad submitted yesterday." My mother crosses the room to hand me the envelope. "Technically you're still the squad's captain."

I toss it on my desk dismissively. "Yeah, but for how long?" The way my life is going, it won't be long. So there's no need to worry myself with coordinating our fundraisers this semester."

"I think it's important you honor your obligations through all this," my mother says. "Once it's behind us, you'll be able to pick right back up like it never happened."

I turn back around in my chair. "Except it did happen, Mama, to *me,* not you."

It takes a few seconds before I hear the door close behind me. I suspect my mother was lingering in the doorway, searching her mind for words that would ease my anxiety, and decided to leave when she realized there are none.

I refresh my Instagram time line and a photo of Duchess pops up. It's captioned *my heart and my headache.* I assume that the heart and headache she's referring to is the girl with the blond buzz cut who is bent over in the camera frame flashing one of the most infectious smiles I've ever seen. Duchess has an arm draped around the girl's shoulder and is kissing her on the cheek. They're seated at a booth. The black-and-white-checkered floor tells me exactly where they are.

The longer I stare at the photo, the tighter my chest gets. Duchess and I have talked more in the past two days than we have in a while. Maybe that's why her betrayal feels like more of a gut punch than Lana and Giselle's.

I slam my laptop shut, grab my frayed denim jacket off the back of the chair, and charge out of my bedroom. I need to understand why she did this.

CHAPTER TWENTY-ONE

DUCHESS

OCTOBER 20
7:43 P.M.

THE CHEESEBURGER I just ate feels like lead in my stomach. I check the Fox 6 News mobile app again: still no breaking news alert announcing Jax's or Tinsley's arrests. How everything unfolded over the last twenty-four hours is boring deeper into my chest, smushing my insides under its weight. This friction between me and Pops is worse now that he knows I defied him and kept investigating Nova's murder with Tinsley, who's probably moved me up to the number one spot in her burn book 'cause she thinks I betrayed her.

I kinda did, in a way, since I didn't reach out last night or this morning to give her a heads-up that Pops and the chief were going to ambush her to get Nova's phone. I talked myself out of doing it after Pops showed me that surveillance foot-age of her driving near school that night, making me second-guess my gut feelings about her involvement when he started spinning theories about how both her *and* Jax could be involved in Nova's murder.

A chocolate milkshake is suddenly pushed in front of me, breaking my stream of thought. Ev is standing at my booth in Jitterbug's when I look up, an apologetic grin brightening her pretty face.

"A peace offering," she says, looking down at the milkshake. "You can't stay mad at me forever."

"Wanna bet?" I say, and playfully yank from her hand the straw she pulled from the black apron tied around her waist. After tearing off the paper and jamming the straw into the thick shake, I say, "Ev, you made things so much worse between me and Pops."

Last night, after I got home from Tinsley's, Ev came over, giving me so much attitude. Tinsley is guilty; Ev doesn't want to believe anything else. I told her what we found at school, thinking it might get her to see things the way I do. Two minutes later, while I was making myself a sandwich in the kitchen, she marches right into Pops's office and tells him about Nova's phone and us finding the bloodstain in the storage room. Never got to eat my sandwich. Lost my appetite once Pops started yelling.

"I would say I'm sorry, but I'm not." Ev slides into the other side of the booth, slapping down the wet rag she just used to wipe off a table. "I don't want you hanging around that chick. That pic they got proves she's been lying."

"Not necessarily," I say. "I don't think Pops and the chief specifically asked her what route she took to drive home when they first talked to her."

Ev smacks her lips. "I know you're not defending her to me."

"Ev—"

"Ev, what?" she parrots, her voice cracking with irritation. "I don't care what your gut is telling you. It's wrong. Everyone and their mama knows that girl is guilty. And I wasn't about to let her get away with anything because she has fooled you into trusting her again—"

"Hold up," I cut in. "Who said all—"

"She might have snuck back on campus last night to wipe away evidence or erased stuff off Nova's phone," Ev continues, talking over me. "You can't sit here and tell or show me anything that shuts down the possibility she could be working with Jax. And, what—she *claims* she doesn't remember driving by the school because she was fucked up? How convenient."

I sink lower into the booth. Ev has a point. But in the back of my mind, I wonder if I'm so ready to believe what Ev is saying could be true out of fear of being humiliated if it is and I was out here playing myself by not even entertaining the possibility. Justice for Nova. Justice. For. Nova.

"You know what I don't understand?" Ev cocks her head. "This is a chick who you yourself have described as back-stabbing and manipulative, and all of a sudden y'all buddy-buddy again?"

"We're not 'buddy-buddy.' I thought—"

"You thought wrong, just admit it," she interjects, throwing her hands up. "Your beautiful, smart girlfriend was right."

Despite how annoyed I am that she keeps cutting me off, I chuckle. This girl. I love how passionate and animated she gets. She's the only person who can make me laugh even when

I'm mad at her. I decide to let go of the lingering irritation I feel about what she did. I don't want to be fighting with her too. She's been the only anchor holding me down since my entire life blew up. Even if I tried to tell her how Tinsley is a product of her environment, which is a bubble of bigotry and entitlement of Mrs. McArthur's design, explaining wouldn't help.

At the end of the day, I owe Tinsley nothing. We aren't friends. Who cares if she's mad? There's a lot I can be angry with her about, whether she ends up being involved in Nova's murder or not. But feeling that way doesn't stop the guilt tightening in my chest.

"Any news yet?" Ev says, pointing at my phone.

I frown, not immediately catching on to what she's asking.

"About Jax or her," she explains.

"Oh no," I reply, shaking my head.

"If I'd known he could be linked to all this, I would have clued your dad in sooner on what I witnessed between him and Nova."

Evelyn not only outed me to Pops last night, she shed new light on this thread between Jax and my girl.

I sit up straighter in the booth. "So Jax was in here with Nova a few days before the coronation and you didn't think that was important enough to bring up sooner?"

I wanted to ask about it last night after Ev mentioned it to Pops, but him yelling at me for not telling him sooner about Nova's phone and the blood in the storage room stopped me. His concern over how I'm dealing with Nova's death has to be the only reason he didn't ground my ass.

"It didn't register to me as strange," Ev replies to my question. "Jax is always in here pushing up on chicks with his boys, so I assumed he was doing the same with her. I didn't think to mention it 'cause I really didn't think it meant anything. I couldn't hear what him and Nova were talking about that day, but it was clear they got into it about something. She looked like she was about to cry for a sec."

"They had to be arguing about her pregnancy," I say.

"I thought he said something disrespectful that pissed her off." She pauses, a thought shifting her expression. "I *did* overhear him say he wasn't going to let her ruin his life."

I lean forward, stunned by this new detail. "You didn't tell Pops that last night."

"I just remembered it," she says quietly.

Then it must be him! That fuckboy didn't want Nova to ruin his life with a baby *he* helped create, so he killed her? It starts feeling ten degrees hotter. I bite down on the straw in my milkshake, sucking with a creased brow. Ev looks off over my shoulder, nodding and smiling at the customers sitting at one of her tables.

"Hey, bae, let me close out these last few tables and then we can bounce," she says, tossing the rag back over her shoulder as she slides out of the booth.

I nod at her, not really paying attention. My mind is racing with images of Jax hurting Nova.

Tonight's the first time I've been in Jitterbug's since her murder. I was in here almost every day before that, hanging out while she and Evelyn worked. The atmosphere was so different when I walked in tonight. This place is now another reminder of something else I'll never share with Nova again. A framed picture of her in the Jitterbug's uniform sits on the cashier's counter at the entrance, a small wreath of flowers dangling on one corner. The staff's way of memorializing the girl customers always praised for her easygoing personality and great customer service.

As I'm looking around the retro-themed diner, my gaze stops on a family of four seated two tables from my booth. The two small children are feverishly coloring the backs of their kids' menus. I catch their parents glaring at me, and they quickly hide behind their own menus. I shift in the booth, angling my body away from them. I'm pretty sure they go to our church, which means they know who my father is. And if they do, I can add their scrutinizing stares to the collection of disappointed looks I've been getting all week from Black people who have placed solving Nova's murder squarely on Pops's shoulders. Being seen with Tinsley hasn't been a good look either.

"Was everything you said a lie?"

Tinsley slides into the other side of the booth. I sit back, startled. There are veins cording her thin neck as she glares at me from across the table.

"All that stuff about your father being racially discriminated against in the department. You told me that thinking it would win my trust?" she demands. "You thinking I'm innocent; that was a lie as well?"

I'm a little tickled by the resentment outlining the sharp features of her porcelain face. I hide my amusement by pursing my lips. Yeah, it was kind of messed up, what I did. But she's done *much* worse to people, and I ain't about to let her turn this around on me.

"Does it matter?" I reply.

"You really think I did this?"

I ignore the desperation straining her voice and instead give in to the frustration I've had to hold back since showing up at her house to get justice for Nova.

"Why do you care what I think?" I press my hands to the booth's table. "You can say what you want, do what you want, and never face any consequences! Sounds about *white,* doesn't it?"

"Duchess, I swear on a stack of Bibles." She raises her right hand in the air. "I did not kill Nova."

"This is about more than that! It's about you fixing your mouth to say what you did in that video. Mocking her life. For trying to *put her in her place* by reminding her what she didn't have that day in Mr. Haywood's class."

"I didn't mean it like that. I was just—"

"Taking the easy route to hurt her by weaponizing who she was, her character. It's what y'all do. Arrogantly remind us of what we are whenever y'all think we're getting something we don't deserve. And even if you didn't mean for it to come off racist, it does, because it came from *you.* A more-than-privileged white girl who's never had to think about or be excluded from something because of the color of your skin—that is, until you couldn't be homecoming queen because of it."

She picks up a napkin and starts nervously tearing off the edges to avoid the truth in my intense stare. "I thought you were serious about helping me find out what happened to your best friend," she whimpers.

That makes me chuckle. "You know what's funny? You coming up in here with this stank-ass look, acting all hurt, over something I did that you've done who knows how many times to people. You live off using people, manipulating them. Playing games. And now you mad? Girl, please. You can dish it out, so learn how to take it."

"This is serious," she says with a pained expression. "This is my life."

Something inside me snaps. Why is it that every time a white person gets called out about their mistreatment of us, they flip the script by accusing *us* of ruining *their* lives by having the nerve to not sit back and take it? Thank God I didn't defend this girl to Ev.

"Oh no. You don't get to play the victim, not now," I fire back. "Not after the things your family has done to keep Black people down in this town. You wanting to hijack the homecoming elections falls right in line."

Her head pops back and her eyebrows squish together. "I don't understand what you're talking about."

"Of course you don't!"

Even if she didn't kill Nova, what she said obviously inspired someone else to do it. That's what is so annoying about this girl. She acts like she doesn't realize the power she has.

"Duchess, I didn't know my mother would do what she did when I told her you kissed me," she says, lowering her voice. "Is that part of your resentment against me too?"

Deflection! She and Nova must read from the same playbook. Don't want to talk about something? Bring up something totally unrelated.

"It's about so much more than that," I say. "You wished death on a girl, *my best friend,* who meant something important to us. We weren't being underrepresented at school. We were systematically excluded from things you and your friends take for granted."

"This whole time, what was this about?" she says, flicking her hand back and forth between her and I. "Making sure I wasn't covering something up? Or was it some kind of payback?"

"It's about finding out who killed my friend," I say through clenched teeth. "How and if that hurts your feelings will always be last on my list."

She tears the napkin in half, her lips pinched together. I work on steadying my breathing. I can feel people staring at us. I also feel ten pounds lighter after having said all the things that have been pent up inside me, even before Nova died.

"You okay?" Evelyn asks, appearing at our booth.

"I'm good, bae." My voice is still trembling. "Please tell me you ready to bounce?"

"Give me fifteen." Her eyes cut over to Tinsley, who gives her a nervous smile.

After a few seconds of strained silence Tinsley sticks out her hand. "Hi, I'm—"

"I know who you are," Ev scoffs, turning her back to Tinsley so that she's facing me. "Why is she here? Shouldn't she be—"

"Ev, don't," I say, licking my lips, which became dry and cracked during my rant. "I don't think she . . . you know."

Tinsley's eyes fall into her lap when I glance in her direction.

"The privilege of it all," Ev groans, and retreats from the booth.

I gulp, feeling the back of my throat thicken. Ev wants so bad for me to believe in something I don't. Tinsley is the worst, no question about that. But she's not a murderer. I still feel that in my gut.

"That's the girlfriend, right?" she asks.

I roll my eyes and loudly exhale. Then I close my eyes and nod.

"She goes to school with us?" she asks.

"She's in her first year at Cartell Community College."

The stretch of silence that follows stiffens the air between us.

"Duchess, I'm sorry for—"

"What the fuck?" I snap.

My gaze has drifted over Tinsley's head, out the window behind her that overlooks the parking lot, to Jaxson Pafford, leaning against his truck, surrounded by his usual entourage of football players.

Jaxson's cheesy smile deflates the second he sees Tinsley and me charging his way. The Ariana Grande song playing inside Jitterbug's is instantly replaced as the overlapping sounds of revving engines, pulsating music, and the boisterous chatter echoing throughout the sprawling parking lot overwhelm us.

"Shouldn't you be in jail?" I shout.

The gaggle of football players surrounding Jaxson all turn around.

"Calm down, *bro*. Our boy was just giving the police a statement about what he saw go down at school between Nova and the psycho debutante over there," Patrick Dunnard says, tilting his chin at Tinsley. He's a junior and the running back on the football team. "The media's been blowing that shit up to more than it was."

Tinsley and I exchange knowing looks.

"Is *that* what you told them?" she says, glaring at Jaxson. Some of the bitchy confidence I'm used to seeing in her returns. "Well, let me school y'all on why the police really wanted to question your king. It's because—"

"Guys, I'll meet y'all inside," Jaxson interjects, cutting her off. "Let me holla at them for a sec."

The guys don't have to be asked twice. They migrate into Jitterbug's with eye rolls and mumbled asides aimed at us. Once they're out of earshot, Jaxson leans back against the grille of his truck with one leg casually propped against the bumper. I want to smack him.

"Despite how it looks, I didn't do it," he says. "I had to spend two hours proving that."

"And what lie did you tell my Pops?" I demand.

"I didn't have to tell any lies," he says. "I told him the truth."

"Oh, so you told them all about the fight you and Nova had here a few days before the coronation?" I say.

I feel Tinsley look over at me, confused by my question. Jax's arms drop to his sides and his chin trembles. He knows exactly what I'm referring to.

"What did you say to her that night?" I press, giving him this melodramatic look of confusion. "Oh, that's right. That you weren't about to let her ruin your life."

"You bitches are trippin'," he says, biting his bottom lip as he struggles to mold his face back into the cocky façade he prides himself on.

I take a step forward, clenching my fists. "We ain't gonna be too many more bitches, fuckboy."

"Is this why y'all been hanging?" he says, pointing at me

and Tinsley. "Concocting these ridiculous theories about what happened to her, for what? To find out who killed her? Well, y'all got the wrong person."

"Why did you ask her to meet you in the storage room that night?" I say. "We know that's where you killed her."

"And what was with that threatening note?" Tinsley adds.

Jaxson gives her a blank look. "What note?"

The question confuses me too.

"Why can't y'all get it through y'all's thick skulls?" he says, his voice rising. "I didn't hurt her."

"Bullshit!" I hiss.

"I wouldn't do that to her."

"Then why the secret rendezvous in the storage room?" Tinsley asks again.

"You kill her 'cause you didn't want that baby holding you back?" I fume, getting up in his face. "She meant that little to you?"

"Was it because your parents are, like, the absolute worst, and you're more like them than you care to admit?" Tinsley says.

Jaxson's chest hitches. "No! It wasn't like that," he says, his voice quaking.

"Then why'd you do it?" I scream.

"I didn't!" Jaxson shouts back. Some of his spit spraying me in the face. "I couldn't hurt her. I . . . I cared about her too much."

I take a step back. "Boy, please. You treat girls like microwave hoes."

"And that right there is the reason she was scared to ever

tell you about us," Jaxson says, jabbing his finger in my face. Seeing him blinking back tears makes me flinch. "She didn't want to deal with you judging her for wanting to be with me."

Is that why she changed the subject that day I pressed her about why she was posing that question about dating a white person? How long had she been holding that in? Her demeanor at the reception right before I left . . . did it have to do with him and their baby? *Stuff you'd have to promise you wouldn't tell anyone else,* she told me at the coronation. If she and Jaxson cared so much about each other, why would she want to keep that a secret from me?

Jaxson turns his head and quickly swipes his hand across his eyes. This can't be real. Jaxson crying? Nova and I used to make fun of him. And now he's standing here crying over her? What is happening?

"You really cared about her, didn't you?" Tinsley says, her voice softer. "That's why you've been acting so *different* at school. Looking like you haven't been sleeping."

Jaxson's glassy eyes drop to the ground before he nods. "We used to joke about being the next Travis Kelce and Kayla Nicole once I went pro. That ain't happening now."

"Why ask her to meet you in the storage room, though? What happened there?" Tinsley asks again, but this time with a less accusatory tone. "You're the only person we know of who was in there with her that night."

"I didn't meet up with her," he says.

"Liar!" I bark. "We saw the text."

"Yeah, I texted her to meet me in there," he says, "but I never went."

I shake my head, shifting my weight from one foot to the other. This can't be his alibi. This can't be all he had to say to avoid getting arrested.

"That doesn't make sense," Tinsley replies, sort of reading my mind.

Jaxson scratches his head. "Look, y'all were half-right, okay? She and I were arguing a lot leading up to the coronation. She found out she was pregnant a few days before the homecoming elections. And we both agreed to get rid of it since neither of us wanted a baby right now, nor could we afford one. But then she changed her mind. Said she didn't know if she could go through with it since her mother had contemplated aborting her when she first got pregnant."

"Her mother told her that?" Tinsley says.

I'd call him a liar again, but I'd be the one lying, since that sounds like something Ms. Donna would say—especially if she was angry with Nova. Like I said, their relationship was hella complicated.

"I think Donna said it one time while they were arguing," Jaxson continues. "Nova said her mom was sleeping with some married dude when she got pregnant with her. *Anyway,* she tried to make me feel guilty about wanting the abortion by telling me we would have never met and fallen in love if Donna had gotten rid of her. I told her that was nonsense. Tried reminding her that neither one of us has money or families that could support us going to college *and* raising a baby. At school, the day of the coronation, she asked me if I'd change my mind if she knew of a way we could have the baby and not have to worry about money.

"I texted her that night to meet me 'cause I knew what

my answer was. But I ended up not coming to campus. I was avoiding her. That's why I went with Parker and some of the other guys when they showed up at my place and pressured me into going with them to break into Capitol Heights campus and steal their championship trophies—you know, as a prank before the game this week."

"And you never told her you weren't showing up?" I yell, attracting stares from the group of girls walking past us toward Jitterbug's.

Had he met up with her that night, Jaxson's presence might have stopped whoever killed her. Or at the very least, he might have seen who did do it.

"Nova was in such a foul mood that night," Jaxson says. "Her mother was being a super bitch to her," he adds, pointing at Tinsley. "I didn't want to have another argument. I planned on telling her I hadn't changed my mind the next morning, but . . . yeah."

"That doesn't prove you didn't kill her," Tinsley says.

Jaxson sighs. "Capitol Heights reported the break-in, so the police already checked out the story. The school is over forty-five minutes away. We got back late, so I spent the night at Derrick McGillian's house 'cause I knew my parents would trip if I came home past curfew. Derrick's mother confirmed my story to your dad, Duchess."

I jam my hands into the front pouch of my hoodie. I'm right back where I started. Haunted by unanswered questions about why someone would kill my best friend.

"When did y'all start hooking up?" I ask.

If he didn't kill her, I want to know who she was with him. What else there was she kept from me and how long.

Remember her through somebody else's eyes. Someone I would never have thought would care so much about her.

"This summer, while you were away visiting your brother in California," he replies. "I was here by myself, she was working the late shift. We were just joking around. She was giving me that sassy attitude while I was trying to push up on her. But we ended up hanging out all night and just talking. And it felt nice. Different. So we kept talking every night, until . . ."

The euphoric smile on his face gradually disappears. "Shit is hard right now. Trying to walk around and pretend she didn't mean more to me than she did. That she wasn't carrying our . . . Fuck, man! If I had met up with her like I should have . . ."

Then she might still be here.

Jaxson bites down on his clenched fist. He's blinking rapidly to fight back more tears. I turn away to hide my emotions. If I'd known about them, maybe we could have shared this grief instead of suffering alone like we've been. Then the void wouldn't be so huge inside me.

"You okay?" Tinsley asks when I turn back around.

Jaxson is gone.

I look over my shoulder and catch him walking toward Jitterbug's. Evelyn's standing a few feet behind us. She's clocked out and traded her uniform for a black miniskirt, black ankle boots, and a cropped black shirt, under the pink leather motorcycle jacket I got her for her birthday.

"You good?" she asks.

I sniff back tears. "Yeah, I'm good. He didn't do it, though."

"You'll have to tell me about it in the car. The crew is waiting on us."

I let her weave her fingers with mine. I start pulling her in the direction I parked, but she resists.

"Tinsley," she says, "why don't you come with us?"

I spin around. My ribs feel like they're trying to crush my heart. Tinsley is standing in the same spot with one arm folded across her stomach.

"Whatcha doing?" I scoff at Ev.

"Hush," Evelyn says with this coy smile. "Tinsley, come with us. This will be good for you."

"I don't want to intrude," Tinsley says, eyeing me.

I tug on Ev's hand, but she resists. "Stop it! You know this girl—"

"Duchess says you're innocent. I want to see that for myself." Evelyn grabs Tinsley's wrist with her free hand. "Plus, I want to get to know the girl who's been spending so much time with my boo."

Ev doesn't give Tinsley a chance to respond. She just guides her toward my car. She's practically pulling me along too, ignoring every squeeze I'm giving her hand to try and stop her. I call bullshit on her wanting to get to know Tinsley. She can't stand her. Can't stand me being around her. That has to mean she's up to something. Something I already know I'm about to regret.

CHAPTER TWENTY-TWO

TINSLEY

OCTOBER 20
8:05 P.M.

THE MARKED LOVETT Police squad car that followed me to Jitter-bug's had been parked along the median across the street. Given the threat I received tonight, I'm not hating having a police shadow now.

The car turns onto the two-lane road along with us. From the backseat I can see it in the rearview mirror, but I can't tell whether Duchess notices we're being followed. If she does, her fixed gaze on the road doesn't give it away.

The reality of Jaxson's innocence starts to settle in, pulling my body deeper into the backseat. I was wrong. Again. The realization adds to the sobering things Duchess shouted at me back at Jitterbug's.

Maybe her father and my parents are right. We aren't cut out for this. Each time I've been cocky enough to think I figured out who might have killed Nova, I've had the chair kicked out from under me. Now I'm sitting here with no idea where I'm going. Something I kind of allowed to happen out of my desperate need to have someone else believe in my innocence. That someone being Duchess's girlfriend, who clearly doesn't like us hanging together.

She keeps eyeing me in the passenger-side mirror. It's too dark for me to really read her face. Being disliked by other girls used to amuse me. I'm used to it. It's the curse that came with being who I am. Reveling in that mindset is what got me into this predicament. Everyone thinking I could do the worst thing ever. Gotta change the narrative. Prove Duchess wrong about me.

"Did Jax tell y'all why Nova changed her mind about having an abortion?" Evelyn asks Duchess up front.

She asked me if I'd change my mind if she knew of a way we could have the baby and not have to worry about money, Jax said. What could Nova have meant by that? Was she about to come into a large sum of money somehow?

As Duchess and her girlfriend talk, I pull out my phone and swipe to the photo I took at the police station.

Don't do it! Or I'll make you regret it!

Was she blackmailing someone? Whoever wrote that note didn't want Nova to do something. It couldn't have been Jax. He *wanted* her to "do it." Anyone who's ever asked me *not* to do something did so because I knew something embarrassing they didn't want me to reveal. Maybe Nova went after the wrong person with some secret she knew? That's the only plausible explanation I can come up with for that note. Nova didn't really have any enemies.

I tuck my phone back into my jacket pocket as the tires crunch over gravel and look up. I've been so preoccupied I haven't been paying attention to where they're taking me. The small parking lot is stuffed with cars, and a dark, nondescript building fills the view out of the windshield of Duchess's car. I can make out several Black people loitering near the tinted-glass double doors at the center of the building. Most of them appear to be around our age. After leaning forward and squinting, I realize they're all girls.

"Is this a lesbian bar?" I ask as Duchess squeezes her car between a sedan and a black SUV.

She smacks her lips. "No."

"It's this chill coffee shop/restaurant/bar-ish hangout," Evelyn says as she digs around in the purse on her lap.

I press my face against the window. I can make out the sign at the edge of the parking lot. THE DRIP is lit up in flashing white LED lights. The reader board underneath the glowing letters says *Thursday Night Slam Poetry Open Mic 8–10*

"Wait. Is this one of those places where people perform those poems, you know, like in that old movie *Love Jones*?" My hand is already on the door handle, a lightness ballooning in my chest. "I've always wanted to go to one of these!"

Duchess casts an amused glance at Evelyn, who is using the mirror in the passenger-side sun visor to apply a fresh coat of burgundy gloss to her plump lips.

"Girl, whatcha know about *Love Jones*?" Evelyn says after pressing her lips together to even out the coat.

"I love Larenz Tate," I say. "I started watching that show *Power* just to see him. He's like a freaking vampire. He never ages."

"Black don't crack," Duchess quips as she's stepping out of the car.

"Is it gonna be cool for me to be in there?" I ask, the anonymous emails popping into my mind. Anyone with the username *sickofkarens* has to be Black.

Evelyn turns around in the passenger seat with her perfectly arched eyebrows raised. "Girl, chill. You ain't gonna be the only white person in there. It's *us* who need to worry when it's a whole bunch of y'all around."

A pang of shame hits me. This girl already hates me. She probably thinks I said that because I see all Black people as threats. She doesn't know about the cryptic messages I've been getting. She doesn't care that I might be recognized. But then, I'm not alone. I'm with them. There is safety in numbers, right?

I open the door and climb out. As I'm shutting it, I notice my police shadow parking at the other end of the lot. I catch Duchess's eyes flick toward the squad car and then back to me. I bet she knows who the shadowy figure in the driver's seat is. I want to ask, but she looks down and starts fidgeting with the sleeves of her letterman-style jacket.

Evelyn's complex description of the place makes perfect sense once we enter. The exhilarating aroma of roasted coffee beans floods my nostrils as soon as we walk in. An array of tables, varying in sizes and shapes, dot the dimly lit room stretching out before us. Everyone seated at the tables is staring at the elevated stage tucked in one corner of the room. It's lit up by the bright spotlight beaming from the DJ booth nestled in another corner on a raised platform behind where we've congregated at the entrance. About twenty feet from the other side of the entrance is a wraparound bar. Two industrial-size espresso machines are stationed at opposite ends, but liquor bottles are neatly arranged along the lighted shelves that make up the bar's backsplash. A glowing sign makes it known that no alcohol is served to anyone without an ID. There are quite a few people here about our age, but quite a few more who are obviously old enough to drink.

"Officer-involved shootings? No, they're modern-day lynchings of our Black men!" the girl onstage shouts in a rhythmic tone that's followed by the steady beat of an unseen drum. The drumbeat, which seems to be a track the DJ's playing, mirrors a heartbeat.

"Come on, my crew is over there." Evelyn grabs my wrist and pulls me behind Duchess, who's already quietly maneuvering her way between the tables.

The girl onstage continues with her anti-police-violence manifesto as Evelyn leads me to the group of people seated in the center of the room around two square tables that have been pushed together. She doesn't let go of me until we reach the table. Four of the chairs are empty and they happen to be facing the stage, so we sit, and the three people already seated turn at the sound of our chairs scraping the floor.

" 'Bout time y'all get here," whispers a fair-skinned Black girl with a shoulder-length bob that's frosted blond at the tips. "You almost missed Briana's piece," she adds, nodding at the stage.

I give the girl a tight smile when she does a double take at me.

"This is Duchess's friend Tinsley," Evelyn leans over and whispers at everyone else I can feel staring at me.

"*Friend* is a stretch," Duchess says, side-eyeing her girl-friend.

The guy sitting next to the girl with the bob is white. He

gives me a quick once-over with his gray eyes before he extends his hand across the table.

"I'm Chance." The beaded bracelets stacked around his wrist click together as I shake his hand. "This is my girlfriend, Nikki," he says, nodding at bob-girl, who gives me a polite smile.

Chance nods toward the person seated to my right, and my smile drops when I see who it is.

"And that's—"

"Trenton," I finish for Chance, forgetting to keep my voice low. My outburst elicits a few annoyed glances from the people sitting behind us.

Trenton Hughes's sneer uncoils a tightness in my chest.

He leans over to Duchess and whispers, "You didn't tell me you were bringing *her* with you," loud enough for me to hear.

"Bullshit," she says. "I texted you when we left Jitterbug's and told you she was with us."

Trenton leans back in his chair. "Well, I didn't think you were serious."

Chance and Nikki eye one another. In my desperate attempt to avoid the disapproving glare of the boy who went on the evening news to emphatically proclaim my guilt, I look around. I lock eyes with a girl seated three tables to our right. She nudges the girl seated next to her and points at me.

I reach into my jacket pocket for my phone, hoping I can hide by looking down at it.

Evelyn reaches over to cover my phone screen with her hand. "No phones while folks are performing. The light is distracting."

Briana's voice has picked up in pitch and tempo, as has the drumbeat now thumping like a racing heart. I no longer feel

Trenton leering at me, but disdain radiates from him like heat from a radiator, warming the right side of my body. My heart starts to sync up with the rush of the synthetic drum pulsing through the sound system.

I can feel Trenton's leg shaking under the table, and I bite the inside of my lip, my anxiety building.

He's gonna make a scene. Please, God, don't let him make a scene.

I'm so preoccupied by my growing paranoia I don't realize Briana is done with her performance until bright lights flood the room and enthusiastic clapping explodes around me.

"Girl, you killed it!" Nikki tells her as she drops into the last empty seat at our table.

Briana tosses her butt-length braids over her shoulder with dramatic flair. "Thank you, thank you. No autographs, please." Her eyes narrow on me.

"Bri, this is Tinsley," Evelyn says with a wave in my direction. "She goes to school with Trenton and Duchess."

Briana's tight expression indicates that she already knows who I am (and probably has strong opinions about me). I catch a flash of amusement ripple across Evelyn's face. My stomach is doing flips. I don't want everyone at this table hating me.

I lean over to Briana. "Your poem was really good," I say. "Like, really timely."

Everyone's eyes fix on me, but I can't read their expressions. Did I just make things worse?

"You ain't gonna go back to the White People Meeting and report me, huh?" she asks and my mouth drops open. Everyone bursts into laughter and I start shaking my head. "Relax, girl. It was a joke," Briana adds. "Duchess, please don't tell me you brought some sensitive-ass white girl around us. You know only the ones with swag, like Chance, got thick enough skin to deal with our foolishness."

I join in their laughter this time around, hoping it'll disprove Briana's theory about me.

The announcer calls another girl to the stage. She performs a piece deconstructing the disparities between white feminism and Black feminism. Conversation at the table resumes when the lights go back up and the announcer says there'll be a thirty-minute break before the next performance. I mostly sit on the sidelines of their discussion, which flip-flops between their thoughts on some of the earlier performances we missed and on-campus gossip—which confirms for me that Nikki, Briana, and Chance attend Cartell with Evelyn.

Listening to their quick-fire verbal jabs at each other is amusing. It feels nice to be a part of a group again—even if it's with a bunch of people I don't really know. This feels familiar. Safe. Something I haven't felt since Friday.

I catch Trenton watching me. His eyes dart across the table toward Chance and Nikki the second he realizes I caught him.

"Tinsley!" Evelyn nudges me with her shoulder. "You ignoring us?"

"Huh?" I respond, blinking at her.

"Briana was talking to you," Evelyn replies, smirking as she's pointing across the table.

"I'm sorry, what?"

"I was asking if you wanna come with us to Jackson this weekend." Briana crosses her arms in front of her on the table. "We're thinking about joining in on the protesting."

"You mean all that stuff over that gardener they think killed that couple?"

Briana, Chance, and Nikki all nod.

I scratch the side of my neck, worried how my response will make me look. "Oh, I don't think my mother would let me participate in that."

"Shocker," Duchess drawls.

"My sister is obsessed with that case," I add quickly. "She's convinced that guy is innocent."

"Well, of course he is," Nikki says. "That's why I don't blame everyone for looting and burning down shit to show the police we're tired of them taking our lives for granted and getting away with it."

"Maybe you guys can have that same energy for me," I say.

I regret it as soon as I see the way Trenton and Duchess turn to me, their brows creased and mouths tight.

"Excuse me?" Briana asks.

"You didn't just try to equate what you're going through to what they're doing to Curtis Delmont," Nikki says as Chance drapes his arm around her shoulder. "He's in jail. You're not. Thanks to your pretty white skin. It's hardly the same."

"I—I—I never said it was. But I mean, technically. He's being accused of something he says he didn't do, and so am I."

"Girl, please!" Evelyn says. "That Black man is sitting in jail all because he was in the wrong place at the wrong time. And because a bunch of white people *think* he did something. And yet, here you are, *free,* despite the fact there's a viral video of you saying you want to kill someone who coincidentally turned up dead the next day—"

"Which is why I'm struggling to understand why you running around town with this chick," Briana interrupts, looking at Duchess, who's avoiding the glances I'm darting at her, silently begging to be recused.

"You don't get to cast yourself like some victim when you still have the freedom to walk around and clear your name—which Curtis Delmont can't do right now," Evelyn says. "And he may never get the chance, because the police already decided his fate. And they don't need *unequivocal* evidence to do it. Had he done everything you did, they'd probably have him in the electric chair by now."

There's a lump in my throat the size of a tennis ball. This wasn't about getting to know me or trying to understand why her girlfriend thinks I'm innocent. Evelyn brought me here for this. To attack me about the same things Duchess already did at Jitterbug's.

"Since we're on the subject, Tinsley," Chance says, "I'm a little curious to hear why you used the term *reverse racism* as an argument in opposition to your school's homecoming queen election policy." Chance retracts the arm he draped across the back of Nikki's chair, propping his elbow on the table. "You know what a lot of the problem in this country is: white people acting like every racial group has the power to oppress other marginalized groups systemically on multiple levels. Like Black prejudices don't affect our rights or our way of life anywhere near the way our bigotry and hate affects them."

And now I literally want to die.

"This is almost like those white people who complained about affirmative action. What did they think legacy status at all these Ivy League schools is?" Chance continues. "Basically affirmative action but for white people, even though we've never had a problem with it."

"I'm not this horrible, bigoted person," I argue, desperate for them to understand my side. "Okay, yes, I said things I shouldn't have. I didn't realize how deeply they would hurt people."

"That's what happen when you don't understand your privilege," Nikki interjects.

"I still can't get over you hanging around this girl," Briana says to Duchess. "You know people talking—and it ain't good."

"Y'all not defending me?" she replies, her shoulders drooping.

Briana turns to me, ignoring Duchess's question. "I still wanna hear her defend what she said about the school's policy. She's got the right one here to educate that ass."

Something inside me snaps. I can't take any more. There's one person at this table who shouldn't have allowed this to happen.

"You are such a fucking bitch!" I snap at Duchess, shooting up out of my seat. "It wasn't enough that you already told me how horrible a person I am, you needed your girlfriend and your friends to do it too?"

I don't wait for her to respond. I charge toward the exit.

"Tinsley, this wasn't me," I hear her shout behind me.

I spin around to find she's right on my heels.

"I don't even know why I bother with you," I hiss.

"*You* bother with *me*? No, boo boo, it's the other way around. 'Cause honestly, I should have punched you in the throat the day you rolled up on me at Nova's locker. What you can't stand about me is that I'm not afraid to call you out on your bullshit.

You don't know how to handle that 'cause you're used to everyone bowing down to you like you're some queen."

"Yes, I was a horrible person! Yes, I was manipulative and a bitch! But I don't deserve any of this!"

"And cue the violins!"

"Y'all, stop," Chance says, appearing next to us. "Everyone is looking."

To think, I figured it would be Trenton causing an embarrassing scene.

"I guess you know everything, right?" I fire back at Duchess. "Well, everything except literally anything your *supposed* best friend was going through."

Seeing the hurt flash in Duchess's eyes makes my heart beat faster.

"I totally understand why Nova kept so much from you. And you have to feel like shit knowing she thought you were so judgmental she couldn't tell you she was in love. Does it keep you up at night that there might be some other secret that got her killed? Maybe if you had been a better friend, she'd still be alive!"

I leave Duchess and Chance standing in the middle of the room.

Only to get outside in the parking lot and remember that I rode here with her.

Shit.

I'm eyeing the squad car that followed me. My phone is telling me the nearest Lyft is more than twenty-five minutes away. Do I go over and persuade whoever's inside to give me a ride back to Jitterbug's?

"Hey, ain't you ol' girl they're saying killed that Black homecoming queen at Lovett?"

I've barely looked up from my phone before I'm surrounded by three girls. All of them Black. All looking super pissed.

"Yeah, this her," the one to my left says, dismissively waving her hand at me.

"You had a lot to say on that li'l video," the first girl follows. "Why would you say some messed-up shit like that?"

"What did that girl ever do to you?" the third girl barks.

I don't realize I've been slowly walking backward until I nearly trip over a concrete parking block in front of the building. I regain my footing and say, "I'm just waiting for my ride. I'm not here to start any drama."

I frantically search the parking lot and suddenly realize we're the only people out here. I stumble backward around the corner of the building and lose sight of the squad car. I should scream. I need to. But my voice is trapped in my throat.

"I'm so sick of you white girls thinking you can get away with saying and doing anything you want," the second girl says. I recognize her. She's the one who pointed me out to her friend inside.

"It should have been you that got busted in the head and dumped in a cemetery, not her!" she rails, folding her arms across her chest with a sneer.

It should have been you, not Nova. Same thing sickofkarens said in that anonymous email. My chin starts trembling. I need to shout that I didn't kill her. Not that what I say would mean anything to them. But the words come out in whimpers as tears prick my eyes.

"Save yo' white tears, sweetie," the second girl says.

"Y'all Karens love to weaponize your tears once you get called out for yo' racist bullshit," the third girl follows.

I'm not racist, though. I'm not!

"Rather kill a Black girl than let her be queen after y'all privileged behinds been wearing the crowns since the dawn of time," the first girl says.

The second girl steps up in my face. "It would serve you right if someone did the same thing to you!"

"Yeah, hashtag Justice for Nova," the third girl chimes in.

When I take two steps backward, the back of my head knocks up against the side of the building with a deafening thud. I'm trapped. With no way to escape but through these girls. Is this how Nova felt before she was fatally struck in the head in that storage room? Crippled by the feeling that someone hated her enough to want her dead?

"You lucky I'm a Christian," the first girl says, jabbing her finger in my face. "Old me might have caught a case tonight to teach yo' entitled ass a lesson about talking reckless against Black women!"

I squeeze my eyes shut, pushing the tears down my cheeks. The back of my head is throbbing. Never has my life felt as fragile as it does now.

"Hey!"

My eyes pop open. The girls all turn.

Trenton is standing to the side, holding up his phone. His face hardened by a scowl.

"You sho' you ready to go to jail tonight?" He waves his phone in the air. "Cops already on their way."

The second girl twists her upper lip at Trenton. "Calm down, ain't nobody touch her. She's just scared of Black people."

"Tinsley, come on."

Trenton is holding out his hand to me. He's the last person I thought would ever come to my rescue, but I'm so glad he did. I snatch his hand. The lifeline I never expected (and maybe don't deserve).

"Watch yo' back, Becky!" one of them says as Trenton pulls me away with him.

He tugs me to a silver Nissan Maxima. "Come on, I'll give you a ride home," he says after I pause.

"My car is at Jitterbug's."

"Then I'll give you a ride there. Get in."

I climb in on the passenger side. My heart still feels like it's about to explode and my mind is spinning. Why is he deciding to be this hero to me, the girl he accused of murdering his friend on the local news?

This has to be his mother's car. It has a Delta Sigma Theta license plate decal. I know that's a Black sorority because Giselle's mother is also a member. Trenton starts the ignition and the soulful bass line of an R&B song I don't immediately recognize engulfs us, blasting from every speaker. The bass thumps my heart harder. He changes the radio station with a meek grin before we pull out, opting for Hot 100 hits instead. The awkward silence thickening between us helps to calm my nerves.

"Thanks," I mumble after my breathing becomes somewhat normal again.

It takes a few seconds for him to weakly reply, "Yeah, you welcome."

The silence continues for a few miles. I check the rearview mirror. My police shadow is a few cars behind us.

"I'm sorry."

I heard Trenton utter the words clear as day, but I lean toward him anyway.

"You're sorry? For what?"

"About what I said on the news," he answers.

My mouth slightly drops open. Did he really say what I think he said? Trenton's side-eyeing me. Probably because I haven't responded. But I don't know what to say. Is this why he was out in the parking lot? Looking for me to apologize but stumbling upon my near-death situation instead? I prop my elbow on the door to cup my chin, which is trembling a little.

"I was really angry, really hurt, when I did that interview." His grip on the steering wheel tightens. "And . . . well . . . I—"

"We don't have to do this, Trenton." My voice comes out soft and shaky. I'm not sure I have the strength to handle wherever this conversation is about to go. "I understand. It was kind of obvious you liked her—you know, in more than just the friend way."

"But you don't understand everything. At least, I don't think you do," he says.

His hands keep shifting around the steering wheel. I think he's nervous.

"What else is there to understand?" I ask.

"What I did wasn't all about Nova."

"It wasn't?" I respond.

My hands are quivering. If what he said on the news wasn't him hurt over losing the girl he was secretly in love with, then it could only be about one other thing: me.

"I mean, yeah. I liked Nova, *a lot*," he says. "But I wasn't in love with her like that. Not like you think. I came to terms a long time ago with the fact that girls like you and Nova don't be checking for the nerdy dudes like me until we're pulling in the seven-figure salaries at our tech start-ups."

I lift my hand to hide my smirk. *Nerdy* is definitely how I'd describe Trenton, but he's always come off as too uptight to be self-deprecating. A seven-figure salary is him selling himself short. I could totally see him becoming the CEO of some multibillion-dollar tech company. He's president of the robotics club and the math club, and captain of our debate team. I even overheard some kids say he hacked into the school's security system once just to prove that he could.

He really wouldn't *look* so nerdy if he kept his mini Afro trimmed and stopped wearing those loose-fitting shirts—they only make him look skinnier than he is. Trenton isn't a *terrible*-looking guy. With the right skin regimen and better clothes, he would catch the eye of the girls he thinks are out of his league now.

"Real talk, Nova's friendship was enough for me," he continues. "She was . . . too complicated. She always had so many walls up. I sometimes felt like she wasn't telling me the whole truth about, well, anything. It was like she had been through stuff she had convinced herself none of us would understand or something."

Trenton doesn't have the slightest idea how right he is. But it's not my place to tell him everything I've uncovered about Nova these past four days. Suddenly I want to protect her image, and all I wanted a week ago was to destroy it.

"Why the change of heart?" I ask after about a mile of silence. "The evil eyes you were giving me back at the Drip told a different story."

"It was Duchess."

"What about her?"

I highly doubt she has said *anything* positive about me to him. She made it clear tonight that we'd never, could never, be friends.

"She is judgmental, like you said, but she's also intuitive and rarely wrong about people," Trenton explains. "She dead-ass wouldn't be hanging around you if she really thought you killed Nova."

I look out the window. My eyes well up with tears that I blink back.

I've damaged another relationship. Said things I shouldn't have. I've spent too many years being the person Duchess and her friends think I am. When I'm feeling threatened, attacked, or insecure, my default will always be to lash out and destroy.

"If you tell her I said this, I'll deny it," I say as the flashing marquees of all the hotel casinos and beachfront restaurants come into view, signaling we're about to cross back into town. I let the warmth of the memory of who Duchess and I used to be as little girls wash over me. That might have been the only time I had a friend I didn't treat like a possession. "As much as she irritates me, I actually care what Duchess thinks about me. It's almost like getting her to be my friend again would some-how prove I'm not as horrible as everyone thinks I am. That I'm not who those girls back there said I am."

Trenton doesn't say anything, and after a few seconds I add, "She lives her life so authentically. Everything about my life is so freaking artificial. At the same time, she makes me feel like I'll never win with her. I mean, why do I have to bear the bur-den of my ancestors' sins, you know?"

"Maybe because you haven't been willing to do any of the work it'll take from y'all to undo them," he opines in a warm tone.

The headlights from the car in the opposite lane flood the car's interior as it zooms past. I look over at Trenton and see what I think is kindness in his face.

"Is it true?" he asks.

"Is what true?" I reply.

"That you and Duchess are investigating Nova's murder together?"

"*Was* true. Doubt it is anymore, after what went down tonight."

Maybe if you had been a better friend, she'd still be alive! The guilt of remembering what I said to her presses down on my chest.

"Y'all get any good leads?"

"Nope. Just a lot of dead ends." I sit up straighter, it suddenly dawning on me that Trenton was at the coronation ceremony. After a beat I ask, "You didn't see anything strange at the reception that night, did you?"

"Nah. I cut out right after Duchess and Ev."

He turns onto Highway 675, the winding two-lane highway that leads back to Jitterbug's.

"I'm praying they find out who really killed her," I say, more to myself than to him.

"If they haven't arrested you yet and you didn't do it, does it matter? You're a freaking McArthur. Your family is practically royalty in this town."

I pinch the bridge of my nose. "That's precisely the problem. I'm a McArthur. A McArthur who will have a cloud of suspicion hanging over my head for the rest of my life if they don't close this case. In this town, that's a whole different kind of prison."

"Your family is kinda the reason I said all that on the news."

The sign for Jitterbug's glows in the distance.

So I was right. That was about me.

"This is about what went down between our fathers, isn't it?"

Trenton glances at me. "You know what your father's been doing?"

Why is he speaking in the present tense? The rift between our fathers happened years ago. Everything since then has just been business.

"*Been* doing?" I say. "I just know he beat your dad's company out of a lot of projects and your dad is all bitter about it, which honestly isn't fair to blame me for."

Trenton whips his mother's car into the Jitterbug's parking lot. My convertible is the only car in the lot besides a midnight-black Ford Focus parked more than fifty feet away. He pulls up beside it, but I don't get out.

Something about our conversation feels unfinished.

Trenton swallows hard and shuts off the ignition and the headlights, leaving only the distant chorus of crickets chirping in the night to fill the silence.

"What happened between them was a lot deeper than that, Tinsley," he says, looking over at me. "You have to know that."

"Well, I don't. So explain to me why you've spent the last three years staring at me like I killed your puppy."

"My dad was one of the first hires your father made when he started McArthur Construction."

I nod. That much I was aware of.

"My dad worked as his lead engineer for years, pretty

much helped him build that company when your dad's own father was making it difficult for him to strike out on his own," he says, an edge creeping into his voice. "When construction started really booming around here after Katrina, my father approached your dad about resigning so he could start his own company with my Uncle David. Virgil let him, promising my dad he'd use them as the subcontractor on his multimillion-dollar projects, a lot of which had minority-owned business mandates because they were attached to federal funding."

I was told Trenton's father quit because he became difficult to work with. *Thought he knew everything,* my father said. But I'm not mentioning that, given the conviction in Trenton's face right now.

"But your dad never kept his word. In fact, he worked overtime to sabotage my father's company. Badmouthing him to developers, squeezing him out on bids for government contracts, thanks to his childhood friendship with the mayor."

After a beat Trenton continues, "I'm just going to say it: we think your dad illegally secured a lot of the government contracts that allowed his business to grow."

My heart pushes into my throat. "You can't prove that!"

Trenton sneers at me with the same disdain he showed back at the Drip.

"The day before the coronation, my dad had to file for bankruptcy," he says. "Him and my Uncle David had banked on winning the bid for this massive affordable housing project in the Avenues. It was going to be their big break. But guess who was awarded the contract?"

My chest tightens. *I thought it could help me get ahead of some business mistakes* is what my father said when I confronted him about sponsoring Nova. Is everything Trenton is saying what he was referring to? What Duchess said about my family doing things to keep Black people down pops back into my mind as well.

"He hasn't said anything to my Moms about filing for bankruptcy, but I hacked into his computer," Trenton says. "I think he's gonna lose the business. He's in debt up to his ears. I want to go to Howard University next year. There's no way in hell my parents are gonna be able to afford to send me there."

"How do you even know all this, Trenton?" I say, my voice cracking. "We were like one when Katrina happened."

"Because it's all my dad talked about when I was growing up. How Virgil McArthur 'stunted his dreams' after my father helped him build his." Trenton leans his head back on the headrest, casting a faraway gaze out the window. "That's a direct quote from him. Heard it so much I couldn't help but hate your father too."

An awkward silence swells inside the car as I mentally digest everything he just said.

How could Trenton not hate my father? I probably would if I were him. And all the time me willingly ignorant to it while acting self-important and dismissive of his feelings. Duchess is so right. I'm the freaking worst.

"I'm sorry," I say.

Trenton slowly turns to me. Because of the faint smile he's giving me, I notice for the first time he has a dimple in his right cheek.

"I'm starting to think it's unfair to hold what your father did to mine against you."

I give him an apologetic grin I hope he can see through the darkness. "Believe me, I've done enough shitty things to deserve all the stuff you said about me."

We sit in silence a little while longer. My hand is on the door handle, but I have no motivation to pull on it. This bubble of honesty I'm in right now feels good, and opening the door means stepping back out into a world I don't want to face. Suspicion that's making me question everything about who I want to be if I can make it to the other side of these allegations.

"You all right?" Trenton asks, his voice deeper than I've heard it before.

I'm about to respond when headlights flood the car's interior. We both turn and watch a BMW slowly creep into the parking lot and pull up on the side of the Ford Focus the same way Trenton is parked beside my car.

"We can sit and talk some more if you want to," he says.

Trenton's dimple gets deeper as his smile widens. My pulse starts to quicken.

"You seem like you aren't ready to go, and I have another thirty minutes before my curfew," he adds, and his eyes briefly drop down to his lap, and then back up to me.

Wait. Is he kinda into me? I wonder. Is that why he wants to keep talking?

My gaze nervously shifts to the right and the back of my throat thickens. The people who were in the BMW are now standing between it and the Ford Focus. It's a couple engaging in some serious PDA. The man and woman break apart just as I'm about to look away, and when the man's face comes into view my heart drops into my stomach.

"Oh. My. God!"

Trenton whips his head in the direction of my wide-eyed gaze. "What's wrong?"

"I know him!" I lean over the center console, my hand clutching Trenton's knee so that I don't fall in his lap. He leans farther back in the driver's seat as I lean forward and squint to see better.

"Who is it?" he asks.

The man's goofy smile at the woman whose face he's softly caressing is the same one I've seen who knows how many times across our dinner table.

"My brother-in-law!"

"And by your reaction, I'll assume that dark-haired woman isn't your sister."

I jerk back into the passenger seat to dig my phone out of my jacket pocket and I quickly tap open my camera app.

"What are you doing?" Trenton asks as I hold up my phone at Aiden and the whore.

"Making sure my sister can get out of her prenup," I say, taking as many shots as I can.

CHAPTER TWENTY-THREE

DUCHESS

OCTOBER 21
10:07 A.M.

IT WAS A mistake agreeing to speak at Nova's memorial. I don't know what to say.

I tear another page from my notebook, this time after only jotting down one sentence. I toss it with all the discarded pages that have piled up next to my bacon, egg, and cheese sandwich. I prop my head against my fist on the table, frowning at yet another blank sheet. I've been at this for the past thirty minutes. Nothing sounds good enough to say in front of who knows how many people at tonight's game. Nothing I've scribbled down so far feels like me. Or her, for that matter.

This is why teenagers shouldn't have to eulogize our friends. We're supposed to have more time to get this right.

My phone chimes. Most likely another text from Ev. One I plan to ignore, just like I did the one she sent an hour ago. I'm punishing her for last night. I knew she was up to something when she invited Tinsley to the Drip. I had no idea what, though. Until she and the others started going in on Tinsley, that is. She might not have known Tinsley would turn around and lash out at me, but Ev was glad it happened. She was practically beaming as she watched us argue. I gave her the silent treatment afterward the entire drive to her house. The little gang-up they pulled on Tinsley isn't what upsets me the most. It's Ev refusing to trust in my conviction regarding Tinsley.

My best friend is dead. Pops and I are barely speaking. And now my girlfriend is acting like the opp. Her instigating more drama between me and Tinsley doesn't help me get justice for Nova. Especially if I'm right and her murder is somehow connected to someone wanting revenge on that pampered princess for some fucked-up shit she's done in the past.

I don't know what to say tonight, because my mind is all over the place.

I sit back in my wrought-iron chair and take in the surroundings outside Sunny Side Bistro. Main Street is buzzing with activity. Everyone has places to go and people to meet up with for coffee and small talk but me. We got a text alert last night that campus would be closed for a second day. The morning news said police are still there processing the crime scene. According to the report, tonight's game is still on, but the gym and auditorium will be roped off. School's still hosting the dance in the gym tomorrow night, which seems a little morbid. I definitely won't be there.

I wonder how long it'll take for it to not feel weird about life moving on without her. It's been four years since my mother died and I still struggle with that loss. My gaze drifts across the street, stopping on the wooden bench where I had a hissy fit when I was seven because I wouldn't go into the dress store and let her buy me a dress to wear for Easter Sunday service. The memory of us together on that bench scratches at the back of my throat.

"I don't want to wear a dress," I remember sobbing to her. *"Why do I have to? It's not me. I'm not like all the other girls."*

I didn't understand sexuality then. I just knew I was *different*. And in that moment, my mom realized it too.

My mother gave me the kindest smile ever (God, I miss that smile) and said, "Okay, baby. You don't have to be like them. I want you to be you. Whoever that is. And I'm going to love you to pieces."

Then she kissed me softly on the forehead and took me to another store down the street, where she let me pick out a boys' suit that I wore to church on Easter. And she proudly told everyone giving me strange looks that "Duchess is a leader, not a follower. She's our special baby."

I brush away the tear that dribbles down my cheek as I drop my eyes back down to my notebook. The phantom sensation of her warm kiss tingles on my forehead. It's not fair she's gone. It's not fair I now have to keep on living without my best friend too. Maybe I should put that in my speech. Let everyone know how guilty I feel to keep on living. Especially with Nova's killer still walking around somewhere.

Thinking about that makes me think of Tinsley.

What she said to me last night grinds at me. *"Does it keep you up at night that there might be some other secret that got her killed?"*

I told myself not to let that shit get to me. I don't know if I'm more pissed at myself for lying to myself or at Tinsley for knowing just what to say to shut me down. *Maybe if you had been a better friend, she'd still be alive!* Her words are still twisting around my heart. Squeezing it tighter every time I think about them. I should have pressed Nova harder to tell me what had her distracted at the coronation reception. Maybe it was her pregnancy and the fight with Jaxson. But what if there *was* something else I don't know about and that's the reason she's dead?

A shadow passes over the paper in front of me.

"Should I assume by that pile of crumpled paper you're having some trouble penning the next great American novel?" a voice says, and I look up. A shaggy-haired guy is standing at my table, smirking.

I sit up, pulling my notebook closer. "Yeah, something like that," I say.

"Maybe I can help unblock your creative well, Duchess," he says, and a chill goes down my back.

It takes a few seconds for me to realize why this dude knows my name. The sweatpants, relaxed T-shirt, and sunglasses threw me off. I'm used to seeing him in khakis and blazers, with his thick black curls a little more tamed than they are now.

"Hey, Mr. Haywood," I say, relaxing. "Didn't recognize you at first."

He looks down at his outfit and laughs. "I tend to dress like I'm still a broke college kid on my days off. Given how little I get paid, maybe this is my broke teacher look now."

I laugh harder than his joke deserves.

"See I wasn't the only one craving a bagel breakfast sandwich this morning." He holds up the brown bag dangling in his right hand.

"Great minds," I say lightly.

"Out here getting homework done on your day off?" he asks. "Given how tough I'm sure things have been for you, I'm impressed by your tenacity."

"That's not homework," I say, trying to keep my voice from cracking as I eye the discarded balls of paper. "That's me not knowing what to say about a person I'm not ready to let go of."

Mr. Haywood pulls out the empty chair across from me and drops down into it, though I'm sure nothing about my demeanor indicates I was looking for company. I smile anyway, since he can be cool at times.

"That's right," he says kindly. "The memorial ceremony at tonight's game. You're speaking, aren't you?"

"Supposed to be." I toss my pen onto the notebook. "As you can see, I'm having a little trouble with that."

"Not to equate what I've been feeling to what you are, but it's been so unexplainably surreal having one of my students get murdered and another suspected of doing it." The empathy in his dark eyes melts more of my resistance to this impromptu conversation. "I thought Nova would become one of those students I'd tell everyone I taught after she became some famous fashion designer. The girl had so much natural talent for sketching."

"My girl definitely used to let 'em have it when it came to her 'fits," I say, smiling at the memories of all the times I watched her rip up, cut apart, and/or sew fire-ass outfits like it was nothing. What Nova didn't have the money to buy, she'd make herself, but with her own spin.

"Does any of the hostility you've been experiencing from some of your classmates have anything to do with this?" he asks, waving at all the paper between us on the table.

I frown, not understanding what he's getting at.

"I might be a teacher, but I hear the gossip," he explains. "I know the students, mostly the Black ones, have been giving you a hard time. You know, because your dad hasn't arrested Tinsley yet."

I shrug. "Well, yeah and no. That's not it."

I'm curious who his source could be. Are students talking about Pops *that much*?

"I know Tinsley comes from a pretty powerful family, but I'm still shocked she isn't facing any charges," he says. "After seeing that video and then hearing about how she threatened Nova, figured all the money in the world couldn't get her out of a mug shot, at minimum."

"Wait," I say. "What threat?"

Bump who's shit-talking Pops to him. Tinsley threatened Nova? When? I slide up higher in my chair.

"That note the police found," Mr. Haywood replies.

Tinsley's invisible ribbon around my heart tightens. She mentioned a note in the Jitterbug's parking lot. Pops hasn't said anything about a threat. I'm not certain he would, though. He's been keeping everything pretty much to himself since I showed up at the police station with Tinsley. The only thing I know they found is whatever they took from Nova's locker.

Could *that* be what Mr. Haywood's talking about?

The crease above the rim of Mr. Haywood's sunglasses disappears when my eyes light up and I take a wild stab to see if I'm right.

"*Oh,* you mean that note they found in Nova's locker," I say casually, which dissolves his confused look. "How'd you hear about that? Your class is in A-Building."

He shrugs and says, "School gossip."

I nod. Strange that I haven't heard about it, and neither has Jaxson or anyone else besides Tinsley. Though what it said is what I'm more interested in at the moment. Maybe I can get him to tell me.

Mr. Haywood takes off his sunglasses. "Was that threat not enough to implicate Tinsley?"

"I don't know. Apparently it's not as cut-and-dried as it seems," I say.

"Really?" he says. "It sounded to me like that note could directly relate to their beef."

If that were true, the chief would definitely have the princess in cuffs by now. Which means they must not be able to prove she wrote it.

"Tinsley didn't write it," I say, hoping it might get him to tell me more.

"That's crazy," he says, raking his hand through his wild hair. "They have any idea who did? Nova seemed well-liked. Tinsley was the only person I ever knew her to have a conflict with."

I shrug. "No clue."

"None at all?"

"Not that I know of. And my Pops has been keeping me updated on everything since this is so personal for us," I lie.

"Huh," he says, sliding his shades back on. "Must not have been anything to it, then. Well, I'll let you get back to work."

As he's standing up, I ask, "If those gossip birds drop any more tidbits on you, will you let me know? You know, so I can drop a line to my Pops."

"Of course," he says. "Good luck with the speech tonight."

He flashes me a quick wave and a tight smile, then strolls off down Main Street. I watch him get into his car and pull out into traffic, my stomach quivering the entire time.

Which usually happens when I think someone has lied to me.

CHAPTER TWENTY-FOUR

TINSLEY

OCTOBER 21

11:00 A.M.

YESTERDAY IS WEIGHING so heavily on me I can't get out of bed. My fight with Duchess, getting accosted by those girls, Trenton's accusations about my father—all of it haunts my thoughts. But it's seeing Aiden nearly engulf that woman's face in the Jitterbug's parking lot last night that's killing my motivation to start my day. I don't want to leave this bedroom. Rachel is here. She was here when I got home last night. Thankfully, she was already asleep in her old bedroom, so I didn't have to face her. My phone felt ten pounds heavier with the picture I snapped of Aiden and that woman.

How do I tell her Aiden's cheating without it coming off like a major I-told-you-so?

I'm lying here regretting every sly comment I've ever made about him. But how could Rachel not have assumed he was cheating? She had to sense something was off about their marriage, given how much he was "working late." Poor Lindsey. Her childhood is about to become a constant shuffling between two homes.

Why did I have to be the one who caught Aiden? I have enough on my plate. Holding up a mirror to her marriage could go very wrong for me. She's probably going to think I'm doing it out of spite. To deflect from what I'm going through. And in the past, she would have been right.

There's a knock on my door, followed by "Tins, it's me."

A balloon expands in my chest.

Fuck you, Aiden, for being a cheating asshole!

"Hold on!" I shout to my sister as I'm kicking off the covers.

I crack open my bedroom door. She's standing there, wearing a pair of old pajamas. They're sagging off her body. Have I been so preoccupied I didn't notice she's lost weight? Probably from stressing over him? Which could mean she already knows. My mother always says women have a sixth sense about these kinds of things.

"Hey," she says. "Just wanted to make sure you're okay before Lindsey and I left. Mama has convinced herself you're going to need AA before you turn eighteen."

I manage to cough up a laugh.

"What's wrong, Tins?" she says. "That constipated look you've had since Saturday is extra strained right now."

"Where's Lindsey?" I ask her.

"Downstairs with Mama." She briefly looks down at her intertwined fingers, then back up at me. "Aiden had another late night at the office and Lindsey fell asleep here watching *Frozen 2* last night, so we stayed. Didn't feel like lugging her across town to an empty house."

I can tell she's struggling to maintain her counterfeit smile.

"Come in," I say. "And close the door."

Rachel joins me on the bed. My hands are trembling as I pick up my phone. My sister watches me, her face clouded with confusion.

"What's going on?" There's a note of impatience in her voice.

"Here."

I hand her my phone with the picture of Aiden's indiscretion pulled up on the screen.

At first, I think I might have accidentally scrolled to the next photo in my album due to her stoic look. I nibble on the end of my thumbnail as I watch her, waiting for her eyes to bulge or her nostrils to flare the way they do whenever she's upset. But her expression never changes.

I'm literally not breathing when she hands me back my phone.

"Where was that?" she asks.

Her tone is even. Her eyes are steady.

"At Jitterbug's," I say.

"He's going out in public with her now. Great."

"I don't know, I mean, I was one of the only people there. I was . . . driving by— Wait. Do you know her?"

She seems more bothered that I know than outraged that her husband is having an affair in the first place. What the fuck?

Rachel shuts her eyes and nods. "She's a cocktail waitress at one of the casinos. I found out about the affair Fourth of July weekend, in the most clichéd way ever. I noticed some charges on our credit card bill—flowers, a motel room, and jewelry. So I followed him one night and, well . . . yeah."

Did she just say Fourth of July?

"You've known for *months*?" I shriek. "Why haven't you said anything? Why haven't you filed for divorce?"

She looks down at her lap, then up at me. "At first I was going to, but then . . ."

"Then what?" I press.

Rachel sighs. "Mama talked me out of it."

Wait. Our *mother* knows too? And she told her *not* to leave Aiden? That can't be right. That woman is the queen of pettiness. She had one of her friends blacklisted from a charity ball just for forgetting to include her name on the donor list. It doesn't make sense.

"Why would she do that?" I say.

"She says that's what men do, especially men with means and social status, like Aiden and Daddy."

Hearing her bring up our father stirs up a faint rippling in my gut. *Daddy didn't cheat, Aiden did!* "Why are you bringing Daddy into this?" I say.

"This is why I've always envied you," Rachel says. "They shield you from anything real. Allow you to live in your romanticized bubble of what you think our life is because you're the youngest."

"That—that's not true," I protest, shaking my head.

Why is she getting so defensive? I'm already regretting this conversation. I should have known she wouldn't want to hear this from me.

"Then why do you look so surprised to hear that Daddy has carried on with other women too?"

My stomach knots. "Wom*en*? There've been multiple?"

Rachel purses her lips. She's acting like I shouldn't be

shocked that she's basically calling our father a fuckboy and our mother an enabler.

"Mama would never put up with that," I say. "She's so overbearing. And Daddy sometimes comes off as a little hen-pecked."

"He doesn't fight because he doesn't have to," she says matter-of-factly. "What's Mama going to do? Leave him? That prenup Grandma made her sign is airtight. She wouldn't get a dime. And you know she'd rather die than go back to being poor."

"But you're not her," I say. "You're a McArthur by blood. You have your own money, and that business degree you never use. You'll be all right if you leave Aiden. Don't you have an infidelity clause in your prenup that forces him to pay you spousal support if he cheats?"

Rachel runs her hand through her black tresses. It dawns on me: Did she dye her hair the same color as Aiden's mistress's, thinking that it would somehow make him stop hooking up with her? Given the time line, it makes sense.

"Aiden's family lawyers made sure to strike that from our agreement. Mama got them to keep a clause granting me financial support if he gets another woman pregnant, though."

"You still don't have to stay in a loveless marriage, Rachel. What kind of life is that?"

One that mirrors our parents'? She can't want that. Rachel is always criticizing how we've grown up. She constantly mocks the Southern aristocratic traditions we were taught to embrace. I don't even know who she is right now.

"Who said it was loveless?" she says.

I roll my eyes.

"Mama says nearly all her friends' husbands have had affairs. It's no reason to leave my marriage when he's giving me security in so many other areas."

"Yeah, let's ignore the women's movement like we do every other progressive thought here below the Mason-Dixon Line."

It's like I've woken up in some alternate reality. Now Rachel is the one regurgitating our mother's convictions and *I'm* the one seeing the fault in her thinking.

"Look, Tins, I don't really care, okay?" Rachel says, throwing her hands up.

I'm not gonna let her do that. It's time we break the cycle.

"I don't believe you," I argue.

"He's a good father, a good provider. Mama said you don't leave your husband because of infidelity. You *manage* it."

I stand up from my bed and I'm hit by a wave of dizziness, so I drop back down and gently place my hands on her forearms. "You are worth so much more than that," I tell her. "You deserve more than that."

Rachel pulls away from me. "Tins, you have enough to worry about right now. Don't worry about my marriage. I know what I'm doing."

"But—"

"And if you mention a word of this to Lindsey, I will kill you," she adds. I watch, stunned, as she gets up and walks to the door. She pauses after grabbing the doorknob and says, "I love you for wanting to tell me. And I love you even more for wanting better for me." She opens the door but pauses again in the doorway. "I'll think about what you said, I promise."

"Wait," I say.

She pauses. "What?"

I may be the only one thinking clearly when it comes to her marriage, but there is something I'm struggling with too. And she's the only person in this house I trust to discuss it with. My stomach is doing cartwheels.

"Do you think I'm racist?" I ask.

"What?" Rachel shuts the door and returns to the same spot on my bed. "Where is that coming from?"

I tell her all the things Evelyn's friends dumped on me last night, how Duchess railed on me at Jitterbug's, and about my run-in with those three girls in the parking lot. And how, after tossing and turning over it all night, I'm starting to feel guilty for some of the things I've said and done, including how I immediately categorized those girls as threats just because they were angry (rightfully so) at me for what I said about Nova.

"I feel like shit for not knowing all the ways my actions could have fed the struggles that Duchess and her friends have gone through," I say. "If only I—"

"Stop," Rachel interrupts. "Don't do that."

"Do what?"

"Cast yourself as the victim or martyr for being ignorant when it comes to systemic racism." Rachel tucks one of her legs underneath her butt as the frustration that outlined her face a minute ago rearranges into serenity. "That won't do anything but piss Duchess off more."

"Then what am I supposed to do?" I say with a shrug.

"Learn. Listen." Rachel leans in, giving me an endearing smile after softly grabbing my wrists. "Don't make your guilt the emotional baggage of others to deal with. It's not their job to hold our hands and make us feel better. Do what I did in college: read books about this stuff, and there are a lot of them. I can give you some recommendations."

I start twiddling my thumbs. "I want to be a better person."

"You can." Rachel squeezes my hand. "You have to work at it, though."

By the time she leaves my room, I feel gutted. My mind spins as it continues to process everything Rachel dumped on me.

Taking a shower doesn't wash away the consternation that has seeped into every pore of my body. The 11" × 17" envelope Ms. Latham dropped off yesterday catches my eye as I'm tying my robe on my way out of the bathroom. I snatch it off my desk, desperate for a distraction, and settle back on my unmade bed, where I dump out the envelope's contents.

The squad's fundraising suggestions are nothing I didn't expect. They basically pitched a lot of stuff we've done before.

Car wash.

Bake sale.

Kissing booth—*disgusting.*

Raffle.

Guess How Many Years Tinsley Will Be Sentenced for Murder. That one was submitted by Lana.

Bitch.

The next list of suggestions chills my blood. I sit up straighter in bed and grab my phone. I pull up my photos and hold the handwritten note next to the picture on my screen. My breath catches in my throat. The slanted handwriting is exactly the same.

I know who threatened Nova.

I charge out of my room.

Please, God, let Rachel still be here!

The entire squad is watching me as I approach. They're in the middle of their pyramid formation on the grassy swathe of land near the back of Beachfront Park. They're practicing here since campus is still shut down.

Don't do it! Or I'll make you regret it!

What could have made Jessica Thambley write that to Nova? Crashing practice seems like a logical way to find out.

"Coach, wasn't it decided that *she* wouldn't be cheering with us tonight?" Lana shouts at Ms. Latham, who's sitting on a concrete bench beneath the shade of an oak tree nearby.

I haven't received any official correspondence from the student council that they've issued a vote of no confidence against me. That's likely because they haven't been able to meet since campus has been shut down these past two days. So I'm still dangling by a thread from all my student leadership positions.

"Relax, Judas, I'm here strictly in a supervisory status," I say. "I mean, I *am* still the captain. It's only right that I'm here to make sure you don't look like complete trash tonight."

I lower my chin to cast an inquisitive glance back at Ms. Latham over the rim of my sunglasses.

"Girls, it's fine." She looks back down at the phone she's cradling with both hands. "Run through the pyramid again. We need to get that tight for tonight. There'll be a lot of eyes on us."

I study Jessica's face from behind my sunglasses. Looking for any change in emotion at the mention of Nova's name. But her ethereal features give nothing away.

The squad scrambles into the formation again. I drop to

the ground and cross my legs, pretending to supervise like I said I would. Several little girls who were swinging on the play-ground equipment across the way from us stop and watch the squad too.

Watching Jessica's barely one-hundred-pound body being tossed back and forth in the sky, I'm baffled. It's hard to believe she had enough strength to deliver a fatal blow. If the police are right, and Nova's scepter was the murder weapon, how did Jes-sica get it? And how could she get the best of Nova, who was at least a foot taller than her?

The skepticism creeping into my thoughts won't over-shadow what I know for sure: Jessica definitely wrote that note. The handwriting matches perfectly.

On my way here, I went over every interaction I could re-member between Nova and Jessica before last Friday. The only thing standing out is the death stare Nova gave Jessica right before she and I got into our fight.

Is that true? Nova had said to her after I implied that the girls on the squad were gossiping about Nova and her uncle. Some of the color had drained from Jessica's face. Nova definitely knew something Jessica was embarrassed about.

Jessica throws her skinny arms in the air, forming a Y, after she gets hoisted to the top of their pyramid for the finishing move. Doubt flickers in the back of my mind again. Even if Jessica had enough strength to knock Nova over the head and kill her, I can't see her being strong enough to cart Nova's body over to the slave cemetery to make it look like I did it. She would definitely need an accomplice to pull that off.

"Girls, that looked flawless! What do you think, Tinsley?"

Ms. Latham is standing over me. The squad has already

dismounted from their pyramid to a round of applause from the little girls watching from the playground.

"Yeah, it looked great." I stand up, dusting off the back of my tights. "Glad we got that knocked out ahead of nationals."

The girls gather in front of me and Ms. Latham, who barks out orders about what time she wants them on campus and in uniform for tonight's game. As soon as she dismisses them, I make a beeline for Jessica. Confrontations haven't worked well so far, so I'm taking a different approach with her.

I remove my sunglasses as I approach the cluster of girls who retreated to a nearby picnic table.

"It shouldn't be much longer before things go back to normal," I say. The girls all turn to me. "The case should be closed soon and my name cleared."

The shade from the nearby tree is needed relief from the heat and humidity that already has my hoodie sticking to my back. I'd take it off if wearing it wasn't serving a purpose.

"I'm kind of liking this new normal. What about the rest of y'all?" Lana takes a swig from her bottled water, her eyes locked on me the entire time.

Giselle and some of the other girls nervously look away. Jessica is pulling out the rubber band that was holding her thick blond hair in a ponytail. She uses her hand to fluff out her hair, unconcerned with what's going on around her.

"Anyway," I say, "I heard from the police today. They found a note in Nova's locker from someone who threatened to kill her." That stops Jessica cold. "Duchess Simmons's father says they have a good idea who wrote it and could make an arrest before tonight's game."

Jessica turns her back to the rest of the group. Her shoulders slump as she bends over to zip up her duffel bag, which was on the bench connected to the picnic table.

"Yay," Lana drawls, rolling her eyes. "Well, I'll see the rest of you ladies later tonight. I need to skedaddle to pick up my dress for the dance. Nathan helped me pick it out."

Lana doesn't get the jealous reaction from me she probably hoped she would. Given how much they're on Instagram lately, I assumed they were going to the dance together. Besides, I'm solely focused on Jessica, who has snatched up her duffel and is speed-walking to the parking lot.

Trying to catch up with her, I nearly walk into a couple jogging the park's winding trail.

Jessica is parked three spaces down from me. By the time I make it to the edge of the parking lot, she's already in her car. But from the looks of it, she's sitting in the driver's seat, frantically talking on her phone. I eye the police car on the other side of the lot. I need to ditch it if I'm going to carry out my plan.

I make sure Jessica isn't about to pull out of the lot before hopping in my car. Rachel pops up from where she was hiding in the backseat as soon as I shut the driver's-side door. I left the doors open for her to sneak in once she arrived five minutes after I got here.

"Did she take the bait?" she asks.

"Yes! Where did you park?" I start pulling my hoodie over my head.

"Two spaces to the right," she replies. "Your shadow didn't see me."

"Good."

It takes less than a minute for Rachel to put on my hoodie. She moves into the driver's seat while I inconspicuously crawl out on the passenger side. I remain crouched between my car and the Ford Explorer parked next to it, out of sight from the officer following me today.

Rachel tucks as much of her hair as she can into the hood. Still squatting beside the Ford Explorer, I watch as the squad car follows Rachel when she drives my car out of the parking lot. Once they're both gone, I stand up and shoot over to Rachel's car. She left the keys in the ignition.

Jessica is turning onto Beachfront Boulevard by the time I'm backing out. I maintain at least a two-car-length distance as I follow her. We drive for another ten minutes, past the hotel casinos, the country club, and the beach. Apparently, she's not going home—she lives in Plantation Hills, like me. She turns onto Prescott Boulevard, a four-lane highway where most of Lovett's newer construction and businesses are located. It's lined on one side with multifamily housing built up within the last seven years. And on my left are countless strip malls anchored by big-box stores like Walmart and Target. This part of town is mostly populated by young singles, college students, and newlyweds not ready to move into starter homes before having kids.

Jessica slows down as we near a cluster of townhomes. She parallel parks in front of a white-and-canary-yellow one.

"Where is she going?" I say to myself.

I keep driving, then turn right at the next corner and park near a stop sign a few blocks down from where Jessica parked. From where I am, I see her get out of her car and start walking in my direction.

I drop down, stretching my body across the center console so she can't see me as she struts past. My heart is pounding in my ears.

She crosses the street toward another cluster of townhomes on the block behind us. I wait until she's completely out of sight before I get out of Rachel's car. I speed-walk down the street but hang back enough so that she doesn't see me. Jessica pauses in front of a beige-and-sky-blue townhome. I quickly dodge behind a tree before she glances up and down the sidewalk. What if she knows she's being followed?

I wait until she disappears around the side of the townhome before I dash after her.

"What are you doing here?"

I stop abruptly and spin around. Duchess is pulling off her hood as she approaches from across the street.

"Are you following me?" I huff.

"Nah." She glances past my shoulder in the direction Jessica went. "Looks like I might be on the right track, though."

"Why are you here?"

Duchess folds her arms across her chest. "You first."

I groan. "I don't have time for this. I need to—"

"Keep following Vanilla Barbie? What's up with that?"

I cast an anxious look at the townhome over my shoulder, eyeing the spot where Jessica disappeared around the side. "I really don't have time to walk you through it right now," I say.

"Either you tell me, or I can call my Pops and ask if they know you somehow ditched the officer assigned to follow you." She pulls out her phone with a raised brow.

Why is this girl so infuriating?

"All right!" I yell, throwing up my hands. "There's something I didn't tell you. It's what the police found in Nova's locker earlier this week."

"The threat?" she interjects.

My eyes stretch wider. "Yeah," I say. Then add, "I thought you didn't know about that."

"I didn't until this morning. What did it say?"

"'Don't do it! Or I'll make you regret it!'" I answer after a beat.

Duchess's eyes go wide.

"I didn't mention it—"

"'Cause you knew I'd accuse you of writing it," she says, "thinking it was about the elections."

"Well, Jessica wrote it."

Her eyes narrow. "Vanilla Barbie? Why?"

"That's what you're interrupting me from finding out," I reply, irritated but relieved that she believes me. "I think whatever secret Nova knew about her, she came here to do damage control."

"To Mr. Haywood's house?"

I glance back at the townhome. "Our art teacher?"

"It's why *I'm* here."

Duchess tells me about her conversation downtown with Mr. Haywood. And how his knowledge of the note and line of questioning about it set off all kinds of alarms for her, rightfully so. How does he know about it?

"I found out where he lives and was sitting in my car contemplating how I was going to knock on his door and prod him some more about it," she explains. "That's when I saw Jessica, and then you roll up."

"But why is she here? And how did he . . ."

My words trail off as we lock eyes, and we both realize the same thing at once. We take off running around the side of Mr. Haywood's townhome.

All the windows are curtained, which sucks. We can't look inside. But it also means that Jessica and Mr. Haywood can't see us out here either.

A wave of relief hits me when we round the back corner. There's a patio and, more importantly, a sliding glass door that has the Venetian blinds pulled up. I crouch, gesturing for Duchess to follow me, and carefully head toward it. Slowly, I stand when we reach the sliding door. Duchess remains crouched, stepping in front of me so she can crane her neck and see inside as well. I'm reminded of when we were little girls, sneaking around like this at the country club on make-believe spy missions.

We have a clear sight line into what looks like a dining room with a connected kitchen. In the distance, a living room can be seen through an elaborate archway. The townhome is moderately decorated in lots of beige and browns.

"You see her?" Duchess asks. "'Cause I don't see anybody."

"Maybe she's upstairs," I whisper.

A stick breaks somewhere in the backyard and my heart slams into my throat.

Duchess and I both turn at the same time in the direction of the noise. A squirrel standing up on its hind legs tilts its tiny head at us, then scurries up a tree. I press my hand to my chest. My heart feels like it's literally about to burst.

The silence is interrupted by the sound of muffled shouting, and it's definitely *not* a squirrel this time. It's coming from inside. I can't make out what they're saying, though. I stretch up on my tiptoes to get a better look inside, and Jessica suddenly pops into view descending the staircase that divides the living room from the dining area.

Duchess pulls back, pressing herself into my legs as she tries to stay hidden. I still can't hear what's being said, but I can see Jessica, who's waving her arms as she talks.

"You see him yet?" Duchess whispers.

My breath catches as Mr. Haywood steps off the staircase.

He gently cradles Jessica's face with his hands, and then he kisses her.

CHAPTER TWENTY-FIVE

DUCHESS

JESSICA STOPS DEAD in her tracks the second she sees Tinsley and me leaning against her car.

I'm perched against the driver's side, arms folded across my chest. Tinsley is on the other side, propped against the passenger door. Even from twenty feet away, I see the dread shadowing Vanilla Barbie's perfect face as she reluctantly approaches us. She's trying to come up with a story to explain why she's on this side of town, which I'm guessing Nova would know all about.

"Hey, Jess!" Tinsley says with a cocky grin. "Enjoy your after-school *art lesson*?"

"Whatever y'all *think* you know—" she starts, but before Jessica can finish her sentence, Tinsley holds up her phone, showing the picture she snapped of Jessica and Mr. Haywood kissing through his sliding door. The blood drains from her face.

"Did you follow me?" Jessica says, now standing at the front bumper of her car.

I shake my head. "No. We're the ones who'll be asking the questions here," I say.

"Like, how did Nova find out about you and Mr. Haywood?" Tinsley says, making Jessica's doe eyes widen. "That's why you threatened her, right? Because you were scared she'd tell someone about your dirty little secret? And you weren't even brave enough to deliver your threat face to face. You snuck it into her locker."

Jessica turns to me, her brow furrowed. "Is it even true that your father knows I wrote that note?"

"Not yet," I say. "But once we tell him, he'll definitely understand why you and Mr. Haywood killed her."

"We did *not* kill her!" she says, holding up her hands, her gaze darting back and forth between Tinsley and me.

"Your note literally said, 'Don't do it! Or I'll make you regret it!'" Tinsley's neck jerks forward as she enunciates each word in Jessica's threat. "How else would you make that happen—her *regretting* it?"

"'Cause it's looking a lot like it means y'all killed her," I say, shrugging and pursing my lips.

My mind is still spinning, trying to digest all this. Vanilla Barbie never would have crossed my mind as a suspect.

"Y'all don't know what you're talking about!" she shrieks.

"Then help us understand," I say.

Jessica wrinkles her nose at me.

We stand in silence for a few moments before I drop my

arms. "Tinsley, fuck this," I say, holding eye contact with Jessica. "Let's just call my Pops. He'll get this THOT to talk."

"Fine!" she yells, then looks up and down the busy street, as though to make sure no one can hear her, and says, "Can we get in my car first? Then I'll tell you everything."

I look across the hood of the car at Tinsley. She waits a beat before nodding assent.

The whizzing sound of the traffic zipping down Prescott Boulevard lessens to a rhythmic hum once we're in her car with the doors closed. I scoot into the middle of the backseat and lean forward through the gap.

"Nova caught us in his class one day after school—the day the election results were announced, actually," Jessica begins, her voice trembling. "She didn't say anything until the next morning. She cornered me in the bathroom, before first period. Said she had gone to Aaron's class after dance practice that day to ask for a letter of recommendation to apply to some fashion design school. She saw us, you know, through the small window in the classroom door."

I've never heard Mr. Haywood's first name, so it takes a second for it to register whose class she's referring to.

"'Aaron'?" I repeat. "Y'all on a first-name basis? But then, I guess you are. Yeah, you a full-on THOT."

Tears well up in Jessica's eyes. "Tinsley, please, please don't use this against me," she says. "He could lose his job. Go to jail. Oh God, he's going to kill me now that y'all know."

"Like he killed Nova?" Tinsley prods.

Jessica's hands fall from her face to her lap. "He didn't kill her. He didn't!"

"Gurl," I drawl. "Stop capping."

Wanting to avoid the career-ending scandal and prison time their affair would mean is a strong enough motive for Mr. Haywood. And they had ample opportunity to commit the murder. They were both at the coronation reception. Either one of them could have slipped away that night and followed Nova into that storage room, and then gone back later to move the body.

"Then why threaten her?" Tinsley asks.

Jessica presses her thin pink lips into a tight line. She looks out the window, her hands fidgeting in her lap.

"He didn't even know I wrote that note. He was so mad when he found out." She sniffs, choking a little on her tears. "Even though you told him the police don't know who wrote it, he's being so paranoid. Called me stupid for doing it. As if I was supposed to know that Nova would turn up dead before she ever read it."

"So you *did* slip it into her locker?" Tinsley says.

Jessica nods. "After cheerleading practice last Friday, before the coronation."

"Why threaten her with 'I'll make you regret it'?" Tinsley beats me asking. "What did that mean? Did you have something on her too?"

"No." Jessica uses her hand to brush away the tears that have dribbled down her cheeks. "It was an empty threat. I just reacted after she confronted me, acting all self-righteous. We'd hardly ever said anything to each other before that day, but all of a sudden she was pretending like she cared so much about my well-being. Kept saying she'd be obligated to go to Mrs. Barnett if I didn't stop sleeping with him. Like, who is she to judge me?"

Tinsley's eyes shift to mine. We're both thinking the same

thing: Nova linked her childhood sexual abuse with Jessica's inappropriate affair with our teacher. After what she went through as a little girl, I can see her not being able to let another older man abuse his authority with a younger girl, even if what they're doing is consensual. Though no one will ever convince me that these types of relationships are consensual.

"Aaron says I should have come to him after Nova confronted me," Jessica continues. "But I didn't want him to freak out and end things. I thought I could, I don't know, scare her into keeping quiet."

"You gonna have to come harder than this if you expect us to believe anything you just said proves y'all didn't kill her," I say. "I'm honestly not convinced you didn't tell *Aaron* that Nova knew, given all he stands to lose once it gets out he's been sleeping with one of his students. If that ain't motivation to kill her and then try and frame Tinsley to make sure it doesn't link back to y'all, I don't know what is."

Tinsley nods. "And we know y'all had the opportunity to do it. So let me guess. When you saw Nova sneak off to the storage room, Mr. Haywood followed her and killed her. And then once everyone was gone and the reception was over, you both went back and dumped her body at that slave cemetery since my video was already going viral by then."

"That's not what happened at all! We . . . I . . . ." Jessica has this pained look on her face. Her hands are shaking, and her eyes are darting everywhere. What could she possibly be conflicted about saying?

"Are you saying you lied to the police, then?" Tinsley pulls out her phone, swiping to a picture it looks like she took inside the police station. She pinches the screen with her fingers to zoom in on something in the picture. "We know you told the police you were at the gym cleaning up at least until ten or ten-thirty."

"I lied, all right!" Jessica screams, slamming the steering wheel with her hands. "We left way before that. I didn't stay behind that whole time to clean up. Aa—he and I went to a motel afterward. Grady's Inn."

Tinsley scrunches her nose. "Eww! That place is a dump."

"A dump on the other side of town that hardly anyone we know would be caught dead at." Jessica sniffs back more tears. Her hands are trembling in her lap. "We were there *all* night. I lied and told my parents I was staying with Kimberly Weathers."

"And you expect us to just believe that?" I ask.

"Why would I lie when y'all are threatening to tell the police we killed her?" Neither Tinsley nor I respond to her desperate look. "Call the motel if you don't believe me. He always checks in under the name Keith Haring."

"That artist we learned about who died of AIDS?" Tinsley asks, surprise creasing her face.

I pull out my phone. Jessica and Tinsley's heads whip around to the backseat when I start typing *Grady's Inn* in my Google search window. When it appears in the results, I tap the number and hit call.

"What are you doing?" Jessica asks, urgency in her voice.

"Calling and checking," I reply with a nonchalant shrug.

"What are you going to say?" Tinsley asks.

I press my index finger to my lips, asking for her silence and put the phone on speaker.

"Grady's," answers a male voice that sounds like glass scraping against concrete.

"Hi, sorry to bother you, sir, but I need a huge favor," I say, enunciating every syllable and speaking with a higher inflection to make it harder for him to tell I'm Black. "I was there a week ago with my . . . gentleman friend. And I think I left my favorite pair of earrings behind in the room. Please tell me you found them."

"Depends," the man says. "What room y'all was in?"

"I can't remember, I had a little too much to drink that night," I say. "But the reservation was under the name Keith Haring."

We hear papers rustling and mumbling on the other end of the line. "Ah, Room Two Fifteen," the man says seconds later. "Checked in around nine-forty-five that night. But I thought I remember that young guy telling me he was staying the night with his little sister, not his girlfriend. You the little pretty blond girl that was waiting in the car, huh? You looked way too young to be—"

I hang up. He's told me all I need to know.

Jessica tosses her hair back, rolling her eyes at us. "Told ya," she says.

"You're not completely out of the woods, sweetie," Tinsley retorts. "How do we know y'all didn't just register there to have an alibi?"

"In case of what, Tinsley?" Jessica snaps. "If we were really suspected of killing her, why would we want to pretend to be together at a seedy motel? You know, since y'all were eager to remind me that he'd go to jail."

She has a point.

"Tins, please, please don't tell anyone. I'm begging you." Jessica gently places her hand on Tinsley's knee. "I'll do anything you want. I swear, we had nothing to do with Nova's death. But please don't out me. I can't lose Aaron. I love him, and he loves me."

Ugh.

"We aren't hurting anyone by being together," she goes on. "I never should have written that note, but I was desperate. He . . . he means too much to me."

Tinsley flicks Jessica's hand off her knee. "Yeah, yeah, yeah, fine," she says. "We believe you."

Wait. I jerk forward. "We do?"

Tinsley shoots me a serious look and nods and I sit back while Jessica makes Tinsley promise not to go to Mrs. Barnett or the police at least three more times.

"Let me find out you lied to us about anything, just know it'll be my Pops you're talking to instead of us," I say before getting out of the car.

Tinsley and I both slam our doors shut and we watch Jessica peel off down Prescott Boulevard.

"Real talk," I say. "I don't know if I'ma be able to keep that shit to myself. It ain't right."

"Yeah, me either," Tinsley says.

"But you promised her—"

"I promised I wouldn't tell the cops or Mrs. Barnett," Tinsley says with a sly smile.

I mirror it back to her.

We walk in silence until we stop next to a white Tesla SUV.

"You really believe her? Her alibi?" I say as she walks around to the driver's side.

My mind doesn't want to let go of the possibility they could have killed Nova. Maybe because we don't have any other leads to follow now.

Tinsley shrugs. "I think so. Not one hundred percent, though. Think you could put a bug in your dad's ear to check it out further without letting on how we know about the note?"

I think about it. "Maybe."

Tinsley lets out a big breath. "My God. Nova found out she was pregnant, was being pressured by her boyfriend to have an abortion, was trying to out a teacher/student affair, and she was dealing with her depraved uncle getting out of jail all in the same week. But you'd never know it from her demeanor."

"Black women been doing that for years." I pull my hood back over my head. "We smile through all the bullshit this world puts us through to be strong for everyone else."

"I'd be a fucking mess."

"Yeah, we know," I reply, then take off across the street to my car. Leaving Tinsley behind with a grimace I'm sure she wore all the way home.

CHAPTER TWENTY-SIX

TINSLEY

OCTOBER 22
11:15 A.M.

RACHEL KNOCKS ON my bedroom door and opens it before I can respond.

I'm nestled in the recliner with my laptop balanced on the armrest. I'm reading an article published in this morning's paper. The headline: *The Girl Who Couldn't Be Queen.* While I spent this week running around town like Nancy Drew, a reporter from the *Lovett Bugle* was interviewing the victims of my past machinations. He used all the deceitful things I've done to them to build an argument around my possible guilt. He even got quotes from the president of the NAACP, who spouted off a lot of the same things Duchess and her friends said about how my privilege and my family's wealth are protecting me from being charged.

"Can I ask you something?" Rachel stops in the center of my room.

She and Lindsey spent the night here again last night. All three of us stayed up late eating junk food and watching movies.

"I'm reading it now," I say dryly, never taking my eyes off my computer screen. "I'm not fragile. I don't care what these people say or write about me anymore."

Maybe if I keep saying that out loud it'll become true.

"Huh?" Rachel cocks her head with a frown. "Oh, that. Yeah, I saw it. But that's not why I'm here. I . . . I need a favor."

I close my laptop. "Cashing in already for helping me yesterday?"

"Something like that." Rachel's eyes bounce around the room. "Will you come with me to the country club? I'm meeting with a divorce attorney for lunch."

I sit up straighter. *Did I really hear her say "divorce attorney"?* "Are you serious?" I say.

"Shhhhhh, not so loud. I don't want Mama to know yet. I'm not one hundred percent sure I want to leave him, but I want to . . . I *need to* see what my options are."

"Yeah, sure." I stand up. "*That* I'd love to do."

I really hadn't planned on doing anything today. With no more threads to pull that could clear me of suspicion, I'm out of options and therefore have no reason to leave this room.

I don't know what happened within the last thirty-six hours to change my sister's mind, and I don't care. I'd like to think that what I said to her yesterday worked. A small victory I needed. If she's going to leave that lying piece of shit, I'm all for it. It's time we both stop living in our parents' shadows. Chart our own destinies. I don't know yet what mine will be if I can ever get out from under this cloud of suspicion, but I know the life I used to have, the things I thought were important to me, just aren't anymore.

Rachel lies to my mother, who agrees to babysit Lindsey while we're gone. I barrel out the door behind my sister before my mom has a chance to bring up the news article.

The hostess who greets Rachel and me as we enter the restaurant at the center of the country club's expansive waterfront property does a double take at the sight of me. I adjust the oversize sunglasses I'm wearing, as if pushing them higher on my nose will hide more of my face.

"Table for three, please," Rachel tells her. "We're meeting someone."

The restaurant is moderately full, which isn't unusual since it's Saturday. Today's the day most members use the club's amenities, like the golf course, the tennis courts, and the spa. Saturdays were usually the day I came here with my parents. Lana and Giselle would often come with theirs, and we'd hang together while our dads played golf and our mothers "played tennis," which meant day drinking in the bar. The room is drenched in the sunlight pouring through the floor-to-ceiling windows that make up the restaurant's back wall and offer a panoramic view of the Gulf.

I turn away from it. The sky's vibrant color reminds me of Nova's eyes.

The white linen tablecloths and napkins, glistening table settings, muted earth tones, wood finishes, and jazzy instrumental music momentarily lull me into a sense of comfortableness I haven't felt in days. But the sideways glances we're already getting from the people seated at tables near the hostess station yank me back into my new reality.

"One moment. Let me see what we have available, Mrs. Prescott." The hostess casts another awkward glance in my direction before she scurries off.

"They're not serving breakfast anymore?" I ask.

Rachel looks up from her phone. "What are you talking about?"

I point to the sign on the hostess stand that says BREAKFAST NOT SERVED UNTIL FURTHER NOTICE.

"Oh yeah. Started last week. One of the chefs got fired." Rachel looks back down at her phone. "Aiden came home bitching about it right in the middle of me trying to get in touch with you after seeing the news about Nova."

Something about Rachel's explanation doesn't connect for me. But I don't get the chance to sort out why before the woman reappears and gestures for us to follow her.

As we're zigzagging around the tables, I spot Jessica Thambley's mother and father seated at a two-top in the back. Both unaware of the scandal their daughter is involved in. I'll need to change that somehow. Just not today.

The lawyer Rachel is meeting arrives about ten minutes after we're seated. She's a dark-haired woman named Allie Sullivan who is apparently a sorority sister. Allie dresses like she stepped out of a fashion magazine. I'm already impressed. As we order food, she and Rachel make small talk, which is mostly gossip about which sorority sisters they think post the most lies about their lives on social media.

"Please tell me you're talking my sister into leaving her fuckboy husband and somehow will make him pay for it," I say after our server places a bread basket on the table.

Allie chuckles and says, "If she wants, I'll damn sure try.

Her prenup is pretty airtight, but there are some workarounds we could use against him. Rachel tells me you have something for me."

"You're talking about the picture I took of him and the slut?"

"I like her, Rach," Allie says, shooting my sister an amused smile.

"You don't happen to practice criminal law, do you?" I say as I pull out my phone. "If you haven't heard, I may need a good lawyer soon too."

"Tins, that's not funny," Rachel says.

I pull up the photo and hand Allie my phone.

She studies it with a raised brow for a few moments, then says, "Email me that. Receipts are everything."

"You got it," I say.

I frantically type as Allie tells me her email address. I've always found that photos are the best tools for blackmail. Thank God for smartphones.

"You'll need to be prepared for a fight, Rach," Allie says. "Aiden's family is just as wealthy and influential as yours. He might push back . . . and hard."

My sister's eyes lock with mine. I give her a reassuring smile. I want her to know she can do this, and I'll be right here to support her.

"You know he'll want to save face any way he can," Allie continues. "Which means he could get personal if you try to paint him in a negative light."

I swipe right on the picture of Aiden and his mistress, and the photo I took at the police station appears. While Rachel expresses her concerns for my niece and how a nasty divorce might impact her, I study the photo again.

I zoom in on the picture. I've focused so much on Jessica's note, I haven't really looked closely at the rest of the image. Toward the bottom of the picture, Trenton's name grabs my attention. I scan down, and underneath that are the names of the girls from the squad who I know volunteered to work the reception. I pull the picture down, and above the list of names are the words *Students principal says stayed behind to.* Then the photo ends. I'm guessing the rest of that sentence is *clean up after reception.*

But why is Trenton's name listed? He told me he left the reception not long after Duchess did.

CHAPTER TWENTY-SEVEN

DUCHESS

OCTOBER 22
12:53 P.M.

BU-DONK-PAT!

Another brick. I run and scoop up my basketball before it rolls down our driveway and into the street. I haven't made a single basket since I've come out here to toss the ball at the portable basketball hoop in front of our house. I'm so rusty that if Pops and I play our weekly one-on-one game tomorrow, he'll pull off a rare win against me. He's still barely talking to me, though, so tomorrow will probably make two Sundays in a row with us not having our daddy-daughter game. The back of my throat starts aching at the thought of it.

I stop dribbling, popping the ball against my hip as I look down the street, which is lined along its entirety with single-family brick homes fronted with modest yards like ours. Pops didn't come to Nova's memorial at last night's game. He was asleep in his home office when I got back, snoring with his head down on his desk and paperwork from Nova's criminal file strewn on top of it. I'm guessing he has reached a dead end in his investigation of Nova's murder, just like me and Tinsley. I'm starting to think he might be avoiding me because he doesn't want to let me down by not uncovering Nova's killer.

Stuff you'd have to promise you wouldn't tell anyone else.

Nova's words have been echoing inside my head all morning. That's why I'm too distracted to concentrate on making a shot. *What was she talking about?* I keep wondering.

I snap out of my thoughts when Briana's silver Kia sedan whips into our driveway, jerking to a stop a few inches in front of me.

"You play too much," I say, bending down to roll my basketball toward our house.

I've been out here tossing hoops since Ev gave me the heads-up they were passing through before their drive to Jackson. Ev showed up at the game last night even though I had been ignoring her texts all day. Neither of us apologized or really talked about why we're annoyed with one another. And for now, I'm fine with us acting like nothing happened. I got too much other shit on my mind.

Ev steps out of Briana's car on the passenger side. She's in a pair of cutoff jean shorts and a white V-neck T-shirt. She walks up and kisses me, letting go as Briana, Chance, and Nikki climb out of the car.

"Make sure y'all look out for each other while y'all protesting," I say, squeezing Ev's hand. "Try not to get arrested. Heard on the news they locked up more than a dozen folks last night."

"You sure you don't wanna come with?" Nikki cups her

hand over her brow to shield her eyes from the glaring sunlight and holds up a red bandana. "You can tie one of these over your mouth to hide your face. Chance brought 'em in case they tear-gas us."

As much as I would love to go to Jackson and join the growing protest over Curtis Delmont's arrest, I'm not about to add to Pops's stress. If the chief or any of the other police officers found out, it would cause all types of trouble for him. He got chewed out by the chief after I retweeted something Marc Lamont Hill said about defunding the police. Pops has stalked my social media accounts ever since. I've often wondered if Chief Barrow holds the kids of his white officers to the same standards.

"My girl is gonna hold it down for the both of us," I reply, pulling Ev close so I can peck her on the cheek.

"Y'all should have heard my boo last night at Nova's memorial," Ev says as we walk around to the passenger side of Briana's car arm in arm. "She had so many people in tears."

The speech I had quickly jotted down after I got home from the confrontation with Jessica was forgotten the second I stepped up to the mic. The hush that came over the crowd, the energy resonating in the stadium, and the moving tribute the band, the cheerleaders, and the dance squad had put together motivated me to speak from my heart instead. That involved telling the hundreds of people crowded in the stands that Nova's murder is a reminder of how quickly life can change. How every day isn't promised. That even the best friendships can have their secrets. That Nova's legacy isn't about inclusion. That her focused campaign to become the school's first Black homecoming queen was a sad reminder that we must twist the arms of white people just to have opportunities to be seen as someone worthy of celebrating.

"It's all Ev's been talking about," Chance says.

"Ad nauseam," Briana says, flicking her eyes toward the sky.

I don't like her tone, but I'ma let it slide.

"What you getting into while I'm gone?" Ev asks.

I prop my arm on the passenger door. "I don't know yet. Thinking 'bout checking in on Ms. Donna. She didn't come to the game last night. I'm a li'l concerned."

"That would be nice," Ev says, rubbing my forearm.

I peer inside the car. Posters and signs are stacked on the passenger seat. *Innocent until* proven *guilty—unless you're Black!* is scribbled in bold letters on the sign on top.

I rapidly blink at what I see written on the corner of the one poking out from underneath it.

"Wait a minute." I bend over to reach inside and pull it from the stack. I hold it up and read it aloud. "'If Curtis is guilty, so is Tinsley McArthur! Lock her up!' Y'all can't be serious with this."

Ev, Nikki, and Chance each look down at the ground when I turn to them. Briana lowers her chin with a pinched mouth. "It's what everyone has been saying, including you," she asserts.

"That was before," I respond, flinging the poster back on the passenger seat.

"Before what? You started hanging with yo' li'l friend again?" Briana taunts. "Drinking that champagne Kool-Aid?"

I don't know why I look over at Ev. I know better. She turns away from me. Of course she's not going to defend me. Not when Briana is being her mouthpiece right now.

"She didn't do it, so her getting charged for it is counter-productive," I retort.

Briana snorts. "See, told y'all she was gonna do this now that she buddy-buddy with that white girl."

"Do what?" I shout.

"Not a goddamn thing!" Briana snarls, her braids flailing like tentacles as she jerks her head. "But I've come to expect that with you and your father."

Ev tries to grab hold of my arm, but I yank it away. I should be yelling at her, but since Briana seems to want all the smoke, I'll give it to her. I can feel my pulse speeding up. It's already a lot having to defend Pops to people who aren't trying to understand his motivations for putting on that uniform every day but love to question his character for doing it. I'll be damned if I let my so-called friends disrespect him.

"Tinsley being arrested accomplishes nothing with regard to Nova's murder," I argue.

"Y'all, chill," Nikki pleads.

"This is about showing white people they aren't above the law," Briana says. "That we're tired of them changing the rules when it comes to us."

"And we do that by arresting innocent white people?" I counter in a sarcastic tone.

"They've done it to us for decades!"

"So this is about going tit for tat—not about fixing the system?" I snap. "I was under the impression we were fighting for equality. Marching to prevent the scales of justice from tipping one way or the other based on the prejudices of those in power."

"We are!"

"Tinsley getting arrested doesn't help do that!" I yell. "Nova deserves justice. I want whoever killed her buried underneath the jail! I'm not interested in some symbolic arrest to placate Black people by having them think the same injustices can happen to white people too."

Ev's hand gently presses into my back. I recoil from it. I pause to take a deep breath. Stop myself from getting any more worked up.

"Bri, I understand where you coming from, I do," I say. "But there are more layers to this. I want a system that works the same for everybody. Black people getting away with crimes because white people do ain't it for me. Not when there are people and families who deserve answers when it's our friends and loved ones dead. It pisses you off every time a Black mother has to watch a white police officer get a paid vacation and avoid jail time after they've killed her unarmed son. Well, Nova is that unarmed Black man for me. And Tinsley being arrested even though she didn't kill her means that whoever really did is getting a paid vacation to continue living their life free of consequences."

The ringing of my phone cuts through the silence that has swelled between us. I look down at the screen. Briana sees Tinsley's name flashing across it. She groans and slumps back in the driver's seat.

I wait until I've stepped underneath our carport to accept the call.

"What's up?"

"Hey . . . you okay?" Tinsley says. "You sound . . . I don't know. Tense."

"I'm good. Talk."

My heart is pounding from the blowup with Briana.

"What's up with Trenton? Like, is he trustworthy?" she asks.

I feel the back of my throat closing. *I can't with this!*

At the game last night, Trenton kept asking me if I was still hanging with Tinsley. I got irritated and told him I thought he didn't like her so why did he care. He claimed they came to some kind of *understanding* after he drove her to her car from The Drip. He had the same twinkle in his eyes that he used to have when he was crushing on Nova—up until she told him she only liked him as a friend. Which means now he's crushing on Tinsley. And judging by this call, it's worse than that: she must be crushing on him too. Why can't I get rid of this chick?

"Are y'all trying to kick it or something? What the hell happened between y'all Thursday night?" I say.

"Nothing," Tinsley replies. "Wait, did he say something?"

I sigh. "I ain't got time to play love connection."

"That's not why I'm calling." She lets out a big breath. "I just . . . I don't know . . . he . . . ugh!"

"Spit it out," I snap. "I'm kind of in the middle of something."

"Oh, I'm sorry. It was nothing," she says, her voice trembling. "Just forget I called. Bye."

Ev is standing behind me when I turn around. Everyone else is watching us from inside Briana's car.

"No, we ain't doing this too," I blurt just as she's opening her mouth to speak. "You don't wanna have my back—cool. We can just—"

"*Stooooopppppp,*" she interrupts, grabbing my flailing arms by the wrists. "Take a breath, calm down."

She starts lightly stroking my forearms. I look away from her and stare down the street as I try to steady my breathing. This tension between her and me over Tinsley is starting to feel like an impasse. Something we can't continue to sweep under the rug. Something that could break us up. Every muscle in my body feels sore from strife that has been bubbling up between us.

"I'm sorry," Ev says.

The apology draws my gaze back to her. Ev's chin is pointed toward the ground, but her eyes are looking up at me. They're the softest I've seen them all week.

"I'm sorry for going behind your back and telling your father about Nova's phone and that bloodstain," she continues. "I'm sorry for being petty and inviting Tinsley to The Drip just so we could be shady to her. And I'm sorry for not defending you just now. You were right."

The tension in my body starts to dissolve.

"God, I honestly hate being Black in this country sometimes," she says, throwing her head back. "Nothing is ever easy for us to process. And sometimes I feel like it never will be."

"Trust me, I know."

"I do trust you." Ev holds up my fists, giving each one a quick peck. "You're one of the only people in this world I trust besides my family. And no matter how I feel about her, I should have been trusting in you and what you believe instead of coming between you and your father, and her."

A smile tugs at the corner of my mouth. I don't think she'll ever like Tinsley. But what she's saying right now is everything I wanted to hear. Needed to hear. It's reminding me why I fell in love with her: she shows up for me when I need her most.

"This is personal for you, and I haven't respected that, bae," Ev says. "I'm supposed to be supporting you right now, not acting like the opp. I love you. And I don't want you to ever feel like I'm questioning what's important to you."

I weave my fingers with hers. "I love you too."

"You want me to stay?"

"No. Go with them. That's important too." She kisses me. "But don't let Bri talk any more shit about me."

"I won't." She gives me that flirtatious smirk that has made me weak since the day we met.

She promises to rip up the sign about Tinsley, and we kiss again before she turns and goes back to the car. I stand in the driveway, watching Briana pull out, and stay there until the car disappears down the street. The call from Tinsley prickling in the back of my mind.

CHAPTER TWENTY-EIGHT
TINSLEY

OCTOBER 22
4:40 P.M.

THE KNOTS IN my stomach keep tightening the closer I get to Trenton's house. Tonight's the homecoming dance. If Trenton is going, he'll probably be leaving soon, especially if he has a date. I mash the accelerator harder, eyeing my police shadow in the rearview mirror. I don't want to ditch him today, not while I'm doing this. Not when I'm unsure what I'm about to walk into.

Please, God, let there be some logical explanation why Trenton lied. Like he just misspoke. Not because he killed his friend.

No, Tinsley, I tell myself. *Don't think like that. Not yet.*

The driveway of the two-story Colonial-style house I pull up to is empty. I figured out where Trenton lives through a reverse search on his cell phone number, which is listed with his Facebook account. I turn off my car and climb out. If there weren't lights illuminating several of the windows, I'd think no one was home.

No matter how much I rub my hands across my jeans as I walk up the narrow cobblestone path to the front door, I can't get rid of the slickness on my palms. I press the doorbell, my heart thumping a mile a minute.

I sneak a glance over my shoulder to make sure my police shadow is parked nearby. It is, along the curb between Trenton's house and their neighbors.

Be cool. Flirt a little. Do. Not. Look. Nervous, I tell myself just as the door swings open.

Trenton is barefoot in gray sweatpants that are cut into knee-length shorts and a navy-blue T-shirt with HOWARD across the chest. He has a dazed look.

"Tinsley? Um, wassup?" he says with a crooked smile. "What are you doing here . . . at my house?"

"I, uh, was in the neighborhood and . . . I . . ."

His eyebrows lift. "You were in *my* neighborhood?"

"Yeah. Is that so hard to believe?" I force myself to smile.

His mouth slacks. "Uh, yeah."

I do that thing when I laugh and look away, then slowly shift my eyes back to who I'm talking to after my face goes serious. Being flirtatious might get him to let his guard down. Duchess does seem to think he likes me. "I was driving around, you know, thinking about our conversation the other night," I say. "How nice and unexpected it was."

"Real talk, it's been on my mind too." He rubs the back of his neck, shifting his weight from one foot to the other. "You wanna come in?"

I nod, then step inside.

"You not going to the dance tonight?" I ask after he closes the door.

"Nah, that's more your crowd—if you know what I mean."

A smirk pulls at the corners of my mouth as I remember Duchess's earlier comment.

We stand by the door, staring awkwardly at one another a few seconds. My mind is struggling for a way to ask him why he lied.

I crane my neck to look into what I think is the living room, which is to my left. The room to my right is dark, but I can tell it's the kitchen from the tile flooring and the silhouette of a table and four chairs I see in the shadows. A carpeted stairwell is right behind me. The air smells like warm apple pie.

"Where is your family?" I ask lightly.

"My little brother is at the movies with some friends. My parents . . ." Trenton's eyes drop to the floor and he starts rubbing the back of his neck again. "My dad told my mom about the company going bankrupt today, and, well, they're at dinner trying to 'figure things out.' Whatever that means."

I grimace and say, "Oh, I'm sorry."

"Nah, nah, it's not your fault." The sincerity in his voice makes me believe him. "I meant it when I said I won't hold what went down between our fathers against you. It's just . . ."

"It's just what?"

"Moms told me this afternoon they probably won't be able to afford to send me to Howard. She wants me to apply to some community colleges, you know, just in case."

I want to reach out and hug him. Apologize again for the role my father played in blocking him from something he wants so badly. I'm feeling even guiltier for never having to worry about money like this.

"But you're smart as hell," I say. "Couldn't you get a scholarship?"

"Yeah, but it wouldn't be enough to cover out-of-state fees and everything else." He scratches his mini Afro. "No offense, but I'm really not trying to get into all that right now."

"Of course, sorry." More silence and awkward staring. "So what does *your* crowd do on the night of the homecoming dance?" I ask.

An infectious grin transforms his face. "I was up in my room, working on a project for Robotics Club."

"Show me," I say. The words fly out of my mouth in a knee-jerk reaction.

His brow knits.

"I mean, if you want to," I add.

"Come on," he says, nodding for me to follow him up the stairs.

Every part of my body is quivering. I don't remember feeling this on edge when I confronted anybody else I mistakenly suspected of killing Nova. Maybe coming here, trying to do this alone, was a mistake. If I'm right this time, the cop parked outside the house is too far away to be any help. If Trenton does anything to me, he just won't be able to get away with it as easy as he did with Nova.

Stop, Tinsley, I tell myself. *You have no proof that he did anything. Only that he lied.*

Trenton's bedroom is exactly what I expected. A floor-to-ceiling bookshelf takes up an entire wall on the right, every shelf filled with perfectly aligned books, Funko Pop bobbleheads displayed neatly among them. The ones Trenton has are either superhero-related or cartoonish replicas I recognize from

Stranger Things and *Lovecraft Country*. A desk tucked into a corner of his room is crowded with so many computer parts and electronics it looks like he could communicate with NASA. The color scheme is a mix of muted neutrals.

"You can cop a seat over there." He waves at his bed.

I respond with a tight smile before sitting on the edge. He doesn't shut the door, which eases some of the tension in my body. At least I have a direct line out if things turn. Trenton sits down at his desk, picking up some silver pencil-looking thing he cradles between his index finger and thumb, as if he were eating with chopsticks.

"I gotta finish up this robot to show Mr. Netherton next week," he says. "The district robotics competition is next month."

"Cool."

The boy builds robots for fun. He wants to go to college. He's not a murderer. *Please* don't let him be a murderer.

"You don't really think it's cool, do you?" he says with a playful grin and a raised brow.

I fake another smile. Do I just say *Why did you lie about leaving the reception early?* And if he tries to say he didn't, do I tell him how I know he did? And when I do, what happens after that? Maybe I should send my location to Rachel.

"I mean it, Trenton. It's cool." I reach around to casually dig my phone out of my back pocket. "But if you tell anyone I said that I'll deny it."

That makes him laugh, and I drop my hand from my pocket. "But how would you explain being in my house, in my bedroom?" he asks, his gaze growing sharp.

He's looking at me like I'm this mesmerizing thing he's desperately trying to understand, and I realize it would probably have my stomach fluttering in a good way if I weren't afraid he might have killed someone. My gut has me thinking I have to be wrong. That I'm overreacting. No one this unassuming is capable of murder. There's no way.

"We can still talk while I work on this," he says, "if that's what you came over for." He picks up a square-shaped motherboard—the only thing on his desk I can identify, thanks to that computer science class I had to take sophomore year. He places it on his lap. "Or I can stop if you want. Not trying to bore you with this."

"Don't mind me," I say, flashing him a smile. "I don't want to interrupt. I wanted to get out of the house. I was tired of staring at my bedroom walls."

Trenton begins jabbing the silver pencil-looking thing into the motherboard, sending up sparks every so often.

"Does that mean you and Duchess have given up on being . . . whatever female odd-couple amateur sleuths there are in pop culture?" He smiles at his own joke. "Nova would be shitting bricks if she knew y'all were hanging tight now."

"Really? Why is that?" I say, driven by a growing curiosity to understand who Nova was.

"Come on, Tinsley, don't play dumb. You wouldn't be slumming it with us if you hadn't fallen from grace."

Ouch. That kinda hurts.

"I don't consider it slumming."

Trenton looks up at me. "Oh. What do you consider it, then?"

"Making new friends," I say with a heartfelt smile.

Trenton smiles back, then lowers his head to continue whatever he's doing.

I look around the room. He asks what I did this weekend and I tell him half-truths that omit Jessica Thambley's affair with Mr. Haywood. I ask him about the tribute to Nova, my curious eyes bouncing from the knickknacks on his mirrored dresser to the posters and pictures on his wall as I pretend to listen to his response. My gaze stops on the neat row of sneakers lined up against the wall next to his closet door.

He's babbling about some drama in the robotics club, but I'm barely listening. From where I'm sitting, I can see inside his closet, and I spot something that makes my breath catch. It's the black suit Trenton had on in all the pictures from the coronation reception. I realize that I don't have to ask him about lying. There's another way I can find out what I need to know.

"Hey, you got anything to drink?" I say, touching my throat. "I'm like, *dying* of thirst right now."

He drops the pencil-thing on his desk and says, "Oh shit. My bad. I didn't even ask." He stands up and heads for the door. "You want Coke? Sprite? Water?"

"Have anything a little stronger?" I ask with a devilish smile.

"I could raid my parent's liquor stash. What does the lady request?"

I ask for a glass of wine, which I can tell surprises him a little by the way he tilts his head and his eyes get big.

"Sit tight. I'll be right back," he says.

When I hear him descend the stairs, I spring into action. I pull out my phone, turn on the flashlight, and start inspecting the suit. Even though there was a stain in the storage room, it looked like someone had cleaned up most of the blood. And there's no way you could kill someone, clean up, and carry the body to a second location without getting blood on you.

Though he could have had it dry-cleaned by now, I think.

My heart racing, I rummage through the pockets of the suit coat and pants. I have no idea what I'm looking for. Which I guess doesn't matter, since they're all empty. I look down at the closet floor. He must have worn the black patent-leather shoes to the reception—they're the only ones that would go with a suit. If he walked in Nova's blood or was out at the cemetery, there would be evidence on the bottoms.

I drop to my knees, picking up a shoe to inspect the sole. The bottom is scuffed, but other than that, it's pretty much immaculate.

I pick up the left shoe, flipping it over to confirm that it's just as spotless as the right one. When I do, something falls out and hits my knee. I look down and a flower-shaped silver-and-diamond pendant twinkles in the halo of the flashlight on my phone. An icy spike slides down my spine.

Nova's necklace!

The one I rarely saw her not wearing. The one she had on that night. The one Duchess's father said was missing.

I suddenly feel sick.

Something moves in the corner of my eye and I spin around to see Trenton standing in the doorway, the glass of wine I asked for in his hand. The excitement in his eyes shifts to alarm the second he looks down and sees Nova's necklace dangling from my hand.

"Hold up. Let me explain."

I jump to my feet, still clutching the necklace. I'm trying to speak. Mouthing the question that's reverberating in my head. *Why did you do it?* But my voice is lodged in my throat, behind a scream that bubbles to the surface as Trenton takes a step toward me.

There's a thud from me backing up into the bookshelf. It makes him stop.

"I know how this looks, Tinsley, but it's . . . complicated."

I'm trapped. With no way out but through the door he's blocking. Yeah, it was so dumb for me to come here by myself.

"If you give me a minute, I can make everything make sense," he says, and slowly bends over, sets the glass of wine on the floor. His eyes remain on me as he does it. The maneuver creates a narrow pathway to the door. And most importantly, out of the room. It's the only chance I'll probably get, so I take it.

Trenton must have anticipated what I was thinking. When I make a lunge for the door, he jumps right, catching me in his arms. Squeezing me in the tightest, most terrifying hug I've ever been in.

That's when the scream that has been lodged in my throat comes out. I kick and squeal. I punch at him. But I never let go of Nova's necklace.

"Shut up!" he yells. "Shut up! Please!"

I claw at his face, digging my nails into his cheek like I want to tear his skin off.

"Aaaaagggghhhh!" he yelps.

His grip on me loosens. I'm able to gain a little more control. I use the opportunity to jump and propel myself backward, sending us flying onto the bed. I bounce out of Trenton's arms on impact. Before he can regroup, I take off running out the bedroom door.

He's right on my heels as I barrel down the stairs.

"Tinsley, stop! Wait! Please listen to me!"

Is he freaking crazy?

He nearly grabs hold of my sweatshirt as I'm nearing the bottom of the stairs. I scream again, pivoting on one foot to hold out the other, causing him to trip on the last two steps. It sends him flying in the opposite direction, into the living room. He slides across the room, almost in a fetal position, which gives me enough time to twist open the lock on the front door and dash out of the house.

"Tinsley, wait!" he's yelling. *"Please!"*

I keep running, straight across the front yard, toward the Lovett Police car that's still parked in the same spot. My shadow. Thank you, Chief Barrow!

I bang on the window, and the young officer who peeked into Captain Simmons's office the day I snuck back there and took the photo jumps.

He rolls down his window and I scream, "He's trying to kill me!" Tears are spilling down my cheeks.

"Who?" he replies, poking his head out the window to look up and down the quiet street.

"Trenton Hughes!" I yell back. "He killed Nova!"

CHAPTER TWENTY-NINE

DUCHESS

OCTOBER 22
8:26 P.M.

FINDING OUT THROUGH a breaking news alert that your homeboy was arrested for killing your best friend really knocks the wind out of you. I've been at the police station for nearly two hours and I'm still struggling to catch my breath. I just can't understand it.

Pops has me sequestered in his office, so I'm out of the way while he and the chief question Trenton and Tinsley separately. I've been pacing so long in here I'm getting dizzy. I stop the moment Tinsley and her parents whip past the doorway.

I run into the hall. "Tinsley!"

They stop. She turns around first. Her eyes are bloodshot, and the collar of her sweatshirt is ripped. The harsh overhead lighting is giving her a ghostly glow. She breaks away from her parents and bolts toward me, and we collide in an awkward hug.

"What the hell? This can't be right," I say when she pulls back. Her body is shaking, her eyes darting every which way, like nothing around us makes sense to her anymore. "Trenton? Ain't no way. I know him. I don't understand. . . ."

"I know, but he had her necklace. The one that was missing. It all—"

"What?" I interrupt. "Makes sense? This is crazy. I. Know. Him."

"Apparently not as well as you thought," Mrs. McArthur says behind us.

I roll my eyes at her over Tinsley's shoulder. "Help me understand," I say to Tinsley. "How could you think . . ."

My heart gradually slides into my stomach as Tinsley talks me through what led her to go to Trenton's house tonight. Hearing about how she discovered Nova's necklace and how he attacked her has my ears ringing. Trenton can be hot-tempered, but violent? It's like I never really knew him.

"Why would he hurt Nova?" I ask.

"Chief Barrow thinks he was in love with her and he might have killed her in a fit of rage because she wouldn't reciprocate his feelings, *or* because he knew about her relationship with Jaxson."

" 'Might have'?" I repeat.

"Your dad says Trenton hasn't admitted to it yet—killing her."

"Do *you* think he did it?"

The way Tinsley's brow is creased and the tightness in her face has me thinking she might be doubting his guilt too.

Her bottom lip starts trembling. "What am I supposed to think? He admitted to—"

"Tinsley," her mother says, walking up to us, "let's go. We're leaving *now*!" She grabs Tinsley's arm and yanks her away, practically dragging her down the hall. Midway, she stops and turns back to me. "Now you have the answers you wanted. It's not Tinsley's fault if you don't want to accept them."

"You could show a little compassion. Trenton was my friend!" I shout after Mrs. McArthur turns away.

She whips back around, still clutching Tinsley's arm. "Oh, like the compassion you had while helping them pin this on my daughter?" she says. "From the second you waltzed into our house, I knew you couldn't be trusted."

My dislike for this woman swells into a simmering anger that crawls over my skin.

"Bet that has more to do with my natural-born tan," I say through clenched teeth.

"If that's what you need to tell yourself, honey, be my guest." She spins back around and yells, "Virgil, let's *go*!"

Tinsley's father looks as pained by the exchange as Tinsley does. It doesn't stop him from obeying his wife's order, though. Before they disappear into the lobby, Tinsley turns to me and mouths, "I'm sorry."

But I can't be certain what she's sorry for—her mother's insensitivity, or what's happening to Trenton.

Pops is posted in the middle of the hallway when I turn around.

"Pops, talk to me," I plead. "What did he say? He admitted to killing her?"

Pops pinches the bridge of his nose. "No. Says he didn't. Claims he found her dead in the storage room while they were cleaning up after the reception. He was in the process of calling nine-one-one when someone sent him the video of Tinsley's rant on the beach. Claims that his anger over that, plus what her father did to his over the years, motivated him to go home, change clothes, and then sneak back onto campus later that night to move her body to the cemetery as a way to throw more suspicion Tinsley's way. He hacked into the school's security system—that's why there was no footage of him returning to the school."

My stomach clenches. Trenton lied about the school installing new firewall protection when I asked him to hack into the security system earlier this week.

"He said he was sick of the McArthurs thinking they could do and say whatever they wanted without repercussions," Pops continues. "He saw Nova's murder as an opportunity to bring shame on the family. Told us he took Nova's necklace because he intended to plant it somewhere that would further implicate Tinsley. He was ready to do it the night you guys hung out together and he drove Tinsley back to her car, but he changed his mind."

Motivation? It's all things I already know—that Trenton has harbored contempt for the McArthurs because of years of their intercepting his dad's business, including edging him out of lucrative government contracts. Trenton even said that Mr. McArthur got the contract for an affordable housing development in the Avenues illegally. And that contract was what forced Trenton's father to file for bankruptcy, for some reason. Which meant Trenton wouldn't be able to attend the college of his dreams. Framing Tinsley was his way of payback.

Now it feels like I've been punched in the gut.

"Listen, the chief is on my ass about getting him booked

and processed," Pops says. "He's already getting calls from city officials about the way things were handled with Tinsley. He's gonna use Trenton's arrest as a way to get back in their good graces. We'll have to talk later."

I nod, trying to process everything he just told me, the most he's said to me since I blew up at him the night after Nova's body was found.

Knowing I won't get more information today, I head out of the station. When I'm alone in my car, the tears fall. This week, I've lost two friends. None of it makes sense. Even if Trenton did set out to frame Tinsley, his killing Nova isn't connecting like it should. It was months ago when Nova told him she didn't like him in a romantic way. He was disappointed, but he never acted like it fazed him. He kept it moving.

I guess everything doesn't have to connect when the spotlight is on us. Arrest warrants get handed out like candy when a Black suspect enters the conversation.

My eyes feel like sandpaper by the time they dry. I use the rearview mirror and a T-shirt that was flung across my backseat to clean my face. I'm about to turn the key in the ignition, but something occurs to me.

Nova's necklace.

A conversation Nova and I had about it plays in my mind, now colored by what I've learned about her this week. Its meaning feels different. I turn back and charge to the station, taking the steps two at a time up to the front entrance.

I walk in on Pops seated behind his desk, frowning at whatever he's reading on his laptop.

"The necklace!" I say.

He looks up, one hand cupping his chin. "What about it?"

"When Nova got it for her birthday, I commented on how expensive it looked. She shrugged me off, saying it was a good fake she found online. I believed her, knowing Ms. Donna could never afford the real thing—and neither could Nova herself."

"Uh-huh."

I lean over, pressing my hands on my Pops's desk. "I think she was lying. She kept a lot of things from me, Pops. And if she lied about it, maybe the necklace is a clue to the secret she was hiding. She would never take it off. It must have had sentimental value, right?"

I'm tingling all over. That necklace *had to* be connected to whatever "stuff" was bothering her at the coronation reception. The stuff she was going to make me promise not to tell anyone. I'm practically panting as I try to read Pops's face. He's stoic at first; then his hand drops from his chin and the corners of his mouth curl into a proud grin.

Does he not believe me? The thought tightens my chest.

"What's funny?" I say. "I'm serious."

"I wish you'd rethink becoming a cop," he says. "You'd make a good detective, baby girl."

He turns his laptop around so that I can see the screen. A picture of Nova's flower-shaped diamond pendant fills what looks like an online ordering webpage.

"I had the same thought, so I googled the name that was engraved on the back of one of the petals," he says, holding up the plastic evidence bag Nova's necklace is sealed in. "It's a high-end boutique in Atlanta."

I round his desk as he turns the laptop back toward him.

"Trenton is smart enough and had the motive to frame

Tinsley, but that kid wouldn't hurt a fly," he says. "I remember that time he was at our house and begged me not to kill a spider, said it 'served a purpose in the ecosystem.' Boy helped me catch and release it instead. That kind of person doesn't take another person's life."

Pops looks back down at his laptop, but I can't take my eyes off him. My lungs expand, the air filling some of the void that's taken up residency in me. *This* is why having him on the police force is important. The chief is ready to lock Trenton up. But Pops knows Trenton, and knows the struggles Black people face in the justice system, so he digs deep for the truth instead of accepting things at face value like his white counterparts, who only want to see Black people one way. These are the moments I wish his haters could see.

"Pops, I didn't mean it," I blurt out.

His brow knits. "Huh?"

"What I said about Mama and you promising you wouldn't let her die. I didn't mean it. I was angry. That's all. You're my hero, even when I don't understand why you still show up to this place. Times like this, I'm glad you do."

"I know that, baby girl." He stands up, pulling me into his arms. "I know you've had to put up with a lot because I have this badge. I expect a lot out of you."

"But I never want you to think I think of you like they do," I sob into his chest. "This week, I did for a moment. And I didn't defend you like I should have to some of the kids at school who were giving me grief about y'all not arresting Tinsley. It just hurt, losing Nova like I lost Mama."

He pushes me away so he can look down at me. "I'm sorry for being hard on you. It was coming from a place of love. Of me not wanting you in danger, because . . ." He chokes back tears of his own. "Your brothers and you are all I have left of her. I wasn't about to risk losing you like we lost Nova."

I bite my lip, tasting the saltiness of the tears that have drained into my mouth.

"And there ain't nothing you could do or say that would ever make me love you less," he continues. "We are solid, you hear me?"

He pulls me into a suffocating hug. Listening to his heartbeat calms me. Makes me feel for the first time in a while like everything will be okay.

"Now, about this necklace." We break apart and he drops into his desk chair. I hover over his shoulder and use my sleeve to dry my face. "The thing costs about five thousand dollars."

My mouth drops open. "Who could have spent that much bread on her?"

"Sugar daddy, maybe?" Pops says.

"That'd be hard for me to believe, given what she went through with her uncle," I say. "It would also be super hypocritical, given how she was about to out Jessica's relationship with our teacher."

"Huh?"

"I'll tell you later." I turn Pops's head back to the computer screen. "Is there a way we can find out who bought it for her?"

"I was getting ready to call the shop before you walked back in here." He picks up the receiver of his office phone and starts dialing the number at the bottom of the webpage. He replaces it and puts the call on speaker once the line starts ringing. "You be quiet. Let me do all the talking."

"Sparkling Creations, how can I help you?" a woman answers.

"Yes, I'd like to speak to the owner," Pops says.

"Speaking. This is Johanna Kurns."

My heart is doing flutter kicks in my chest as I listen to Pops explain who he is and why he's calling. Finding out who gifted Nova a five-thousand-dollar necklace feels like the answer that's been staring us in the face this entire time.

"Captain Simmons, I'd be happy to help in any way I can," Ms. Kurns says. "Lucky for you, I keep meticulous records of our customers to maintain our mailing list. Most people become repeat buyers of my pieces. I've only sold a handful of those flower pendants."

The sound of rustling papers comes from the other line. "When did you say the pendant was purchased?"

"Maybe sometime between April and May of last year," Pops said.

"And you're in Lovett, Mississippi, right?"

"Yes, ma'am."

"Ah, here we go . . ."

I put my hand over my mouth, worried I'll breathe too loud and miss what this woman is about to say.

"That pendant was purchased by a man," she continues. "McArthur. First name Virgil."

CHAPTER THIRTY

TINSLEY

OCTOBER 22
9:15 P.M.

MY PARENTS HAVE been lying to me.

They told the first lie the morning I woke up to the news of Nova's murder. It hits me as we're pulling up to our house—why hearing about the country club temporarily suspending breakfast service didn't sound right. If that's true, then it's impossible that my parents had breakfast there last week, like my father told me when I asked why they weren't home when I woke up the day after the coronation. Of course, he could have just misspoken, given how frantic I was. That's what I would have thought if it weren't for the second lie. I've been thinking about it since I locked myself in my bedroom.

In actuality, it's only a *possible* lie. But after witnessing the weird exchange my parents had about Trenton's arrest as we were getting into the car this evening, I'm ninety-nine percent sure it's a lie.

As I was climbing into the backseat, my father mumbled something to my mother over his shoulder before he walked around to the driver's side.

My mother replied, "Virgil, it's over. Just let it be," as she slid into the front passenger seat.

To which my father said, "That boy doesn't deserve—"

And then my mother hissed, "Virgil, don't test me. I said: Let. It. Go!"

I think my mother's been lying about her suspicion that the house cleaners have been stealing from us, which she claimed was the reason she lashed out at them in front of Duchess. I was so caught up in not having Duchess think we were racist snobs that I allowed the absurdity of her reasoning to fly right over my head.

A few years ago my mother thought one of our gardeners had stolen some equipment from our shed, and she immediately fired him. She had no proof that he'd actually done it, but that didn't stop her from letting him go. If she truly thought those women were in our house taking things, they would have never been allowed back inside. And that leads to the question I've been pondering for the past thirty minutes: Is there something in the display case she didn't want them to see? That's the only logical explanation for her not wanting the cleaning staff near it. The answer has my stomach in knots.

And what about my father's words *That boy doesn't deserve*—

Trenton doesn't deserve what? What did my mother stop my father from saying?

Trenton's swearing that he didn't kill Nova echoes in my mind as I quietly open my bedroom door. The hallway is pitch-black. There's a sliver of light coming from the crack under my parents' bedroom door when I step barefoot onto the hall's icy hardwood floor.

I tiptoe to the stairs, my knotted stomach driving me downstairs to the display case that holds the family crowns and scepters.

Your mother was being a super bitch to her, Jaxson told me the night we confronted him outside Jitterbug's. I try to push the memory down as I reach the bottom of the stairs. My mother's a bitch to everyone. That doesn't mean—

Stop! I tell myself. *You're overthinking this.*

But it doesn't loosen the tension in my stomach.

Most of the lights are off downstairs. Rachel decided to go home tonight, since Lindsey started asking about Aiden. I think my niece senses something is wrong between her parents.

There's a light coming from under Daddy's office door. You would think his drinking binges would be over now that Trenton has been arrested and my name has been cleared. Maybe tonight's the first night he's actually in there working.

The glass display case is haloed by the moonlight seeping into the room through the windows. I can barely feel my fingers as I dash over to it like I'm a bad-ass spy breaking into a museum to steal some precious artifact in a popcorn action movie. For a few seconds I stand in front of the case, staring at the crowns.

Everything inside is arranged as it always is. But the gnawing suspicions in the back of my head persist. I open the case and pick up my mother's crown. Holding it up in the moonlight, I inspect it as if I've never seen it before. I don't know what I'm looking for, but at the same time, I do.

Blood. Any drop of blood. In case my mother—

But that's absurd.

I replace the crown on its stand on the top shelf. I've let this girl's murder turn me into a paranoid freak. These are my parents. This is my *mother.* Yeah, she's done some fucked-up stuff—like turning on her best friend, who was raped at a party they attended together. That doesn't mean she's capable of murder.

Does it?

I pick up her scepter next, inspecting it the same way I did her crown. The moonlight illuminates the engraved inscription below the bulb and my blood turns to ice.

NOVA ALBRIGHT

I barge into my parents' bedroom waving Nova's scepter in my trembling hands. My mother is sitting at her antique vanity in lavender silk pajamas.

"What are you doing with this?" I demand.

My mother pauses in the middle of plucking her eyebrows, casting a confused look at me in the vanity mirror. It's brief, but I catch her eyes as they stretch wider before she shifts her weight in her seat and relaxes her face.

"What on earth are you talking about?" She leans forward into her reflection to resume the work on her eyebrows.

"This is Nova's scepter!" I stomp into the middle of the room, stopping in front of the fireplace facing my parents' king-size bed. "Why do you have this? Where is yours?"

"I must have picked hers up by mistake the night of the coronation." My mother tosses the tweezers down on the vanity with all the other creams, perfumes, and makeup tools cluttering its polished surface. "Why are you standing there looking at me like that?"

I shake my head as I study my mother's nonchalant demeanor in the mirror, my body subconsciously responding to another lie she's told. I tried to believe that Nova's scepter was in our house because my mother had mistakenly picked it up, but hearing her say it confirms how ridiculous that is.

"You're lying," I say through clenched teeth.

"I'm what?"

"You're *lying*!" I shout. "Because if you have her scepter, it would implicate . . ."

The words get caught in my throat like a piece of dry bread.

My mother slowly turns, her jaws clenched and her freshly plucked brows knitted. Her eyes are devoid of emotion and her mouth is set in a tight line.

"What exactly are you implying, *sweetie*?"

She says "sweetie" in the icy tone that has always been able to stop me in my tracks. Tonight, it turns my disbelief into hostility.

"Explain how you could have picked up Nova's scepter by accident," I say. "Tell me, or—"

"Or what?" My mother stands up. "You are in no position to threaten me, young lady. Now go return that scepter to where it belongs and then carry your little pretty self to bed. You've had a stressful week—we all have."

My bottom lip is trembling when she steps up and starts petting my hair. "Nova's killer is in jail. And that's the end of that."

"No it's not!" I push her away, stumbling back into the fireplace mantel. "He didn't do this. You did, didn't you?"

"You don't know what you're talking about." My mother turns her back to me.

"Why would you do this? Because she won homecoming queen over me?"

My mother spins back around. There's a feral intensity in her eyes and mouth. "Don't be absurd. Just do what I say and *go to bed*!"

I'm struggling to catch my breath. "You and Daddy lied about eating breakfast at the club last Saturday. I know because the club was closed for breakfast. One of their chefs got fired."

"Tinsley, get out, *now*!" she yells. "Before you *really* upset me."

"And then what?" I ask, surprising myself as I say it. "You kill me, like you must have killed her?"

"You shut your goddamn mouth!"

She did it. I know she did. But it doesn't make sense. What could Nova have done to her to deserve death?

"Why would you do something like that?" I'm choking on tears. "Was it because of me?"

My mother shoots out of the chair so fast she's in my face quicker than I can blink.

"Shut your fucking mouth, you little bitch!" She rips the scepter out of my hand, waving it at me with such venom I have to take a few steps back to avoid getting hit by it. "You have no idea what the truth is. None! And you could never handle it. It's over. She's dead. Your name is cleared—"

"He didn't kill her." I know it's the truth as soon as I say it out loud.

"But you won't ever breathe a word of that, do you hear me?" My mother's face is inches from mine. "Now get out, and never speak to me about this again."

How could she kill someone and then go on with her life like it never happened? It's like she's done this before, killing and then moving on. Our conversation about the chief's sister pops back into my mind, taking on new meaning considering what I know now.

"Was all that stuff about Regina Barrow a lie too?" I say.

It happens so fast I don't register that she's slapped me until I feel my cheek burning. My mother is practically foaming at the mouth as I touch my face, my eyes frozen on her in shock.

"Charlotte, get away from her."

We both turn. My father is framed in the bedroom doorway, his bitter gaze locked on my mother.

"You heard me. Get. Away. From. Her."

My mother takes a few steps back, but she's smacking the scepter's bulb in her open palm, giving my father an icy look. "Are you here to tell your daughter the truth?" she asks him. "Would that free your weak conscience? Bury the memories you've been drowning in whiskey all week?"

"Daddy, what did y'all do?" Tears are dripping into my mouth.

My father runs a hand through his hair.

"Virgil," my mother persists, "your daughter asked you a question."

"I heard her, dammit!" my dad screams.

"Then tell her!" my mother says. "Tell your daughter what we did."

"What *you* did!" he retorts, pointing at my mother. "I had no part in it."

"Oh, dear, you had every part in it," my mother says. "It happened because of you. Because of how you disrespected me."

My father's gaze ping-pongs between me and my mother. His face is twisted with something I don't think I've ever seen in him before. Fear, and maybe regret. How could he be connected to Nova, and what my mother did to her?

"Daddy, what is she talking about?" I sob.

"Tell her who Nova was, Virgil. It's about time she knew all about your dirty little secret."

"Shut up, Charlotte," my father barks.

My mother is sneering at him. She's enjoying this, while I feel like I'm about to have a heart attack.

"Tinsley." My father says my name like it takes every ounce of strength he has left. "Nova was . . ."

"She was what?" I prod, terrified about what he's going to tell me.

My father raises his eyes from the floor. They're glistening with tears. "She was my daughter."

My heart falls to my feet.

I feel my knees buckle. I have to reach out and grab on to the fireplace mantel to stop myself from dropping to the floor. This has to be some kind of horrible nightmare. My parents are staring at me, waiting for a reaction to the bomb my father dropped.

"Wh-wh-what are you talking about?" I say to him.

"She was my daughter, Tinsley. Your sister."

But how? When? Why?

"Mama, this isn't true," I say. "It can't be true, right?"

My mother turns her back to me, tossing Nova's scepter onto their bed.

"That's why your mother did what she did." My father crosses the room, coming toward me, but I throw up my hand, commanding him to stop. "Nova threatened to tell everyone who she really was."

"No," my mother says. "I lost control and bashed that little witch over the head because she threatened to extort money from you, and I knew you would be gullible enough to let her do it. Like you were suckered into sponsoring her behind my back, despite how that would make the daughter you raised feel."

"I owed her that after everything you did to them!" my father shouts.

"You owed me more for fathering a child with that piece of ghetto trash," my mother retorts. "You think I'm going to let the Albrights, the likes of *them,* take away what I sacrificed and fought for?"

"I'm not a fucking piece of property!" my father yells.

"No, you're a pathetic man who can't keep it in your pants!" my mother fumes, dropping down into her vanity chair.

"Stop it!" I scream, my hands pressed to the sides of my head.

My mind swirls as I try to keep up with everything they've said. So much regarding Nova's actions leading up to her murder now make sense. Was that why she changed her mind about the abortion? Because being a part of our family would allow her the means to raise a child?

And Jaxson said Nova's mother got pregnant by a married man. Unbeknownst to me, that man was the one I call Daddy. The conversation with Rachel in my bedroom two nights ago connects the rest of the dots.

I stumble toward the chair next to the fireplace and collapse into it. The *him* Leland Albright referred to the day I was at Nova's house must have been my father, not Jaxson. And the day Nova and I got into that fight—she made that remark about a missed opportunity to be close like sisters.

My head snaps up.

"How did Nova know?" I say. "How did she know you were her father?"

"She didn't find out until she and Donna moved back into her grandmother's house," my father says, his eyes locked on my mother. "Nova found a bunch of old love letters and notes I wrote to her mother when she worked for me. She was the first secretary I had when I started the construction company."

"Those were from *you*?" I say, realizing what was in the box I found. The notes weren't discolored from moisture in the air-conditioning vent. They were just old.

"Your mother saw Nova sneak off during that reception," my father explains. He sits down on the end of the bed, his elbows propped on his knees. "I didn't know it at the time, but she followed her. Was going to threaten Nova to make her stay away from you and the family after you spotted us together."

My mother tosses down the brush she's been stroking her hair with while my father was talking. "Because clearly her mother wasn't honoring our agreement anymore."

"What agreement?" I ask.

"I wasn't about to let his tragic little mistake make me look like a fool," my mother says, turning so that she's facing my father. "Could you imagine how the people in this town would talk to learn not only that your father cheated on me with someone like *her*, but that he fathered a child with her too?"

So this was about her pride. Her fragile status in the world she married into.

"But that day at school, you acted like you didn't know Ms. Albright," I say.

My mother locks eyes with me in the vanity mirror. I recall the fleeting look of confusion Ms. Albright gave her after my mother pretended to not know who she was. My mother's performance must have thrown her off.

"You've been lying this entire time," I say to her.

"Nova was innocent," my father says.

"That bitch was going to take what is rightfully my daughter's!" my mother yells. "Besides that, *I* am the only mother of your children! That was the agreement."

I can't take anymore. I'm going to be sick. My mother takes evil to another level. I shoot up from the recliner and dart toward the double doors that open onto the master balcony. I knew I wouldn't make it to the bathroom in time. The food I taste in the back of my throat explodes from my mouth just as I slam into the balcony railing. More tears dribbling down my face with every heave that causes my stomach to press harder into the ridges of the railing.

My mother killed Nova.

My stomach heaves.

Nova was my sister.

Another heave.

My father knew and has been helping her cover it up.

I have to cough up the spit stuck in the back of my throat.

"Tinsley."

I spin around. My father is standing at the balcony doors.

"Why would you help her?" I say. "If Nova was your daughter, how could you help Mama get away with that?"

"She blackmailed me to do it," my father says. "Everything

your friend Trenton said about me illegally securing government contracts is true. And your mother has the receipts to prove it."

"I call them my loophole to our prenup," my mother says, walking past my father with a towel in her hand.

"Get away from me!" I scream, taking a step back from her. "You killed Nova to maintain a lifestyle you never truly deserved."

"You have no idea the sacrifices I had to make to give you and your sister a life I only dreamed about in that godforsaken trailer park."

I don't care what she has sacrificed. Nova didn't deserve to die because of them.

"You killed her!" I scream.

In the blink of an eye, my mother has ahold of both my shoulders. "Lower your damn voice!" she whispers loudly.

Stepping up to try to pull my mother off me, my father shouts, "Charlotte, let her go!"

But she won't let go. Her nails are digging into my flesh. "Do you have any idea how much I had to put up with to get where I am?"

"Let me go!" I yell. My heart is racing. I've never seen my mother like this. Like a woman possessed.

"You shut your *fucking* mouth!" she shouts. "You'll take this to the grave with you!"

"Charlotte!" my father yells.

My mother squeezes me tighter and I push as hard as I can to get away.

"Get off me!" I scream, digging my nails into her flesh, hoping it will get her to release me.

She pulls me tighter, thrusting her face into mine. "Do you hear what I say? You don't say a word—"

"Charlotte!" My father has his arms wrapped around her waist, yanking her away from me.

"Let me go!" I yell.

My father finally manages to rip her off me. But the force of our separation sends me flying into the balcony railing so hard that my feet lift off the ground.

I hear my father shout my name. As I'm falling back, my hands flail in the air, trying to latch on to something but feeling nothing but air. My father reaches out to me, but it's too late. My fingers graze his just before I tip over the railing.

For two seconds I'm weightless before gravity pulls me down.

I see a flash of blinding blue light. The last thing I hear before everything goes black: my mother's bloodcurdling scream.

CHAPTER THIRTY-ONE

DUCHESS

OCTOBER 23

11:18 A.M.

ONLY ONE WORD can describe the last fourteen hours.

Insane.

Every theory I had about why Virgil McArthur might have bought Nova a five-thousand-dollar pendant was wrong. Never in a million years would I have thought he was Nova's father. Although nearly all of my theories involved money and him killing her over it. Turns out he did it to keep people from finding out he fathered a child with his former secretary, something Nova was threatening to expose after he refused to give her any more money or expensive gifts to keep quiet. The "stuff" she was going to tell me before she died is now out for the public's consumption. Nova was straight-up this whole other person I really didn't know. And Ms. Donna isn't any better in my eyes. A part of me believes she *had* to know on some level that Mr.

McArthur was behind it. Was she so afraid of the man that she was going to let him get away with murder?

Mr. McArthur's arrest has already made the national news. I'm sure everyone in town is talking about it, but I've been at the hospital since Tinsley was admitted last night.

Her sister was waiting bedside with me at first. Now her mother's here. Mrs. McArthur and her resting bitch face arrived this morning after she was released from questioning with regard to her husband's arrest. Tinsley apparently figured out what her father did around the same time as Pops and me. When he called a little while ago to check in on Tinsley's condition, Pops gave me the rundown on everything Mrs. McArthur said to them. That she was trying to stop her husband from attacking her daughter after Tinsley confronted him with the truth. And that Tinsley fell off the balcony during their struggle.

Thank God Pops got there when he did. Might've had two dead girls to mourn had he not. Whether I like her or not, I wouldn't want to see her die. Not like that.

The persistent beeping of her heart monitor fills the silence between her mother and me. Both of us are acting like the other isn't here. She's seated on the other side of the room and I'm on the side of the bed closest to the window. The steel-gray skyline outside adds to the room's dankness. The only thing her mother has said to me was right when she got here. And that was that I could leave. She turned her nose up when I said I wasn't going anywhere until Tinsley was awake.

My eyes flick up from my phone right as Tinsley's fingers start twitching. I jump out of my chair and dart over to her bed, her mother close on my heels.

"Tinsley," I whisper. Her eyes blink open at the sound of my voice. "Was starting to think you wouldn't ever wake up."

She squints at me from the sting of the overhead light. But her face softens as she starts to recognize mine. Her mouth opens, her tongue darting in and out across her chapped lips. She attempts to sit up and I gently press down on her arm.

"Keep still. Yo' body must feel like it was hit by a ton of bricks," I say.

"Sweetie," her mother says, leaning over her daughter, "you gave me a pretty good scare."

Tinsley's arm tenses beneath my touch and her eyes nearly pop out of her head. "Get away from me!" she shouts in a hoarse tone, recoiling from the hand her mother was about to place on her forehead.

I slowly pull my hand back, confused by what just happened.

Mrs. McArthur's nervous glance flits in my direction. She gives her daughter a tight smile. Tinsley is straight-up looking at her mother like *I don't want this woman anywhere near me!*

"Calm down, sweetie. You're in shock," Mrs. McArthur says, reaching out again but pauses when Tinsley flinches. "I know you're still reeling from what your father did, but it's okay now. You're safe."

I lean forward again. "Yeah, he's—"

"Let me talk to my daughter, okay?" her mother snaps at me.

The nurse assigned to Tinsley's room block breezes into the room, telling us she saw a shift in Tinsley's vitals on the monitoring equipment out at the nursing station. Mrs. McArthur and I step aside so she can check Tinsley. There's a weirdness in the air that even the nurse picks up on. She keeps looking back and forth between Mrs. McArthur and me, and Tinsley's mother starts pacing between the chair and the door. My insides have twisted into a knot.

Why would Tinsley pull away from her mother like that? The woman saved her life from her murderous father.

"Relax, okay, honey?" the nurse says. "You've got a broken arm and a serious concussion. I'll be back in a few with the doctor. I'm sure your friend and your mother will catch you up on *things*."

She says that like learning how your father killed his illegitimate daughter, then almost killed you too, is a normal Sunday occurrence.

"You mind stepping outside while I talk to her?" Mrs. McArthur says to me after the nurse leaves. The placid smile she's giving me doesn't align with the distress in this woman's eyes.

I look over at Tinsley. The way she's staring at me raises the hair on the back of my neck. A thread starts slowly unraveling in the back of my mind. This wasn't supposed to be like this, feel like this. Where is the tearful hug and proclamations of answered prayers I imagined there would be between mother and daughter after what they survived?

Why does this feel so wrong?

"You want me to leave?" I say to Tinsley.

"*I* asked you to leave," her mother interjects.

"I been here since you were admitted." I march back to her bedside as if I can't see or hear her mother. "Pops was rolling up to your house when you fell from the balcony."

"The blue lights." Tinsley squints, looking up at the TV

behind me with this faraway glaze in her eyes. "That was your dad? Why was he there?"

"Captain Simmons was there to arrest your father," Mrs. McArthur answers before I can. "They know Nova was his daughter. And that he killed her."

There's a shift in Tinsley's face. "Wh-what—"

"Don't concern yourself with talking," Mrs. McArthur instructs her. "Save your strength." Then she turns to me, her mouth set in a tight line. "Can you please leave . . . *now*? My daughter and I need to talk."

Tinsley avoids my inquisitive stare by peering past me out the window. I catch her bottom lip tremble.

Something is definitely not right.

"How did you figure it out?" I ask her. "Your Pops? Tell me how you put it together."

She side-eyes her mother, who I can feel glaring at me.

"My daughter has been through enough. She doesn't have time for this."

"Did you figure out that he bought her that five-thousand-dollar necklace for her birthday?" I say, ignoring her mother.

"She means the necklace she *extorted* out of your father," her mother hisses. "Now leave, before I call security."

I shrug and say, "Why would he—"

"No! Get out!" Mrs. McArthur points at the door. "Get out now."

"In a minute," I snap at her. "I'm just a little confused. If Nova was extorting your husband for money, why did he buy her a necklace from an Atlanta boutique during a business trip? That seems like such a personal gift. Nova never really wore a lot of jewelry. So it's odd she would ask for that instead of money. And it's odd to meet someone blackmailing you out in public, the way Mr. McArthur did with Nova. The daughter he killed because he supposedly *didn't* want anyone to know of his connection to her."

It catches me by surprise when Mrs. McArthur stomps over to my side of the bed and snatches hold of my shirt.

"Get out!" she demands, yanking me back.

I latch on to the bedrail. "It doesn't make sense, does it, Tinsley?"

Her eyes are glistening with tears. She's hiding something. I know she is.

"How did you figure it out? Tell me!" I beg.

"Shut. Your. Mouth. And *get out* of my daughter's room!"

Tinsley turns away from me. Whatever she's hiding, she's not going to say.

Why am I not surprised? Of course she'll always choose her mother over me. Her idol. The mold from which she was born. I jerk myself free of Mrs. McArthur and head to the door. I'm gonna find out what they're hiding. And won't give up until I do.

"Duchess," Tinsley says.

I pause, my hand on the doorknob. When I turn around, Tinsley's jaw is set, her eyes locked on me. The angst that was written on her face a few seconds ago is gone.

"Tell your dad to go to our house and check the glass display case in our formal dining room," Tinsley says.

"Tinsley," her mother says, "don't you—"

"He'll find Nova's scepter where my mother's should be," Tinsley finishes.

"*TinsLEY.*" Mrs. McArthur says it like a warning and clenches her fists.

"Where's hers?" I ask, my hand falling off the doorknob as a chill runs through my body.

"I don't know," Tinsley says. "She had to get rid of it after she used it to bash Nova over the head."

Mrs. McArthur charges at her daughter. "You spiteful little bitch!" she roars.

I don't make it to Tinsley in time to stop her mother from taking hold of her and violently shaking her.

"Let go of me!" Tinsley cries.

"Get off her!" I yank on Mrs. McArthur's sweater, pulling with all my might.

"You get off of *me*!" she barks.

She shoves me with so much force I go flying over the chair. The back of my head slams into the wall. White-hot pain turns my world into pulsating dots. The room goes topsy-turvy. I can't grab anything to steady myself or get up. Then hands wrap around my throat and I can't breathe.

"Mama, no!"

I hear Tinsley scream but can't see her. The dancing dots are everywhere, shadowed by a dark silhouette.

"You changed her!" Mrs. McArthur screams, shaking me. "You changed my daughter!"

Her spit hits me in the face. Her screaming vibrates my eardrums. Her hands tighten around my throat. I claw at them. Need to get them off. I can't breathe. I kick my legs and jerk my body back and forth, but I can't loosen her grip around my neck. I can't get this psycho bitch off me.

"I'll be damned if I let you have my daughter!" she screams. "She's mine!"

My throat is on fire.

"Help! Please, somebody help!" Tinsley's screaming, but she sounds so far away.

"I'll kill you before I let the likes of *you* take everything from me!" Mrs. McArthur screams. I gasp for air that doesn't come.

There's shuffling somewhere around me; then I hear "Ma'am. *Ma'am!* Please stop," and *"Security!"*

My head gets slammed into the wall again. Searing pain stabs me in the temples.

"Mama, let her go!" Tinsley screams.

Everything hurts.

"Join your friend in hell, you nosy little degenerate!"

"Mama, stop!"

The darkness around the edges of my white-hot pain starts closing in. The numbing peace it brings with it feels good. It eases the burning in my lungs.

Mama. I think of Mama. Her face glowing in front of me, telling me not to give in to the dark quiet.

I miss you, Mama.

Duchess, hang on! she yells.

Mama, why do you sound like Tinsley?

"Stop it! You're killing her!"

This surge of cold air punches me in the chest.

There's scuffling.

"Don't touch me! Let me go!" I hear Mrs. McArthur shout.

The pressure releases from around my throat. My body collapses onto the cold, hard floor.

I'm lifted by someone else. Their arms squeezing me, but

I can still breathe. The person pulls me close. They smell like apples and jasmine. Tinsley always smells like that.

"Just breathe. Breathe," she says in a soothing voice. "It's gonna be okay."

I do. Deep inhale. Slow exhale. Again. Then again. Then again.

Warm tears wet my face. They aren't mine, though. They're hers. Tinsley's, who I can now see holding me as the pulsating dots begin to fade.

"We're okay. We're okay. We're okay," she keeps repeating.

No one can pull us apart until Pops arrives.

CHAPTER THIRTY-TWO

TINSLEY

OCTOBER 26
2:05 P.M.

BY THE LOOKS of him, you would think my father has been locked up in the county jail for four years instead of four days. I'm taken aback by how disheveled he is when he enters the visitation room. His beard is knotted, his hair wiry and wild. The gray-and-white-striped jumpsuit sags on his body. His eyes are dull until they lock on me sitting alone at the table across the room from him. His face lights up with a smile. I want to return it, but I can't. I'm still confused, too angry. Seeing all that reflected in my face flattens his smile.

The back of my throat starts to ache as he makes his way to me. The prison's visitation room reminds me of the cafeteria at school. The room is flooded with sunlight from the wall of windows to my left. White metal square tables dot the spacious room, their seats connected to the base and bolted to the concrete floor. A correctional officer is posted in each of the corners of the room, monitoring everything happening. And there is a lot happening. It's crowded in here, many of the other tables filled with family members sharing enthusiastic reunions with their incarcerated loved ones.

I can't believe this could really be my life for who knows how long.

My father eyes the cast on my arm as he approaches. He pauses for a few seconds, then continues and sits down across from me. His skin is blotchy and his eyes are a little red.

"Tins, I'm glad you finally— Thank you for coming." His voice even sounds rougher than usual. "I've been asking about you . . . a lot."

I know. Rachel tells me every time he does. She and Lindsey have been staying with me since my mother's arrest made me an orphan. She says serving as my guardian is giving her purpose now that she's divorcing Aiden. That, and trying to sort through the shambles that is my father's company. The feds have opened an investigation into his business dealings. She told me this morning our father could be facing all kinds of additional charges besides the double accessory to murder for Nova and her unborn baby.

Our mother hasn't been cooperating with the police, but my father has. He confessed to helping her cover up Nova's murder by going out to the beach the morning after the coronation to toss my mother's scepter into the Gulf.

So many pieces are now connected, but there are still answers I need. That's the only reason I agreed to see him.

"I'm not here for pleasantries," I tell him. "I have questions, and I want answers. That's it."

He folds his hands on the table. "Of course you do. I know this has been a lot on you girls."

"A lot?" I scoff. He can't be serious. "That's an understatement, Daddy. *A lot* was when I had my face splashed all over the news as a *person of interest* in a murder investigation. We've sailed right into the fucking insane column now. The murderous Southern socialite who killed the bastard child of her husband—that's literally going to be the description under the Netflix original movie about all of this. Mark my words. I've barely eaten or slept since Rachel brought me home from the hospital. So, Daddy, it's more than *a lot.*"

"Sweetie, I know you're angry. I understand."

He's giving me this wounded look that makes my hands start twitching. How dare he act all hurt by what I said? Not after everything he's done.

"You know what I don't understand?" I lean forward, resting my casted arm in my lap. "How you could help your wife cover up the murder of your illegitimate daughter. If you didn't want her, you should have never created her."

My father's chin quivers. "I only did that be—"

"Because she blackmailed you? Yeah, I know."

I can hardly look at him right now.

"It was more than that, Tinsley. Much more." He runs a hand through his hair, which doesn't make it look any better. "I thought I was protecting you and your sister from my mistakes. From the possibility of losing your mother if she went to jail for this. I didn't want y'all to suffer for something I never should have allowed to happen. But don't you think for a second I wasn't torn up, that the guilt wasn't killing me inside."

"Which guilt, Daddy? The guilt of being married to the

woman who killed the daughter you weren't there for? Or the guilt of knowing you could have spared your other daughter the humiliation and stress she went through because everyone thought she killed the sister she didn't know she had?"

My father's eyes fall to his lap. This feels good. Getting out the anger that's been pent up inside me these past four days after reflecting on all the ways my parents sat on the sidelines and watched me go through hell for a crime *they* committed.

I turn toward the barred windows. The prison parking lot stretches endlessly on the other side. Somewhere in the sea of cars, Rachel and Lindsey are waiting for me. My sister thought it best I talk to our father alone. I scan the room.

"Have you visited your mother since . . ."

"No. I can't. I barely want to sit here with you."

That image of my mother choking Duchess in my hospital room has permanently imprinted itself in my mind. Just like flashes of how possessed she looked when she was shaking me on the balcony is on a loop in my thoughts. I don't think I'll ever be able to see her as anything different from now on.

"I know you think we ruined your life—"

"How could you bring a child into this world and ignore her?" I interrupt. I don't want to hear his regrets. I want to know how he could treat Nova and her mother the way he did. "Do you have any idea how hard Nova's life was? That she was molested by her uncle?"

His mouth drops open. "Who told you that?"

"Was protecting our family image that important? How did you live your life knowing you had a child out there and sleep peacefully at night?"

"I didn't know about her. Not for a long time." He rubs the

back of his neck. "It wasn't until she and Donna moved back here last year that I found out. And that's only because I ran into them downtown one day. When Donna introduced Nova as her daughter, well, I did the math. And I had this feeling. I can't explain it. I just knew she was mine."

"She has your eyes," I say, yet another clue that's been staring me in the face this entire time.

"Donna wouldn't admit it at first, but after I kept pushing her for the truth, she finally did," he says. "That's when I learned about everything your mother had done to keep me from finding out."

He tells me he and Nova's mother were involved in a year-long affair seventeen years ago. He even claims he was deeply in love with Donna Albright, which got under my mother's skin. Unlike other trysts he had apparently had, which sound more like one-night stands while he was away on business, he and Donna had mutual interests. She made him feel wanted and needed. Not like a status symbol, the way my mother did.

That would be hard to believe if I didn't know my father. He has always colored outside the lines of our upper-class Southern tradition. He defied my grandfather by not carrying on the family's riverboat casino franchise and opted instead to start his own legacy with his construction company. His mother wanted him to marry Regina Barrow, but he went after her best friend, my mother, who everyone thought was beneath him. Marrying her was another middle finger to anyone who tried to tell him who he should be. His affair with Nova's mother must have been him acting out again, since my mother had become so obsessed with being accepted in the world he harbors such disdain for.

"She was this broken woman who had never experienced

real love," he says, referring to Nova's mother, "and I saw how much it meant to her that I could give her a piece of that, and I got addicted to it—to her."

His stupidity infuriates me. "So on top of being an accomplice to murder and a cheat, you have a white savior complex?" I say. I read about the topic last night in one of the books my sister recommended on systemic racism. They've been the only thing distracting me from the disaster that is my life. Given the confused look on my father's face, I should send him a copy to read while he's in here.

"Go on," I say, when my father looks unsure of what to say next.

"I should have known your mother would feel threatened by Donna," he says. "She was once the outsider who desperately clung to me. The way Donna did. Made me feel needed and wanted. Someone different from prissy debutantes your grandmother and everyone else expected me to be with."

"Like Regina Barrow?"

After a beat, he nods. "Your mother found out about Donna and me somehow. Maybe because I had become so withdrawn from our marriage. She also learned before I did that Donna had gotten pregnant. She demanded that Donna have an abortion.

"Unfortunately, Donna didn't realize the snake she was dealing with. Charlotte hired some PI who uncovered how ill Donna's mother was back then. The woman was struggling with a multitude of health issues—cancer, diabetes, just to name two. Donna's mother had no health care and no way to afford the treatments she needed to even fight to stay alive. It was the perfect thing for your mother to exploit, so she did. Promised Donna's mother the best health care to prolong her life, but only if Donna left town with our baby, never came back, and never reached out to tell me."

I run my hand through my hair, hold it back for a second, and then release it so that it falls back forward, framing my face. This is what my mother was talking about when she told Rachel women must "manage" their husband's infidelity. For her, that involved ruining a child's life.

"Your mother even made Donna sign a nondisclosure agreement stating that if she broke their agreement, she'd be on the hook for all the money your mother secretly paid toward her mother's medical expenses. Donna used her mother's house as collateral in the agreement, so violating it would put her in financial ruin and they'd be homeless. It just wasn't worth it to her to cross your mother by telling Nova and me who we were to each other."

"Oh my God," I cry, pushing my cast into my clenching stomach.

Another puzzle piece to this saga locks into place.

"The night I came into your office to confront you about sponsoring Nova." I hold up my casted arm as the memory pops into my mind of him passed out in the chair, clutching a sheet of paper. "You were holding an NDA. But you put it away when you caught me trying to read it."

"I had visited Nova's mother earlier that day to offer my condolences and to beg her to let me pay for our daughter's funeral," he says.

It dawns on me why Donna seemed so amused when she mentioned that I'd nearly run into the visitor who had been there before me.

"Donna told me about the NDA, so I tore the house up and

found a copy of it that your mother was hiding," he continues. "It wasn't until you came home at the beginning of the semester, voicing your frustrations about the Black girl who everyone was saying would be the shoo-in for homecoming queen, that your mother found out Donna and Nova were back here. She was ready to go after Donna, probably confront her about the NDA, but I threatened to divorce her and send her back to the trailer park I plucked her out of if she did anything against them."

There's a hint of tears in my father's turquoise eyes. But they annoy me instead of softening me to the turmoil he's been going through.

"You were secretly trying to establish a relationship with Nova?" I ask.

"Maybe. I don't know." He sighs. "Nova acted like she didn't need me. Didn't want me around if I hadn't chosen to act like her father before then. But once y'all's little rivalry over homecoming started, she began reaching out again. I think to get under your skin. She never said it, but coming back here and seeing the life that could have been hers probably made her resent you too."

"And the fact that I was a grade-A bitch to her."

"Yeah, and that," my father says with a smirk.

"You sponsored her because you felt guilty?"

He nods.

I've lost count of the lies my parents have told me now.

"Did you know she was pregnant?"

He shakes his head. "Not at the time."

"I think she wanted to keep it. I think she was going to ask you to help her financially."

We sit in silence for a moment. I feel him watching me as

I look down at my lap. "You talk about her like she was an object. Like she was this *thing,* and not the person who you helped bring into this world. And I treated her like she was irrelevant. She had every right to resent us. I resent us."

I lift my head to look my father dead in the eyes and I add, "I've never been more ashamed to be a part of this family."

CHAPTER THIRTY-THREE

DUCHESS

NOVEMBER 7
4:25 P.M.

"I'M SORRY."

I think Tinsley is talking to Nova at first. We're standing at her grave. But she's looking at me when I lift my eyes from the headstone that reads *Lovett High's First Black Queen. May She Rest in Eternal Peace.*

"Sorry for what?" I ask.

"Being everything you accused me of at Jitterbug's." She looks back down at Nova's headstone. "For trying to make you feel guilty for Nova's murder. For what my mother did to Nova . . . and to you."

This is the first time she's acknowledged what happened in her hospital room. I reach up and touch my neck. I haven't wanted to talk about it either, so it hasn't bothered me that she didn't.

"You ain't gotta apologize for her," I say. "Not after what you sacrificed to stop her. We good."

We buried Nova yesterday. Hundreds of people came to the funeral. Tinsley chose not to. That's why we're here today. She wanted to pay her respects in private, not be a distraction from the services. The media's presence was distracting enough. Nova's funeral served as the grand finale to their weeklong coverage of her murder and the arrest of Tinsley's parents. The national news outlets all packed up and rode out of town last night, leaving us to deal with the shattered fragments of the damage.

Trenton showed up. He was released the morning after Mr. McArthur was arrested. Pops is working with the DA's office on a deal. It's likely he'll only have to serve some probation once the charges are downgraded. Like Tinsley, he hasn't returned to school yet. The funeral was the first time I've seen him in weeks. I slip my hand into the front pocket of my joggers, grazing my fingers across the folded edges of the one-page letter Trenton asked me to give Tinsley. Now feels like as good a time as any to do that.

"Here," I say, holding it up to her.

She frowns at it before taking it from my hand. "What's this?"

"It's from Trenton."

Pensiveness shadows her face. "What does it say?"

"Read it and find out."

She takes her time unfolding it. Maybe because her hands are trembling. Remembering my conversation with him yesterday still weighs on me.

"Dear Tinsley," she reads aloud. *"Hate does something to you if*

you hold on to it for too long. It can turn you into the very thing you've been taught to loathe. That's the only way I can explain what I did. Growing up, all we heard in my household was that the McArthurs were heartless, selfish, and unscrupulous. All of it poisoned me. It was all I could think about as I was looking down at Nova's lifeless face that night. Not because I thought you had killed her. After seeing that video right after finding her in the storage room, the years of hatred my father instilled in me reflected hardest back at me as I stood there dazed by what I found. I know you'll probably never forgive me, and I don't expect you to. Just know I've hated myself enough for the both of us since that night. Only a heartless, selfish, and unscrupulous person could have done what I did. What I ultimately wanted to do to you. That night in my mother's car changed everything. Made me realize how we've both suffered and been affected by the sins and expectations of our parents. That's why I couldn't go through with framing you for Nova's murder. But what does it say about me that I even tried to?"

Tinsley reads the rest in silence. I bet it says some of the same things Trenton told me when he pulled me aside at the funeral. She wipes away a tear as she refolds the letter and stuffs it in the pocket of her jacket.

"He apologized to me yesterday," I say.

"What did you say to him?"

"That I need time. That I'm hurt by what he did, how he tried to use our friend. He could have really kept us from learning the truth. He said he understood." Tears begin to well in my eyes. I blink a few times to push them back down. "I don't know if I'll ever be able to look at him the same again."

Watching Nova's casket get lowered into the ground has filled in the rest of the void her murder left behind. Now her memory has settled in my heart. Next to the one I carry around of my mother. It'll take a little time before I make room for Trenton.

"Since you brought it up, I have wondered what made you do it?" I say as a breeze brushes my cheek. Tinsley gives me a confused look. "Turn on your mother. You could have easily kept that secret. Kept her, you know."

"I didn't want to live with that, allowing her to get away with hurting another girl." She chews on her bottom lip. "I had to end the cycle Trenton so accurately characterized. I didn't want to end up like *her*. And I wanted to do right by Nova. And you."

"Still haven't talked to your Moms?"

Tinsley tucks her hair behind her ear. "I'm not ready yet. Don't know if I'll ever be."

My phone chimes. It's a text from Ev.

"Oh," I croak.

"Something wrong?"

"Nah. Ev sent me an article." I have to squint to read some of it because the sunlight is shadowing my phone screen. "Curtis Delmont got released and all the charges related to the murders of the Holts were dropped."

CNN aired a story last night on how his lawyers uncovered the gun used in the shootings, which belonged to Thomas Edgemont. Thomas was having an affair with Monica Holt, the wife. He killed them after Monica refused to leave her husband for him.

"'Bout time they got it right," Tinsley says.

"Well, they didn't have us to do their jobs for 'em."

Tinsley steps around the fresh mound of dirt to place the bouquet of white roses she brought among the many flowers crowding the headstone. She and I have hung out pretty much every day since she came home from the hospital. I've been dropping off her school assignments. She's become a shell of the person she once was. Kind of a good thing, I guess, but sad too. I don't know how to be a friend to her. What to say. Or what to do. Ev says me showing up every day is probably enough. "Sometimes folks just need someone who won't pull their hand away when they need someone to hold on to," she told me.

She hasn't been throwing any shade at me about Tinsley. She does roll her eyes if I bring her up too much, though.

"Oh, forgot to tell you. They're arresting Mr. Haywood this afternoon," I say.

Tinsley's face lights up . . . a little. "Really?"

"Whatever you told her mom worked. Pops said Mrs. Thambley called the station to report him after she went through Jessica's phone and saw all the inappropriate text messages between them. I think there might have even been some pictures also."

"*Ew!* From him?"

Who knew one girl's murder would uproot so many scandals?

Tinsley ambles her way back to me. We stand silent for a few minutes. The sun warming our backs.

"I've been stalking her social media pages," she says. "Dissecting every caption. Studying every detail. Trying to absorb as much information as I can about her. I'm becoming obsessed with wanting to know who she really was."

She means Nova. "It's funny," I say. "Her being the first Black homecoming queen really had me walking around thinking we had accomplished something great. But representation isn't enough. It isn't the liberation I thought it was. The home-coming elections policy, the racial quotas, it's all another form of performative activism. It doesn't really fix the issue if the same oppressive systems remain—in this case, the AP/standard curricula. *That's* really the problem. That's why the Black kids and the white kids don't know each other and aren't motivated to. If our school wasn't so segregated, we'd have more classes together. Be socializing more. We wouldn't need to force diversity; it would happen organically. Trying to force it creates new tensions."

"We could always blow up the system," Tinsley says. "Trust me, some of the kids in AP aren't there because they have the grades. I know how we could prove it."

I raise an eyebrow, curious. "We?"

"Well, I'm still student council president since the council dropped their crusade against me. 'Bout time I use the position to really do something impactful." She turns to me and adds, "I wouldn't be able to do it alone. I still have a lot to learn, and this is complex territory. You're the only person I trust. Would you be opposed to teaming up again?"

I let my agreeable smile serve as my answer.

"You ready to bounce?" I ask a few minutes later.

"Can we stay a little longer?" she asks. "I like the quiet."

"Cool."

It catches me off guard. Her weaving her hand into mine. I don't pull away. I squeeze tighter. Pull her a little closer. Let it wash over me that even though there's an unsettling chill in the wind, we might be okay on the other side of everything that has happened.

ACKNOWLEDGMENTS

People were right. Publishing can be a roller coaster ride of incredible highs and depressing lows. Thankfully, I have a great champion on my side in my agent, Alec—or as I like to refer to him, "the whitest, straightest man I know." Alec, you promised to keep knocking on doors until publishing paid attention to me, and here we are, with the first of what I'm sure will be many books for us. I never could have gotten this far without you. See, I was able to write this without profuse exclamation marks. Aren't you proud of me?

Krista, you have lived up to everything I've hoped and dreamed for in an editor. You understood my vision for this book and pushed me until it was everything I wanted it to be and more. Thanks for loving Nova, Duchess, and Tinsley just as much as I do. Lydia, thank you too, not only for falling in love with these girls but for talking about all things Housewives when we weren't discussing edits. And to the rest of the team at Delacorte Press/Penguin Random House: You helped make this vision a reality. Y'all are the best.

To my parents: Mom, you were my first fan. Reading everything I wrote on the typewriter you bought for me one

Christmas when I was in middle school. You've spent years praying for this dream of mine to manifest, and I'm convinced those prayers played an integral part in it becoming so. Dad, you say I'm your hero. Well, you're my rock. You show up when I need you most and love me harder than I could ever love myself. I hope I've made you proud. I hope I've made both of you proud.

Kita, I couldn't have asked for a better sister. You're always cheering me on from the sidelines. The smile we share always brightens my day. You've given me so much, including Leah, Riley, and R.J., who make me feel like the luckiest uncle in the world.

Adekunle, thank you for bringing Nova to life through your haunting and inspiring artwork. And thank you, Casey, for designing a cover I could have never dreamed up myself.

There are so many friends I'm grateful for: G.M.B. (Koi, "Craig," Kim, Tat, Jennifer, and Strozier), y'all keep me humble, keep me laughing, and never stop rooting for me. Southern University Jags just do it better, and we're proving that every day. Melody and Katara, we've shared so many laughs and ups and downs. You both showed me early on that it's okay to live in my truth because there are people in the world like you two who will be there for me no matter what. You both hold a special place in my heart for supporting me when I thought no one would. Lance and Mikey, a world without two of my very best friends is a world I don't want to live in. The two of you constantly remind me what this world could be like if we all truly listened and cared for each other. And, Lance, thank you especially for being my personal photographer. To Kermit and Keith, y'all are the Dorothy and Rose to my Blanche—you two can fight over who's Rose (even though we all know who that is, wink, wink).

Then there are my "writer friends." The gang of misfits who understand the struggles that take so long to describe to anyone outside the publishing industry. Jess, you believed so passionately in this book during its infancy. You have held my hand through this entire journey. I can never repay you for all the words of wisdom and insight you have given me, but I'm going to try anyway. Brian, my brother in prose, you are so freaking talented, and I can't believe we get to go on this journey together. I couldn't have asked for a better CP. Brooke, your insight on the early draft of this book really helped me shape Tinsley's voice. You're truly a gem, please know that.

Andrea, you planted the seeds that sprouted this story. I'll be eternally grateful. To my Pitch Wars and #DVPit friends and supporters: You helped me believe in myself when I had doubts. Truly the supportive community everyone talks about.

I'm also grateful to all the teachers (and there were many) who encouraged me to write and never give up. Most importantly I must thank my fourth-grade teacher, Mrs. Fleming, who allowed me to write my first play for the school's "Just Say No" campaign, and then cast my friends in it to perform in front of the class. The applause I received from my classmates is what began my obsession with entertaining people through stories from my imagination. And to my extended family and friends, of whom there are too many to list, this brown boy writing thanks you from the bottom of his heart for your support.

Toni Morrison said you should write a story you want to read, so I did. But there are still so many more I want to share. And maybe, just maybe, Duchess and Tinsley will pop up again in some of them. ;)

ABOUT THE AUTHOR

Jumata Emill is a journalist who has covered crime and local politics in Mississippi and parts of Louisiana. He earned his BA in mass communications from Southern University and A&M College. He's a Pitch Wars alum and a member of the Crime Writers of Color. When he's not writing about murderous teens, he's watching and obsessively tweeting about every franchise of the Real Housewives. Jumata lives in Baton Rouge, Louisiana.